Captain Calhoun's smile went wolfish.

His fist whipped around with no hesitation, and caught Jellico squarely in the side of the head. Jellico went down amidst gasps from everyone surrounding him.

"Get out of here!" Jellico said, rubbing his head. His eyes weren't focused on anything; Thul could practically hear Jellico's head ringing right from where he was standing. As Calhoun turned and walked out of the door, Jellico shouted, "I'll have your rank for this, Calhoun! Do you hear me? You are gone! You are finished! Do you hear? Finished!"

STAR TREK
THE NEXT GENERATION®

DOUBLE HELIX

BOOK FIVE OF SIX

DOUBLE OR NOTHING

PETER DAVID

Double Helix Concept by John J. Ordover and Michael Jan Friedman

POCKET BOOKS
New York London Toronto Sydney Tokyo Singapore

An *Original* Publication of POCKET BOOKS

POCKET BOOKS, a division of Simon & Schuster Inc.
1230 Avenue of the Americas, New York, NY 10020

ISBN: 0-671-03478-2

First Pocket Books printing August 1999

10 9 8 7 6 5 4 3 2 1

POCKET and colophon are registered trademarks of
Simon & Schuster Inc.

Printed in the U.S.A.

DOUBLE OR NOTHING

Seven Years Earlier . . .

1.

VANDELIA TRIED TO CONCEAL her astonishment when her rescuer's face fell off.

She had not been expecting a rescuer at all, much less one whose visage suddenly abandoned him. Only five minutes before, her situation had seemed utterly hopeless. Not that it was in Vandelia's nature to admit that any situation was hopeless or in any way outside of her control. It wasn't that she was eternally optimistic. She was just too damned stubborn, not to mention extremely fierce-natured.

She was a sinewy Orion woman, with thick green hair that cascaded about her slim, bare green shoulders. She was scantily dressed, as was the custom of her kind, in a clinging outfit that concealed almost nothing and accentuated that which it hid. Orion females preferred such attire because it made them more formidable fighters. After all, how was an opponent expected to concentrate fully on his own defense when there was so much exposed flesh coming at him? A male never quite knew where to look first, and consequently he never quite reacted properly to an assault. Before he knew it, razor-sharp fingernails would be slashing across his face, or filed teeth would be ripping a chunk of his jugular from his throat. Even Orion men were daunted by their females. Indeed, it explained the se-

3

rious population problem that Orions were having. Granted, each new generation of Orions was stronger and tougher than the last. That was out of necessity, since only the hardiest of Orion males dared to try their luck with their females. Survival rate of such engagements was roughly 83 percent . . . less if the female in question happened to be in heat, a biological drive that was probably the only reason Orions hadn't vanished from the face of the galaxy centuries earlier.

The sinewy Orion girl pulled with renewed determination at her bonds, but she had absolutely no more luck in severing them this time than she'd had the previous times she had tried to muscle herself free of her imprisonment. Even her formidable fingernails were incapable of severing her restraints. More out of a sense of pure frustration than any true belief that success would result from the efforts, she strained against the bonds, her clearly defined muscles undulating beneath her dark green skin. Still nothing. She was held tight.

Matters might have been slightly improved if she had only had an idea of where "here" was. Unfortunately, she had no clue at all. She had been captured, in her sleep of all things. How cowardly was that? How craven on the part of her captors.

Vandelia was a business woman, a professional entertainer. She danced at parties and social functions, and not only was she very good at it, but she had been extremely canny in investing the financial gains that her performing had garnered her. She had millions of credits stashed away as a result of her seven-plus years of playing to a crowd, plus additional activities on the side.

She had been dancing this night . . . except she realized that she had no reason whatever to assume that this night was the same night. She had no idea how long she had been unconscious. One night, two, five . . . no clue at all, really. The only thing she knew was that when she had woken up, she had been ravenous. Nevertheless, when some flunky had shown up in her bare-bones room to bring her food, she had spat it back in his face. He had cleaned the food off himself without a word. The next time he came to her, he had two assistants along, and they had pried open the woman's mouth and poured the food straight down her throat. Obviously the actions did not endear them to her. They could not have cared less.

The flunky was not of a race that she recognized. He was short and squat, wider than he was tall, bald and jowly and with bright red skin. The assistants he brought with him had similar coloration, albeit different builds. But as far as Vandelia was concerned, if she never saw any members of the entire race again, she'd be the happier for it. She did, however, feel some degree of alarm when she started wondering what the coloration of any offspring would look like. She hoped like hell that she wasn't approaching her heat cycle. Being out of control of her mating instincts was simply not aggravation that she needed.

They (whoever they were) didn't *have* to keep her trussed up. There were, after all, various electronic devices capable of controlling her. Collars, wrist bracelets with shock devices, and many other options. But they had chosen none of those, instead going for something barbaric and debilitating to the spirit such as total immobility through heavy-duty ropes. It was as if her captors were almost daring her to slice her way free. If what they were trying to do was totally muck with her head, then they were succeeding. She was becoming angrier, more frustrated, more of a seething volcano with each passing day. The most frustrating thing of all was that she knew they were doing it just to anger her . . . and yet she couldn't help herself, couldn't do anything to fight back the mounting ire.

On her third day of captivity, she met her host.

He was red-skinned, like the others, but he sported a series of elaborate tattoos on his forehead and also at the base of his throat just above the collarbone. He had high cheekbones and deep set eyes that glittered fearsomely. He dressed primarily in loose-fitting black clothes, with a loose-sleeved tunic and black pants tucked into the top of knee-high black boots. He had an air about him, Vandelia thought, that made it seem as if he didn't care one way or the other whether the individual he was looking at was dead or alive. Furthermore, he didn't seem to care whether he was the one responsible for that death or not. Vandelia was most struck by his hands, which were huge in comparison to his admittedly muscular arms. Every so often, as he spoke to her, his hands twitched slightly as if he was envisioning what it would be like to be crushing someone's windpipe.

5

"Greetings." His voice was amazingly soft-spoken for one so large and apparently threatening. She had to strain to hear him, and she realized that that was partly his purpose for speaking so quietly. "Have you been enjoying your stay?"

She said nothing, merely snarled at him.

"You are a feisty one. That's what I like about you. There's not enough feisty females in the galaxy."

This time, she spoke. "Come to my home world," she said between clenched teeth. "You'll find more than enough feistiness to keep you busy."

"I daresay." He bowed slightly at the waist as he said, "My name is Zolon Darg. And you are Vandelia."

"And you are dead."

The smile never wavered from his thin lips, but one of his meaty hands swung around so fast that she never even saw it coming. One moment his arms seemed relaxed and at his sides, and the next the hand was smacking her in the face. She lowered her head a moment, trying to compose herself and failing utterly. When she glared back up at him, it was from between strands of hair that lay upon her face, and her lips were drawn back in a snarl revealing her sharp teeth.

"Mind your manners," said Zolon Darg. "This will take as long as it has to take."

"What is 'this'?" she asked.

"Why, to make you mine, my dear," Darg told her. "I saw you dance. I was one of your many customers, your many admirers. But unlike others, I choose not to admire from afar. I wish to draw close, to be . . . personal."

"Go to hell," Vandelia said.

"Yes, yes . . . I'm sure you would like that," he said in a condescending tone that made it sound as if he were addressing a child. "That will not be happening anytime soon, I'm sorry to say . . . for your sake."

"So that is all that this is about?" Vandelia demanded to know. "You kidnapped me because you find me attractive? How pitiful. How mundane."

"You misunderstand me." He smiled, and although he did not have sharpened teeth as Vandelia did, his smile looked no less threatening than hers. He looked perfectly capable of biting a piece out of her if it suited his purposes. "It is not simple attraction. You are a challenge. There are few enough true challenges in this galaxy, and I take mine where I can find them. When I saw you dance, I knew instinctively that you'd be impossible to tame. But I thrive on impossibilities."

"Then think about some impossible things you can do with your own anatomy." Then she spat at him.

He hit her again. And again. The smile never wavered, his pulse never sped up. Three, four, five times and more, and again and again, across the face with those huge hands, first one cheek and then the other. The first couple of times she tried to voice, at the very least, a snarl of inarticulate rage, but when he'd slapped her the twentieth time, she'd stopped. She simply sat there, her head hanging, trying to breathe and laboring because of all the fury that had tightened her chest. She couldn't get a sound out. He folded his arms and stood there with a quietly smug expression. He had the air of someone who was utterly confident as to precisely who was in charge.

"I'm sorry, my dear," he told her, although he didn't sound especially sorry. "I very much wish that I could tell you that there is some deep, greater meaning to your being here. That in fact you have something I need, or that you've actually got a microchip with secret information hidden beneath your skin, or you're actually a long lost princess, or perhaps you and you alone are capable of finding the cure for a terrible disease. But it's none of those things. You're an amusement, a diversion." He crouched down then, going to one knee so that he could regard her at eye level. "A pleasant diversion, granted . . . but that's all."

"Is this what you do?" Her lips were starting to swell up a bit from the pounding she'd taken, but she was determined not to acknowledge the pain. Even so, when she spoke her voice sounded thick and a bit uneven. "Divert yourself? Is this how you . . . pass your days?"

"Not at all," said Zolon Darg. He straightened up and then bowed slightly at the waist as if presenting himself in most courtly fashion. "I will have you know that I am one of the premier weapons suppliers in the territory."

"Are you now." She didn't sound impressed. "So what. You help people kill each other. As if that makes you someone of consequence."

"You do me a disservice, woman. You oversimplify. I have supplied freedom fighters who battle for their crippled rights. I have supplied governments who fight to protect themselves from evil and unappreciative mobs of rebellious ingrates. I am always, always, on the side of those who are in the right."

"And what makes one right and one wrong?"

"Money, my dear girl," he smiled.

She spat in defiance once more. But this wad didn't even manage to cover the distance before it splattered impotently to the floor. Darg didn't give it a glance. "You amoral pig," she growled.

"The moral high ground, my dear Vandelia, belongs to whomever can afford to pay the toll."

She said nothing, merely glowered at him. He smiled thinly, clearly finding the entire encounter very amusing.

Since she was seated, he naturally towered over her. But he took the opportunity to crouch and bring himself to eye level with her. He studied her thoughtfully, and then said, "Let me tell you what's going to happen. We're going to start putting you on a somewhat erratic eating schedule, for starters. Sometimes you will find yourself starving, your belly aching so pitifully that you'll feel as if it would gladly rip through your body and go off in search of food on its own. Other times we will suddenly feed you in such copious amounts that we will literally be shoving it down your throat. The five or so gentlemen who have been overseeing your trips to relieve yourself in delicate lady-like fashion will be assigned other duties. We will simply leave you tied up at all times, so that you can wallow in your own waste products. When you begin to fall asleep, loud noises will be blared at you, blinding lights shined directly into your face. We also have one or two fairly belligerent empaths at our disposal . . . individuals who will be able to project into your mind whatever emotions it amuses me to have you feel. You have a very strong mind, Vandelia. At the outset, you'd likely be able to resist them. But that will only be at the outset, and we have a very long time available to us. We will, in short, do all that we can to disrupt you, discommode you, and utterly break you."

"And once that's done?" she asked levelly.

"Why then, at that point . . . you will be reeducated. Reprogrammed. The personality, the attitude that you have now . . . that will be like a bad dream. It will go far, far away where it can never be of any harm to you again." As he spoke, his voice almost seemed soothing in its confidence. "Instead, it will be replaced by a calmer, more loving personality. Oh, but don't worry. You will continue to dance. But you will perform your seductive dances . . . only for me."

She looked at him with utter contempt. "You have no idea, do you."

"What do you mean?" His head was tilted in a curious manner.

"My dancing. You think somehow that's separate from who I am. That is, after all, what attracted you to me. You poor, pathetic fool, Darg. When I dance . . . that is an expression of my personality. And that personality holds you, and all your kind, in the utmost contempt. When I dance," and she lowered her voice to an almost sultry tone, "I know that you all caress me with your eyes. I know that you think of what you would like to do to me. How each of you envisions possessing me. But you're all too stupid to realize that in my gyrations, I'm letting you know just how little I think of your desires. I don't dance to seduce. I dance to let you know what you can never, ever have. Let us say," she continued as if warming to the topic, "that you somehow manage to break my personality. Make me less than I am. Do you seriously think that if I'm even capable of dancing again, it will bear the slightest resemblance to anything you saw before? You will sit there and shake your head in frustration, wondering what happened to the passion, the fire, the sheer raw sexuality that drew you to me in the first place. And when you sit there in discouragement, when you mourn the loss of something that you truly adored . . . why then, my friend, you will have only yourself to blame. Only yourself. And even if you manage to have your way with the body you see before you now . . ." She grinned ferally. "Even if you manage that . . . you will never have me. I will be long gone, beyond your ability to touch or harm or seduce or even interest. Do we understand each other now, Zolon Darg? Have I made things sufficiently clear for even a brainless pig such as yourself?"

He smiled mirthlessly. "Abundantly clear, yes."

"But it is still your intention to hold me here?"

"Yes. You see . . . it doesn't particularly matter to me if you wind up being destroyed as part of my endeavors. At least I'll know that I was able to bring you down, and I will allow myself to take some pleasure in that."

Then he slapped her several more times. There seemed to be no particular reason to do so. But he did it anyway. Vandelia, for her part, couldn't even muster the ability to spit.

That was when the alarm went off.

Vandelia was positive that that was what it was the moment she heard it. The loud, screeching klaxon jolted Darg, and he looked around in confusion as if he weren't quite certain that he was in fact hearing the noise that was threatening to deafen the entire place. For the first time, Vandelia saw a momentary bit of uncertainty pass across Darg's previously smug face. She was extremely pleased to see it. Her only regret was that she wasn't the cause of it.

He tapped a comm unit that he wore on his wrist and said, "Central. This is Darg. Report: What is the cause of the alarm?"

"We have an intruder, sir," came back a voice crisply.

"How do we know that, Kapel?"

"We found Dikson down on level three. Apparently he'd been in a fight. Someone broke his neck, and they did it very cleanly and very efficiently."

Clearly, it took a lot more than the discovery of a corpse to throw Zolon Darg off his stride. "Will you shut that damned alarm off? How is anyone supposed to concentrate on anything with that godawful noise howling in our ears?" A moment passed and then the alarm, obediently, was shut off, although the lights were still rapidly dimming and glowing. Vandelia viewed the flickering with grim amusement. Since the alarm had likely made everyone in the area deaf, dimming the lights was probably the only remaining means of alerting all concerned to the fact that there was a problem.

"Now then," Darg said slowly, once he seemed satisfied that the alarm was no longer going to assail his ears, "We don't know absolutely for certain that Dikson's death means that we have an intruder. He had a history of gambling, as I recall. Could this be retaliation of some sort for money owed?"

"Sir," came back the voice of the one who'd been addressed as Kapel, "his debts were his protection? Who's going to kill someone who owes them money? Rather difficult to collect."

"Hmm. Yes. Yes, you're right," Zolon Darg said after a moment's consideration. "All right, then. I want everyone throughout the base on full watch. Have all shifts report in. I want tech teams scouring level three. Perhaps Dikson discovered this possible intruder performing some sort of sabotage act. If so, it has to be found and rooted out immediately. Is that clear, Kapel?"

"Yes, sir."

"I will be right up."

"Yes, sir."

He clicked off his comm unit, and then turned to Vandelia. "I have to leave, darling. But rest assured, we will have time together. Not only that," and he ran a finger along the line of her jaw, "but you will dance for me . . . and only for me."

Her head struck forward like a serpent's, her sharp teeth clacking together, but he deftly moved his hand away lest he lose a finger. "Feisty," he said once more in approval . . . and then swung a vicious roundhouse punch. He connected with her on the point of the jaw with such force that it knocked her completely over. The chair crashed heavily to the floor. Vandelia's head lolled back, her eyes closed.

He turned and walked away from her. When he got to the door, it slid open . . . and standing there waiting for him was another of his race. The new arrival was slightly shorter than Darg, and slimmer. He seemed momentarily startled, apparently not having expected the door to open right up. "Zolon Darg," he said, recovering quickly. "The . . . the alarm . . ."

"I heard it," Darg said impatiently. His eyes narrowed as he stared at the other Thallonian. "What is your name again?"

"Qadril, sir," said the Thallonian. "We met not long ago. I'm a friend of—"

"Yes, yes, I remember. Qadril . . . attend to her."

"To her, sir?" He looked uncertainly in Vandelia's direction. "Are you sure—?"

"Of course I'm sure," Darg told him, his temper not becoming any gentler with the constant need for repetition. "Haul her chair upright so that she's not simply lying about on the floor like that. And keep your fingers away from her teeth, would be my recommendation."

"Yes, sir."

With that, Darg headed out.

Qadril glanced right and left. Vandelia knew this since she was watching him carefully. Her eyes were narrow slits as she saw him draw closer, closer. She suspected that he would be of no more use in freeing her than anyone else, but she looked forward to sinking her teeth into him during an unwary moment. His howls of pain would bring her great pleasure, and be a further reminder to Darg that she was going to make every moment that he held her captive as much of a living hell as she could manage.

Qadril hesitated a few feet away, and then he went around her and gripped her chair from behind. She was mildly surprised when he did not grunt under the weight of hauling her back into an upright position. He didn't *seem* all that strong. Obviously he had some muscle, although one wouldn't have known it to look at him.

But, just as obviously, he was remarkably stupid, for the poor fool was actually in the process of exhibiting something akin to concern for her. He walked in front of her and took either side of her face in his hands, tilting her head back so that he could try and see into her eyes. "Can you hear me?"

When he said that, there was something different in his voice. He sounded rougher, more brusque than he had mere moments ago when speaking to Darg. Darg he had addressed in a manner that was fairly simpering. But not now. Now he sounded more dynamic, more confident and sure of himself.

It was probably, she assumed, because she was unconscious. In fact, he was probably trying to determine if . . . yessss. Yes, that was it. He wanted to see if she was still out cold so that he could have his way with her with impunity. Oh, and wouldn't that be something for him to boast to his friends about. She could practically hear his weasely voice bragging of how he had "tamed" her, made her beg for his attentions. Her fury began to bubble over the imagined liberties that he was about to take.

He had momentarily distracted her from her purpose with his feigned concerns as to her well-being. She was annoyed with herself that she had allowed that to happen, no matter how short a time her determination had actually wavered. As if to make up for it, she attacked with speed and viciousness that would have done any Orion female proud.

Just as he was making another inquiry as to her wakefulness, her head whipped around and she sank her teeth into his left forearm. She had envisioned chomping through his flesh, all the way down into the bone if she were lucky. If not, then at least she would take some pleasure in tearing out a large, dripping hunk of the man's arm and spitting it back into his face while his blood trickled down the sides of her face.

But she did not come into contact with flesh or bone. Instead her teeth bit through the cloth of his sleeve and hit metal.

"No!" he shouted.

What in the world? The thought flashed through her mind even as she quickly yanked her head back. Perhaps, she thought, he was some sort of cyborg or android.

Sparks flew from the section of his arm that she had mutilated, and she saw a few quick sparks dancing along his shirt sleeve. He tore at the sleeve, pulling off some sort of device that had been strapped around his arm.

It was at that moment that his face fell off.

Vandelia gaped in confusion as the red skin cracked and crumbled away, cascading to the floor in a powdery heap. Not only was his skin color different, but the very shape of his visage had altered.

The man who only moments before that been calling himself Qadril had gone from having a fairly round face to one that had a good deal more definition to it. His chin was cleft, his nose somewhat irregular, as if it had been broken. Instead of being bald, he had a thick mop of black hair. His skin was no longer red, but instead a paler shade that was more evocative of human beings. Even his eyes had changed color, going from a sort of pale blue to a vivid purple. Most striking about him to Vandelia, however, was a scar that ran the length of his right cheek. Considering the skin graft and dermaplast techniques that were so readily available, Vandelia couldn't recall ever having seen a facial mutilation that was quite so severe.

She found it rather attractive.

"Perfect," he growled, dusting away the remains of the red

13

material that had been obscuring his true features. "Just perfect. You had to do that. You just had to."

"Who are you?" she demanded.

"The one who was going to get you out of here. At this point, though, I'm half-tempted to leave you." He made an impatient noise, blowing air from between his clenched teeth, and then he seemed to make up his mind. "All right," he sighed, "we'll just have to make the best of it. If I free you, will you give me your word that you won't attack."

For a moment, despite the fact that he was offering her aid, she couldn't hold back a contemptuous sneer. "Are you that afraid of me?"

"No," he said reasonably. "But you're a splendid looking woman, and I try to minimize the number of splendid looking women I kill in the average day."

The words were light, the tone quite flip, but she looked into his eyes and there was something in there, a flat, cold stare that caused her to realize that there was nothing cavalier about his attitude. He really did believe that he was capable of killing her. Moreover, she began to get the impression that he might actually be able to accomplish it.

"You would take the word of an Orion?" she asked after a moment.

"Look," and it was clear from his tone that his patience was starting to wear thin, "I'm not interested in passing judgment on a species just now. I'm asking you, personally, if—"

"Yes, yes, all right, you have my word I will not attempt to hurt you," she said at last.

He had a knife hanging from his right hip. He pulled it out and briskly cut through the ropes that bound her. "You use that knife as if you really know what you're about," she commented.

He said nothing, but instead simply slid it back into its sheath. He glanced around the room they were in as if he were trying to see if anything could be used as a weapon.

"What was that device you were using to disguise yourself?" she asked.

"A Zynterian Camouflage Field," he replied as he went to the wall and ran his fingers along it. He seemed to be probing for something. He had been wearing gloves, which one would have thought was simply for ornamentation, but now she realized it had been to hide the true color of his hands.

"Zynterians? They're a passive race. They have no espionage interests that I've ever heard of," said Vandelia. She was busy rubbing her wrists, trying to restore circulation to them. She was a bit unsteady on her legs as well, but was determined not to let the weakness show.

"True enough. But they don't use it for espionage. It's a sex aid."

"A what?" She didn't quite think she'd heard him properly.

He cast an impatient look at her, as if he couldn't quite believe that he was wasting time explaining it to her. "They believe sex in any form is inherently evil, and so they use the camouflage field to disguise themselves as members of other races when they're . . . involved. That way they can pretend that they themselves are remaining pure. It's a sort of ritual."

"I see." She didn't, actually, but it seemed the thing to say.

"Generally Zynterians are the only ones who can use them. Other races who have tried to employ the device for other pursuits—such as espionage, as you mentioned—find that the device tends to sear the flesh from their bones. However, we Xenexians are close enough biologically to Zynterians that we can get away with using them. It causes considerable pain, but otherwise no lasting damage."

"Pain? You were in pain the entire time you were using that thing? I couldn't tell."

"I'm very stoic," he said, never taking his eyes from the wall as he continued his probe of the room. "For instance, my impulse is to throw you to the ground and take you like an animal right here. But you'd never be able to tell."

His voice was so flat, so lacking in inflection, that it was impossible for her to tell whether he was joking or not. She felt a headache coming on just trying to keep up with him. "Who are you?" she demanded.

"Call me Mac," he said over his shoulder. "Ah."

"Ah?"

He had his hand against a section of the wall that looked no different from any other. However, he pushed it and suddenly the wall swivelled around, revealing what appeared to be some sort of passage. She couldn't quite make out any details, although she did see small, flickering lights lining the upper section.

"Come on," he told her.

"But . . . where does this go?"

"Away from here. For the moment, that's good enough."

She mentally shrugged as she realized she had nothing to lose. This strange individual, whoever he was and wherever he was from, at least seemed to have some idea as to what he was about. She really couldn't be much worse off than she'd been a few minutes ago.

They headed down the narrow passage. Moments after they'd entered, the wall had slid back into place on noiseless hinges. The action dimmed the corridor slightly, but not significantly.

"How did you know that was going to be there?" she asked. "That false wall, I mean."

"I didn't. Not for sure. But we've done a good deal of research on Darg, and it seemed a reasonable guess. He had a similar hideaway on Estarcion IV, and he'd laced it with catacombs with similar entrances. He likes to get about unobserved and show up unexpectedly. He feels it keeps his people on their toes."

"It probably does." She paused and then said, "Who are 'we'? I mean, the 'we' who did this research?"

"You don't need to know that either," he said brusquely.

"Listen," and her temper started to flare, "I'd better start getting some answers, or—"

"Or what?" He turned to face her there in the confines of the passage, and there was unmistakeable danger in his tone. "Look: You weren't in the plan. I found out that you were here when I was already inside. You're an innocent bystander who's in the wrong place at the wrong time. I decided that it wouldn't be right to simply leave you to die. So I am risking myself to save your neck. I didn't have to. I still don't. If you want to go off on your own and take your chances, go right ahead." He flattened against the corridor wall so that she could pass by him. "My guess is that it branches off just ahead. You can go on and take your chances. I'll give you a five . . . no, three . . . minute head start. You'll go your way, I'll go mine, and that'll be that. Or tell me now if you're going to stick with me but are going to continue to irritate me, because if you are, then I'll put you down right now and be done with it. I don't need the distraction or the grief. Life's too short and on the verge of getting even shorter. Your only other option is to shut up so I can get both of us out of here in one piece. Once we're out of here and safe, you can be as arrogant and irritating as you wish. It won't bother me then because you won't be putting us at risk. Now have I made myself clear?"

"Yes," she said tightly.

"Now are you going to be quiet?"

No reply.

"Good."

She took some small measure of satisfaction in the fact that he actually appeared surprised that she had quieted down.

As she followed him, she said softly, "May I ask a less inflammatory question?"

"If you must."

"You've been talking as if we have a deadline. Why is that?"

That was when a massive explosion rocked them.

She stumbled against him as the passageway vibrated uncontrollably around them. He steadied her and muttered, "Idiots. They must have found it and tried to defuse it."

There was now an unmistakeable rumbling all about them, and he grabbed her wrist and yanked. "Come on." There was urgency to his voice, but he didn't sound close to panic. Clearly this was someone who was accustomed to handling difficult situations with aplomb.

She picked up speed and now they were heading at a full dash down the corridor. There was the sound of a second explosion, and a third, and they staggered as they ran. From a distance they could hear shouts and the sounds of running feet, and voices being raised in alarm.

There was a sensation of heat from directly behind them. "I wouldn't look back if I were you," the man called Mac warned her.

She looked back.

A gigantic ball of flame was roaring down the passage behind them.

She looked forward once more, suddenly wishing that she'd done as he suggested.

The seam in the wall that indicated a door barely had time to register on her and then Mac was pushing both of them through. They stumbled out into a main hallway that hardly seemed to be much better in terms of being a safe haven, for men were running about in total panic and any one of them might notice the escaping prisoner. Giving no heed to the danger that being spotted presented, Mac slammed the door back into place just as the jet of flame caught up to them. The wall instantly became superheated, but Mac had blocked off the passageway just in time, and the flames within passed them by harmlessly.

"Come on," and he pulled her roughly. "We've got to get to our ride. This place doesn't have much longer."

It was the first opportunity that Vandelia had had to see anything of her place of capture aside from the one room in which she'd been imprisoned. The place was massive, stretching upward as far as she could see. There were crosswalks and catwalks far overhead and then, when she looked down she saw that they descended to a great depth as well. Everything had been constructed so that everything was visible to some degree from elsewhere within the complex. It was all rather clever; it meant that Darg could keep his eye on just about everything from any point.

Under ordinary circumstances, she and Mac wouldn't have had a prayer of getting ten feet without attracting attention. But these circumstances were far from ordinary. She continued to hear explosions, some further away, some closer, and the entire place had spiralled into chaos. "What did you do?" she cried out over the shouts of others who were running around without noticing them.

"I'll tell you later, provided there is one!"

"You!"

Vandelia's heart sank. She recognized the voice immediately, of course.

It had come from behind them, and they turned to see Zolon Darg. He was on a catwalk above them, looking down, and he had half a dozen men with him. He had spotted Vandelia, and more, he obviously realized that it was Mac who was the intruder. Perhaps it was the fact that Mac was wearing the same clothes as the supposed red-skinned guard had been sporting a short time earlier. "You did this! You! Stay where you are!"

"You don't have time for this, Darg!" Mac shot back. "These explosions you're hearing so far are nothing! A chain of bombs to distract you from the real threat: The fact that I set two of your main boomers in your central weapons room to overload. Once those go, you can say good-bye to this entire place! You've got only a couple of minutes to get clear! Are you going to waste them coming after me, or are you going to save your own neck?"

The choice seemed fairly straightforward to Vandelia. Unfortunately, it was less clear-cut to Darg, who did not hesitate to aim a fairly lethal weapon squarely at Mac and fire.

Mac yanked Vandelia forward, barely getting them clear of the shot. "Get them!" they could hear Zolon Darg shout after them, but they didn't look back. Instead they bolted as quickly as they could along the catwalk. "Get back here!" Darg's voice came, and a disruptor blast exploded just ahead of them, missing them but blowing the leg off a hapless individual who was trying to save his own skin. He hit the ground, crying out as he clutched at the stump of his knee. Mac and Vandelia did not slow down, but instead simply vaulted over him and kept going.

They angled left, then a quick right, and they were on a rampway that was heading downward. Vandelia had no idea whether Mac truly knew where they were going, or if he was simply guessing with sufficient confidence to allay her concerns. But she was quite certain that the source of the explosions which were wracking the entire area was below them, and heading toward that source was the height of folly. She yanked her hand from his. He turned and looked at her in confusion. "Come on!" he called to her.

"We're going the wrong way! We're heading towards the explosions! It's suicide!"

"There's no time for this!"

But she wasn't listening. Instead she turned and ran.

Her legs moving like pistons, she charged back up the ramp, found another turn-off and took it. Someone tried to get in her way. She didn't even slow down, didn't take time to look at his face. She just slashed out with her fingernails and ripped across his face. He doubled over, blood welling up from between his fingers, and she shoved him aside and kept going.

19

Suddenly she was hit from the back, a flying tackle as some-one took her down. She hit the floor, taking most of the impact on her elbows which sent a shock straight up her arms. But she did not cry out, instead keeping the pain within. That was how she was going to get out of it, she had decided. She would focus all her anger, all her agony, and it would drive her forward to safety. At least, that was the theory.

Unfortunately, the weight of the person atop her was such that, not only had the wind been knocked out of her, but she couldn't get the leverage to thrust upward and knock him off her back. She struggled, she snarled, and then rough hands grabbed her by either arm and hauled her to her feet. She tried to angle her head around to bite one of her captors, but another pair of hands came in behind her, grabbing her by the back of the head and snapping her skull back. Her attempts to pull her head forward simply resulted in her nearly tearing her hair out by the roots.

Zolon Darg stood in front of her. He was staring at her with enough cold fury to peel the skin off her face just with the force of his glare. "Where's your friend?" he demanded.

"What friend?" From closer than she would have liked to hear, an explosion sounded. Several of Darg's men flinched or looked about nervously. Darg didn't even glance in the direction of the noise.

"I understand now," he said evenly. "Very elaborate. Very clever. You trick and seduce me into bringing you here so that your mysterious associate could follow you and track you to our hidden location."

"You idiot! I'm the victim here! You're giving me entirely too much credit. You've created some elaborate conspiracy theory where none exists!"

Darg circled her. "Then why did he stop to rescue you?"

"I don't know! Ask him!" She tried in futility to pull free. "I don't know if you've noticed, but this entire place is going up!"

"I have my best people on it," Darg replied confidently. "They will locate whatever further boobytraps your partner has laid and dispose of them. As for you . . ." And he aimed a dis-ruptor squarely at her forehead. "Call your partner. Summon him, right now."

"He's not my partner!"

"Call him." His tone didn't waver.

"He's probably long gone by now, because you've been too busy playing games with me!"

He fired a warning shot to her right. It grazed her upper thigh. To her credit, she still didn't cry out, as much as she wanted to. The bolt almost struck the man who was standing behind her, holding her immobile. Aware of the near-hit, he cast a nervous glance at his associates.

"Last warning." This time he aimed it straight at her face. The man who was holding her head steady angled around so that Darg would have a clear shot.

Realizing she had nothing to lose, Vandelia called out, "Mac!"

"That's better. Call him again."

"Maaaaac!"

"Mac what? What is his full name?"

"I have no idea."

He activated the disruptor's energy feed, preparing for another shot that would take her head off.

"Mac Morn Michelity," she said without further hesitation, reasoning that they likely weren't going to be around long enough for Darg to learn that she had no idea what she was talking about.

Suddenly there was a brief clatter from further down the rampway. Vandelia couldn't help but notice that Darg and his men were well-trained: Half of them looked in the direction of the noise, but the rest of them looked instead behind them, just in case the noise was a diversion to allow Mac to get in behind them.

Nothing, however, seemed to come from either direction.

Darg waited impatiently for another noise, and when none was forthcoming, turned back to Vandelia and said—with very little trace of sadness—"It appears your friend has deserted you. Farewell, Vandelia." He levelled the gun right at her face.

That was when the deafening roar sounded from behind them.

As one, they turned just in time to see a monstrous creature, reptilian in aspect, with leathery skin and a huge mouth filled with teeth that seemed capable of rending or shredding a shuttlecraft. It was poised above them on its hind legs, its whip-like tail snapping about with such ferocity that anyone within range of it would have been crushed instantly. When it roared, the hot, foul vapor of its breath washed over them, and the sound drowned out yet another explosion in the near distance.

The response among Darg's men was instantaneous. With a collective shriek of terror, they broke and ran as the creature advanced on them, each stomp of its massive feet causing the rampway to shudder beneath it. In doing so, they released their hold on Vandelia. Her immediate instinct was to try and attack Darg, but the shot he'd taken at her leg had done her more damage than she'd first realized. It went out from under her and she found herself barely able to walk, much less capable of lunging to the attack.

The only one who did not break and run was Darg himself. He stood precisely where he was, utterly paralyzed. His mouth hung open, his eyes were wide and looked almost lifeless as he stared at the monstrosity before them.

Suddenly Vandelia's view was blocked . . . by a rope which had just dropped directly into her line of sight. She glanced up and saw, on a rampway above her, Mac. He was holding the other end and mouthing the words, "Hurry up!"

She did not hesitate, but instead grabbed the rope with both hands and held on as tightly as she could. Mac pulled, and she was surprised how quickly and effortlessly he hauled her aloft. He had looked rather unprepossessing, but there was clearly more than ample strength in his arms if he was able to yank her upward so easily. He drew her upward, hand over hand, one foot braced against the hand railing, his mouth set and his eyes burning with a quiet intensity. He did not grunt, nor make any sound to give away any strain he might be feeling.

Darg still hadn't budged. He was indeed so frozen by what he was witnessing that he didn't appear to have noticed that Vandelia was no longer there. The monster roared once more, a particularly high-pitched shriek, and something in the piercing nature of the howl caused Darg's finger to tighten spasmodically on the trigger. The disruptor ripped out a shot and it went straight through the creature without the monster even acknowledging that it had been hit.

It took a moment for Darg to register for himself what he

had just seen. Then his eyes narrowed and he fired again. Once more the creature was utterly unharmed by the disruptor blast.

He shouted a profanity and suddenly looked around . . . and then up. He did so just in time to see Vandelia being pulled over the railing of the overhead rampway, and he caught a glimpse of Mac looking down at him. Vandelia saw the two of them lock eyes, two enemies truly knowing each other for the first time.

"Get back here!" bellowed Darg, and he fired. Vandelia and Mac ducked backward as the blast sizzled past them.

"Come on! And stick with me this time!" Mac admonished her. The last thing Vandelia wanted to do was admit that her thigh was throbbing, so she gritted her teeth and simply nodded. Mac grabbed her wrist and they started to run. It was all that Vandelia could do not to limp in a most pronounced fashion. "What was that monster?" she called out.

Without glancing behind himself to address her, Mac said, "Holo unit. Pre-set monster, emanating from a disk about the size of my palm."

"That was the noise we heard . . . you activated it on a time delay and then tossed it down—"

"You're going to hear more noises than you'll want to hear if we don't hurry—"

The rampway shook beneath their feet. There seemed to be a series of seismic shocks building, one upon the other, throughout the structure. Mac glanced around. There was a network of ramps some thirty feet away from them, and between them was a deep well that seemed to fall away nearly into infinity. The ramp trembled once more.

Suddenly there was a screech of metal and the ramp started to twist at an angle. "Hold on," Mac said with a sort of resigned calm. He yanked off his belt buckle, twisted it, and suddenly he was holding a device that looked like a small gun. He tapped a button on the side and the end of the device was ejected, trailing a cord behind it. It "clacked" onto an upper rampway across the well.

At the far end of the ramp that they were upon, Darg was suddenly there. He was howling with fury, heedless of the chaos around him, as he charged straight toward them. He was firing his disruptor indiscriminately, no longer aiming but instead just shooting in their general direction. He lurched toward them, gripping the handrail, apparently not even aware that the ramp was in danger of collapsing.

Mac didn't even bother to glance at him. Instead he gripped the device in his palm, threw an arm around Vandelia's waist, and launched off the rampway. Vandelia had a brief glimpse of the ground, unspeakably far below, but it was all a blur, and suddenly they were on the other side. Mac snagged his legs around the railing and shoved Vandelia onto the ramp.

Zolon Darg brought his disruptor to bear, aiming at them across the divide, and then with a roar of metal the rampway that he was standing upon gave way. He tried to clutch onto something for support, but couldn't find anything. The sounds of the tearing metal drowned out Darg's shrieks as he tumbled downward and landed with a thud on the rampway below. He had about a second's respite before the falling metal of the upper rampway landed on him. The last that Vandelia saw of him was his face twisted in fury before he was completely obscured by the mass of twisted metal that crunched down atop him.

Mac, for his part, didn't appear to give it any notice. He seemed far more concerned about other things, such as survival. "This way," he said, and pulled her wrist. She limped after him.

"But we're heading toward the explosions!" she cried out to him, the same objection that she'd been raising before. But she was at that point somewhat resigned to her fate, convinced that she had only moments to live anyway. As if to underscore the point, there was another explosion, even louder than before.

"Here. Right here!" Mac called out to her. He hauled her over to a spot near a wall that was quivering from the most recent explosion. Then he stood perfectly still. "Don't worry," he said confidently.

"Don't worry!"

"That's right. Don't worry."

From deep within the well that the rampways surrounded, there was an explosion that was so loud Vandelia felt her teeth rattle.

Orion beliefs had one aspect in common with human theology. They shared a belief in an afterworld for the evil that was a scalding pit of torment. At that moment, Vandelia was suddenly convinced that she was within that very pit, for the air around her started to sizzle. She found it impossible to breathe, the air searing her very lungs. The entire area seemed bathed in light. She looked down into the well around which the rampways hung, and she saw a massive fireball roaring up toward them. Within seconds it would envelop them.

Part of her wanted to scream, to curse, to agonize in loud misery over the hideous and unfortunate set of circumstances which had brought her to this pointless end of her life. Instead, somewhat to her surprise, all she did was turn to Mac and say, sounding remarkably casual, "Can I worry now?"

He sighed. "If you must."

And she saw a flash of amusement in his purple eyes . . . at which point his eyes abruptly started to haze out in front of her. Then she realized that she, too, was disappearing, as the entire area around them demolecularized. Considering the circumstances, it was understandable that she didn't quite realize at first what was happening. *So this is what death is like* went through her head before she truly had a chance to register that she was not, in fact, dying, but that instead she was in the grip of a transporter beam.

Then the world reintegrated around her and she found herself in the back of some sort of small transport vehicle. Somewhat larger than a runabout, it seemed like a small freighter more than anything, designed for short runs with cargo that was generally contraband. The smaller the vessel, the less chance there was of attracting attention. Then she fell, for Mac was no longer supporting her. Instead he had moved quickly off the transporter pad and was at the helm. "Hold on!" he called.

"Hold on! To what?!" she cried out. Ultimately it didn't matter; the freighter suddenly leaped forward, sending Vandelia tumbling backward, her feet up and over her head. She clambered to her feet, her leg still throbbing but starting to feel improvement.

She could see that they were on the surface of a planet, but the freighter was already firing up and leaping skyward. Vandelia lurched to the front and dropped into the copilot seat next

to Mac. He barely afforded her a sidelong glance as he checked
readings on the control dash. "How's the leg?" he asked. Considering the circumstances, he sounded relatively calm.

"Getting better."

"Good. Let's see if we can keep the rest of you intact."

He urged the freighter forward, and it rocketed upward,
faster and faster.

"That place you had us stand. It was a preprogrammed
transporter point," she said.

"Yes," he said tersely. "I didn't know the exact layout of the
place, but I knew they had scanners that would detect transporter homing beacons or comm units, as well as any beam-
ins. So I had to sneak in on my own, and make a guess as to
coordinates when I set a time and place for a beam-out."

"You could have explained that."

He didn't reply. The chances were that he wouldn't have
done so anyway, but he was actually handed an excuse for not
continuing the conversation as several explosions around them
caused the freighter to rock wildly.

"Oh, now what?" demanded Vandelia.

"We have company," Mac muttered. "Computer, rear view."

A section of the screen in front of them shifted. It was only
then that Vandelia realized they weren't looking through a window, but instead through a computer-generated representation
of what was outside. Most of that view remained, but now part
of it had altered to present the view from behind them. Three
small vessels were approaching them most rapidly. They were
so small that they appeared to be one-man fighters each, but
because of their diminutive size, they were fast and very ma-
neuverable. The odds were that they would be able to catch up
with the freighter in short order.

But that wasn't the only thing that attracted Vandelia's attention. What she noticed in particular was a tall tower in the distance. It was surrounded by rich and green forest, but stood
high above it, almost a mile high, it seemed. It had a wide
base, becoming progressively narrower as it got higher. It was
silver and gleaming and would have been far more impressive
if it hadn't been for the huge gusts of black smoke wafting out
of a number of places. Then, as Vandelia watched, the lower
third of the tower was engulfed in flame. She saw the upper

two thirds start to wobble, teeter, and then tumble over in ex-
cruciatingly slow motion.

"Impressive," was all she managed to say.

Then the pursuing vessels began to fire. Mac's fingers flew
over the board, handling the freighter's course with astonishing
confidence, sending it zigzagging one way and then another,
dodging a number of the blasts with facility even as he continued them on their upward course. Nevertheless, the freighter
shuddered as several of the shots got through.

"Rear deflector at eighty percent and dropping," the computer informed him.

"Concentrate all deflector power to rear shields. Shore it
up," he ordered.

"We're not going to make it," Vandelia said.

The vote of no-confidence didn't seem to perturb him.
"Then we don't make it."

"You seem rather sanguine about the prospect."

"Would you rather I started to panic?"

"No."

"Then shut up."

She opened her mouth to reply, but came to the realization
that perhaps shutting up would indeed be the smarter course of
action.

The freighter angled down abruptly. The ground seemed to
be approaching them at horrifying speed and Vandelia was certain that there was no way, absolutely no way, that they were
going to forestall a crash, at which point the freighter zoomed
upward once more. Mac tapped the control board again, and
Vandelia was surprised to see on the rear view that a suddenly
great gust of white was billowing behind them. "Are we hit?
Are we leaking something?"

"No."

For a moment she could see nothing on the rear view, and
then the pursuing vessels burst through the mist and continued
after them. But then Vandelia noticed something: Their hulls
were starting to change colors.

"What's happening to them?"

"Watch," he replied. He hadn't taken his eyes off the front
view, but she could see a touch of amusement at the edges of
his mouth.

The vessels that had been pursuing them were slowing, and then Vandelia looked on in amazement as she saw their lower hulls start to be eaten away. Huge spots of corrosion appeared on them and then rapidly spread. With each moment it spread faster and faster, eating through the exterior of the ships with the greed and velocity of a hungry child being handed a handful of sweets. Breaking off the pursuit, the three vessels dove as quickly as they could for the ground, but they didn't quite make it in time. Within seconds the ships had fallen apart completely, and Vandelia watched with smug delight as the erstwhile pilots of the vessels tumbled toward the ground, waving their arms and legs in a most entertaining manner. She felt as much remorse and pity for them as they likely did for her . . . which was to say, of course, none.

Seconds later, the freighter tore lose completely of the planet's surface, spiralling into space. "We're clear of the planet's atmosphere and gravity," Mac announced. "Taking her to Warp One."

"This ship has warp capacity?" Vandelia said in surprise. But then she reined in her surprise with clear amusement. "Well, why shouldn't it? Apparently it packs some sort of gas that eats ships."

"Only unshielded ships. We were lucky. Vessels that small don't pack enough power or equipment to generate anything beyond the most minimal of shielding. They count on their speed to avoid attackers. Leaves them vulnerable. Warp on line."

Space twisted slightly around them and the ship leaped into warp space. Vandelia leaned back in her chair, shaking her head in amazement. "I still can't believe it," she said. "An hour ago, everything seemed hopeless."

"An hour ago, it was. Things change."

She turned to face him. "I owe you my life."

"Yes," he said matter-of-factly, without even looking at her.

"And what do you want."

At that point, he did afford her a glance. "Want?"

"Yes. Want." She cocked an eyebrow.

To her surprise, he seemed to laugh slightly to himself, and he shook his head. "It's some world you live in. People do things because they want something in return. Everyone's out for themselves. No one does something for the common good."

She seemed puzzled by what he was saying, "That's right. That's my world. Yours, too."

"And it's impossible that I could have helped you just because it seemed the right thing to do at the time."

She sat back in the chair, her arms folded tightly across her breast. "Everyone wants something in exchange. No one does anything if it doesn't serve their interests, first and foremost."

"You're probably right," he said with a sigh.

"Which brings us back to what you want."

He appeared to give it a moment's thought, and then said, "There's a changing area and hypersonic shower in the back."

Now here was something she understood. In a way, it was almost comforting to her. Her entire world view was predicated on the selfishness of all those around her, particularly males. The last thing she needed was someone coming along and shaking up the very foundations of her philosophy. "So . . . you want me to strip and shower, is that it?"

"Yes. You've been slapped around, tortured, shot at . . . you've worked up quite a sweat, and it's detectable. So please shower it off. And there's a jumpsuit you can change into."

She was stunned. There was no interest in his voice at all. He wanted her to stop smelling. Beginning, middle, end of interest.

Then, of course, she understood.

"I see. You prefer men."

Mac looked at her, and then laughed. He didn't even reply, but instead continued to laugh softly to himself while shaking his head.

Without another word, Vandelia went to the shower and washed herself thoroughly. Even though it was merely a hypersonic shower, it was still a tremendous relief to her. It was particularly soothing for the injured thigh, the hypersonics caressing it so that, by the time she was done, there was not the slightest hint of pain in her leg.

She put on the jumpsuit, and walked back into the main cabin. Mac didn't even appear aware that she was back. Instead he was finishing issuing some sort of report as to the completion of the "mission." When he did notice she was there, however, he ceased the recording, or perhaps it was a transmission. Vandelia couldn't be sure.

"Who are you?" she asked as she dropped into the seat next to him. "Are you some sort of spy?"

"If you wish," he said.

"Who do you work for?"

"Myself."

"Someone must be sponsoring you. You must report to . . ."

"Get some sleep. We'll be at Starbase 18 before too long. I'll be dropping you off there. There'll be a connector flight there which will take you wherever you wish to go."

"I . . . do not know what to say."

" 'Thank you' will suffice."

She considered that a moment. Then she rose from the chair, went to his, and draped herself across his lap, straddling it.

"What are you doing?" he inquired.

"Saying 'thank you.' " She undid the fastenings of the jumpsuit and slipped it off her shoulders. It dropped to her waist, leaving her nude from the waist up.

He stared at her. "Apparently it's cold in here," he said.

"We'll warm it."

"Vandelia . . ."

She put a finger to his lips, and grinned in a most wolfish fashion. "I'm going to return the favor you've done me, Mac. And when I'm through," and she put her hands behind her head, arching her back, "you'll never think about having sex with men."

"That's probably true," Mac said.

And she began to dance. And for the first time in her life, she danced only for one person . . . only for him.

It was not possible that anyone should be able to haul himself from the wreckage of the tower. Not possible that anyone should have been able to survive. Particularly when one was considering that the candidate for survival had had his body crushed by falling metal.

All this, Zolon Darg was most aware of. Nonetheless, as he lay there on the ground, staring up at the twilight sky that was rapidly becoming night, it was impossible to overlook the fact that he had, in fact, survived.

It was also impossible for him to move. Sheer fury, pure force of will, had pulled him from the flaming wreckage that had been his headquarters. That, and the memory of a green woman with a defiant gleam, and a man . . . a man with purple eyes and a scar on his face. A man he would never, ever forget.

He tried to feel something below his neck, but was unable to. Nothing would move, nothing would respond to the desperate commands that his brain was issuing.

He drew in a breath, and it was an agonizing effort. But it was worth it, for it allowed him to exhale, and when he did so, what he breathed out were the words, "I'll . . . kill them . . ."

Then he lay there, a sack of broken bones and bloodied meat, and wondered when the dark gods he worshipped would see fit to do something about his condition.

He remained that way for three days before he received his answer . . .

Now . . .

1.

DOCTOR ELIAS FROBISHER was 43 years and one day old, and he couldn't quite believe he had made it. When he woke up, he had to pinch himself to make certain that he had really managed to accomplish it. When someone had lived under a bizarre death sentence for the last decade or so, as he had, the achievement felt particularly noteworthy. He lay in his bed, breathing in the filtered air of the cone-shaped space station, but never had that air felt quite so sweet. It felt like a glorious day. Granted, concepts such as day and night were entirely subjective, created and controlled by the computer core of the station. There was neither sunrise nor sunset, and this was something that had taken Frobisher some time to get used to. He had been planet-bound most of his life, and the curious and unusual life which existed in space was a difficult adjustment that Frobisher had made because he'd really had no other choice.

Quite simply, he'd had no other choice. He'd had to get away from the Guardian.

He took a long shower that morning, and felt that he had earned it. It was pure water rather than hypersonic, a rarity that Frobisher was revelling in that morning. As he did so, visions of the Guardian came to him unbidden, as they were wont to do. Frobisher shuddered, thinking about the hideous shadow he had lived under all these years.

Then he started to tremble more and more violently. He had lathered up his thinning brown hair, and the shampoo dribbled down into his eyes, but it barely registered upon him. The soap slipped from his hands, his legs went weak, and he sagged to the floor, still unable to control the spasms which had seized him. Paradoxically, he began to laugh. It was a bizarre sound, that choked laughter, a combination of chuckling and sobbing that grew louder and louder, so much so that it could be heard in the hallway outside his quarters. His assistant, Dr. David Kendrow, heard it, and started banging on the door. Normally Kendrow, a thin, blond man, was overly mannered and reserved in his attitudes, but one wouldn't have known it at that point as he was fairly shouting, "Doctor Frobisher? Are you all right, sir?"

"Yes! Yes," Frobisher called back to him. "Yes, I'll . . . I'll be fine." It was all that Frobisher could do to pull himself together. He hadn't expected to react in that manner, but really, it was inevitable when one looked at it with hindsight. The amount of anxiety that had built up as he approached his 43rd birthday had been truly horrific. The knowing, and yet not knowing. That insane combination of certainty and doubt, warring within him as each passing day had brought him closer and closer to the inevitable . . . except, maybe not.

And he had made it. He had survived his birthday. It really was true, what they said: Today is the first day of the rest of your life.

He emerged from the shower and, as he towelled off, looked at the gut that had been building up on him. As the dreaded day had approached, he hadn't been bothering to exercise or take care of himself. He'd had a fatalistic attitude about him, and that was certainly understandable. But now the joke was on him, as was the extra flab. He was going to have to do something about working that off. After all, it wouldn't be particularly attractive to women.

Women. His face lit up as he dressed. Relationships. He had been afraid to begin any, because the prospect of condemning some poor woman to become an early widow. Oh, certainly he could have had a string of casual relationships that went nowhere. Love them and leave them, and rationalizing that, since he was a walking dead man, it was the only way that he could conduct his life. But he was a highly moral man, was Dr. Frobisher. Highly moral, and more than that: He knew that one woman after another, used and tossed aside, was simply not for him. He wanted companionship, he wanted someone who, he knew, was going to be there for him. He wanted someone to wake up to, someone who would cheerfully kiss him in the morning and loved him so much that it wouldn't bother her if he hadn't had a chance to brush his teeth yet. Someone he would be able to look at across the breakfast and smile at. Someone who wanted to spend a lifetime with him . . . a real lifetime, not the truncated thing that had been handed him.

Oh, and someone who was a brilliant engineer in the field of artificial intelligence and computerization, of course. That was a must as well.

There were a few likely possibilities, actually. To give himself some vague bit of hope, something to cling to even though he was certain that it was hopeless, Frobisher had had the Omega 9 run a scan of potential mates. It was unbelievably quaint, even absurd: Using a creation as infinitely advanced as the Omega 9 for the purpose of, essentially, computer dating, seemed absurd on its face. But he had done so nonetheless, and the list that had been drawn up had been quite impressive. Now that the dreaded day had passed, he was looking forward to trying to act upon the possibilities. As he headed to the lab, having had his customary quick breakfast, he patted the data chip in his pocket to which he had copied the information that Omega 9 had obtained for him. His mind was already racing with possibilities. He would pick the most likely prospect, "likely" being derived from personality profile, shared interests, age, background, etcetera. He'd subtly do some checking to see if she was otherwise involved and, if not, he would find a pretense to begin a correspondence with her. Hopefully, he would be able to develop it into something substantive and sufficiently personal that she would be prompted to come out to the Daystrom Station where he worked and meet with him.

And then . . . who knew? Who indeed knew?

"I knew," he said rather cheerfully to no one. "I knew, but I didn't know. But now I know, and it's great knowing and not knowing!"

He entered the lab, his lanky legs carrying him across it with a jaunty speed. Kendrow was already at work, but he was casting a watchful eye upon Frobisher. "Good morning, David!" called Frobisher.

"Good . . . morning, sir." The surprise in his voice was unmistakeable. He wasn't used to Frobisher sounding so cheerful in the morning . . . or ever.

Frobisher glanced over the station log, and frowned slightly. "Some sort of glitch in the standard running program?" he asked.

"Yes, sir, I just noticed it. It's minor systems failures . . . so minor that we hadn't even been noticing when they'd been going down. I'm running diagnostics checks on them, sir. I'm hoping to get it locked down by this afternoon."

"Oh, you'll get it sorted out, Kendrow." He patted him on the shoulder. "I have the utmost confidence in you."

"Th—thank you, sir." Kendrow stared at him as if he were concerned that Frobisher had been replaced by a lookalike, lighthearted alien.

"Not used to seeing me this chipper, are you, Kendrow?" asked Frobisher.

"To be blunt . . . no, sir. I'm not."

Frobisher laughed, and then sighed to himself. "Between my attitude now and what you heard earlier . . . you must be somewhat puzzled, eh, Kendrow?"

"Yes, sir. I am, sir."

"Sit down, Kendrow."

Kendrow looked down at himself. "I am sitting, sir. Already, I mean."

"Oh. Yes, of course." Frobisher leaned against a console and smiled broadly. "I'm sorry, Kendrow," he said earnestly. "The truth is, this last week, leading up to the day I've dreaded for so long, seemed almost to fly by. Now I know I've been out of sorts the past few days . . . weeks . . ."

"Try months," Kendrow muttered, but then looked immediately apologetic.

Frobisher waved it off. " 'Months' is probably more accurate, to be honest," he admitted. "And yesterday was probably the worst of all."

"Well, I have to say, your behavior was rather pensive considering it was your birthday. I know that some people become daunted by the prospect of turning forty or fifty . . . but forty-three." He shrugged. "It seemed . . . odd. You seemed to want to do everything you could to ignore it."

"Believe me, I did want to ignore it. Although I'm surprised that my parents did. Usually they send me a greeting on my birthday, but this year . . . nothing."

"Had you told them not to?"

"No. No, I kept my unease to myself . . . or at least I thought I did. But perhaps they picked up on unspoken signals nonetheless. Ah well . . . no use worrying about it now. You see . . . there's been a reason for my concerns. Do you know what I used to do, Kendrow? Before I joined Daystrom, I mean, to work on the Omega 9."

"You were involved in some sort of archaeology project, I think, sir."

"Not just some sort. This was THE project. The Guardian of Forever."

Kendrow blinked in surprise. "The time portal? I'd heard about that, but I'd almost thought it was a myth."

"Oh, it's not a myth, I assure you. It's real." Despite his newly achieved state of bliss, Frobisher shuddered slightly as he recalled the image of that cheerless place. It wasn't just the Guardian itself that so spooked him. He couldn't get out of his head that eerie, mournful howl of the wind that filtered through the remains of the ruined city around the Guardian. It was as if ghosts of a race long lost still haunted the place, laughing and taunting. "It's . . . all too real."

He was silent for a moment. Prompting him, Kendrow said, "And you studied it?"

"People . . . tend to come and go there," Frobisher told him. "Oh, they're excited at first. Word spreads, after all. And it's an irresistible proposition: Studying the past, seeing it unspool before you. How can anyone pass that up? And yet . . . people burn out, very, very quickly. Six months, a year at most, and suddenly you see complete turnover in the staff there. I didn't understand why. But now I do." He laughed softly to himself. "Now I do. It just . . . gets to you after a while."

Kendrow tilted his head slightly as he regarded the doctor. "What happened there, sir?"

"I . . . saw my future. At least, I thought I did."

"The future? But . . ." Kendrow shook his head. "I thought that the Guardian only shows the past, not the future."

"That was my understanding as well. That's what they told us, at any rate. But I will never forget it, nonetheless. I had been there two months . . . well," and he smiled ruefully, "two months, seven days, eighteen hours. I was monitoring a playback on the Guardian. No two are exactly the same, you know. Even if you ask for the exact same scenario to be replayed, there's always slight variances in the scene. Some of them can be extremely minor . . . but they're there. That's one of the things we study: The reasons for it all. It truly supports the notion that time is in a constant state of flux.

"In any event, I was monitoring . . . and there was a rather fearsome ion storm overhead. Not low enough to be of any direct danger to me, but I was getting apprehensive just the same. In fact, I was even considering packing it in for the day. Still, I was doing my job, my tricorder picking up the events as they hurtled past on the time portal's screen.

"Suddenly, overhead, there was this . . . this burst of ionic energy. Despite the awesome artificial intelligence that the Guardian displays, it's still just a machine. Perhaps the most sophisticated machine that ever existed . . . aside from the Omega 9," he smiled, and then continued, "but a machine nonetheless. Perhaps the ion storm interfered with its working for just a moment . . . or perhaps it was my imagination all along . . . I couldn't be sure. But the screen flickered in a way I'd never seen before, and then I . . . saw it . . . or at least, thought I saw it . . ."

"Saw what?" When Frobisher didn't immediately continue, Kendrow repeated, "Saw what, sir?"

"A report. A news report . . . a printed one, actually. It flew by so fast, my eye barely registered it. And it said . . ." His mouth suddenly felt dry. He licked his lips. "It said, 'Elias Frobisher Killed on 43rd Birthday.' "

"You're joking."

"Do I look like I'm joking?" Even though the awful day was behind him, he still couldn't keep that feeling of dull terror completely out of his thoughts. He had lived with the knowledge for so long . . . and had never shared it with anyone. How could he have, after all, inflicted that upon another human being?

"No, sir, you certainly don't." He let out a low whistle. "That's . . . truly awful. To be carrying that with you all this time. Are you sure of what you saw . . . ?"

"No. That's the worst part. I wasn't sure, not completely. It happened so quickly and then it was gone. Not only that, but no matter how many times I played back my tricorder record of the event, there was no trace of it. My tricorder hadn't picked it up either. Then there was the 'knowledge' that the Guardian only played the past, not the future. Every credible, scientific measure that I had available to me only served to underscore the impossibility of what I was sure I'd witnessed. And yet . . ."

"You couldn't be sure."

"Could you?" he asked. Kendrow shook his head. "Well, neither could I. I couldn't help but wonder if I'd been given this . . . vision . . . for a purpose. Except what that purpose might have been, I could only guess. Was it a warning? A random attempt at torture? Was it something avoidable, or was I supposed to surrender to fate? I remember . . ." The recollection was painful to him, even after all this time. "My last day there, I stood in front of the Guardian and just screamed and kept on screaming, wanting to know what the purpose to all of it had been. And the thing just sat there, replying in one of its preprogrammed ways that it was there to be my guide. No man should know his fate, Kendrow, or the time of his demise . . . even the possible time.

"The events that I experienced on that world shaped—'distorted,' might be a better word—the way in which I handled the rest of my life up to this point. I had no idea whether I had imagined it, whether it was to happen irrevocably, or whether it was one of the assorted possibilities that trickled through the Guardian but wound up being swept away by the rivers of time. I spent about six months barely functioning as a human being before I pulled myself together enough to carry on with . . . well, with whatever it was that I was going to be left with.

"But you know what, Kendrow?"

"What, sir?"

Slowly he walked over to the interface console of Omega 9. The flashing pad blinked its hypnotically entrancing lights at him. The pale blue pattern was rather soothing to him. "If not for that experience . . . it's possible the Omega 9 might not exist. When your mind reaches a point where it can't function in its normal patterns, it seeks out new patterns. And my thoughts eventually brought me in the direction of the Omega 9. I saw . . . possibilities," he whispered the word. "Circuits, possibilities, revealed themselves to me, one unfolding upon another. And when I saw them, ignoring them was not an option. That's what brought me to the Daystrom Institute. The years hurtled past, Kendrow. I almost didn't notice them, because I was so busy working to produce the Omega 9."

"I just wish . . ." Kendrow began to say, but then he stopped.

"No, it's all right, Kendrow." He folded his arms and leaned back against a console. "What's on your mind?"

"Well . . . the top secret turn this entire project has taken." He gestured around him, at the banks of computer circuitry and nannite growth technology that was in place. "It's . . . well, this outpost is fairly remote, sir. Somewhat lonely."

"I prefer it that way, Kendrow. My theories, my work is off the beaten path. I'd prefer that I remain that way as well. The fortunate thing about the Daystrom Institute is that they understand and respect the concept of creative vision. Once they're convinced that they're dealing with a true visionary . . . such as myself, I modestly admit," and he laughed at the obvious pretentiousness of the viewpoint, "then they're willing to provide as much or as little help as required, as much or as little in terms of equipment as needed. And the precise working environment to foster the best work. I wish . . ." and he shook his head, "I wish I could have met Daystrom himself. Poor fellow. What a tortured genius he was. That incident with the *Enterprise* a hundred years ago . . ."

"Sir . . . about this working environment . . ." He coughed politely. "To be honest, I haven't spoken to you about it since I first came here six months ago because of, well . . . your attitude, and the tension that seemed to, frankly, ooze from every pore. But since we're being open and straightforward now, I feel inclined to ask . . . doesn't our presence here make us something of a target, sir? The Omega 9 . . . ?"

"Of course not." Frobisher laughed at the notion. "The work we've developed here is going to be made available to all. There's nothing for anyone *to* steal. And even if we did . . . we have enough internal defenses here to hold them off until help comes. And those defenses were built by very paranoid Daystrom executives who have the exact same mindset as you, Kendrow. You should be pleased . . . or maybe you should be afraid, I'm not quite sure." He clapped Kendrow on the shoulder. "Be of good cheer, Kendrow. I feel like I have a new lease on life. Tell you what: Let's track down that glitch you were talking about, and then we can actually take the rest of the day off from work. Have you put Omega 9 on the trail of this glitch?"

"Oh, sir, that's kind of like using photon torpedoes to kill an insect. It's just some sort of elusive little bug. Why waste the O-9's time on it?"

"Kendrow, for all its advancement, for all the potential it displays . . . it's still just a machine. It's not as if we're going to hurt its feelings or insult it by asking."

"Sir, perhaps . . ."

"Kendrow, for crying out loud, cheer up! Life's too short." He walked over to the Interface station and placed his hand against it.

"Interface activated," came the calm tone of the Omega 9. Despite the ominous name of the computer itself, the machine's voice was that of a young female, not more than ten years old. One of the scientists back at the main institute, in the early days of the computer's development, had patterned the voice on his daughter's as a sort of birthday surprise for her. He had intended to change it subsequently, but Frobisher felt it was so charming that he opted to retain the voice for the Omega 9.

"Interface prepared," said Frobisher. "Activate nannotech for link."

He felt the familiar tingling along his palm. The most difficult thing he'd ever had to accomplish in the early days of the

Omega 9 was develop the confidence to allow the machine to work as intended. It had taken something of a leap of faith for him, and he still saw it as the one possible drawback in the widespread acceptance of the Omega 9. But he hoped that that, too, would pass.

"Nannotech on line," the computer informed him. Already he could sense the computer's voice not outside of his mind, but within. "Link established."

"Doctor . . ." Kendrow seemed to be trying to get his attention.

But it was too late. Frobisher's mind was already deep within the Omega 9. He felt the usual, intoxicating rush that came to him at such times. It took an act of will for him to steady himself, to avoid being swept away into the morass of the complex machine's innermost workings. The nannotech helped keep his mind focused, and then he turned the Omega 9's formidable abilities to the fairly minor task at hand.

His mind plumbed the depths of the machine, information coming in from all over, giving Frobisher a link to every part of not only the computer, but the entire station.

At times such as this, Frobisher rarely had any true sense of time. Usually, he felt as if he were inside the machine for at least an hour, perhaps more. Invariably, though, he was there for less than a minute.

This time it was only seconds. But when he emerged from the machine, his eyes were wide and his face pale. Slowly he turned his gaze toward Kendrow. "What . . . have you done?" he whispered.

"Done, sir?" Kendrow appeared politely confused.

"You've . . . taken down our defenses. Slowly, gradually, subtly . . . done it in such a way that the computer detected no attempt at sabotage. Rerouted systems, drained away energy . . ."

Kendrow started to voice a protest, but one look from Frobisher was enough to silence him.

". . . and your work . . . affected the chronometers," Frobisher continued, as if speaking from a place very far away. "You probably didn't even realize it. It was an accident, an unexpected side effect of your tampering. It sped the chronometer up. That's why time seemed to fly by. It wasn't just subjective. The computer core was actually malfunctioning, shortening hours and minutes, eventually days over the past week or so. At night, while we were sleeping, we lost even more time. At his point, we've misplaced about twelve hours. Which means . . ."

Kendrow's expression was one of frightened understanding. "I'm . . . I'm sorry . . ."

"Which means . . . today is still my birthday," Frobisher said tonelessly.

At that moment, the entire station shuddered as something smashed against the exterior. Frobisher, at one with Omega 9, felt the shock as if it had happened to him personally. Alarms screeched throughout the station, and the Omega 9 registered that a group of unknown beings had just materialized in one of the station's upper sections. There was a ship, a massive war vessel of some sort with utterly unknown markings, in orbit around the station. The sensors and early detection devices had all been taken off line, as had communications and weaponry.

So . . . here it was. His destiny, staring him in the face.

Oddly, he had never felt more calm. He had spent so many years worrying, wondering, angsting over his known-but-frightening future, that now that it had arrived, all the fear dissipated. Instead he marshalled his concentration and dove into the Omega 9 with all the speed and precision that he could muster. All the damage that Kendrow had done was laid out before him, and he had only seconds to choose what would be the most effective thing to undo. Shields? Too late. Weaponry? Likewise. That was all created to deal with potential intruders while they were still outside, but they already had unknown enemies rampaging through the station.

Communications. That was the only hope. Again, seconds were what remained to him . . . but a second for a computer is quite unlike a second for anyone else. Frobisher envisioned himself within the Omega 9, saw his hands moving through the circuitry like an electronic ghost. Like a father gently kissing a scrape on a child's knee in order to make it feel better, Frobisher untangled the knots of interference that Kendrow had tied. Kendrow, good lord, how could Kendrow have done this to him? He had hand-picked the man out of a field of twenty-seven applicants as the man who seemed most capable, most intelligent, who had the most on the ball. And Kendrow had betrayed him to these . . . to whoever these people were.

He had allowed his mind to wander. That was pure foolishness, something he should not be permitting himself to do. He had little enough time as it was.

Using the Omega 9, he punched through the comm snarl that Kendrow had created and immediately sent out a distress call. He didn't have to record it, didn't have to speak. His mind shouted into the computer, "This is Daystrom Station, we are under attack, repeat, we are under attack. Any Federation vessel in the area, please assist. This is Doctor Elias Frobisher of the Daystrom Station, we are under attack, please assist . . ."

A comm message suddenly sprang into existence within the computer's program. That was fast, miraculously fast. Perhaps there might be a hope in hell of salvaging this situation yet. Frobisher's mind opened the message . . .

It was from Earth. It had been sent hours ago. There was an elderly couple, smiling at Frobisher. The man looked like an older version of Frobisher himself.

"Elias, darling! It's Mom and Dad! Happy birthday, son! We ran a little late, but this should still get to you in time, and we wouldn't want you to think we forgot your very special day!"

And suddenly Frobisher felt himself yanked out of the Omega 9. He fancied that, from very far away, he heard the alarmed cry of a young girl's voice . . . the voice of the Omega 9, pleading with him to come back, asking that she not be left alone.

Frobisher staggered, the nannites slipping away from him, scurrying back into their techno hidey-hole. The world around him appeared flat, one dimensional, as his senses fought to cope with reintegrating themselves with reality. The world snapped into two-dimensions, then three, and Frobisher found himself handled roughly by an alien being of undetermined origin. His skin was brown and leathery, and he had thick tusks jutting from beneath his upper lip.

There were several others nearby, a mixed bag of races, and one being from a race he did recognize, for they had been very much in the news lately. It was a Thallonian. He was very oddly built, however. His head seemed smaller in proportion to his massive body than it should have been. Frobisher attributed it to body armor.

Beg for your life, the suggestion came into his head. *You might still get out of this. Beg. Beg to live.*

Frobisher was not a fighter, not a hero, and not particularly brave. But he felt an anger, implacable and unstoppable, bubbling up and over. And he realized that all these years of living in fear, all the years of frustration, he had carried incredible resentment within him. The problem was, he had never had anyone to be angry with. No one had done anything to him. No one had forced the knowledge upon him. He had simply stumbled upon it, like a scientist out to probe the secrets of the universe and inadvertently finding more than he had bargained for.

But he resented it nonetheless. Why had the fates done this to him? What in the world could he have possibly done to deserve this awful foreknowledge of the time of his demise? He had been a good person his entire life. Never cheated anyone, never tried to hurt anyone that he knew of. And yet he had been handed this hideously raw deal.

For years, for more years than he cared to think about, he had wanted someone, anyone he could strike against. A target upon which he could vent his anger, anger which had grown exponentially as years had passed. Wasted, wasted years . . .

The being who was leering over him was bigger, broader, infinitely stronger than he. It was the kind of situation where, under normal circumstances, Frobisher would have put up his hands, surrendered, and prayed . . .

. . . and given over control of his life one more time.

In his mind's eye, he saw the Guardian staring at him. That thing, that monster, that machine had cast a long shadow over so much of his life. Built by beings unknown, functioning in ways no one knew. The Andorians had their own name for it: The T'Sh'Iar, which meant "God's Window."

God had looked through the window, seen Frobisher peering through, and had punished him for absolutely no reason at all. Taken away his destiny by sadistically handing it to him.

Frobisher saw the blaster hanging at the hip of the alien with the brown, leathery skin, the being who looked like a giant serpent. There was a throbbing in Frobisher's head. The tall red alien nearby was addressing him, but the pounding in his head drowned it all out. All the rage, all the anger, everything that had ever infuriated him over the hopeless wreck that his life had become as time's inexorable march had carried him unwillingly toward his doom, it all exploded from him at once.

There was no way that Frobisher should have been a threat to the serpent man, no way. The serpent man was paying so little attention to the possibility of Frobisher as a threat that he never even saw the trembling fist that Frobisher's fingers had contracted into. Furthermore, his skin was so hard that even if Frobisher were to land a punch, he shouldn't even have felt it.

Frobisher's years of anger congealed into that fist, and without listening to a word that the red-skinned alien was saying, he spun and swung his fist into a powerful roundhouse. In his entire adult life—for that matter, throughout his childhood and adolescence—he had never thrown a punch in his life. The roundhouse was his very first.

It was perfect.

It caught the serpent man squarely in his lantern jaw. The impact immediately broke Frobisher's knuckles. It didn't matter. Frobisher never even felt it. But the serpent man most certainly felt the blow as his head snapped around and he let out a startled squeal that seemed totally at odds with his hulking demeanor. He staggered, and that was all the opening Frobisher needed. He yanked the blaster out of the holster at the serpent man's side, swung it around and aimed it squarely at the red-skinned man who was clearly the leader.

The red-skinned man looked mildly surprised.

It was the single most exultant moment in all of Frobisher's life. Given a half second more, he would have fired the blaster.

He never saw the blow from the serpent man coming. The alien swung his fist like a club, and it caved in the side of Frobisher's head. His arm swung wide. His finger squeezed spasmodically on the trigger and the shot went wide, exploding harmlessly against the far wall. Frobisher collapsed, his head thudding to the floor. He heard a sort of distant buzzing, saw a thick liquid dripping in front of his eyes that he did not recognize as his own blood. He reached out a hand, and it touched something warm. He couldn't tell what it was, but a female voice seemed to be singing to him.

His lips puckered together. He drew in a breath with effort, and then with even more effort expelled it. It rattled from his throat and out through his mouth, and in his mind's eye he saw candles flickering in front of him. With the gust of breath from his lungs, the flames disappeared. All out at once.

I hope I get my wish, thought Frobisher as he died.

Zolon Darg stared at the corpse on the floor, and then slowly levelled his gaze at Shunabo. Shunabo, for his part, seemed extremely irritated with Kendrow. The brown-skinned, leathery Shunabo approached Kendrow with a stride that was an odd combination of swagger and slink. "You said he wouldn't be a problem," Shunabo said, his irritation causing him to over enunciate every syllable. "You told us—you told *me*—that he was a quiet, reserved, run-of-the-mill human who wouldn't offer up the slightest resistance." His soft voice began to get louder. "Oddly, you didn't happen to mention that he had a punch like a berserker Klingon, or that he was capable of coming within a hair of *shooting Zolon Darg's head off!*"

In point of fact, Zolon Darg knew that Shunabo was right. He had been caught completely flat-footed, and this little scientist, this no one, this weakling, this nothing, had nearly succeeded in accomplishing what some of the greatest and most accomplished bounty hunters in two quadrants had not. Darg had gotten sloppy, very, very sloppy, and Shunabo had saved his ass.

It was a situation that had to be addressed immediately.

In two quick steps, Darg was directly behind Shunabo. He slapped a hand around Shunabo's chest, yanked him backward, grabbed the top of his head and twisted quickly. The sound of Shunabo's neck snapping echoed through the suddenly silent lab.

There was still a flickering of light in Shunabo's eyes as Darg snarled in his ear, "I was in no danger. I could have handled him. And you were under specific instructions to keep Frobisher alive." That last, at least, was accurate, and really, in the final analysis, one point was all that was necessary. Zolon Darg spread wide his arms and Shunabo sank to the floor. Before Shunabo even landed, Darg turned away from him disdainfully. He towered over Kendrow, and he could see that

Kendrow's legs were trembling. Kendrow appeared to be keeping himself standing by bracing himself against a table.

"Are you going to be able to do the job in Frobisher's place?" he demanded.

Kendrow's mouth moved, but nothing audible came forth. Darg scowled in a manner that seemed to suck the light right out of the lab. "Well?" continued Darg. "Are you capable of speech at all?"

"Probably not at the moment, Zolon."

The voice behind them, in contrast to the increasing bellow of Darg, was remarkably mild. The individual to whom it belonged likewise seemed mild in appearance. He was a Thallonian like Zolon, but whereas Zolon Darg was massive, the newcomer appeared quite slender, although it was hard to tell since he was wearing fairly loose black and purple robes. He had a neatly trimmed, yellowing beard, which indicated his age to anyone who happened to know that Thallonian hair tended to yellow with age rather than turn gray or white, as occurred with humans. His face was carefully inscrutable. Only his eyes seemed to burn with an inner light. The rest of his presence was so minimal that one's gaze could easily have passed right over him.

"Is that a fact, General Thul?" Darg said. But despite the defiant sound of the words, there was nothing in his tone that was challenging. It wasn't out of fear, of course. It was more from a sense of respect. And it was quite possible that General Gerrid Thul was the one individual in the galaxy for whom Darg was capable of showing that sort of deference.

"Well, look at the poor man," Thul said. He crossed the room toward Kendrow, and didn't seem to walk so much as glide. "You seem to have scared him terribly. Am I correct, sir?"

Kendrow slowly nodded.

"There? You see?" The General clucked sympathetically. "You know, Darg . . . you used to be a much calmer, understanding individual. The difficulties you've encountered in the past years have not mellowed you. You must learn to be calmer. You will live longer."

Darg smiled in a rather mirthless way. "I shall be sure to remember that."

"See that you do. Now, Mr . . . Kendrow, is it?" When Kendrow nodded, the one called Gerrid Thul continued, "Mr. Kendrow . . . you have been paid a significant amount to cooperate with us, have you not."

"Yes, sir. I have, sir."

"Articulate speech. You are capable of articulate speech. That is good, that is very good. Now then, Mr. Kendrow . . . since the good Doctor here," and he tapped Frobisher's corpse with the toe of his boot, "is not in any condition to provide assistance to us, it is important to know whether you are going to be able to continue in his stead."

"I'm . . ." He cleared his throat. "Do you really want an honest answer?"

General Thul smiled in an almost paternal fashion. "Honesty is always to be preferred."

"Truthfully, I'm not sure. I tried to familiarize myself with all aspects of his work, but the Omega 9 was such a uniquely personal, and truly amazing, piece of work . . . I can't pretend that I know or understand all the parameters and aspects that he brought to it. I know and understand the basic interface options, I can program the—"

Thul stopped him with a casual gesture. "It is not necessary to go into details, Mr. Kendrow. Your honesty is appreciated. Is it safe to assume that you can aid us in transporting the key components of the Omega 9 to our ship, and that you will, at the very least, give us your best effort in adapting and understanding the possibilities this amazing device provides?"

Kendrow's head bobbed so eagerly that it seemed as if it was about to tumble off his shoulders. "Yes. Yes, absolutely, sir."

"That is good. That is good to hear. So, to summarize," and he placed a hand on Kendrow's shoulder, "you will help us . . . and we will allow you to live. And if you cease to help us, either due to lack of cooperation or lack of knowledge, why . . . you shall meet the same fate as Doctor Frobisher. Except your demise will be far slower, much more protracted, and will involve an impressive array of sharp objects. Do we understand each other?"

Kendrow gulped deeply.

Zolon Darg, for his part, smiled. For a moment there, he had been concerned that Thul was going to be entirely too sympathetic. He realized that he should have known better. After all, when someone was interested in obliterating almost all sentient life, as General Thul was, such an individual was not about to be concerned about sparing the feelings of one insignificant little scientist.

"Well, Mr. Kendrow?" General Thul prompted once more. "Do we understand each other?"

Kendrow nodded.

"Well, then!" Thul said, and he clapped his hands and rubbed them together briskly, "let's get to work, shall we?"

And as they got to work, the distress call continued to issue forth, searching for someone . . . anyone . . . who might be able to save what was left of the day . . .

II.

COMMANDER WILLIAM RIKER felt as if all the eyes in the Ten-Forward lounge were upon him. He kept telling himself, however, that he was probably imagining it. He found a table off in the corner and signalled to the bartender that he'd like a drink. One was quickly produced and he proceeded to sip it in relative peace that lasted for a whole seven seconds.

He glanced up as Lieutenant Palumbo looked down at him. Palumbo was half a head taller than Riker, with black hair slicked back and a rather open manner that Riker wasn't quite sure how to react to. Palumbo clearly considered Riker something of a curiosity; one might even have said that Palumbo came across as being in awe of him, as if not sure how to respond to the presence of the Great William Riker aboard the *Starship U.S.S. Independence.*

"So . . . what's it like?" asked Palumbo without preamble.

" 'It,' Lieutenant?" Despite the breach of protocol, Riker couldn't help but feel some amusement at Palumbo's manner.

Palumbo promptly dropped down into a chair across from Riker. "Being related to one of the original signers of the original Resolution."

"Well . . . Lieutenant," Riker felt constrained to point out, "the Resolution of Non-Interference was signed nearly two

53

hundred years ago. Granted, I'm related to one of the original signers. But it's not as if Thaddeus Riker was someone that I spent a good deal of time with. In point of fact, he died more than a century before I was even conceived."

"Even so. Even so," Palumbo's head bobbed as if he were furiously agreeing and disagreeing simultaneously. "It must make you proud, right? Am I right?"

Actually, Riker had never given the matter all that much thought. Riker had always considered himself somewhat self-sufficient. He was determined to carve his own career and obtain his own notoriety, and he wasn't the type of person who rested upon the achievements of those who had come before him.

Still . . . he had to admit that there was something to be said for it. He'd done a good deal of reading up on Thaddeus Riker as the bicentennial had approached, and the more he'd learned, the more impressed he'd been.

"You're right," agreed Riker.

Palumbo slapped the table. It shook from the impact. "See, I knew I was right!"

"Is this guy bothering you, Commander?"

Lieutenant Mankowski had come up behind Palumbo. During their shift, Palumbo operated conn while Mankowski was at ops, so they were accustomed to working tightly together. When Mankowski spoke, it was with a faint southern drawl. Riker couldn't help but notice, to his amusement, that Mankowski was keeping one eye on his reflection in the observation glass nearby, running his fingers through his wavy brown hair to make sure that it was "just so."

"No, Mankowski. No bother at all."

"Thanks for being so concerned, Joe," Palumbo said in obvious irritation. "What, you trying to embarrass me in front of the Commander here?"

"Oh . . . please. You needn't concern yourself about that, Lieutenant," said Riker. "Really. It's not a problem. To be perfectly honest, if I were in your position, I'd probably be reacting in exactly the same way."

"Well, that's good to hear, sir. Very understanding of you." There was one other chair at the table, and Mankowski sat in it. Riker chuckled softly to himself as he saw that Mankowski straddled the chair in the same manner that Riker habitually did. "Look . . . to be honest, sir, there's a goodly number of people on this ship who would love to bend your ear about all manner of things. Not just about your ancestor, but about you yourself. You've had a hell of a career, after all."

"It's been . . . interesting."

"You're being too modest, sir."

"Oh, yeah. Way too modest," echoed Palumbo.

"Now me," and Mankowski tapped his chest, "I'm not that kind of person. The hero-worshipping sort, I mean. I think people have a right to be proud of their accomplishments, but that's no reason to elevate them to some sort of bigger-than-life status. In fact, I was just saying the other day to—"

From across the lounge, a crewman called, "Hey, Joe! Joe! Got a second?"

"Hey!" Mankowski shot back, clearly annoyed. "Can't you see I'm talking to Commander William T. Riker here? *The* William Riker?"

The crewman held up his hands, palms out, in mute apology for butting in.

Riker put a hand in front of his mouth and laughed into it.

"It's just that," Palumbo jumped in during the momentary lull, "it's just that, well . . . the truth is, I've been a fan of yours ever since I was a kid."

"A *kid?*" Riker couldn't quite believe his ears as he stared at the young officer. "Lieutenant, for God's sake, I'm not *that* old."

"Well . . . not a little kid," Palumbo amended hastily. "Just since, well . . ." He considered it a moment. "Since I was a teenager."

That still seemed a hideous age discrepancy to Riker, and he said, "That can't be right. I haven't been at it that long . . . have I?" His voice trailed off on the last two words.

"Oh, sure," Palumbo said with a cheerfulness that Riker couldn't help but find disturbing. "My dad was—is—in Starfleet, and he talked about officers who were on the fast track. He especially thought the crew of the *Enterprise* was top-notch."

Riker quickly did the math in his head and realized that Palumbo was exactly right.

"Those were the good old days, huh, Commander?" Palumbo asked.

"Ohhhhh yes. The good old days." Riker was suddenly starting to feel as ancient as Thaddeus Riker.

"Mike . . . I think you're making the Commander uncomfortable," Mankowski said cautiously, glancing from Riker back to Palumbo.

"Nah! Am I? I didn't mean to . . ."

"It's . . . all right," Riker said. He generally had a fairly ready smile and it didn't fail him this time either as he was able to appreciate the more amusing aspects of the situation. "It's just that, well . . ." and he tapped his chest, "in here I feel like I joined the Fleet only yesterday. I'm not entirely sure at what point I went from eager young cadet to gray eminence. It's a disconcerting transition, that's all."

"Do you think Captain Picard went through the same thing?"

"The captain?" Riker smiled puckishly. "Absolutely not. The truth is that Captain Picard was born forty years old. He didn't have the time or patience for child or adolescence. He simply went straight to the status of 'authority figure.' "

"I believe it," said Palumbo. "He came and lectured to one of our classes once. He scared the crap out of me. But . . . don't tell him that next time you see him, okay?"

"My lips are sealed," Riker assured him.

They chatted for a few minutes more, although Palumbo and Mankowski seemed more and more interested in crosstalk between the two of them, leaving Riker serenely to his thoughts. And, naturally enough, those thoughts turned to Thaddeus Riker.

The truth was that the Resolution was indeed one hell of an accomplishment, and Thaddeus Riker had been one of the main architects. The Resolution of Non-Interference had been a sort of United Federation Bill of Rights. It had pulled together a number of fractured members of the United Federation of Plantets into a basic position paper that put forward, in language so plain and firm as to command their assent, the basic philosophies that the UFP hoped to pursue. Many historians felt that the Resolution was not only the turning point in the UFP's early development, but the basics for some of the Federation's most fundamental philosophies—including, most notably, Starfleet's Prime Directive—had its roots in the Resolution of Non-Interference.

Thaddeus Riker, one of the principal drafters of the Resolution, had affixed his name to it along with some fifty other representatives of assorted worlds, outposts and colonies. That important event had occurred nearly two hundred years ago, and a major celebration on Earth was in the works. Indeed, that was the reason for Riker's presence on the *Independence*. The starship was en route to Earth anyway, and the ship had been instructed to pick up Riker and bring him along. For other officers, the easy assignment would have been considered something of a paid vacation. That was not the case with Riker. He thought it a colossal waste of time, and tried to convince Starfleet that this endeavor was worth neither the time nor the effort as far as his presence was concerned. He could think of a hundred more constructive things he'd rather be doing than putting in an appearance at some high-profile function, no matter how historically important that function might be. Unfortunately, as so frequently happened in cases like this one, Starfleet wasn't able to come up with any.

Which was how Riker had wound up aboard the *Independence*, being made to feel old by two young officers who seemed bound and determined to worship Riker to bits. They chatted on with Riker barely listening, and hoping against hope that something—anything—would distract them from the unwanted attention they were lavishing upon him.

That was the moment that the yellow alert klaxon went off. Without hesitation, Mankowski and Palumbo high-tailed it out the door, as did the other patrons of the Ten-Forward. Within moments the place was empty, leaving a disconsolate Riker staring at the glass still in his hand. His very soul cried *"Foul!"* as he thought of where he was during an emergency as opposed to where he'd prefer to be.

On the other hand . . . he was a guest. Guests should be, and are, accommodated whenever possible. And perhaps he was a guest who could lend a hand, presuming the captain was interested in the extra help.

Couldn't hurt to ask him, Riker reasoned. Couldn't hurt at all . . .

* * *

Captain George Garfield, a man of modest height but booming authority, looked surprised to see Riker striding onto the bridge. Garfield's face had a craggy ruggedness about it, and his gray hair was so tightly curled that some felt it was possible to slice one's finger open on it. "Is there a problem, Commander?" he asked.

"No problem at all, sir. I just . . ." On the face of it, it seemed absurd to make the offer now that he was there. It was an insult, really, an implication that the captain was unable or unwilling to handle the situation on his own. First officer Joe Morris was watching Riker warily. He was a lean man with thinning hair and a foxlike face. He tended to smile a lot for a first officer, and he had a habit of taking pains to display his perfectly arrayed teeth whenever possible.

Garfield smiled grimly and nodded in apparent understanding. "When there's a red alert, you don't exactly feel comfortable with the prospect of hiding down in your quarters, is that it?"

"Exactly it, sir."

"Very well. As long as we remember whose ship this is."

There was a bit of a ribbing quality to the comment, but at the same time, a very clear, somewhat territorial warning. Riker didn't have to be told twice. "I'm just a spectator, captain."

"Spectate from there," Garfield said, indicating the vacant counselor's chair. The ship's counselor, Lieutenant Aronin, hadn't been feeling particularly well as of late, and had been confined to sickbay under orders of the ship's CMO, Doctor DiSpigno. "And don't you worry. Once we attend to whatever's going on, I assure you we'll give you a smooth ride to your destination."

"Much obliged, sir."

Riker promptly slid easily into the chair.

"Talk to me, Mr. Palumbo," Garfield said.

Palumbo scanned the board and reported, "Distress signal, sir. I believe it's coming from the Daystrom Institute Outpost."

From the tactical board, Lieutenant Monastero called, "Confirming, sir. Putting it on screen."

The image of a gentle-looking man appeared. But the background behind him was extremely strange. It didn't seem to be an actual place so much as an environment of pulsing energy.

"Good God," said Morris. "What's that?"

"This is Daystrom Station, we are under attack, repeat, we are under attack," said the man on the screen. "Any Federation vessel in the area, please assist. This is Doctor Elias Frobisher of the Daystrom Station, we are under attack, please assist . . ."

"It appears to be computer generated," Mankowski said. "Not an actual image, but one composed by a computer. Question is, why?"

"No, Mr. Mankowski, that's not the question at all," Garfield told him in no uncertain terms. "The question is, 'How fast can we get there?' "

"At maximum warp . . . ?" Mankowski did some rapid-fire calculations. "Three hours, eighteen minutes."

Morris had stepped over to the ops station and was glancing over Palumbo's shoulder. "We appear to be the closest ship in the area, sir."

"Lieutenant, best speed to Daystrom."

"Aye, captain." Mankowski immediately punched in the course, and the *Independence* angled sharply away from its then-current heading and headed with all possible alacrity toward the scene of the distress call.

The captain shifted in his chair and looked at Riker with mild apology in his eyes. "Seems we're going to be late getting you to your appointment with fame, Commander. Regulations clearly state . . ."

"That any Starfleet vessel capable of responding to a distress call must lend assistance whenever possible," Riker recited with a smile. "Captain, there's a number of regs that I would be the first to dispute . . . but that is most definitely not one of them. The only question is, is there going to be anyone or anything left by the time we get there."

"I don't know," Garfield admitted. "We can only do the best that we can do, Commander. The thing is, a science station such as Daystrom's outpost isn't like a planetary treasury or some such, where you just go in, raid the riches and depart. Whatever these possible raiders want—whether it's technology, files, information, what-have-you—it's probably going to have to be handled with delicacy. That means they'll have to take their time extracting it for fear of damaging it, and if they take enough time," and he nodded grimly, "then we've got them."

There was little talking for the remainder of the trip. Riker watched the crew of the *Independence* going about their business. It was an odd sensation for him. He was, after all, part of his surroundings and environment. And they were all Starfleet, after all. They might be spread out among various ships, but they were a unit nevertheless, each capable of helping one another and functioning as a team.

But just as he was a part, he was also apart. He had his rank, certainly, but he had no place on this vessel. He was simply a passenger, with no more intrinsic importance to the ship than cargo being carted down in the hold. It was a very, very strange feeling. Every so often Garfield or Morris would engage him in polite conversation, but it seemed to Riker that it was more a matter of form than any real interest in him. Then again, he might simply have been imagining it.

"Approaching Daystrom Station," Mankowski announced finally. "Sensors indicate that the company hasn't left the party yet."

"Magnify," ordered Garfield.

The screen rippled briefly, and then the conical shape of Daystrom station appeared in front of them. Sure enough, in orbit around the station was a vessel the likes of which Riker had never seen before. It was low slung, built for speed but, at the same time, clearly heavily armed . . . an assessment that Monastero confirmed a moment later from tactical.

"Disruptors, phasers . . . and some sort of plasma weapon as well. They're well armed, all right. Nothing our own weaponry and shield can't handle, but I don't think I'd care to face them in anything less than a starship."

"Thank you, Mr. Monastero. Open a hailing frequency, please."

"Open, sir."

Garfield leaned back in his command chair, crossing his legs in a rather casual manner as if he were having a comfortable chat in his living room. "This is Captain George Garfield of the *Starship Independence*. Please identify yourselves immediately and prepare to be boarded. Thank you."

"Captain," warned Mankowski, "they're powering up their weapons."

"Didn't their mothers teach them that 'please' and 'thank you' are the magic words?" said Morris.

"I know mine did," said Garfield. "Shields up. Maintain hailing frequency. Unidentified ship, please stand down your weapons immediately, or we will be forced to defend ourselves."

"They've opened fire!" Mankowski said. Sure enough, plasma torpedoes were hurtling across the void and spiralling straight toward the *Independence*.

And both Garfield and Riker called, "Evasive action!", the latter doing so by reflex. Immediately realizing his error, he looked with chagrin at Garfield. Fortunately, Garfield seemed more amused than usurped.

Mankowski spurred the mighty ship forward, and the *Independence* gracefully angled down and away from the brace of torpedoes. "Return fire," ordered Garfield.

"We're not yet at optimum distance for full effectiveness."

Garfield glanced over his shoulder. "Indulge me."

Monastero nodded as his hands flew over the tactical array, and the phaser banks flared to life. But the distance was indeed too great, and although the phasers scored a direct hit upon the opposing vessel, the damage done to their shields was virtually non-existent.

"They're moving off!" Mankowski said.

Riker realized that Garfield was faced with a dilemma. If he attended to the space station, took the time to send down an away team, then the delay might give the other vessel time to get away. But if there were wounded or dying people at the station, then a chase after the attacker might delay the *Independence* for so long that no aid to the station personnel—should there be any surviving—would be possible.

An obvious solution immediately presented itself to Riker, and out of reflex he was about to suggest it. But as Riker opened his mouth to speak, Morris said, "Captain, I've readied the shuttle bay in case . . ."

"You read my mind, Number One. Bridge to security."

"Security. Petronella here."

"Mister Petronella, scramble a security team and med unit

and get yourselves down to the shuttle bay. Attend to whomever needs help aboard the station and remain here until we return."

"Aye, sir."

Garfield noticed Riker's still-open mouth out of the corner of his eye and asked, "Is there a problem, Commander?"

"No, sir. Obviously no problem at all."

"Good."

"Enemy vessel preparing to go to warp, sir," Mankowski announced.

"Stay on her, Lieutenant," Garfield said calmly. "Mr. Monastero, fire a warning shot. See if we can persuade them to stay and chat."

As the *Independence* hurtled toward the station, closing the gap, Monastero fired the phasers. One blast coruscated against the enemy ship's shielding, while the other went across her bow, intercepting the vessel's momentary trajectory. But the unknown vessel spun out of the way and moved away from the station, picking up speed with every passing moment.

"Shuttle away!" called Palumbo.

"Chase them down, Mr. Mankowski," said Garfield.

"Aye, sir." Mankowski grinned in a slightly devilish manner. If there was one thing he liked, it was a pursuit.

The *Independence* darted straight toward the alien vessel, but the other ship immediately kicked into high gear. It was a burst of speed that was a bit surprising to those on the bridge of the starship, for it hadn't seemed as if the other ship had that much power to her. But they were only momentarily daunted. "Looks like we're in a race," observed Riker, and no one disputed that.

The "race" continued for some minutes, and then for an hour. Every so often, the opposing vessel would scatter something behind them: A plasma torpedo, or a bomb. But the *Independence* adroitly kept out of the way. Unfortunately, the starship wasn't drawing close enough to do any serious damage with her own array of weaponry.

"Sir . . . we're approaching Thallonian space," said Mankowski. "I know that she's been opened up ever since the collapse of the Thallonian Empire . . ."

"But there's still an 'approach with approval only' mandate on it. I know, Mr. Mankowski. But this is likely where they were heading in hopes that we were going to break off pursuit. Are you interested in quitting the chase, Mr. Mankowski?"

"No, sir," Mankowski said with a grim smile.

"Maintain course and speed, then."

Riker found the give and take between the captain and his crew to be a bit amusing. Garfield was older than Picard, and yet he seemed to take a somewhat paternal air with his crewmen. It was a very different command style, and certainly not Riker's own during the times when he'd been in command, but it was certainly a viable one nonetheless.

"Engineering to bridge." A formal British accent came over the comm unit.

"Bridge. Garfield here," replied the captain. "Go ahead, Mr. McKean."

"Captain . . . may I inquire as to whether we will be reducing velocity in the near future? I am uncertain whether I will be able to maintain maximum thrust for all that much longer."

"No promises, Mr. McKean."

"Sir, I'm not asking for a commitment. But I do wish to be able to provide the velocity you require if and when you require it. As things stand, I am unable to guarantee said velocity will be yours for the asking. The warp core is, if you'll pardon my poetic language, complaining bitterly. All the velocity in the galaxy will be irrelevant if the ship has exploded."

"Understood, Mr. McKean."

"Captain!" Mankowski suddenly called. "The other ship is slowing down."

"Is she turning to fight?"

"Doesn't appear to be turning, no, sir. Perhaps their engines are overtaxed."

And from down in engineering, McKean could be heard muttering, "Perhaps their bloody captain listens to his engineering officer and reduces speed when reasonable."

It was all Riker could do to repress a grin. It was comforting to know that there were some universal constants, and chief engineers appeared to be one of them. For his part, Garfield kept a poker face as he said, "Mr. McKean, we still have an open channel."

"Oh." There was a pause, and then another, "Oh. Uhm . . . McKean out," and the connection was broken.

Turning back to business, Garfield said, "Bring us ahead slow, Mr. Mankowski. Let's see what we've got. Monastero, open a channel."

"You're on, sir."

"Unidentified ship, this is the *Independence*. Please respond."

On the screen, the vessel they'd pursued all that way had come to a complete halt. She wasn't dead in space, but she wasn't taking any action at all. She just sat there.

And Riker couldn't keep his mouth shut. "Sir, I don't like this. With all respect . . ."

"No apologies necessary, Commander," Garfield said, rubbing his chin thoughtfully. "I'm not sure I like it either. Smells like some sort of set-up."

"My thoughts exactly, sir."

"We can't exactly go running away from a ship we chased down this far, and which isn't even firing at us. But still . . ." He thought a moment and then said, "Sensors on maximum. Sweep the area."

"Sweeping, sir," said Mankowski. "Not picking up anything."

"Nothing on tactical sensor scans either," Monastero affirmed.

"Checking the . . ." Suddenly Mankowski's voice caught. "Picking up an energy discharge, sir. Consistent with the patterns detected . . ." He turned and looked straight at the captain. " . . . detected when a Romulan shp is decloaking, sir."

"Where?" demanded Garfield.

"To starboard, sir. At 813 Mark 2."

A moment later, everyone on the bridge saw that Mankowski was correct as a Romulan vessel shimmered into existence to the ship's starboard . . .

. . . and then, a moment later, to her port. In the meantime, the ship they'd been pursuing had come around. "Enemy ship approaching. They're weapons hot, sir," said Mankowski.

"Captain . . ." Riker said in a tone of warning.

Garfield surveyed the situation arrayed against them and nodded his head. "I believe it's time to make like a shepherd and get the flock out of here. Reverse course, Lieuten—"

And then two more ships materialized, one forward and one

after. They were now completely surrounded by Romulan warbirds, all of them combat-ready with their weapons prepared to discharge.

Despite the fact that they were overwhelmingly outnumbered, Garfield did not appear the least bit perturbed. Instead, acting as if he still maintained the strategic advantage, he called out, "Attention all ships. This is the starship *Independence*. The vessel we have been pursuing has illegally entered, and attacked, an outpost in Federation space. This is not your concern, and I strongly advise you to veer off before it's too late."

And then, to their surprise, a voice crackled back across the channel. It was a female voice, and the moment Riker heard it, a chill went down his spine. The voice said, in a mocking tone, "Too late? Too late for whom? For us? Or for you?"

"This is Captain George Garfield. Identify yourself, please."

The image of the ships around them momentarily vanished from the screen, to be replaced by the face of a female Romulan. She had tightly cut blonde hair and an expression that seemed to radiate contempt. "Very well," she said. "We are the ones who are going to kill you. Is that sufficient identification . . ."

Then her gaze flickered toward the officer seated in the counselor's chair, and her eyes went wide with sadistic delight. "Well, well. It's been ages, Will Riker."

"Sela," Riker said tersely.

Garfield didn't even pretend to understand what was going on. "Commander, do you know this . . . individual?"

"Her name is Sela. She's the half-Romulan daughter of a deceased woman from an alternate time line."

"Oh, well, that clears things up," Palumbo could be heard to mutter.

"If you know this individual, then I suggest you advise her against any rash actions."

"You heard the man, Sela. Don't look for a fight where there need not be one. It's not as if you're in the best of relations with the Romulan government at the moment. You can't afford any more military disasters."

"How kind of you to care about my well-being, Riker," Sela replied, "considering that all of my past 'disasters' can be placed squarely at your door. But," she added thoughtfully, "you're right. I don't need more blemishes on my record."

"As I said . . ."

"Instead, I need to blow you all to hell. All vessels," she called out, "you're tapping into this communication. Directly in the middle of us is one Will Riker. Let me tell you, I've been waiting to say this for ages." Her lips drew back in a feral smile of triumph. "Fire at Will."

And as the Romulan ships, as one, opened fire, Riker felt the world explode around him.

III.

IT WAS THE WEEKLY poker game, and all the usual suspects were grouped around: Deanna, Data, Worf, and Geordi. As Riker studied his hand, Geordi leaned forward and said without preamble, "So there's this mighty sailing ship, a British frigate, cruising the Seven Seas, and one day the lookout shouts down from the crow's nest, 'Captain! Captain! There's two pirate ships heading our way! They mean to attack! What should we do?' And the captain, he says, 'Bring me my red shirt.' So they bring him his red shirt, he puts it on, and leads his men into battle. It's difficult, and there are a number of casualties, but they manage to beat back the pirates. That evening, after the survivors have gotten themselves bandaged up, they ask the captain why he called for his red shirt. And he says, 'Because if I'm wounded and bleeding, I wouldn't want the sight of my blood to destroy the morale of my men. But if I'm wearing my red shirt, no one will see it.' Well, the crew thought, 'Wow. What a captain.'"

By this point, every eye at the card table was on Geordi. He continued, "So the next day, another shout, even more worried, comes down from the crow's nest. And the lookout says, 'Captain, my captain! There's ten pirate ships heading our way, and they mean to board us! What should we do?' The fright-

ened crew turns to their captain, but he doesn't flinch. He doesn't hesitate. And he calls out, 'Bring me . . . my brown pants!' "

Laughter echoed around the room, although Worf was naturally somewhat restrained. Even Data, thanks to his newly installed emotion chip, was able to laugh in appreciation. Suddenly Geordi immediately stopped laughing as he looked at something over Riker's shoulder. Riker turned and promptly fell silent, as did the others.

Jean-Luc Picard was standing there. It was impossible to tell how long he'd been there, for he'd entered fairly quietly and everyone had been engrossed in the joke. It was also impossible to tell what was going through his mind. He had a small, enigmatic smile, but that was no indicator. Picard had a standing invitation to join them for poker, but he almost never took them up on it. And of all times, that was the moment he had chosen to make an appearance at the game.

They all waited.

And at last, without the slightest change in expression, he said, "I don't think jokes about cowardly captains are very funny." With that observation hanging in the air, he turned and walked out.

Then the room jolted under Riker, tossing Troi, Worf, Data and Geordi to the floor, and the recollection dissolved into reality.

It took Riker a few more moments to sort the confusing real world from his recollection of times past. The jolt had been rather sudden and, when Riker had been thrown from his chair, he had hit his head rather severely. It had dazed him and sent his mind spiralling back to a time with his shipmates where, somehow, things had seemed simpler. But then, didn't times past always seem that way, no matter how complicated they were?

His lungs began to ache. He wondered why, and then the full realization of his situation imposed itself upon him. The bridge was thick with smoke.

The flame-retardant chemicals were already being released and were controlling the fire adequately enough, but that still didn't help the wreck that the bridge had become. It had all happened so fast, so decisively, that it was difficult for Riker to fully grasp.

Then he saw Palumbo's unmoving body slumped backward in the chair, with half his scalp torn away and a huge metal shard buried in his skull, and the full reality of it sank in quite quickly.

His immediate impulse was to stop, to mourn, to dwell on how just hours before he had been chatting in relaxed and casual fashion with this young man who had considered Riker someone to emulate. And now he was gone, just like that. No more aspirations, no more dreams. Nothing.

And the others, my God, the others. First Officer Morris was also gone, buried under a pile of debris that had broken loose from overhead.

Then Riker, from long practice, pushed such sentiments and concerns aside. There would be time enough later to mourn . . . presuming there was, in fact, a later.

Mankowski wasn't moving either, tilted back in his seat, his head slumped to one side. But he seemed to be breathing at least, albeit shallowly, and he was moaning softly. There was a streak of red down the side of his face, but apparently the wound was under his hair because Riker couldn't immediately discern it.

As for the captain . . . Garfield was unconscious. He was slumped over the ops console, and Riker realized that Garfield must have tried to take over when Palumbo went down. But there was only a blackened shell where the ops console had been. Apparently the entire thing had blown up in Garfield's face. His uniform was torn, his face was blackened, and there was blood everywhere. That Garfield was breathing at all was nothing short of miraculous.

"Commander . . ."

The voice came in a croak. Riker turned and saw Monastero, the security chief, rising from the wreckage like a ghost. "We've . . . got to get them out of here . . ."

"Report, Lieutenant," Riker said through cracked and bleeding lips. "Where are the attackers."

"We have to get out!" Monastero repeated.

"Give me an update, Mister!" Riker was starting to become irritated. Monastero appeared to be in shock.

"A report." Monastero pulled himself together and then fired a dark glare at Riker. "Sensors are down. We're dead in space. Impulse engines off line. Emergency distress signal has been activated. And thirty seconds ago, we got word from engineering that there's a warp core breech."

"What? Riker to engineering." He wasn't quite sure that Monastero, who had a dazed look in his eye and appeared to have gone several rounds with a brick wall, was fully reliable. On the other hand, he was the only person still coherent on the bridge.

There was no response to Riker's hail. But at that moment, the computer voice of the *Independence* said with its customary *sang froid*, "Warp core breech reported. Four minutes, eighteen seconds to final detonation. Evacuation of ship proceeding . . ."

Monastero spread his hands in a "Told you so" gesture.

It was not a situation that gave Riker a warm, squooshy feeling. Outside the ship was an array of Romulan vessels, and he was quite certain that they weren't about to be sporting about the emergency situation. The only hope they had was that the Romulans had moved off upon detecting the rupture of the warp core. The explosion was going to be rather intense, and nobody wanted to be in the vicinity when it happened.

Of course, that included the crew of the *Independence*.

"Are the turbolifts functioning?" Riker asked. Monastero's look said it all. "No, of course not. That'd be too easy," Riker continued, answering his own question. "All right then." He hauled Mankowski out of the chair and draped him over his shoulders in a fireman's carry. "The captain. Get the captain."

Monastero was already ahead of him. He draped Garfield over his shoulder and headed for the emergency exit. Riker followed quickly, while the computer calmly informed them that in just four minutes, the ship they were presently residing in would be nothing more than a large patch of space dust.

When the *Enterprise* had suffered a warp breech, they had been able to separate the saucer section from her and make their escape that way. But that option was not open to the *Independence*. With the impulse drive down, the saucer section would have no means of propelling itself away from the blast area. They'd go up in a ball of fire the size of Topeka. The only hope they had was the individual escape pods which would be able to hurtle away from the ship with sufficient speed to reach a safe distance from the explosion. At least, that was the theory.

Riker just prayed they were still functioning. The escape pods were on a separate, emergency system from the mainline computers, just for this sort of emergency. Still, with everything else down, who knew for sure? But there was no other option. It was either the escape pods or blow themselves out the photon torpedo tubes and pray that they suddenly developed the ability to breathe in a vacuum.

Climbing through the emergency hatchways under ordinary circumstances was problematic enough. Doing so with the slumped body of Mankowski over him was particularly challenging. Every so often Mankowski would flutter on the light side of consciousness, muttering something incoherent—once it was something about a beautiful waltz, another time it related to triangles—before passing out once more.

Monastero, for his part, was utterly stoic. He hauled his captain to safety without complaint or even the slightest grunt. One would have thought he was carrying a bag of katha chips for all the effort he was displaying. He was definitely stronger than he looked.

They arrived at the lower deck which led to the nearest set of emergency pods. "Let's hope there's some left," said Riker.

"Let's hope a lot of things," replied Monastero.

They stumbled down the corridor, and Mankowski had recovered enough of his wits to be able to haul his own weight. Garfield was still out cold. His color—what was discernable of it beneath the burns—did not look good. Riker was no doctor, but he gave Garfield a fifty-fifty chance at best. Then he spotted the sign, glowing in the half-light of the hallway, pointing the way to the escape pods. "There! This way!"

"I know that! It's my damned ship!" shot back Monastero.

They made it to the pods. Other crewmen were hurriedly launching themselves into space, but when they saw the captain was there, several of them stopped what they were doing and helped load him into a pod. It was a gesture that Riker couldn't help but appreciate. They were placing the survival of their commanding officer above their own. That was a true measure of the mettle of Starfleet officers, particularly in a time of crisis. Riker wished that the remaining pods allowed for more than one person; in his condition, the captain could really have used someone with him. But it simply wasn't an option.

"Captain away!" called Monastero. But rather than jump into a pod himself, he helped Riker load Mankowski into an escape pod. Only after that had been fired off into space did Monastero turn to head for his own means of escape. He paused for a moment, however, turned to face Riker, and—despite the fact that such gestures were all-but-unknown anymore—snapped off a crisp salute to Riker. The commander returned the gesture and then climbed into his own pod. He ran through the launch protocol as fast as he could, trying not to think about the dwindling time left to him. The seal slid into place, and Riker engaged the "eject" sequence. Seconds later, the escape pod shook violently around him, and the next thing Riker knew, he was watching the *Independence* spiral away from him.

Through the small viewing porthole of the pod, he couldn't believe the damage he was seeing once he was outside. There was scarcely a section of the ship that hadn't been scored or ruptured. Warp core breech? The amazing thing was that the starship had held together for as long as it had. One warp nacelle had been blown away completely, and was hanging like a severed limb nearby the ship's hull. Air was venting into space, the seals having failed. Even the ship's name, etched proudly on the saucer, was covered with carbon scoring and was barely visible.

"Bastards," breathed Riker.

Then he saw the ship begin to tremble violently, and he realized that the moment of total destruction was very close. Unfortunately, so was he. The escape pod was moving quickly, all right, but he wasn't confident that it was quick enough to put enough distance between himself and the ship.

And then, with a final shudder, much like a death throe, the engineering section of the *Independence* erupted. Riker looked away, partly from the emotion involved in seeing such a magnificent vessel destroyed, and also simply because such a detonation was blinding.

The unleashed energies of the all-consuming warp core enveloped the remains of the *Independence* like a high-speed cancer, and seconds later the ship was gone. In its place was a massive, dazzling blast, with a shock wave radiating from the midst of it that was overtaking Riker's escape pod with horrifying ease.

Riker braced himself, and then the wave overwhelmed the escape pod. It propelled him, faster and faster, and Riker set his jaw and didn't cry out. He wasn't entirely certain why he felt the need to keep it in. It wasn't as if there was anyone around. But he kept his mouth sealed just the same, closing his eyes against the spin of the pod.

Throughout all of it, he was struck by the silence of it all. The blast happened in relative silence, and as he spun about in space, caught up in the force of the detonation, the main sound he was able to hear was that of his own breathing . . . and possibly the pounding of his own heart. He braced himself within the pod, grasping the grips on either side to steady himself. He felt his gorge rising and pushed it back down. The last thing he needed to do was vomit in the confined space of the escape pod.

The momentum continued to carry him as he rode the crest of the wave, tumbling end over end, and the incandescence was simply overwhelming. He was shoved along, a pebble at the edge of a wave. Images flashed before him, people he loved, people he'd worked with, people long gone and people he wondered if he'd ever see again. He realized his life was flashing before his eyes and all he could think was, *How terribly cliché.*

It was only belatedly that he realized the light was fading. He peered through the viewport and saw that the explosion was dissipating. He had made it, had tumbled beyond the blast range. There were some other pods within his field of vision, but it was impossible to tell who it was or how many of the crew had survived.

Now that he was clear, he activated the pod's propulsion system. It wasn't as if the escape pod had a ton of maneuverability. To be specific, when compared to the propulsion and maneuver capacities of a starship, the pod was equipped with little more than a pair of oars. Then again, since the pod really was a glorified lifeboat, that was fairly appropriate.

The problem was, there wasn't really any place for Riker to head *to*. He wasn't situated near any planet . . . and even if he was, there wouldn't be any guarantee that it would have been hospitable. Up to that point, he'd been more reacting than acting. The idea had been to get away from the dying starship rather than be concerned about getting to someplace. Now his main concern was steadying himself and returning to the other pods. If there were a hospitable planet in the area, then the smart thing to do would be to head there as quickly as possible, touch down, and wait for rescue. But with nothing around and Riker uncertain precisely where they were, the only reasonable thing to do was keep together as a group and hope that a ship responded to the rescue call that had been sent out . . .

Just as we responded to a rescue call, Riker thought ruefully. Well, this rescue mission had turned out just wonderfully, hadn't it.

He saw a cluster of escape pods floating to his right, and was about to try and open up a comm channel so that he could discern who it was . . .

. . . and that was when a huge burst of light detonated. Reflexively he shielded his eyes. He didn't even have to look, though, to know what had just happened.

They were moving in, vultures converging on a wounded and helpless herd. Two Romulan cruisers were coming in. *Only two,* he realized. Obviously the *Independence* had not gone out without giving a good account of herself. The other warbirds, as well as the ship they'd been pursuing, had either been destroyed or else so badly shot up that they had had to return to home base—wherever that was—for repairs.

Unfortunately, two warbirds were going to be more than enough to handle the life pods. In fact, considering that the pods were for life maintenance only and contained no offensive capacity, a single Romulan warrior with a phaser cannon could probably dispose of them handily. So two warbirds, in this instance, was overkill.

They were taking their time, the damned sadists. They began fine-tuning their shots; instead of disposing of a group of pods, as one of the ships had just done, they started picking them off one at a time. *Target practice,* thought an infuriated Riker. *They want to drag it out, have some "fun."* Naturally they weren't interested in rescuing any of them. Romulans habitually did not take prisoners. The only time they had that Riker knew of was the imprisonment of Tasha Yar which had resulted in the birth of Sela, and apparently that had been a rather unique set of circumstances.

He wondered if Sela was aboard one of the ships now, or whether she had been on one of the ones that was crippled or destroyed. "She's there," Riker muttered. "She's definitely out there, taking her time, making us suffer. That's her style."

Another pod picked off, and another still. There was no way for them to know who was in which pod. There was no mission to try and seek out particular individuals. It was simply an exercise in barbarism.

"Selaaaa!" Riker shouted, even though she couldn't hear. Even though no one could hear. "Sela . . . I'll find you! Even after I'm dead, I'll still find you, and drag you kicking and screaming to whatever hell you're destined for!"

One of the Romulan warbirds slowly started to turn in his direction. A more fanciful turn of mind would have prompted Riker to think that Sela was in that ship, and that she had heard him. And that she was about to give her reply in the form of phasers aimed right down his throat. At that moment, he thought about the joke. About being faced with a situation where the odds were utterly hopeless.

Never, in all his career, had Riker been as close to death as he was at that moment. A Romulan warbird staring at him, her weapons fully charged and ready, and he had no means of escape, no ability to defend himself. Nothing. He was a sitting duck. And it was just he in the pod. He was faced with the moment of his death, and if he cried out, or sobbed, or broke down in frustration, or shouted out curses at the unfair universe that had left him in such dire straits . . . no one would ever know.

He levelled his gaze straight at the warbird's gunport . . . and then he straightened his uniform jacket, tugging down on the bottom to smooth it.

"Farewell . . . Imzadi," he said to one who was not there. Then he tilted his chin slightly, like a prize fighter daring a challenger, and he said, "Take your best shot."

It wasn't a phaser that the warbird fired, as it turned out. It was a photon torpedo, and it streaked from the ship's underbelly straight at Riker. There was absolutely no way that it could miss. Through the silence it came at him, and within a second or two, it would blow him to bits.

At least it would have . . . had not a phaser blast lanced down from overhead, spearing the photon torpedo with surgical precision and detonating it while it was still a good five hundred yards from the pod.

"What in the—?" said a confused Riker, which was no doubt what they were saying aboard the warbird as well. A shadow was cast over them as something blotted out the light from the nearest star.

Down the starship flew, normal space twisting and roiling around it as the mighty vessel leaped out of warp, firing as it came.

If the warbird could have let out a shriek of surprise, like a genuine bird, it would have. The warbird literally backflipped out of the way as the new arrival unleashed another phaser barrage that clipped the warbird's warp nacelles. Riker was impressed at the precision. Whoever was manning tactical aboard the starship unquestionably knew what he was about.

The other warbird peeled off from its steady annihilation of the life pods and opened fire on the starship. The warbird's phaser blasts danced around the starship's shields, even as the starship returned fire with a photon torpedo barrage that bracketed the warbird, leaving it no where to go, keeping it in position for another well-placed phaser blast.

The first warbird tried to move upon the starship, operating in tandem with its mate, but the starship would have none of it. In what had to be the most insane maneuver that Riker had ever witnessed, the starship actually barrel-rolled via thrusters. As it did so, it unleashed phaser fire that pinwheeled around it, tracing such a bizarre arc that the warbirds didn't know where to maneuver in order to avoid them.

"Who the hell is flying that thing?!" Riker said in shock.

The first warbird moved in the wrong direction and paid dearly for it as the phasers sliced straight across her underbelly, slashing through what remained of the warbird's shields. A plume of flame blossomed from the ship's lower decks. Naturally the vacuum of space quickly snuffed it out, but it didn't matter as the interior of the ship blew apart. Pieces of warbird scattered everywhere, all in eerie silence.

The second warbird, seeing the fate that had overtaken the first one, apparently didn't need to see anymore. It whipped around and, seconds later, had leaped into warp space and was gone. If it had so chosen, the starship could have gone after it, but much to Riker's relief, it chose to stay and attend to the floating life pods.

The ship slowly cruised over him, and he was finally able to make out the name of the vessel as it drew near enough: *U.S.S. Excalibur.*

"I should have known," Riker said. Indeed, he should have. The *Excalibur* was the primary starship that had been assigned to Thallonian space. Still, considering they weren't *that* far into Thallonian territory—indeed, that they were relatively close to the borders of Federation space—the rescuer could have been anyone. However, it was cosmically ironic that it was the *Excalibur* because it meant that, any moment, he'd likely be hearing the voice of—

"All lifepods, this is *Excalibur*, Commander Shelby speaking," a familiar voice came over the pod's speaker system. "We'll be beaming you all aboard momentarily. Please be patient."

"Shelby. Naturally it would be Shelby," Riker said.

To his surprise, her voice came right back at him over the comm. "Commander Riker . . . is that you?"

He blinked. He'd been unaware that the two-way was on, but he realized somewhat belatedly that it was. Still, considering that Shelby had likely gotten numerous responses to her opening hail from other escape pods, it was nothing short of amazing that she'd been able to single out his voice.

"It's me, Commander."

"Hold on." Clearly she was busy getting a track as to which pod his transmission was coming from. "My God," she said after a moment, "you're in the one that we intercepted the torpedo for."

"That would be me, yes. Kudos to the timing of you and your CO."

"I just wish we could have gotten here sooner."

"So do I," he said regretfully, thinking about the crewmen who had been lost.

Suddenly the pod seemed to dematerialize around him, and then he found himself standing on a transporter pad with a number of other shaken-looking former crewmembers of the *Independence*. Elizabeth Paula Shelby, who had served under Riker as his second-in-command when he'd captained the *Enterprise* against a Borg invasion, was standing in the transporter room with her hands draped behind her back. "Welcome, all of you," she said briskly. "Please report to sickbay immediately. We have a medteam just outside who will escort you down."

There were murmurs of "Thank you" as the crewmen filed out. The last one out was Riker, who stopped within a foot or two of Shelby. "Be certain to tell me as soon as you have Captain Garfield's status confirmed . . . whatever that might be."

"I certainly will. It shouldn't take too long to find out. We're utilizing all the transporter rooms to bring the rest of them aboard even as we speak," she said.

He nodded.

She actually smiled. "It's good to see you again, Commander," and she sounded like she meant it. Considering that she and Riker had spent most of their time at each other's throats the last time they'd served together, he considered that a genuine compliment.

"Good to see you too, Commander," he replied. "For a little while there, I thought I wasn't going to be seeing anyone again."

"It must have been terrifying when that thing had you targeted."

He gave it a moment's thought and then said, "Well . . . at least I didn't need my brown pants."

She stared at him. "Oh. Well . . . good. That would . . . clash with your uniform top."

He nodded and walked out, as Shelby stared after him and scratched her head in obvious confusion.

IV.

CAPTAIN MACKENZIE CALHOUN was sitting behind his desk squeezing two small, green rubber balls together when Commander Shelby entered. She stared at him for a short time and then asked, "What are you doing?"

"Relieving tension," he said.

She watched him for a moment longer. "Squeezing those relieves tension?"

"Absolutely. A friend got them for me, many years ago. Would you care to try?" He held up his hands, and there was a green ball in either one. They were fairly small, but the rubber was sturdy and was able to withstand pressure with relative ease.

"No. Thank you."

"Because you look tense."

"I'm not tense."

"You look it."

"Mac . . . I'm not tense."

"All right." He leaned back in his chair. "So . . . bring me up to date."

"We managed to rescue 374 crewmen. The rest either died during the initial Romulan attack, or else when the two ships returned and starting picking people off. Starfleet has been in-

79

formed and has told me that they'll be sending a transport. We're supposed to be hearing back from them once they've firmed up the rendezvous point."

Calhoun shook his head. His face was fairly impassive, which was not unusual for him; he didn't tend to keep his emotions up near the surface for casual display. But the disgust was evident nonetheless. "Not honorable. Picking off helpless people. Not honorable at all."

"The Romulans don't particularly care about such things as honor."

"They used to." He put the balls down on the desk and tapped his computer console. "I've been doing some research. They've always been in opposition to the Federation . . . but they used to be far more honorable than they are now. It's very odd. The Romulans used to focus on honor, while the Klingons were the dastardly race you wouldn't dare turn your back on. But they've switched places in their racial conduct. Curious."

"You can find it curious if you want. What I want to know," and she sat down opposite him, "is what they were doing out here in Thallonian space."

"So would I." He considered the question. "The *Independence* was lured here by that unknown ship they were chasing. The Romulans were waiting for them. Which suggests one of two things: Either the vessel they were chasing signalled ahead, picked this area at random, and instructed the Romulans to rendezvous here. Or else . . ."

"Or else the Romulans have a base somewhere hereabouts, and this was a pre-arranged rendezvous point," finished Shelby. "If that's the case . . . we should find it."

"Excellent idea. Considering that space is infinite in all directions, which way do you suggest we look first?"

"I never pretend to have all the answers, Mac. I leave that to captains."

He smiled thinly and then shifted gears. "Speaking of that . . . how is the captain of the *Independence?* Or at least what was the *Independence*"

"He'll live. He was one of the lucky ones, actually, to have survived that shooting gallery from the Romulans."

"They'll pay for that," Calhoun said with quiet conviction.

"It's not the job of the *Excalibur* to carry out acts of revenge."

When he'd spoken earlier, he had been staring off into space, but now Calhoun swivelled his head so that the gaze from his purple eyes was squarely levelled upon Shelby. "Don't kid me, Eppy," using the nickname—a collapsing of Elizabeth and Paula—that he knew so irritated her. "If we find ourselves in a battle situation with the warbird that got away, or that ship they were chasing, you'll be hoping I blow them out of space. You know it. I know it."

"That's the difference between us, Mac," she said softly, even a little sadly. "I wouldn't revel in it. Two wrongs don't make a right."

"Yes. They do."

"But—"

"They do," he told her firmly. "Someone commits a wrong, a wrong is committed against them in turn . . . that comes out right."

"I'm speaking from a moral point of view, Mac."

"So am I," he said mildly. "That's the joy of morals. They're not absolute."

"There are absolute standards of right and wrong, Mac."

"You should know better than that, Eppy. Physics are absolute. But anything that man can conceive from his own skull is up for debate."

"You see, Mac . . . you would think that. Because you're someone who thinks that rules apply to you when you feel like it, but can be discarded when you consider them an inconvenience."

"Not always."

"No. Not always. Sometimes you have your moments. Sometimes you realize the importance of regs. I like to think that I've contributed to that somewhat. But most of the time . . ." She shook her head and let out a long, exaggerated sigh. "Sometimes, Mac, I just don't know."

"Fortunately enough, I do. But then again, I am a captain. As you said, either I know, or pretend that I do." He paused and eyed her in a slightly amused manner. "So . . . getting reacquainted?"

"What?"

"With Commander Riker."

"Oh. Him." Shelby absentmindedly picked up one of the green balls and started squeezing it. "There's not that much to get reacquainted about."

"Really." He drummed his fingers on his desk. "From what I've heard, the two of you had some interesting chemistry together."

"Chemistry? We didn't have chemistry, Mac. We had fights. Riker is . . ." She shook her head and squeezed the ball tighter.

"Riker is what?"

"Oh, he's an arrogant ass. So self-satisfied, so smug. Spends his entire career hanging onto Jean-Luc Picard's coattails. Now Picard, there's a quality officer . . . as you well know. And Riker, he thinks he's the moon to Picard's sun, basking in the reflected glory."

"Very harsh, Commander. From what I've read, he handled himself in exemplary fashion during the Borg encounter when Picard was assimilated."

"He had his moments, I suppose. But it's . . ."

"It's what?" He cocked an eyebrow. "Eppy?"

"He's got potential, all right? Potential. There's something there. Possible greatness." She was speaking all in a rush, the words tumbling one over the other. It was hard to tell whether she was angry or frustrated or sad or some combination of all those. "I can tell. I can tell these things because I've just got a knack for it. He could be one of the great ones, one of the truly legendary captains . . ."

"But I thought you said—"

"He's got to come out from Picard's shadow, though!" she said in frustration, as if Mac hadn't spoken. "I don't know why he's so satisfied to hide there! And when you talk to him about it, he gets all defensive and his jaw gets so tight and his eyes get all hard while the edges crinkle up . . ."

"Oh, do they?"

"But he's just so . . . so . . . so . . ." Her voice became louder and a bit more shrill with every word. " . . . so . . . so . . ."

The ball popped.

Shelby jumped back in her chair, startled by the sound and reflexively her hand flipped the broken rubber shell away from her. It "thwapped" onto Calhoun's desk rather pathetically.

Calhoun stared at it and then, as if handling a rotting carcass, he picked it up delicately between his thumb and forefinger. "I've had the set for nine years. I didn't think it was possible to do this."

When Riker entered sickbay to check on Captain Garfield, he was momentarily surprised to see Doctor Selar checking over one of the *Independence* crewmembers. He remembered her from her time on the *Enterprise,* and hadn't been aware that her new assignment was the *Excalibur.* He remembered that he'd always been quite impressed with her. She didn't have the most delicate bedside manner, but she was a superb diagnostician and extremely efficient. Plus, because she was a Vulcan, she had the customary Vulcan reserve.

He walked up behind her and said, by way of greeting, "Doctor Selar . . ."

"What do you want?!"

He had never, in his life, heard a Vulcan speak above normal conversational tone, much less have one bellow at him. And it had been, to put it delicately, completely unprovoked. And the oddest thing was probably the fact that no one in sickbay seemed to feel that this was behavior that was remotely unusual for a CMO, let alone a Vulcan.

Remembering the accelerated strength that Vulcans possessed, to say nothing of such techniques as the Vulcan nerve pinch, Riker suddenly felt that it would probably be wiser for him to take a few steps back. He promptly did so. Selar had now turned to face him and was staring at him with no hint of recognition.

"Doctor . . . Selar? Commander Riker. Will Riker. We . . . worked together."

"I am aware of who you are, Commander," she said. "I am also aware that we served together aboard the *Enterprise.* I am further aware that I have been working steadily since the arrival of the survivors from the *Independence.* Fortunately I do not require rest and relaxation as humans do. Lack of sleep has absolutely no effect on me whatsoever. What does have an impact upon me is people engaging me in pointless discussion, social niceties, and significant wastes of my time. If you consider it a possibility that you fall into any of those categories, you might want to reconsider your apparent interest in engaging me in extended social intercourse."

"Doctor," Riker said slowly, "I know this isn't my ship. I know I'm a visitor here. But nonetheless . . . I still outrank you . . . and that rank, to say nothing of simple common courtesy, should afford me a degree of respect. Respect that I don't see happening here. Now I'm not entirely sure what you think I've done to deserve this sort of brusque and, frankly, rude treatment. But I suggest you either tell me what's going on, or—"

"I am not interested in your ultimatums, Commander. Nor do I wish to discuss my personal affairs. Kindly tell me what you desire by coming here, or please leave."

"I'm looking for Captain Garfield."

"There." She pointed to a bed in the far corner and, sure enough, there was Garfield lying there, looking somewhat battered and bruised but most definitely alive. His eyes were closed, his chest rising and falling regularly.

Riker was about to say a curt "thank you" but Selar had already moved off. Shaking his head, Riker walked over to Garfield and stood over him.

"That you, Commander?" Garfield's eyes opened to narrow slits. His voice sounded raspy.

"Yes, sir."

"Sorry . . . we weren't able to give you that smooth ride I promised you."

"Don't worry, Captain. I won't hold it against you."

Garfield stared off into space.

"Captain . . . ?"

"I once met a captain . . . in a place . . . a special place," and he didn't quite smile, but it seemed to bring back pleasant memories. "A place for captains. Perhaps you'll go there sometime. We would sit around . . . tell stories . . . and one evening . . . the subject became losing a command. Different captains talked about it . . . but it wasn't addressed with the usual enthusiasm that usually involved discussions at this . . . particular place. And eventually . . . it got rather quiet. Quiet throughout the entire place, as it never had been before. And someone turned to me . . . and asked me if I'd ever experienced . . . such a loss. And I said I hadn't. That I was totally ignorant of what it was like. They looked at one another, the other captains did, and then they raised their glasses and, almost as one, they chorused, 'To ignorance.' They hoped that I would never have to go through it. But I'm afraid that I've had to disappoint them."

"Sir, it wasn't—"

He held up a cautionary finger to silence him. "If the next two words out of your mouth are going to be 'your fault,' I would suggest you keep them to yourself. It's always the captain's fault, commander. Always. No matter what boards of inquiry may decide. No matter what others may say. Do you know why captains are supposed to go down with their ship? It's so we don't have to listen to well-meaning individuals telling us it's not our fault. Because it is always . . . the captain's . . . fault."

It was as if he'd expended all his remaining energy just to get those words out. Then his head slumped back and he closed his eyes. For just a moment, Riker was about to shout an alarm, but then he glanced up at the scanner mounted on the wall and he saw that the readings were steady. He had simply fallen back to sleep.

"He appears to be resting comfortably."

Riker literally didn't recognize the voice at first as he turned to see Dr. Selar standing at his arm. "Yesss . . ." he said cautiously.

"It was very traumatic for him. We have him slightly medicated to ease him through . . . but not excessively."

He tilted his head slightly as if needing to make sure that he was talking to the same person he'd been addressing before. "Doctor Selar . . . ?"

"Yes? Is there a problem, Commander?"

Her attitude and disposition had completely changed. Gone was the edge of anger, the snappishness, the impatience. Now she was a standard-issue, matter-of-fact Vulcan.

"I . . . don't know. *Is* there a problem?"

For answer, she looked not at Riker, but at the bio-readouts over Garfield's bed. "No," she said after studying it a moment. "There does not appear to be. However," and she looked back to Riker, "if you believe there is one, please do not hesitate to inform me. Good day." All-business, she moved on to the next diagnostic table, leaving an utterly perplexed Riker literally shaking his head.

The doors to the Medlab hissed open, and Commander Shelby entered. "Commander Riker," she called.

"Yes, Commander?"

"I was just informed by the captain that we're receiving an incoming message from Starfleet, and apparently our presence has been requested."

"And you came down to get me yourself?"

"I was in the neighborhood and thought I'd drop by."

"I see. Very considerate of you." He headed for the door, stopping only to nod slightly to Doctor Selar and say, "Doctor."

"Commander," she nodded in acknowledgment as she went about her business.

Riker and Shelby headed down the corridor and into a turbolift. Waiting until the door had slid shut and they had privacy, Riker turned to Shelby and said, "Would you mind telling me what the hell is Doctor Selar's problem?"

"Problem? Oh," she said as if just realizing, "the mood swings."

"Is that what those were? It's not Bendii, is it?

"No. Pregnancy. And when the father is a slightly flighty Hermat, with whom the doctor has formed a close psychic bond due to their intimacy which has permeated her entire personality, well . . ."

"Wait a minute. She's pregnant?"

"Yes."

"But the father is a Hermat?"

"That's right."

"Hermats . . . that race that has both male and female—"

"Correct again."

"And they've formed a psychic bond because . . . ?"

"Of reasons too complicated and, frankly, delicate to go into."

"I'm afraid that's not good enough."

She had looked amused at the situation up until that point. But now she studied Riker as if he were a single-celled organism under a microscope and said, "I'm afraid it's more than good enough. I remind you, Commander, that Captain Calhoun is in charge of this vessel, and not you. You are simply a visitor . . . a refugee, if you will. Captain Calhoun obviously feels that Doctor Selar is capable of carrying out her duties. His judgment is not only to be respected, but particularly in your case, it's not to be second-guessed. Do I make myself clear, Commander?"

"Commander," and he folded his arms across his broad chest, "I am not about to try and undercut a CO. But by the same token, I will speak my mind where I see fit."

"You do that. And of course, if you wish to show us the best way to go about running a ship, you can just head back to the ship that you're commanding . . . oh! Wait!" She slapped her forehead with her open palm as if she had just recalled something fairly crucial. "That's right. You don't have a command of your own. Do you? Perhaps the next time one is offered you, it would be in your best interests to take it, because sooner or later, they'll stop offering."

Riker said nothing, but he couldn't help but feel that the temperature in the turbolift had just dropped rather precipitously.

Calhoun glanced up as Riker and Shelby entered the captain's ready room. They walked in several feet, both stopped, smiled gamely in perfect unison, and stood at parade rest. He looked from one to the other.

"Have a tiff, did we?" he inquired.

"Simply a spirited discussion, sir," Shelby said. Riker nodded slightly in affirmation.

"Mm hmm." Believing that it would probably be wiser not to pursue it, he called out, "Bridge to Lefler. We're ready. Put the comm through."

When the face of the Starfleet officer calling them came on screen, no one could have been more surprised than Calhoun. He hadn't been expecting anyone in particular, and yet, despite that, this was the last person he was expecting.

One would not, however, have had any inkling of his astonishment from his voice. Instead, without blinking an eye, he said, "Admiral Nechayev. A pleasure as always. I wasn't expecting to hear from you. This business is a bit outside your normal purview, isn't it?"

Nechayev looked a bit older than when he'd last seen her. A little jowlier, a little grayer. He'd always been impressed how little the strains of her job seemed to weigh on her, but he had to assume that time caught up with everyone ... even the Iron Woman of Starfleet. "My purview tends to expand as the need arises," she said drily. "Commander Riker, it's good to see you hale and whole. Your loss would have been a terrible blow to the public relations plans for the bicentennial."

Riker bowed slightly at the waist. "I appreciate your concern, Admiral."

"There's humanitarian concerns as well, of course, plus Starfleet's interest in the money they've invested in you as an officer ... but those worries would likely be outside my purview, and I wouldn't want to tempt Captain Calhoun's wrath."

Calhoun noticed Shelby hiding a smile behind her hand, but he chose not to comment on it.

Quickly becoming all-business, Nechayev said, "And how is Captain Garfield?"

"I believe Commander Riker was the last one to speak with him." Calhoun half-turned in his chair and looked to Riker.

Riker nodded briskly. "If anything, I'd say he's somewhat in shock."

"If he weren't, I'd think there's something wrong with him. Poor George. A good man. He, and his crew, deserved better than this." She shook her head, a grim expression on her face. Then she continued, "A transport is under way, Captain, as promised. You will leave Thallonian space and proceed to Deep Space 4, where you will discharge your passengers. And you, captain, will join them."

There was a brief moment of unspoken confusion in the ready room. "I'm sorry ... say again, Admiral?" said Calhoun. "I'm joining them on Deep Space 4?"

"That is correct."

"And the *Excalibur* is to remain on station for how long?"

"She is not to wait for you. I will be meeting with you on DS4, to discuss a matter of some urgency. The *Excalibur* is to return immediately to Thallonian space and continue the investigation of this Romulan attack. We've put our best people on it, and they've come up with one or two possibilities: Either it was random chance that the Romulans intercepted the *Independence* where they did, or else there's a secret Romulan stronghold somewhere in Thallonian space."

"Thank heavens we had the best minds in Starfleet to come up with that," Shelby commented. The remark was, of course, not lost on Calhoun. He knew perfectly well that Shelby had come to the exact same conclusions all on her own. It was probably Elizabeth's greatest curse, he decided, to feel that she was consistently undervalued as an officer. Not only was she hungry for her own command and feeling thwarted that she hadn't received it yet, but he knew that she still felt a certain degree of "exile" in her current post as second-in-command to Calhoun. She believed she was ready for a command of her own, and truth to tell, so did Calhoun. That didn't stop him from valuing her contributions and presence as first officer. There was probably no one else in Starfleet whose advice Calhoun would readily listen to, even though he frequently gave Shelby the impression that he was hardly attending to anything she said.

"Either way," Nechayev was saying, "we want the *Excalibur* to look into the matter and see what you can discern either way."

"How long will I be away from her?" Calhoun asked.

"Impossible to say at this point."

But Calhoun wasn't really listening to what she was saying. Instead he was attending to what she wasn't saying . . . and it spoke volumes.

Some years earlier, Calhoun had departed Starfleet under rather acrimonious circumstances. It had been Nechayev who had seen a potential waste of material and had drafted Calhoun to work freelance for The Division of Starfleet Intelligence, that she oversaw. Her connection to SI was not widely known. She had other, more prominent and promoted duties to which she attended, most of which simply served as cover for her SI responsibilities. After all, it wouldn't do for any communiqué from Nechayev's office to immediately carry with it a likelihood that there was something going on with Starfleet Intelligence. Notoriety is counterproductive to secrecy.

But Calhoun, who had done a number of jobs for her on "his own," knew all too well. He also knew that DS4 was an outpost station for SI, another fact that was neatly hidden from the public at large. If Nechayev was meeting him there, it was because she wanted to assign him to something. He wasn't especially sanguine about it, considering those days long behind him. But he was also aware that if Nechayev had targeted him for an SI assignment, then there had to be a pretty damned good reason. She wouldn't be removing him as captain merely on a whim. He trusted her judgment that much, at least. Still . . . he was beginning to wonder whether this might actually be a precursor to an extended departure from the *Excalibur*, or even a permanent loss of command as Starfleet arbitrarily decided that his talents could better be served elsewhere than the bridge of a starship.

As if reading his mind—which he was convinced Nechayev was actually capable, on occasion, of doing—Nechayev smiled and added, "Don't worry, captain. It won't be indefinite. Simply a matter that needs to be attended to. You'll be back with your ship as soon as possible."

"Very well." Although his next remark was addressed to Nechayev, he was looking at Shelby when he said it. "I have every confidence that the *Excalibur* will be in good hands during my absence." Shelby inclined her head slightly in response as if to say, *Thank you.*

"As are we," Nechayev said. "Commander Riker has proven his capability time and again, and we are certain he won't disappoint us this time, either."

The words hung there. Of everyone in the room, it was Riker who seemed the most astounded. "Admiral . . . I assumed that I would be departing on DS4, to head back for the bicentennial . . ."

"Never assume, Commander. It makes an ass of 'u' and 'me.' Well . . . not of me, in this case, but you get the idea. Did they never teach you that at the Academy?"

"Yes, they did, but I . . ."

"The simple fact, Commander, is that we're taking advantage of your presence there. You not only have more experience with Romulans than does Commander Shelby, but you're certainly the most familiar with the operative named Sela. You know how she thinks, how she plans . . . you can likely second-guess her strategies. You will receive a field promotion to 'captain' for the duration of your stay aboard the *Excalibur,* and assume command as soon as Captain Calhoun has departed."

"But Admiral, I . . ." He glanced at Shelby, whose face was a mask, and said, "it's my belief that Commander Shelby is perfectly capable . . ."

"That is my belief as well. But I believe you to be more so, and intend to exploit that. Commander Riker," and there was just a hint of warning in her voice, "are you turning down a command . . . *again?*"

There was a momentary silence, and then Riker drew himself up and said crisply, "No, ma'am."

"I'm glad to hear it. Captain Calhoun, I shall see you shortly. Captain Riker . . . good luck and good hunting. And if you have any difficulties, I know we can count on Commander Shelby to give you full back-up."

"Absolutely, ma'am," Shelby said without hesitation.

"Starfleet out."

No one said anything for a time, and then Calhoun said, "Commander . . . I'm sorry, *Captain* . . . Riker . . . since apparently you'll be here for a time, I suggest you go down to ship's stores and obtain some things you might need, considering that whatever possessions you were travelling with were blown up. Some off-duty clothing, toothbrush, that sort of thing. I'll have Miss Lefler give you a more detailed tour of the ship at your earliest convenience, and introduce you to some of the key personnel. We're a rather . . . relaxed group around here. I'm sure you'll fit right in."

"I'm sure I will, sir."

"Dismissed."

Riker turned and left. Shelby didn't even glance after him. Instead her gaze was focused on the now-blank screen that Nechayev had been on moments later.

"Are you going to be all right, Elizabeth?" he asked with as much genuine concern as he could get into his voice.

"Not . . . immediately. In a while, perhaps . . . but not immediately."

She stopped talking and simply stood there, still staring at the screen. She didn't seem to show any inclination to leave, but she appeared so seized with contained rage that she couldn't quite figure out the best way to move.

Calhoun picked up the remaining green ball. "In point of fact," he said slowly, "it was Nechayev who gave me these . . . well . . . this. Would you care to . . . ?" He extended the ball to her.

She took it from him, stared at it for a moment. Then, her face twisted into a picture of silent fury, she cocked her arm, and let fly.

The ball struck the monitor screen, ricocheted back, and Shelby had to duck to avoid being struck in the head. The ball bounced back from the far wall and landed squarely in Calhoun's hand.

Slowly Calhoun stood up from behind his desk and stared down at Shelby, who sat, shaking her head. "I actually assumed you were simply going to squeeze it. But, as the lady said, never assume." He waited for response and, when he didn't get one immediately, ventured to add, "Not your day, is it, Eppy."

"Not my lifetime, Mac. Not my lifetime."

V.

THE PUBS OF ARGELIUS II were reputed to have the absolutely best dancers in the entire quadrant, and it was there that Zolon Darg had journeyed as part of what had become his eternal quest. He was looking for a dancer who would expunge the memories of . . . her.

After all this time, the recollection of Vandelia still remained with him. When he closed his eyes, he could see the curves and lines of her body. He could see her breasts upthrust. He could see the saucy smile, the come-hither look in her eyes, the temptation and raw sex that radiated from her body with the clarity of light from a star. And most important of all, he could see his hands at her throat, strangling her for the way that she had turned on him, tricked him, brought down his entire operation in flames around his head. Her and that friend of hers, that "Mac."

Darg had many friends and a long reach, but Vandelia was still just one person, and it was a big galaxy with lots of places to hide if one was so inclined. She had probably changed her name, perhaps even left the quadrant entirely. Who knew for sure? If she'd taken it into her head, she might even have booked passage on a ship and gone through the Bajoran wormhole into the Delta quadrant to explore new territories and possibilities there. Who knew? Who cared?

He cared. She was a dangling loose end that he hoped he would one day be able to tie off, and he would do so by tying it off around her neck.

In the meantime, this dancer that he was now watching was a pleasant enough diversion.

She was not Orion, by any means. Her skin was milky white, for starters, and her long black hair managed to tantalizingly cover her bare breasts at all times. It was somewhat amazing, really. She went by the name of Kat'leen, and her gyrating body was a joy to behold. Her stomach was remarkably muscled, and her legs seemed to go on forever. She kept time in her dance with small finger cymbals, and an enthusiastic drummer pounded away nearby. Darg found himself unconsciously keeping time with a steady beat on the table.

He fingered the glass on the table and realized, with a distant disappointment, that it was empty. "Shunabo, get me another drink," he ordered to his second-in-command, and then came to the hazy recollection that Shunabo wasn't there, mostly due to the fact that—in a fit of pique—he had killed him. The action seemed rather harsh, in retrospect. Shunabo had served him well, and it was just remotely possible that he did not, in fact, deserve what had happened to him.

"Well . . . so what," Darg growled to no one after a moment's thought. " 'Deserve' has nothing to do with it. He was becoming full of himself. A danger. If a man's going to watch my back, I have to be sure he's not going to stick a knife in it. I don't need a man who's going to openly defy me." Whether, in fact, Shunabo had openly defied him was a bit fuzzy in Darg's mind. The drink wasn't helping to keep him clear.

Kat'leen's dance drew to its enticing climax, and then she sprawled on the floor, her legs drawn together, her arms spread wide, her hair Darg once again strategically placed in such a way that Zolon Darg began to wonder if the damned stuff had a life of its own. All around him, lights were clicking on and off furiously on the table tops, which was the standard Argelius means of showing approval.

The one exception was a human over in the corner. A heavyset, gray-haired, mustached man, he was pounding on the table and whistling shrilly between his teeth. He had a large bottle of some liquid that appeared to be green positioned in front of him, and he had clearly been at it for a while. His raucous behavior drew glares from some of the more reserved patrons who liked everything "just so." Darg watched in amusement as the owner of the establishment approached the gray-haired gentleman and clearly, with some polite gestures, indicated that perhaps it was time he take his business elsewhere. With a growl and a burst of what was likely some sort of profanity—but spoken with such a thick terran accent of some sort that Darg couldn't even begin to comprehend it—the gray-haired man swayed out of the pub and into the street.

Darg promptly forgot about him, instead deciding that now would likely be the most opportune time to approach the young lady. Kat'leen was just in the process of drawing a type of shawl across her shoulders. Darg found it rather charming in a way. When she danced, it was with complete lack of inhibition as she practically basked in her sexuality. But now that the dance was over, she seemed almost shy. Not in a shrinking, frightened sort of way. Just a bit more . . . modest . . . than she had been.

"Yes?" she said, one eyebrow raised as Darg approached.

"You dance magnificently," he told her.

"Thank you." She seemed to be looking him up and down, trying to get a feeling for the type of man he was.

"I have two questions for you, if you don't mind."

"Not at all."

"First . . . have you ever heard of another dancer . . . an Orion girl . . . named Vandelia?"

"Not that I can recall," she said with a smile that seemed rather mischievous. "Why? Wasn't I enough dancer for you?"

"Oh, yes, you were superb. The second question is, Would you do me the honor of accompanying me for the rest of the evening."

She sized him up once more, but before she could respond, another voice said, "She's mine."

Zolon Darg turned and looked up . . . and up. Darg was certainly no slouch in the height department with his massive build, but the individual confronting him was, incredibly, a head taller and also wider. He had one eye, having apparently lost the other in a fight . . . or, for all Darg knew, in a card game. His head was shaven, his nose crunched in so stylistically that it was difficult for Darg to tell whether he was an alien who normally sported a nose of that style, or whether an opponent had simply crushed it. His lips drew back in a sneer to reveal a neatly pointed double row of sharp teeth. This was not an individual who appeared likely to back down.

Then again, neither was Darg.

"Calm down, Cho," Kat'leen said to the behemoth, and then looked apologetically at Darg. "I'm sorry. Cho is a regular . . . customer. And he gets a bit possessive sometimes."

"I understand," Darg said calmly.

"So you also understand," Cho growled, "that you better back off."

"I will on one condition."

Cho was clearly puzzled. "Condition?"

"Yes. Condition. A simple enough word. I'm sure it's even in your vocabulary."

"What . . . condition."

"I will back off," Darg said calmly, "if you would be good enough to take a step or two back, bend over, and shove your own head up your own nether bodily orifice."

Kat'leen rubbed the bridge of her nose in obvious pain and took several steps back as if to try and get as clear of the area as possible. It was rather evident she didn't anticipate matters going particularly well in the next few minutes.

Cho digested Darg's requested stipulation for a few moments before fully grasping just what it was that Darg had said to him. Then, with an infuriated roar and no other warning, he came straight at Darg. He wielded no weapon. Apparently he didn't feel that he needed one.

Darg, on the other hand, was quite prepared. He extended the fingers of his right hand, and vicious-looking blades snapped out of the tips. Each of them wasn't more than an inch long, but it was not their length that was the main problem for Cho. Rather, it was the fact that Darg's hand moved so quickly that the word "blur" wouldn't even have begun to cover it. One moment his hand was at this side, the next it was across Cho's throat.

Reflexively, Cho grabbed at his throat, and seemed quite surprised when a thick red liquid began to seep from between his fingers, pumped through the gaping wound in his neck that

Darg had just put there. Kat'leen looked from Cho to Darg and back again in confusion. She had blinked when the strike was made and had literally missed it because of that. So she didn't fully grasp what was happening at first. But when Cho sank to his knees, his hand still at his throat and an expression of total bewilderment spreading across his face, that was when Kat'leen understood.

"I believe you're now free for the evening," Darg told her calmly. The blades were still in evidence on his fingers, but they were tinted with red.

Kat'leen let out a shriek, and that was when Darg came to the realization that Cho might have been many things, but what he was most definitely not was friendless.

They started coming in from all sides, bruisers big and small, advancing on Darg. Darg, slightly impaired both by drink and by the headiness of a blood strike, wasn't quite sure where to look first.

Cho burbled something incomprehensible and then fell forward like a great tree, hitting the floor with such impact that the entire establishment shook. That was all that was needed for the attackers to converge on Darg at full bore. Darg readied himself for the attack, and couldn't help but wonder if perhaps, just perhaps, he might have gotten himself into a bit more trouble than he could reasonably handle this time.

Suddenly the man was next to him.

It was no one that Darg knew, no one that he had ever seen. It wasn't one of Darg's entourage, certainly. He'd made a point of leaving them behind for the evening, saying that he wanted some time alone. They had obediently given it to him, and it had seemed for a few moments there that the decision was going to cost him dearly. Not that he wasn't sure that he could have ultimately handled all comers.

The question was rapidly becoming moot, however, thanks to the newcomer. He appeared to be a human, but he wasn't particularly tall, not even all that impressive looking. But he seemed to exude a confidence, display a sort of pure magnetism and force of personality that could not be ignored. He had a neatly trimmed gray beard, and a head of silver hair that was smoothly combed back. His brow jutted forward a bit, and it was his eyes that were the most interesting to Darg. They seemed cold and pitiless. They were the eyes of a man who could easily kill you as soon as look at you. He was dressed mostly in black, and was sporting a long coat that seemed to whip around him like a cape whenever he moved.

In either hand, he was holding a disruptor. In a rather flamboyant gesture, he crisscrossed his arms in front of himself, putting the disruptors at odd angles to one another, and then he started shooting. He did so with such precision that Darg couldn't quite believe what he was seeing.

The instinct when a mob is bearing down upon one from all sides is to fire blindly into the midst of the crowd and try to take out as many as possible. But that wasn't the case with the newcomer. Instead he was targeting one person after another, blasting out precision strikes that were taking opponents in the shoulder or upper arm or thigh. They weren't even being knocked unconscious. They were simply being incapacitated.

"Not the most elegant of weapons," said the newcomer in what seemed an almost conversational tone. "Very restricted settings. There's 'kill' and 'kill some more.' One has to be precise if one doesn't feel like killing. Hold on, please." He fired again and another attacker went down.

The floor was now covered with moaning, groaning individuals who were clutching assorted parts of their bodies. Darg nodded, impressed with the marksmanship. Still, he felt the need to ask, "Why not just kill them all?"

"And leave a big mess for the owners to have to clean up? I'm a regular customer here. I don't need to get the owners mad at me. All right, let's go."

There were still some individuals on their feet, but they were slow to approach. It was hard to blame them, considering the substantial number of people who were scattered about, crying out in agony. No one seemed particularly interested in shoving their faces into the buzzsaw. In fact, a few were even looking down at Cho's unmoving body with what appeared to be grim assessment, as if trying to determine whether or not he was worth their risking their necks for.

One apparently decided that it was, and he tried to pull a weapon. But the silver-haired man moved so quickly that Darg didn't even see it. All he knew was that suddenly there was a man clutching his hand and screaming profanity, while his weapon lay on the floor. He made as if to move for the weapon with his other hand, but the silver-haired terror simply said, "I wouldn't." The wounded man froze.

"As I was saying: Let's go."

Darg glanced around. Kat'leen was nowhere in sight, apparently having ducked out when the trouble started. There didn't seem to be anything to be gained by remaining. "I couldn't agree more," Darg said readily. They moved out back-to-back, the silver-haired man covering their rear while Darg watched in front of them. Moments later they were out the door and halfway down the street, the silver-haired man holstering his disruptors with a brisk and slightly flashy twirl.

They put a couple more blocks between them and the place before they slowed down to a casual stroll. Around them were the sounds of music and laughter, people sauntering about and having a good time. Over just inside an alleyway, a couple was engaging in the galaxy's oldest pastime with lusty abandon. The silver-haired man modestly averted his eyes; Darg watched with unabashed glee for a few moments before turning his attention back to his unexpected companion.

He stopped walking and said, "What's your name?"

"Kwint," came the reply.

"Kwint. Do I know you?"

"Not to my knowledge. Well . . . good evening to you." He turned and started to walk away.

"Wait!" Darg looked at him with open skepticism. "Why did you help me just now? Because I could have handled them myself."

"I have no doubt that you could have."

"Then why?"

Kwint shrugged. "I didn't like the odds. One of you against all of them. Didn't seem right."

"What are you, some sort of hero?"

"No," laughed Kwint. "Just looking to enjoy myself. Get some relaxation."

"And you do that by getting into fights."

"Sometimes, if the mood takes me."

"And it doesn't matter to you what the fight was about?"

Kwint appeared genuinely puzzled. "Should it?"

"Shouldn't it?"

"I don't see why," Kwint said reasonably. "A fight is always between two sides, both of whom think they're right. Usually, they both are . . . from their point of view. So it really doesn't matter which side you take, because it's never really about who's right. It's about who wins."

"Yes. Yes it is." He paused. "You didn't ask my name."

"You didn't offer, I didn't ask. A man introduces himself or doesn't. Makes no difference to me."

"The name's Darg. Zolon Darg." He waited to see some flicker of recognition . . . and got it. "You've heard of me."

"Yes. I have. Weapons runner, correct?"

"Correct."

Kwint studied him skeptically. "I'd heard you were dead. That your operation crashed and burned some years back, and you went with it."

"Obviously not. Whereabout did you hear my name mentioned?"

"I worked with a fellow named Gazillo. Secondary distributor. Bought a shipment of Tolasian night slicers off you about five years back."

"Yesss . . . yes, Gazillo." He stroked his chin thoughtfully. "I heard Gazillo died ugly."

"He did. Because of me."

"You killed him?"

"No," sighed Kwint. "But he wanted to deal with some people who I knew were going to doublecross him. I tried to convince him of it. But he wouldn't listen to me, no matter what I said. He smelled money and lots of it. When he refused to pay attention to what I was telling him, I walked out on him. Within two days, his body turned up . . . or at least, what was still identifiable as his body. If I'd stuck with him, tried harder . . . hell, if I'd just shot and wounded him, prevented him from going to the rendezvous . . ." He closed his eyes for a moment as if reliving it, and then visibly shrugged it off. "Can't change the past. Well . . . good evening to you, Darg."

Once more he started to walk away, and Darg said, "You seem to be in quite a hurry to leave."

"You served my purpose," Kwint said matter-of-factly. "I saw an opportunity to even some odds . . . the opportunity is done . . . and I'm out to enjoy the rest of the evening. Unless, of course," he said, apparently struck by a sudden thought, "you intend to get into some more uneven fights. Then I suppose I could just follow you around, save myself some time. Not have to start from scratch every time."

"It's entirely possible." Darg had to admit it to himself: he liked this Kwint fellow. There was a remarkable devil-may-care attitude about him. In some ways, he very much mirrored Darg's own philosophies, but in others, he was clearly his own man. For one thing, Darg wouldn't have given a second thought to Gazillo's fate. If the man was fool enough to ignore sound advice, then he deserved what he got. But Kwint still regretted Gazillo's loss . . . while at the same time, showing an admirable lack of interest in such niceties as the righteous high ground. He was a cheerful combination of morality and immorality. In short, he was someone that Darg could very likely use.

Suddenly the loss of Shunabo seemed less unfortunate and more an instance of good timing.

He clapped a hand on Kwint's shoulder and said, "You know, Kwint. There's more to life than fights. Let us not forget that which Argelius is most renowned for. Why," and he lowered his voice conspiratorially, "I know a place around here . . . where the women are sooo . . ."

He didn't have to finish. Kwint promptly nodded eagerly and said, "I know the place."

And they headed off into the night.

VI.

"HELLO, MAC. Ready to have the fate of the entire Federation in your hands?"

Calhoun shrugged indifferently as he sat down opposite Nechayev in her office. From the corner of his eye, through the large viewing window in Nechayev's office, he caught a glimpse of the *Excalibur* just before she leaped into warp space and vanished. Calhoun had made a practice of being self-sufficient. When one witnessed as much death and destruction as he had, it seemed the best way to go about keeping one's head screwed on. And yet, as his ship hurtled away into warp, he had the feeling of someone cut off from their family.

Family. Is that what they had become to him? How very, very odd. It was not something he had remotely anticipated, for some reason.

"A shrug? I ask you a question like that, and a shrug is all I get?" There was an element of teasing in her voice, but there was an undercurrent to her tone that was deadly serious.

"My apologies, Admiral. It's just that . . . this came out of nowhere. I simply never expected to be back in this situation before."

"I know, Mac," she said earnestly, "and I wish I didn't have to put you in it. But I think you'll see that, when it comes down to options, you're our best shot."

"I suppose I should be flattered."

"Don't be. You may very well be sorry by the time this is done." She paused and then said, "You look well. Command has agreed with you."

"Well, command and I have had a few arguments along the way. But I think we've got mutual wrestling holds on each other by this point. So," and he leaned forward, attentive, "let's not dance around. What's happened. What's going on."

"Down to business. Good. You haven't changed. All right . . . we've received the findings from the Away team that the late *Independence* left behind at Daystrom Institute. It appears that whoever our friends are that attacked the place made off with the Omega 9."

"*No!*"

"You've heard of it, then."

"No."

She winced slightly. "Walked into that one, I suppose." She folded her hands on the desk. "The Omega 9 could easily be considered the next major breakthrough in computerization: A computer that enables its user to interface with its data base through pure thought alone."

"Thought? You mean like telepathy?"

"The brain sends out electrical impulses, Captain, just like any other machine. The only difference between the brain and a computer is that the brain is generally smaller, but the computer is faster and has more capacity. The Omega 9 is more than simply a computer. It's a gateway, if you will, that simplifies the communication of mind-to-computer. For all the sophistication that we've brought to computers throughout the centuries, one barrier has never been truly broken down. We still have to talk to the damned things, and the information that we draw out of it is only as good as the questions we put into it."

"And with the Omega 9, that's no longer necessary?"

"Correct," she nodded. She held up her palm. "The Omega 9 bypasses conventional speech. Instead the user simply puts his or her palm against an interface padd. Sensors, combined with Nannite technology, form a temporary bond between user and data base so that the user is able to extract information literally with the speed of thought, and can also supply instructions to the computer in the same way. It's taken a long time to perfect the technology. In the initial stages, there was a tendency for the computer to flood its user with so much information that the human brain would simply collapse. Poor devils, those test subjects. They could barely think coherently at all after their exposure to the Omega 9. Eventually, we—"

"Made them into admirals?" suggested Calhoun.

Her eyes narrowed in her best "we are not amused" expression. As if he had not spoken, she said, "Eventually, we were able to help them recover their normal thinking process. But it was a near thing."

"And now the computer is gone."

"Yes. It's not as if the work is irretrievable. Daystrom has duplicate material at its main headquarters. But building another one would take time, and besides, that's only the tip of the iceberg.

"You see, the Daystrom raid was not an isolated incident. There have been a number of thefts in recent weeks, raids on various labs and such belonging to assorted members of the Federation. The common thread is that most of them have to do with some aspect of research on AI . . ."

"Artificial Intelligence, Calhoun said. Slowly his demeanor changed. He seemed harder-edged. There was something in his eyes that no one who had an affinity for breathing would want to see aimed at them. "All right. Go ahead," he said.

"So . . . there seems to be an excessive interest in artificial intelligence research, of which the Omega 9 might well be the most advanced. There has been one individual who has been spotted at the scene of several of them, however. An old friend of yours: Zolon Darg.

"Darg. You're joking."

"Do I look like I'm joking?" She punched in a code on her computer and Darg's picture appeared on it. It was clearly a picture taken by a hidden security camera somewhere. Apparently it was the last shot that particular camera had taken, because in the picture Darg was turning and pointing straight into the shot. No doubt a few seconds later, the observation camera had been blown to bits.

"No. No, I don't think you're joking at all." He couldn't take his eyes off Darg's massive form. Darg had hardly been a weakling when last they met, but he hadn't been the colossus that he was now. "There had been rumors that Darg had survived our encounter a few years ago, but I had no idea he'd gone this active again." He considered the implications of the news. "So Darg is behind these raids—"

"I didn't say he was behind them; merely that he's involved. We believe that the person who is actually behind them is this individual . . ."

A Thallonian whom Calhoun did not recognize appeared on the screen. It was an older individual, with yellowing beard and a surprisingly gentle look on his face.

"He is General Gerrid Thul. He's a Thallonian noble. We don't have any visual proof that he's connected directly to Darg. If he is, then he's been either too lucky or too clever to be caught on camera."

"Then why do you think he is connected?"

"Because the report came in from an intelligence officer who subsequently wound up dead."

"Dead." He frowned. "Who?"

"McNicol."

This prompted a gasp from Calhoun. "McNicol. He was good. He was damned good. He's dead? Are you sure?"

"There was barely enough left of him for a genetic trace, but yes, he's dead."

The news caused Calhoun to look even more intently at the image of General Thul which sat on the screen. He could almost imagine a look of contempt in Thul's expression. Whatever it was that Thul was playing at, a personal face had suddenly been attached to it: The face of Jack McNicol, a dedicated and clever agent who had paid the ultimate price in his pursuit of keeping the Federation safe.

Nechayev, for her part, didn't seem to be giving McNicol any further thought. It was as if she needed to move on to the next crisis immediately. "Thul has had a rather rocky career. He was imprisoned for a while on charges of treason and attempted murder, but served his time and was released. At the tail end of his tenure in prison, he managed to convince the powers that be that he was a changed man. It's possible he is . . ."

"People don't change."

"You did," she pointed out.

He fixed a gaze on her. "No, I didn't. At heart, I am as I always was. I've simply gotten better at covering it, that's all. Watch . . ."

And just like that, he seemed to relax his guard. Nechayev looked into his eyes, and there was a world of hurt and anger and cold, calculating fury, all warring for dominance behind those eerie purple eyes.

Then, just as easily, he "veiled" his eyes once more. They went to half-lidded, and he seemed so relaxed that he might have been mistaken for a sleeping man . . . or possibly a corpse.

"You see?" he said softly. "It's all still there. M'k'n'zy of Calhoun, the warrior, the slayer of Danteri, the liberator of the planet Xenex. The barbarian who had no place in Starfleet. I keep him locked away . . . for when I might need him. So . . . my point remains. People don't change."

"I could still endeavor to argue that, but I don't see the need right now," she said diplomatically. "You see, in this instance, I happen to agree with you. I don't think he's changed either. From what we were able to gather from McNicol before he was lost to us, Thul has some sort of personal grudge against the Federation. McNicol was a bit unclear on it, and didn't have the opportunity to clarify it before he died. But apparently someone dear to Thul died under unfortunate circumstances which he blames the Federation for."

"And is he right to do so?" asked Calhoun. "Was the Federation responsible for the death of this individual?"

"Considering that the whole of the Federation, every world with sentient races, certainly wouldn't deserve to suffer if that were the case, do you really think it matters?"

"It might. To him."

"And does it to you?"

Once again that veiled look passed over his eyes. He didn't answer, but instead simply said, "What do you want me to do, Admiral?"

She bobbed her head slightly, as if acknowledging Calhoun's having skipped over a potentially problematic part of the conversation. "Despite his being an outspoken critic of the

Federation in the past, Thul has now positioned himself as a supporter of the UFP since the thawing of relations between the Thallonian Empire and the UFP. He's got a good deal of personal charm; he's managed to make some rather high-placed friends. And that means I can't use my normal channels of support in investigating this. You're uniquely qualified for this situation, Mac. You've had more experience with Thallonians than anyone else in the Fleet." She paused and glanced at her computer screen. "There's going to be a reception in San Francisco to launch a week's worth of festivities in connection with the bicentennial . . ."

"The one Riker was supposed to attend."

"Precisely. Thul is going to be there; he's on the guest list. I've arranged with Admiral Wattanbe—who shares my concerns—that you will be there as well. I want you to get close to Thul, find out what he's up to . . . and once you do . . . stop him."

"You're forgetting something, Admiral: There's the matter of Zolon Darg. Even if I do manage to work myself close in with Thul, sooner or later I'll be face-to-face with Darg. He'll recognize me. Perhaps I should go in some sort of disguise . . ."

"Thul's too cautious. If his plans, whatever they are, are coming to fruition, he might not be so quick to welcome a complete stranger into his ranks. But you have a reputation as a maverick, Mac. You've had a publicized 'falling out' with Starfleet before. Dissatisfaction and a willingness to break the rules will be believable coming from you. The fortunate thing is, if you do run into Darg, he has no reason to assume that you were working with SI or had any Starfleet or UFP agenda."

"Meaning I can always pretend I was acting in a freelance capacity for a rival, so that he won't automatically assume that my presence now is part of a covert operation."

"Precisely."

"That's all well and good as far as it goes. But even as a 'freelancer,' I did happen to blow his operation to hell and gone. He might be the sort who carries a grudge."

"Perhaps. But I have every confidence that you'll be able to handle him."

"I'm flattered."

"Report to research and development, two decks down, room 18. The Professor will provide you with some specialized tools and weaponry that might be of use to you."

"It's starting to seem just like old times, Admiral. Of course, we're both a little older . . ."

"But probably no wiser, else I wouldn't be sending you into this." She sighed. "Mac . . . be careful. I'd hate to lose you."

"I'd hate to be lost," he replied, and as he started to walk out, he stopped at her door, turned and said, "By the way . . . I'll want my vehicle. And this time I'll want to keep it, rather than returning it to SI. Signed over to me, so no matter what happens in the future, it will go with me rather than being part of Starfleet equipment."

"That shuttle isn't your property, Captain."

"That's somewhat the point, Admiral. I want it. Think of it as an incentive bonus."

"Think of yourself," replied Nechayev, "as a Starfleet officer who does what he's told."

"I've tried that. It doesn't work."

They locked gazes . . . and then Nechayev fought to hide a smile as she said, "Fine. I'll put through the paperwork."

"Thank you, Admiral."

"In all probability," Nechayev added, "the entire question will be moot, since you'll probably wind up dead as a result of this mission."

"So you win either way."

"Well," and she shrugged, "being an Admiral does have its perks."

The room was empty. Calhoun checked the markings just outside to make certain that he'd come to the right place. There were some counters, table tops, a few cabinets. But nothing was laid out, and there didn't appear to be anyone around. "Hello?" Calhoun called out. And when no reply seemed forthcoming, he called once more, *"Hello?"*

"You don't have to shout. I'm not deaf."

Calhoun turned and looked in utter confusion at the man standing behind him. He could have sworn that there had been no one else there, but this fellow had simply seemed to show up out of nowhere. He was wearing a Starfleet uniform. He had a somewhat long face, and dark, curly hair, but the thing that Calhoun noticed the most about him was the singular air of arrogance that hung thick around him.

"I didn't see you here," Calhoun said. "Are you the Professor?"

The man looked at Calhoun oddly. "Why do you want to know?" he asked.

"I'm here to get weapons. That sort of thing."

"The survival of Galactic civilization is hinging upon you, you know," the presumed Professor told him. He spoke in a rather strange manner, as if he were lecturing from a very great distance.

"So I've heard."

"Perhaps you have, but I don't think you yet fully appreciate the magnitude." He shook his head, seemingly amused with himself. "I must admit to being somewhat intrigued to see where it all winds up, providing humanity—and the rest of the Federation—is allowed to continue through to its natural conclusion rather than an aborted one. That would be something to see."

"I couldn't agree more," Calhoun said, deciding it'd be best to humor him. "So . . . what have you got?"

"Well, there's some interesting things here. There's also some things that can be improved upon." He started opening cabinets and pulling out an assortment of materials, looking each thing over and inspecting it closely. "The trick is going to be enabling you to avoid whatever weapons detection devices they might have. But such devices are only as good as their programming. That is to say, if they don't know what to look for, they won't find it. Here."

He held up what appeared to be a tooth, but when he tilted it, Calhoun could see that it was hollowed out inside. "Here. Slip this over one of your molars." Calhoun did as he was told, and then the Professor said, "Now press the back of it with your tongue."

He did so, and to his surprise, three identical replicas of himself appeared around him. They did not simply mirror him, however. Instead each one moved and reacted in its own, individual manner.

"Portable holo-generator. It generates hard-light holograms, just as you have in holodecks. So not only can they serve as distractions, but you also triple your manpower in one shot. Push it again with the back of your tongue to shut it off."

Calhoun did so, and then the Professor handed him a scar. Calhoun took it and stared down at it. It was an exact replica of the scar on his face.

"It's an explosive," said the Professor. "Hide the weapon in plain sight."

"Am I risking blowing my head off?"

"Not at all. Nothing can set it off as long as the circuit isn't completed. You simply take the two ends and twist them around each other. That engages it, and the chemicals inside it begin to interact and build toward detonation. Once the chemical reaction has begun, there's no stopping it. You'll have about fifteen minutes to clear the area before it blows."

Calhoun held the scar gingerly. "Oookay," he said slowly. He lined it up with the scar on his face and pressed it against it. He heard a small hiss of air and a seal was promptly engaged, adhering the fake scar to his face. The metal of the cabinet was highly polished, and he was able to see in his reflection that the blend was perfect. If he himself had not known, he wouldn't have been able to tell.

"This is almost standard issue by this point," said the professor. He extended a fairly nondescript ring which contained a round emblem at one end. "Push it firmly against someone's skin, and it injects a subcutaneous transponder which sends out a homing signal. You'll be able to track anyone."

"Convenient. No woman will dare brush me off again."

The professor didn't seem amused. "Now . . . this next thing is a pip."

"What is it?"

"It's a pip." And sure enough, he held up what appeared to be a standard-issue pip that indicated rank. "If you're not in uniform, you can still easily attach it to a collar or other article of clothing."

"What's significant about it?"

"Put it on." When Calhoun had done so, the Professor said, "Now say, 'Activate transporter, right.'"

"Activate transporter, right," Calhoun said, wondering why

he was doing so. Then, to his astonishment, he suddenly heard a familiar hum around him . . . and an instant later, he was standing on the other side of the room.

"Short range personal transport device. Moves you ten feet in whichever direction you indicate you want it to go. Just be careful, though. You wouldn't want to move into the middle of a solid object."

"Definitely not." He studied the pip. "I didn't think Federation technology had anything like this."

"Officially, It doesn't. Now . . . here. You can probably use an offensive weapon as well. He produced from a cupboard a pair of boots that were exactly Calhoun's size. He turned them over and, from the right one, removed the heel. He proffered it to Calhoun for closer examination, and Calhoun immediately saw the small, tell-tale barrel of some sort of phaser weapon inserted neatly into the inner edge of the heel. "Squeeze the middle with thumb and forefinger top and bottom, that'll produce a stun blast. Squeeze in at the sides, that'll get you level two power. It will only respond to your DNA imprint, so you actually have to be holding it."

"You mean I don't have to worry about stepping down too hard and shooting myself in the foot."

"Something like that," said the Professor. "The left heel contains a communications device. I'll show you." He tapped the middle of the heel and a small, palm-size device slid out. He removed it and held it up. "Under normal circumstances it would only get you standard range, but I've improved it."

"Improved it . . . how?"

"Total security bypass."

"Total security bypass?"

"That's correct, yes. Plus its broadcast will piggyback on any other signals it detects giving it almost unlimited range."

"Oh really." He tapped the comm button and said, "Calhoun to Admiral Jellico, Starfleet headquarters, San Francisco. Come in please. Admiral . . . my men are under attack by a squad of berserk Amazon women and I can't get them to leave. Please advise."

He smiled wanly at the professor, and then the smile froze as back over the communicator came the unmistakeable, and clearly irritated, voice of Admiral Jellico. "This is Jellico. Amazon women? Who the hell is this? Calhoun, is that—?"

Stunned, Calhoun said in a high-pitched voice, "Sorry," and shut down the line. Then he gaped at the professor.

There was no smile on the professor's face, not a hint of amusement or triumph. He simply stared at Calhoun impassively.

"That's very impressive," Calhoun said slowly.

The professor took a step toward him, and in a low voice tinged with warning, said, "Yes it is, isn't it? Apparently you have been selected to be the champion of the galaxy. I've decided to give you a slight edge. The rest is up to you."

Calhoun stared into those implacable eyes for a long moment. "Who are you?" he demanded.

"Me? I'm simply the fellow in research and development who hands out the weapons." With that, he turned and walked out the door. Calhoun quickly followed him out . . . but saw no sign of him.

VII.

"I WILL ATTEND TO IT, Captain Riker," Si Cwan said with confidence. The Thallonian noble made a few more notes as he looked across the desk of the captain's ready room at Riker. "I have certain ... avenues ... I can check. If there is a hidden Romulan base, I might very well be able to get some indication of where it is."

Seated next to him was Robin Lefler, who was also taking notes. In addition to her position at Ops, Robin had taken on the additional duty of personal aide to Si Cwan. Riker felt himself to be something of an aficionado of the ways in which the human heart moved, and as he watched Lefler try—perhaps a bit too hard—to be all business with Cwan, he had the funny feeling that there might be more motivating her than simply trying to be a good officer or find ways to fill the day. Then again, it wasn't really any of his business or his place to comment. So, rather wisely, he kept his opinions on the matter to himself.

"Do you want me to send out the messages?" Lefler asked him.

Si Cwan shook his head. "No ... no, I think it'd be best if these came directly from me. Thank you for the offer, though."

"And thank you, Lord Cwan, for your assistance in this matter," Riker said.

" 'Lord' Cwan." He smiled slightly at the title.

"Did I miss a joke?"

"It's simply that I cannot recall the last time I was addressed with the title. Here on the *Excalibur,* they tend to address me simply by my name."

"And you tolerate that?" Riker asked in amusement.

He shrugged slightly. "I tolerate the familiarity. They, in turn, tolerate my presence. A philosophy of mutual tolerance, I suppose you'd say."

"I am rather pleased to hear it, Lord Cwan . . . particularly considering the rather incendiary nature of our last meeting."

"Incendiary" had hardly been the word for it, as Riker recalled. The first, and last time, that he had seen Si Cwan was right around the time that the Thallonian empire was beginning to crack apart. Si Cwan, exiled but still imperious, had sought out the Federation for aid, and Riker had been present at the meeting where that aid had been decided upon.

"I have not forgotten, Captain," Si Cwan said with a measure of respect in his voice, "your contribution to that meeting. You not only took my side in the discussion . . . but it was you who recommended the assignment of this vessel to Thallonian space. If not for you none of this would have been possible."

"Someone else might well have suggested it," Riker said, "but nonetheless, I appreciate the thanks. Although as I recall, your being posted to the ship was not part of the plan."

"There was a change of plan," Si Cwan said with a combination of dignity and deadpan.

"Yes, and he changed it," Lefler put in with a slightly teasing tone.

"I was invited by Captain Calhoun to serve as a sort of guide and lead diplomat in Thallonian space."

"After he was caught as a stowaway."

Si Cwan turned in his chair and looked at Lefler with something approaching disapproval. "In my opinion," he said slowly, "you are deriving far too much amusement from the situation." He turned back to Riker and said, "I admit, my arrival on this vessel was not the most . . . dignified. But I am here now, and there are no regrets." He fired Lefler a look. "Although I am beginning to have one or two in regards to certain personnel."

"This is all very interesting, and I would certainly like to hear all about it at some future date," Riker said readily. "However, at this point, I do have other matters to attend to . . ."

"And we shall be more than happy to allow you to attend to them, sir." Si Cwan rose, and seemed to keep rising. Riker was impressed, not for the first time, by the sheer presence of the man. He seemed someone who was genuinely entitled to be referred to by the term "noble." He bowed slightly, a gesture which the now-standing Riker returned, and then he turned and left. Lefler, however, remained where she was. "You told me earlier I should stay after the meeting?"

"Yes. There's a matter I wish to discuss with you. A matter regarding one of the bridge crew . . ."

"Shouldn't you be discussing it with Commander Shelby, sir?"

She had a perfectly valid point. In fact, Shelby was probably the person he should really be dealing with. The problem was, he wasn't entirely certain that Shelby would be anything other than defensive, no matter how diplomatically he tried to handle the matter.

He had no desire to say that, though. So instead he said coolly, "Actually, I thought it best to speak with you first since you work with him fairly closely."

"Ahhh." She sounded as if she knew precisely what was going to be said. "You're talking about McHenry."

"Yes. That's right. When you and Si Cwan came in here, I caught a glimpse of McHenry out the door and it appeared he was . . . well . . ."

"Sleeping. At his post."

He nodded. "Lieutenant, I admit I feel a bit like I'm walking on eggshells here." That was no exaggeration. Riker still remembered, all too clearly, the time that Admiral Jellico had taken command of the *Enterprise*. Despite the fact that the assignment was purely temporary, Jellico had wasted no time not only imposing his command style upon others, but going head to head with the senior staff in a manner that was unnecessarily harsh and certainly aggravating. At that time, Riker had made a solemn promise to himself that if he ever found himself in a similar position, for whatever reason, he would do everything he could not to disrupt the preestablished routines of the vessel. It was one thing when one was coming aboard as permanent commander, but Riker was not about to lose sight of the fact that he was a visitor. Still . . . when he saw something that so set his teeth on edge as a crewman displaying total lack of professionalism, he couldn't keep silent. Delicately, he continued, "I'm aware that Captain Calhoun's command style is somewhat different than mine . . . or Captain Picard's . . . or, in fact, anyone that I can think of offhand. Very much a 'live and let live' philosophy, a tendency to celebrate the little differences in people. And by all means, there is much to be said for that. But there is also such a thing," and his voice hardened, "as maintaining at the very least a bare minimum of acceptable preparedness. And having the helmsman asleep in his chair simply doesn't fit that criteria."

"He's not asleep," she said with the air of someone who was not explaining this for the first time. "It only seems that way. Actually he's just deep in thought, but he's completely attuned to everything that's going on. One hundred percent alert."

"I see."

"Also, I admit. . . . he's probably a bit worn out. I still don't think he's sleeping on the job. But his exhaustion is understandable. He's been through something of an emotional wringer."

"How so? Unless you feel it's none of my business."

"Well, sir . . . probably it's not your business, no." With that mandatory disclaimer out of the way, Lefler quickly and eagerly sat down, elbows propped on her knees.

Riker noted with quiet amusement that she was displaying one of the oldest mindsets of young humans, stretching back centuries: The slightly guilty joy of dishing gossip. No matter how advanced humanity became, no matter how many horizons were explored, no matter how many adventures were pursued, no matter how great and noble the race aspired to be . . . there was simply something irresistible about chattering about people behind their backs. Riker, the older, wiser, cooler head, was relieved that he himself was above such things . . . and then leaned forward so as not to miss anything.

"Okay," continued Lefler, "the fact is that for a while

McHenry and Burgoyne 172 were quite the couple, if you catch my drift."

"Not really."

"Well, Burgoyne is a Hermat."

"Hmm. A Hermat." He understood why she said it that way. Not since the Deltans had there been a race whose sexual mores and practices had engendered more interest than the Hermats. He stroked his chin thoughtfully. "There aren't all that many in Starfleet. It's somewhat amazing that two were assigned to this vessel."

"Two?" The tops of her eyebrows knitted together in quiet surprise and confusion. "What two?"

"Well, the Hermat who is involved with McHenry, and the one who is involved with your CMO. At least, I was told the father . . . mother . . . whatever . . . that that individual is the father of Doctor Selar's child."

"Right. That's Burgoyne. Same person."

Riker stared at her. "The . . . *three* of them are involved . . ."

"No, no. You see . . . well, yes, kind of," and she started ticking off major elements on her fingers. "Burgoyne was interested in Selar. But Selar wasn't interested in Burgoyne. At least, she was trying to pretend that she wasn't interested, but she really was, but part of it was as a result of this whole Vulcan biological thing. They don't like to talk about. There's all kinds of different stories about it. It's a personal, private cultural thing and far be it from me to pry.

"Anyway, Selar apparently changed her mind, but Burgoyne was involved with McHenry by that point. So Selar approached the captain about 'accommodating' her. Apparently he said okay . . ."

"He said *what?*"

"He said okay. Apparently it was part of his Xenexian duty to be accommodating about something like that." At Riker's shocked expression, she quickly added "It's a life or death situation."

"Apparently so." For some reason, Riker was suddenly relieved that Calhoun hadn't been in command of the *Enterprise* when Lwaxana Troi had shown up with a quadrupled sex drive. He was sure that Lwaxana would have convinced Calhoun that hers was a life and death situation as well. "You seem to be rather up on everything that's going on around the ship, Lieutenant."

"A starship is like a small town, Captain. Everybody hears everything. Fortunately enough," she said with a touch of irony, "there's some of us who work hard to make sure that accurate information is being disseminated."

"Bless you."

"Thanks," she said, with a grin. "Anyway, some other stuff happened, and Doctor Selar wound up with Burgoyne after all. Now she's pregnant."

"I see." He was intrigued in spite of himself. "And how does McHenry feel about all this?"

"Well, he was okay with it, but really stunned when he found out that Burgoyne was pregnant too."

"What?" He felt his head starting to spin.

"Yeah. At about the same time that Selar announced she was pregnant with Burgoyne's child, Burgy announced that s/he was pregnant with McHenry's child. Poor Mark. Passed right out. Fainted dead away. Since then, he's just thrown himself into his work. I don't think he knows quite how to approach Burgoyne about it. He feels embarrassed about fainting, I know that, and I sure don't think he was prepared for the notion of being a father."

"Well, he's going to have to deal with it sooner or later."

"I think he's angling for later, sir."

"Computer . . . service record of Burgoyne 172. I think," Riker said slowly, "that I very much want to meet Burgoy—." His voice trailed off as he stared at the screen, and his eyes widened. "Burgoyne is the *chief engineer?"*

"Yes, sir."

"Is this individual *stable* enough?"

"Oh yes," Lefler said cheerfully. "S/he's as stable as the rest of us."

Riker wasn't sure if that was a good thing or not.

They walked out of the Captain's ready room. Shelby was seated in the command chair, and made as if to stand up and give way to Riker, but he waved her off. "That won't be necessary, Commander. Presuming everything is calm here, Lieutenant Lefler is going to help familiarize me with the ship."

"As you wish . . . Captain."

There was just that moment of hesitation, and Riker wondered if something vaguely insubordinate was meant by it. But there was nothing about Shelby's attitude or deportment that seemed to indicate it, and Riker chalked it off to his imagination.

His gaze shifted to Mark McHenry. McHenry was exactly as Riker had seen him before. He was tilted back in his chair, his eyes closed. He wasn't snoring. He didn't even quite seem alive. No one else on the bridge, however, was taking notice of it.

Shelby noticed what had caught his attention, and she smiled slightly. "I went through the same thing," she said. "Trust me . . . it's fine. He's completely attuned to the ship. Check if you want."

Riker paused, wondering how one could possibly "check" such a thing. Then a thought occurred to him. He walked over to the tactical section of the bridge, quietly gesturing for the man on duty there to step aside. He did so and Riker glanced over the array. He tapped a control . . . and the ship's primary defense shields snapped on. There was no signal of an alert, although there was a slight rerouting of energy that was part of the natural defense systems process.

The effect on McHenry was instantaneous. He sat bolt upright, glancing at his board and looking at the main screen at the same time. "Are we under attack?" he asked.

Riker couldn't believe it. He looked to Shelby, who shrugged in a "told you so" manner.

"He'll do," Riker said after a moment, and then walked out of the bridge with Lefler right behind him, leaving a puzzled McHenry checking his readouts.

They walked briskly down the corridor, Lefler saying, "Ensign Beth down in engineering said that Burgy is down in the holodeck, working out. She checked with Burgy, though, who said we should feel perfectly free to come by."

" 'Burgy' is what you call him?"

"That's what everybody calls *hir*. Hermats have their own pronouns. 'Hir (H,I,R)' and 's/he.' "

He shook his head. "Hard to be—"

Then he stopped as a woman headed down the hall toward

him. She was a dark-haired, older woman, with a rather aristocratic air about her. And she looked stunningly familiar.

"Hello, honey," she nodded to Robin.

Lefler kissed the woman lightly on the cheek. "Mom . . . this is Captain William Riker. He's in temporary command of the ship while Captain Calhoun is on another assignment. Captain, this is my mother, Morgan Lefler."

"An honor." She shook his hand firmly and then tilted her head in polite confusion. "Is something wrong, Captain?"

"It's just that . . ." He couldn't take his eyes off her. "You just . . . you remind me of the mother of someone else I know."

"It's entirely possible, I suppose. I have gotten around quite a bit."

"Mom's very long lived," Robin said cheerfully.

"Aren't they all," Riker said. He couldn't take his eyes off her. "I'm . . . sorry, Mrs. Lefler. It's just . . . the resemblance is uncanny."

"Yes, I'm sure it is. Well, you go on about your business; I'm sure you have far more important things to do than standing around, ogling me. I'll see you for dinner, Robin," and with that, she headed off down the hallway.

"Incredible," Riker said as he watched her go. "They could be twins. It's like looking at the same woman. Voice, attitude, everything."

"Captain—?"

He shook it off. "I'm sorry. I shouldn't allow myself to get distracted by things that probably don't mean anything."

They chatted about assorted other matters as they walked to the holodeck. When they arrived, Riker leaned close to the door, frowning. He could have sworn he heard something that sounded like . . . growling. "What is Burgoyne doing in there?" he asked.

"Let's find out." She tapped the control padd on the doors and they obediently slid open.

The sight that greeted them upon entering was a rather astounding one.

Burgoyne was dressed in a skintight workout suit, and s/he was surrounded by a forest environment. There was a vista of trees as far as the eye could see. The ground was uneven around them, with dirt and gravel that made traction difficult.

At that moment, Burgoyne was perched in a tree, crouched on a branch, and s/he had hir mouth drawn back in a feline snarl like a cornered cat.

Below her was roaring a massive creature with thick white fur, leaping up at hir and swinging its clawed hands, trying to get a piece of hir and drag hir down from the branch.

"Lieutenant Commander Burgoyne," Lefler said, "this is—"

Burgoyne leaped from the branch, seeming not to have heard Lefler or even noticed her presence or that of Commander Riker. Hir speed carried hir between the outstretched arms of what looked to Riker like a white furred monster, and drove the creature flat onto its back. They rolled across the floor together, hissing and snarling at each other. Then the monster braced itself and twisted, hurling the lighter but more agile Burgoyne back. S/he landed on hir feet, and the way that s/he had her hands poised, s/he looked for all the world as if s/he had claws.

Riker had had enough. "Lieutenant Commander, I hate to break in on your exercise . . ."

And suddenly Burgoyne was flattened from behind.

What looked to Riker's surprised eyes like a white furred creature was atop hir, roaring its fury. Burgoyne twisted around within its grasp and grabbed it by either wrist. S/he managed to get the creature's hands from around hir throat, but apparently it was everything s/he could do to stop it from tearing hir to pieces.

"*Computer, freeze program!*" shouted Riker. Burgoyne, intent on hir opponent, didn't seem to hear him.

The creature was straddling Burgoyne, and appeared to be doing its level best to kill the struggling Hermat.

Believing there to be a holodeck malfunction, Riker didn't hesitate. He charged toward the creature and leaped onto its back. He braced himself, putting all his strength into trying to haul the monster off Burgoyne. It didn't seem to be paying any attention to him at all, focusing all its efforts on annihilating its chosen prey. For that matter, Riker wasn't entirely sure what he was going to do in the event that the monster actually noticed him, because the odds were that it could kill Riker without any great effort. But Riker was determined that he wasn't going down without a struggle.

He saw Lefler standing there . . . and she was shaking her

head, looking more bemused than anything. He couldn't understand it. Here she was faced with a clear emergency, and she didn't seem to have a clue how to react. *"Security! Get security down here!"* Riker shouted.

"Commander," Lefler began, "this is—"

Burgoyne snarled, trying to fight back, but s/he seemed to be losing the struggle.

"I gave you a direct order, dammit! Now follow it!"

With a troubled frown, she tapped her comm badge. "Security, this is Lefler, in holodeck 4A. Get someone down here, fast." But there was absolutely no sense of urgency in her voice.

Is everyone around here insane? Riker wondered as he redoubled his efforts to haul the creature off Burgoyne. And if he did manage to accomplish that feat, his only hope then was that Burgoyne would recover quickly enough to aid him in subduing the creature. Or at the very least, they could hold out long enough for security to get there. And why was Lefler just standing around? Granted, she was rather slight in comparison to Riker and Burgoyne, but dammit, she could certainly find something to do besides just watching it happen.

The doors slid open and a walking land mass entered. The security guard took up the entirety of the door frame. When he moved, it was slow and ponderous. He had no neck, his head apparently attached directly to his shoulders, and his skin in the dim lighting of the holodeck looked like solid granite.

"Hi, Zak," said Robin.

"Hello. You called?" he rumbled.

Riker couldn't believe it. They genuinely *were* all insane. A security officer had just walked into the middle of what was clearly a life-and-death holodeck malfunction, and he didn't seem quite clear on what had to be done.

"Stop this thing before it kills someone!" shouted Riker.

The guard called Zak stood there for a moment, taking in the situation. He didn't move. Instead he spoke four words:

"Janos." Zak shouted, "Janos! Knock it off." Zak's loud voice almost shook the moon.

The white furred creature stopped in its tracks. Then, with a sigh, it stood fully upright rather than in the hunched position it had been using until that point. Riker was still hanging on its back, dumbfounded.

"Sir? If you don't mind?" asked the creature, and the question was clearly addressed to Riker. "Apparently, this exercise period is over." Riker, feeling as if sanity was slipping away from him, released his grip and dropped to the floor. Burgoyne, for hir part, was picking hirself off the floor and dusting hirself off.

Zak looked back to Lefler. "Anything else?"

"No, that should about do it."

He inclined his chest slightly, which was his equivalent of nodding, and then he turned and walked back out the door.

VIII.

GERRID THUL WAS EMINENTLY pleased as he looked around the room of dead men.

That might not have been the most accurate of terms, he reasoned. Not all of them were men, for starters. A goodly number of males of the species were there, yes, but there was a vast array of females as well. All equally deserving, equally titled, equally dead. And to be absolutely, one hundred percent correct, he would have to admit that none of them were actually, in point of fact, dead.

Yet.

Never had the word "yet" been so delicious, held so much promise. Yet. Definitely, indisputably, yet.

As he walked through the grand reception hall that hosted the first of what was intended to be a number of gatherings celebrating the bicentennial, he couldn't help but be satisfied, and even amused, at the way that others within the Federation were reacting to him. There were nods, smiles, a polite wink or two. And many, ever so many requests for "just a few moments" of his time that invariably expanded into many minutes.

He had been careful, so very careful in making his contacts. And what had been so elegant about the entire matter was that those poor, benighted fools in the Federation had a tendency to side with the underdog. And that was something that Thul had very much seemed. A man who was once great, who had lost everything, and who was now trying to build himself back up to a position of strength and influence. He had come to people seemingly hat in hand, unprepossessing, undemanding. And he played, like a virtuoso, upon one of the fundamental truths of all sentient beings: Everyone liked to feel superior to someone else. It made them comfortable. It made them generous. And best of all, it made them sloppy and offered a situation that General Thul could capitalize upon.

Of course, Vara Syndra had helped.

"Where is Vara this fine evening?" assorted ambassadors and high muck-a-mucks in the Federation asked. But Thul had held her back, and not without reason. Best to build up anticipation, to get them to want to see her, ask about her, look around and try to catch a glimpse of her. Vara knew her place, though, and also knew that timing was everything. She would remain secreted away until the appropriate time had presented itself, and then he would send for her.

He had a feeling that the time was fast approaching.

"Thul! General Thul!" came a hearty voice that Thul recognized instantly. He turned to see Admiral Edward Jellico approaching.

He did not like Jellico. That, in and of itself, was nothing surprising; he didn't like any of them, really. But Jellico was a particularly pompous and officious representative of humanity. Thul hoped against hope that he might somehow actually be able to see Jellico when the death throes overtook him, but that didn't seem tremendously likely. He would have to settle for imagining it. Then again, Thul had a famously vivid imagination, so that probably wouldn't present too much of a difficulty.

"Edward!" returned Thul cheerfully, perfectly matching the pitch and enthusiasm of Jellico's own voice. He had to speak loudly to make himself heard over the noise and chatter of the packed ballroom. Furthermore, all around him the scents of various foods wafted toward him. Thul had a rather acute sense of smell, and the array was nearly overwhelming to him. Some seemed rather enticing while others nearly induced his gag reflex, so it was quite an effort to keep it all straight within him. "It is good to see you again, my friend."

125

"And you as well, General." He gestured to those who were accompanying them. One was another human, a tall and powerfully built human female. The other was a rather elegant-looking Vulcan with graying hair, and that annoying serenity that Vulcans seemed to carry with them at all times. "This is Admiral O'Shea," he said, pointing to the female, "and this is Ambassador Stonn. Admiral, Ambassador, General Thul of the Thallonian Empire."

"The late Thallonian Empire, I fear," said Thul. He bowed in O'Shea's direction, and then gave a flawless Vulcan salute to Stonn. "Peace and long life," he said.

"Live long and prosper," replied Stonn.

One of us will, thought Thul.

"I'm familiar with your good works, Thul," said O'Shea. "As I recall, you were working just last month to seek more humanitarian aid for refugees from Thallonian space."

"Actually," Thul told her, "I have been looking into expanding my efforts. You see, in exploring what needs to be done to help our own refugees, I have stumbled upon other races that could use aid as well. Aid . . . which is sometimes hampered by the Federation."

"Hampered? How so?" asked Stonn.

"It is . . . ironic that I would bring this up now," Thul said, looking quite apologetic. "We are, after all, here to celebrate the signing of the Resolution of Non-Interference, one of the keystone documents of the entire Federation."

"Yes. So?"

"So, Admiral O'Shea . . . it may be time to revisit the entire concept of the prime directive. All too often . . . and I truly do not wish to offend with my sentiments . . ."

"Please, General, say what you feel," Jellico urged him.

"Very well. It seems that, all too often, the intent of the prime directive is corrupted. The letter is followed when the spirit is violated." He noticed that several other people had overheard him and were now attending his words as well. Superb. The larger audience he had, the better he liked it. "The fact is that the prime directive was created specifically so that more advanced races would not *harm* less developed races. But too many times, we encounter situations where it is specifically cited as a reason not to *help* those races. Starfleet stands by, watches them fumble about, and simply takes down notes while observing from hidden posts. Think, my friends. Think, for example, of a small child," and his voice started to ache with imagined hurt, "a small boy, dying of a disease . . . the cure for which is held by those who look down from on high. But do they help? Do they produce a medication that will save him? No . . . no, my friends, they do not. They bloodlessly watch, and take down their notes, and perhaps they'll log the time of death. And who knows if that child might not have grown up to be the greatest man, inventor, thinker, philosopher, leader of that race. The man who could bring that race into a golden age, cut off . . . in his youth. What would it have hurt . . . to help that child? And what tremendous benefit might have been gained. Who among you could endorse such a scenario . . . and believe it to somehow serve a greater good?"

There was dead silence from those within earshot. Finally, Stonn said, "A very passionate observation, Thul. At its core, there may even be some valid points. However . . . interference invites abuse. It was an earthman who stated that power tends to corrupt . . . and absolute power corrupts absolutely. For all of the positive scenarios that you can spin, I am certain that I would easily be able to create plausible hypotheticals of abuse of that selfsame power."

"What Ambassador Stonn is saying," said Admiral O'Shea, "is that if the non-interference directive is, as you postulate, an error . . . isn't it better to err on the side of caution?"

"Two hundred years ago, perhaps. I will certainly grant you that. But of what use is experience if one does not learn from it," replied Thul. "There are people who need help and don't even know that they do. Besides, is not human history rife with such 'interference'? Were there not more advanced members of the human race who went to less-developed, undernourished or undereducated areas and brought them technology . . . advancement . . . even entire belief systems?"

"And in many instances did as much harm as good," Jellico said. "There was also conquest, to say nothing of entire races of people who were annihilated by germs and strains of diseases that their own immune systems were completely unequipped to handle."

"Ultimately, however," and Thul smiled, "things seem to have worked out for you."

"Yes, because we found our own way."

"Or perhaps in spite of finding your own way. Think, though. If older, wiser, more advanced races such as yours, and all those represented in this room were to use their experience, their knowledge of the mistakes that they themselves made to avoid mistakes in the future . . ." He shook his head. "Don't you see. But when there is want and need by other races who have never even heard of the Federation, and who could benefit so tremendously by the help . . ."

"You're saying that perhaps it's time to abolish or reframe the prime directive?" said Jellico.

"At this time? On the anniversary the signing of the document that was its genesis? Yes, that is exactly what I am saying."

There were thoughtful nods from all around, like a sea of bobbing heads. Finally it was Jellico who said, "You may . . . have some valid points there, General. Obviously I can't speak on behalf of Starfleet, and certainly not the Federation . . . but perhaps some serious study should be done as to whether it's time to rethink our intentions and perhaps expand upon—"

"You hypocrite."

The voice had come completely unexpectedly, and the words were slightly slurred. As one, everyone within earshot turned and saw the rather remarkable sight of a Starfleet captain, holding a drink and glaring at Admiral Jellico with as open a glare of contempt as Thul had ever seen.

"You are some piece of work, Admiral. You are really, truly, some piece of work." He took another sip of the blue liquid that was swirling about in his glass.

Thul couldn't quite believe the change that had come over Jellico's face. He had gone from thoughtful to darkly furious, practically in the space of a heartbeat. "Captain Calhoun . . . may I ask what you're doing here?"

"Listening to you reverse yourself," replied Captain Calhoun. "The number of times I've had to listen to you pontificate and talk about the sanctity of the prime directive . . . of how unbreakable the first, greatest law of Starfleet is . . . and how you've used that selfsame law to second-guess and denounce some of my most important decisions. But now here you are, all dressed up at this extremely important gathering," and he added exaggerated emphasis to the last three words, "and this . . . person . . ." and he waved in a vague manner at Thul, ". . . suggests the exact same thing that I've been saying for years now . . . and suddenly you're ready to listen. You act like this is the first time you've heard it."

"Perhaps General Thul simply has a way of expressing his concerns that is superior to the belligerent tone you usually adopt, Captain," said Jellico. Quickly he said to the others around him, "General, Ambassador Stonn, Admiral O'Shea . . . I'm terribly sorry about this. I'm not entirely certain what this officer is doing here . . ."

"I'm here because I was ordered to be here," Calhoun said. A number of other guests were noticing the ruckus, which wasn't difficult since Calhoun's voice was carrying.

"That's strange. My office should have received a memo on that," Jellico said, his eyes narrowing with suspicion.

"Really. Perhaps someone simply forgot. Or perhaps you were too busy getting ready for this little get-together that you didn't have a chance to stay current with your memos. Look, Admiral," and Calhoun swayed ever so slightly. Thul could tell that this rather odd individual had clearly had a bit too much to drink. "Make no mistake. I'd rather be on my ship. But I was ordered to be here because I'm supposed to be representing the Federation's interests in Thallonian space. One of the new frontiers that we brave individuals are exploring and protecting. Here's to us," and he knocked back more of the drink, leaving about a third of it in the glass.

"Of course," said Thul in slow realization. "Captain Calhoun . . . of the *Excalibur.* Am I correct?"

"Correct."

"I am very aware of your vessel's humanitarian mission. It is also my understanding that Lord Si Cwan is among the personnel of your brave ship. I met him once, when he was a very small child. I doubt he would remember me."

"Captain Calhoun was just leaving," said Jellico, "weren't you, Captain?"

"Oh, was I?" Calhoun smiled lopsidedly. "But Admiral, this is a party. Why are you so anxious to have me leave?"

"Captain," O'Shea spoke up, "I'm well aware that you have some . . . issues . . . with Admiral Jellico. But I submit that this is neither the time nor the place . . ."

"Or perhaps it's the perfect time and place," Calhoun shot back. Thul quickly began to reassess his opinion. Calhoun wasn't a bit drunk. He was seriously drunk. Not in such a way that he was going to fall over, but certainly whatever inhibitions he might have about speaking the truth were gone. "The fact is that the good Admiral here has had it out for me for years now. Just because he got it into his head that I was some sort of super officer, and then I didn't live up to the place that he'd set for me. I saved his life, you know," he said in an offhand manner to Thul. "This man would be standing here dead if not for me."

"And because of that, I protected you as long as I could," Jellico said, his body stiffening. "But you're the one who allowed the *Grissom* incident to get to you, Calhoun. Accidents happen, bad things happen to good people. True leaders manage to rise above that."

"And leave their consciences behind?"

"I didn't say that. Look, Calhoun," said Jellico, his ire clearly beginning to rise, "you said you're here because you were ordered to be here. If you're actually obeying orders, it's going to be the first time that I can recall in ages . . . perhaps ever. That being the case, here's another order: Get the hell out of here before you embarrass yourself further, if that's possible."

"Gentlemen," Stonn said, "perhaps you might wish to take this conversation into a private area . . ."

It seemed to Thul that, at that point, everyone in the place was watching them. He also saw several men dressed in UFP security garb threading their way through the crowd.

"I'm sure he'd like that," Calhoun said. "That's how his kind best operates: In the dark, in private, alone, like any fungus."

"That's enough," said Jellico, the veins on his temples clearly throbbing.

"You sway with the wind, Jellico," said Calhoun. "To your superiors and your pals, you say what you think they want to hear. And to the rest of us, you step on us like we're bugs. That's all we are to you. And you can't stand me because I actually stood up to you. Stood up! That's an understatement. I flattened you. I flattened him," Calhoun said to O'Shea. "One punch. I resigned from Starfleet, he tried to get in my way, I warned him, and one punch, I took him down."

"It was not one punch." Jellico looked around, clearly embarrassed. "Not one punch."

"It was. One shot to the side of the head, and you went down on your ass, right after you grabbed my arm . . ."

"All right, that's it. Security!" called Jellico . . .

. . . and he grabbed Calhoun by the arm.

Calhoun's smile went wolfish, and to Thul it seemed as if all the inebriation, all the fuzziness about the man, dissolved in a second. Whatever the man might have had to drink, he was able to shunt it aside in a split second. His fist whipped around with no hesitation, and caught Jellico squarely in the side of the head. Jellico went down amidst gasps from everyone surrounding him.

"That will suffice," said Ambassador Stonn, stepping between Jellico and Calhoun. At that moment, despite the superior strength of the Vulcan, Thul would not have wanted to place bets on just who would win an altercation between the Vulcan and Calhoun.

But Calhoun didn't display the least interest in fighting off Stonn. Instead he simply grinned and said, "See? Told you. One punch."

"Get out of here!" Jellico said, rubbing his head. His eyes weren't focused on anything; Thul could practically hear Jellico's head ringing right from where he was standing.

Calhoun seemed to be enjoying Jellico's disorientation immensely. "One-Punch Jellico, they should call you. That's all it takes," Calhoun called. "That's all it takes to puncture a pompous windbag."

O'Shea helped Jellico to his feet, asking after his health solicitously, but it didn't seem as if Jellico even heard her. Instead, across the room that had now become completely hushed, Jellico shouted, "I'll have your rank for this, Calhoun! Do you hear me? This is the last straw! I don't care who your friends are! I don't care what you've accomplished! I don't care if Picard backs you up! I don't care if the words, 'Calhoun is my favorite captain' appears on the wall at Starfleet headquarters in flaming letters twelve feet high! You are gone! You are finished! Do you hear? Finished!"

"I hear you, Admiral!" called Calhoun as he stormed out of the room. "And I heard you when you said it years ago! And I came back, didn't I? I keep coming back!" He turned and walked out of the room.

"Not this time, Calhoun! Not this time!" Jellico shouted after him.

There was a long silence after Calhoun left from the room. Jellico was flushed red in the face, clearly utterly chagrined at the turn of events. "You've nothing to be embarrassed about, Admiral," said Thul consolingly. "Obviously he was a madman."

"I could tell you horror stories, General, I really could," said Jellico. "Mackenzie Calhoun represents . . . I'm sorry, I should say 'represented' . . . everything that's wrong with the 'cowboy' breed of captain. No respect for rules or for authority. No respect for the chain of command. No . . ."

"No respect, period?" offered Thul.

"Yes. Yes, that's exactly right. He left the fleet once before . . . went freelance . . . did dirty work for whomever would pay him. The only reason he was brought back into the fleet was because he had well-placed supporters, but after this debacle, even they won't back him. Believe me, we're stronger without him."

"And he certainly seems to have no love for Starfleet . . . or even perhaps the Federation," Thul said slowly.

"The Mackenzie Calhouns of this world love only themselves and care about their own skins, and that's all. We were speaking of abuse of power before, General? He's exactly the type that the prime directive was created to ride herd on. Good riddance to him, I say." Jellico rubbed the side of his face. "Let him be someone else's problem."

"Excellent idea," said General Thul. "A most excellent idea."

Mackenzie Calhoun sat at curbside outside the great hall. From within, he could hear the music and voices building up to their previous levels.

He shook out his hand and squeezed it into a fist. It hurt. That was very annoying. His hand shouldn't be hurting. And it seemed to him that Jellico had fallen much faster, and bounced much harder, when he'd struck him years earlier.

"I hope I'm not losing my punch," he said to no one.

"I hope not, too," came a sultry voice, indicating that he had not quite been speaking to no one as he had previously thought.

He turned and looked up.

She was, quite simply, the most beautiful Thallonian woman he had ever seen. She had absolutely no hair, except for two delicate eyebrows that were carefully sculpted. Her neck was long and elegant, her bosom in perfect proportion to her hips. Her legs seemed to go to somewhere up around her shoulders, and when she smiled it was incandescent.

Calhoun automatically rose to his feet.

"Hello," she said.

"Hi. I'm . . ." He thought for a moment, then recalled the information. "Mackenzie Calhoun."

"I'm Vara Syndra," she purred, displaying a remarkable facility for recalling her own name. "Gerrid Thul is interested in speaking with you."

"Will you be there?"

"Yes."

"Then so will I."

133

IX.

"APOLOGIZE, ENSIGN. RIGHT NOW. You too, Burgoyne."

They were in the conference lounge. It was Shelby who had just sternly addressed Burgoyne and Ensign Janos, while a somewhat chagrined-looking Robin Lefler looked on. Riker's face was expressionless. Janos had changed to the Starfleet uniform that he usually wore, albeit uncomfortably, when he was on duty.

"My apologies, Commander," Janos said sincerely. "When . . . exercising . . . my Hermat friend and I can get quite intense. We simply did not hear you call for the program to freeze. Then, when you attacked me, we thought you were joining us. Captain Calhoun does, on occasion."

"My apologies as well," Burgoyne put in.

"Well, then," Riker said, smiling, "a simple mistake. No hard feelings."

"Thank you, sir," Janos said. "But . . . permission to speak freely?"

"Of course," Riker said.

"I am aware that my appearance can be quite startling, even frightening, to those unprepared for it."

134

"All right," Riker suddenly spoke up. His face was still inscrutable. "I see where you're going, and you're right. I shouldn't have made assumptions about you . . . even a 'hologram' of you, based solely on your physical appearance. We in Starfleet are supposed to be above the concept of making judgments based on surface impressions. Therefore, Janos . . . I apologize for jumping to the conclusion that you were a threat and not a Starfleet officer. Perhaps if you were wearing clothing . . ."

"I was, a white jumpsuit."

"I didn't notice. Again, my fault, I apologize."

"Thank you, Captain."

"Sir," Robin Lefler put in at that moment, "I apologize for not taking firmer control of the situation. I could have done what Zak did. I should have been more take-charge, instead of allowing myself to be carried away by the avalanche."

"Yes, you should have," Riker said. "Just try to be a little more aggressive in the future."

"Aggressive. Yes, sir."

"Well, that wraps that up," Riker said, smiling again. "Oh, one more thing. Burgoyne, I understand that you're pregnant. Is exercise of this nature a good idea?"

"Wait, wait a minute," Burgoyne said. "Where did you hear I was pregnant? I'm not pregnant."

Lefler looked utterly confused. "But you are, aren't you?"

"No, I'm not. I think I would know that."

"But . . . you told McHenry . . ."

"What, in sickbay the other day? That was a joke! He knew I was joking."

"Uh oh."

Now both Riker and Burgoyne was staring at Lefler. In unison, they said, "Uh oh?" Janos and Shelby looked at each other in confusion.

"Well . . . McHenry didn't know," said Lefler. "You weren't there when he came to, after he passed out."

"Yes, I know that. While he was unconscious, that's when I was called down to engineering. Worked the eighteen straight hours, as I said. When I finally got back to my quarters, though, there was a message from him. We got together and I let him know it wasn't true. That it was just intended to be a joke."

"You told him that?"

"Yes. A few hours ago."

"Uh oh."

"Why does she keep saying 'uh oh'?" Burgoyne asked Shelby. Shelby shook her head, not knowing the answer.

"Well . . . the thing is, you see . . . McHenry told me. And I sort of told, well . . ." She shifted in her seat, looking extremely uncomfortable.

"You just sort of told, well . . . who?"

Wincing as if she were preparing to duck back from a punch, she said, "Uh . . . everybody."

"What?"

"Yeah, I'm afraid so. How the hell was I supposed to know?" she said defensively.

"You mean everybody on the ship?"

"No, everybody in the quadrant," she shot back. "Yes, on the ship. And not really *everybody.* Just . . . a lot of people."

"Perfect. That's just perfect," moaned Burgoyne. "One casual remark, and suddenly . . ."

At that moment, the doors hissed open and Si Cwan entered.

"Excellent," said the Thallonian noble. "I'm glad you're all here."

"Ambassador, could this possibly wait . . . ?" asked Shelby.

"Narobi II."

Shelby and Riker exchanged looks. "Pardon?" asked Riker.

"I've received word from one of my sources that the Romulans are going to be attacking Narobi II. He's reasonably sure that it's the same pack that you're talking about. The Renegades we'd hoped they return to Romulus to help rebuild after the Dominion War."

Instantly everyone at the table was alert. "How does he know this?" Riker asked.

"He's the type of individual who makes it his business to know such things. In this instance, someone with whom he was connected apparently aided in repairs on one of the vessels that the *Independence* engaged in battle. And this individual happened to hear about one of the next intended targets."

"I'm not sure I like this. It's too pat," said Shelby.

"I agree," Riker said.

"Perhaps. Perhaps not," said Si Cwan. "When you deal with a large operation . . . and this apparently seems to fit that description . . . there's large numbers of people who let things slip. In any event, Captain, you wanted me to try and bring you information. If you're going to dismiss it out of hand, then why am I bothering?"

Slowly Riker nodded. It was, he thought, a valid enough point. "Narobi II. Tell me about it."

"It's a rather unique world in Thallonian space. It's populated entirely by a race who has converted itself into beings of a sort of living metal. They created ultra-durable bodies for themselves that last for hundreds of years. In essence, they've made themselves immortal. They are utterly peaceful, but fully capable of protecting themselves should they be under attack. I'm not entirely certain why the Romulans would choose to target them."

"Neither am I. But we can't afford to let the possibility go. Commander . . . set course for Narobi II."

"Aye, sir."

As they got up from the conference table, Si Cwan suddenly turned to Burgoyne and, to hir surprise, placed a hand on either side of hir face. "What are you—?" s/he began to say.

Si Cwan proceeded to utter a lengthy chant, the performance of which stopped everyone in their tracks. Cwan had a surprisingly melodious voice which floated up and down the register. It was so lovely that no one dared to interrupt as Cwan continued that way for about forty-five seconds, murmuring, chanting, and swaying back and forth slightly as he did so. Then he lowered his hands and smiled.

"What was that all about?" demanded Burgoyne.

"That," Si Cwan said in a booming voice, "was the ancient Thallonian prayer for a smooth and uncomplicated pregnancy, which can only be delivered by one of the Noble house upon an expectant mother. Congratulations, Burgoyne. May you have a child which brings glory to your name."

"I'm not pregnant," Burgoyne said testily, and s/he walked out of the conference room.

There was silence for a moment and then, non-plussed, Si Cwan decided, "Well . . . it's probably for the best. It's been a while, and I was out of practice. Instead of the pregnancy chant, I may have accidentally prayed for hir not to contract root rot."

"Smashing. So the odds of it being effective just went way up," said Janos cheerily.

I've got to get off this ship, thought Riker.

X.

ZOLON DARG WAS RATHER PLEASED with the turnout.

The place that he had chosen for the rendezvous on Argelius was somewhat out of the way, well off the beaten track of most of the places of entertainment and merriment which drew in most of the tourists. Darg, for the get-together that he had been busily arranging, had selected a rather disreputable place which was in violation of at least three Argelian health codes.

He was also drawn by the name of the place: "Kara's," in commemoration of some hideous event which had occurred on Argelius nearly a century ago during which a number of women were slaughtered . . . rather nastily, at that.

Kwint was looking around with open curiosity. They had been out drinking much of the night, but Kwint didn't seem particularly daunted by the amount of alcohol they had been putting away. Zolon Darg was impressed by that. As a Thallonian, he was more than capable of imbibing considerable amounts of alcohol without displaying, or even feeling, the ill effects. Kwint was obviously just a human, yet he didn't seem to be displaying any ill effects at all. Darg wondered if one of Kwint's limbs wasn't actually hollow, enabling him to store vast quantities within.

There was a permanent layer of dirt on the walls of Kara's.

Many of the chairs seemed rickety, and the tables weren't much better. There was a large mirror behind the bar. It was cracked. There were also signs that there had been a fight in the bar not too long ago. Darg wondered absently what had started it, who had won . . . and if anyone had actually survived. Behind the bar, a surly Tellarite bartender named Gwix poured out drinks. Gwix wasn't the type of bartender one poured their heart out too . . . at least, not unless one was a masochist. Gwix had little patience for anything except serving the drinks, getting the money, and closing up for the night. Nonetheless, even Gwix was aware when Darg came in, and tilted his pig-like head in acknowledgment.

"Nice place," Kwint said at length. "Come here often?"

"Often enough."

"You want to tell me what's going on?"

"You'll find out soon enough. Come here." He moved around one of the tables and indicated that Kwint should sit. Kwint did so. Darg, however, continued to stand, and as he leaned on the back of one of the chairs, it was quickly evident why. Just leaning on it would have been enough to break it.

Darg seemed to be assessing Kwint for a long moment, stroking his chin thoughtfully. Finally he said, "You have a lot on the ball, Kwint. I've seen that tonight. First with the way that we met. Then we went to that gambling place, and you immediately nailed the guy who was trying to cheat us. Then we went to the brothel, and you immediately nailed—"

"What are you saying, Darg?" Kwint asked, cutting him off.

"I'm saying that I think you have potential in my organization. An organization that's only going to let larger." He glanced over Kwint's shoulder. "Ah. I see some of our guests have arrived."

They were filing in, one at a time, regarding each other with obvious distrust. Then again, that wasn't all that surprising. The dozen or so beings who had shown up at Kara's were not accustomed to trusting anyone or working together, for they were all from races who were outside of the Federation. Races who, for whatever reason, considered the alliance of the UFP to be suffocating to their own interests. There was an Orion . . . a Kreel . . . a Tan'gredi, all ooze and nictating membranes . . . a Capitano, growling deep in its chest, its eyeless face gazing around with its internal radar taking in the parameters of the room . . . an assortment of others.

"Thank you all for coming," Darg said once everyone was settled. He was all too aware of the suspicion that focused on him from every direction. That was perfectly fine. He could handle that. "Since this is a matter of some delicacy, I know that I can count on all of you for your discretion."

"We're not interested in your compliments or your kudos to our discretion, gun runner," said the Kreel. "We all have other matters to attend to. Say what you have to say."

Darg didn't reply immediately. He'd learned that some extended silence could often be more useful than simply leaping straight into discourse. So he allowed the quiet to hang there a short time before he said, "All of you have grudges and difficulties with the Federation. They, and the races that they represent, have stifled you, interfered with you, operated in manners that are contradictory to your interests. And I'm not speaking of you as individuals, of course—although that much is certainly true—but also for the races that you represent."

There was that slightly nauseating "slurping" sound that always preceded a Tan'gredi before it spoke. "Races do not operate as whole, Darg. There are always different factions. Some of my people—the radicals—speak of joining the Federation at some point."

"True enough," Darg said smoothly. "But let us say that I have contacted you—singled you out as individuals—because I thought that you would be most amenable to the cause I represent."

"What cause is that?" The Orion was idly stabbing the table top at which he was seated with his curved dagger.

"The cause that involves . . . a new time to come. A new era that we think of as the post-Federation era."

"Who is 'we'?" The Kreel, as quick-tempered as most of his type, clearly wasn't interested in vagueness. "And what exactly will make this era of yours 'post'? The Dominion war is over; the Federation is not going anywhere anytime soon."

"I . . . choose at this point not to focus on the specifics."

There was a skeptical groan.

"What I am here to tell you," continued Darg as if they had not made a sound, "is that there will come a time—soon—

when the Federation will not be a consideration. At that point, it's going to be a whole new galaxy . . . and whoever has the greatest technology, the most formidable weapons, and the strongest allies . . . will come out on top. What we—those I represent—are seeking are those who are interested in buying into our vision."

" 'Buying in.' Here it comes," said the Kreel, sneering. "And what exactly does that entail?"

"One hundred thousand bars of gold-pressed latinum from each of you . . . on behalf of the races that you represent."

There was a roar of mixed laughter, disbelief, and outright contempt. Through it all, Darg simply stood there, taking it in, his face immobile, his manner patient. He acted as if he had all the time in the world.

"And if we don't buy in?" asked the Capitano in that remarkable voice that seemed to originate from somewhere in the ground beneath his feet.

"Then you will die."

It was not Darg who had spoken, however. It was Kwint. The attention promptly switched to him, and even Darg was clearly surprised to hear the relative newcomer speak so boldly.

"Is that a threat?" asked the Kreel quietly.

Kwint half-smiled and walked in a slow circle around the gathering. "If someone offered you safe haven from a supernova . . . and you displayed lack of interest . . . and that someone informed you that you were going to die . . . is that a threat? Or is that simply a prediction?"

"Does this human speak for you, Darg?" inquired the Orion. He had stopped sticking the knife into the table, his interest caught by the shift in the atmosphere.

Darg sized Kwint up for a long moment. In point of fact, he had told Kwint absolutely nothing about the plan. Kwint was speaking entirely from conjecture, bluff . . . and attitude. It was, however, an attitude that Darg found most intriguing. "He speaks for himself," Darg said slowly, "but I choose not to contradict him. Make of that what you will."

Apparently feeling that he'd been given a tacit endorsement to continue, Kwint promptly did so. "Yes . . . I am human, as you noted. And there have been any number of times in human history where people were offered an opportunity by those who had vision . . . and the will, drive and resources to bring that vision to life. At the time that these visionaries presented their views of things, there were always those who were skeptical or derisive. Who would gladly turn their back and walk away, not realizing that they were leaving greatness behind. Zolon Darg is connected to that vision. He has seen the dream. He sees a place where there is a galaxy that is unstifled by the rules of the Federation, striving ceaselessly to create a perfect reality that exists only in the minds of those who have an interest in maintaining the status quo. You deserve to come into your own . . . and Zolon Darg, and those he represents, are the ones who bring you there."

There was silence for a long moment. And then the Kreel representative stepped forward and said, "I'm out."

"As am I," said the Orion, "although I'll have another drink first . . . if our generous host doesn't mind."

"Of course I don't mind," said Darg calmly, but his attention was focused on the Kreel. "My friend . . . I understand your concern. And I wish you well in your future endeavors."

He gripped the Kreel by the forearm and nodded firmly. The Kreel eyed him suspiciously, apparently tensing for Darg to make some sort of sudden move. But then Darg stepped away, nodded and said, "Good-bye," and then turned to the others. "I would ask you others to consider the matter a bit more carefully and deeply than our Kreel friend here."

As the Kreel headed out the door, the Capitano rumbled, "You have to at least meet us halfway here, Darg. At least give us some idea of just why you are so certain that you will be able to dispose of the Federation in such a—"

There was a sudden scream from just outside the bar. The voice and tone was unmistakeable. It was the Kreel, and to say that he sounded in distress would have been to understate it.

There was a rush for the door. The only ones who didn't move in that direction were Zolon Darg and Kwint, the latter glancing at the former in silent query. Darg simply nodded and became extremely engrossed in studying his fingernails.

As the others peered out the door, there were gasps of disbelief, a number of profanities, several quick prayers offered up to respective gods, and the sound of the Tan'gredi becoming physically ill ... although considering the somewhat disgusting noises they customarily made, it was admittedly hard to distinguish.

What they saw was the Kreel representative, collapsed on the ground and trying with all his might just to stand up. His skin had become a distinctive shade of green, and gaping pustules had opened up all along his body.

And then the Kreel slumped forward, hit the ground once more and fell silent. His body twitched spasmodically, but that was all.

There was deathly silence in Kara's. Then Darg moved among them, handing out small rectangles with coordinates engraved in them. "If you are interested in learning more of what I've said ... if you are interested in participating ... and if," and he glanced at Kwint in acknowledgment, " ... if you are someone of vision ... then show up at these coordinates precisely five Federation Standard Days from today. We might as well use their units of time measurement," he added in amusement, "for as long as they're vaguely applicable."

"What did that to the Kreel?" the Tan'gredi burbled. "I've seen fast-acting poisons before, but—"

"That wasn't a poison ... was it," said the Orion slowly. "That was some sort of ... of virus. A disease. You gave it to him somehow. What was it? Have you passed it on to us somehow?"

"My dear fellows," Darg said soothingly, "I assure you that you are perfectly safe." And then he added, rather significantly, "for the time being. As Kwint stated, those supernovas can be rather vicious, and I would hate to see any or all of you incinerated."

The Capitano looked at the coordinates and growled, "I know this section of space. There's nothing at these coordinates. Nothing at all."

"There will be," Darg said with a small smile. "There will be."

And with that, Darg made it quite clear that the meeting was over. One by one, the assorted representatives departed, stepping rather gingerly around the remains of the Kreel. "Worry not," Darg said with remarkable cheer, "he'll be attended to shortly enough. I wouldn't advise getting too close for the time being, though." The representatives took care to attend to his advice.

"Well," Darg said once he and Kwint were alone. "That went about as well as could be expected."

"You suspected that someone was going to doubt you . . . to walk out . . . didn't you," said Kwint.

Darg shrugged. "There's always one. Frankly, I was hoping it would be the Kreel. Insufferable race." Then he regarded Kwint more closely. "You spoke out of turn."

"Yes, I did. I considered your proposal intriguing, and seeing skeptical and even disrespectful looks from those . . . individuals . . . was bothersome to me."

"And if something strikes you as bothersome, you feel an obligation to do something about it. Is that it?"

Kwint nodded slightly. "Something like that."

" 'Something like that.' I see." Darg looked Kwint up and down. "You know, Kwint . . . you have potential."

"Potential as what? You mentioned bringing me into your organization before . . ."

"Part of what I was doing during this meeting was keeping an eye on you. Trying to determine what one can expect of you. But you know . . . I'm still not sure. Your speaking up was not particularly wise on your part . . . but on the other hand, it took nerve. I suppose you simply felt you had to 'equalize' things once more."

"In a way."

" 'In a way' is another means of saying 'something like that.' Yes, Kwint, definite potential. If you seem worthwhile, you might definitely be in line for my number two man."

"Me?" Kwint looked like he couldn't believe it. "But we've only known each other for a few hours. Are you sure?"

"I work on instinct a good deal, Kwint. That's how I judge people, and most of the time, I'm right."

"What happened to your previous number two man?"

"I killed him."

"Oh." Kwint didn't seem to know what to say.

Darg, for his part, couldn't have cared less. "I said most of the time, I'm pretty reliable. Everyone has setbacks."

And suddenly his hand was on Kwint's chest, and he was lifting the smaller man up and slamming him against a wall. The pressure on Kwint's chest was such that, not only had the wind been knocked out of him, but he couldn't get any air into his lungs. He pulled in futility at Darg's immovable hand.

"Have a care," Darg said quite softly, "that you do not have a setback of your own." Then his hand opened wide and Kwint slid to the ground, coughing violently as he gulped down air. "Do we understand each other?"

Kwint nodded, still coughing.

"Now . . . you can attend to your first duty as a member of my organization." And he handed Kwint a large sack and a thick pair of gloves. Kwint, having managed to recover his breath, looked in confusion at Darg. Darg simply pointed in the direction of the remains of the Kreel. "Kindly clean that up. That is the first rule of my organization: We pick up after ourselves."

Kwint looked none too thrilled.

"Setbacks," Darg reminded him in a slightly singsong voice. Kwint promptly did as he was told.

XI.

NICE NIGHT TO BE SEDUCED, thought Calhoun.

Indeed, it was a splendid night, one that seemed to be filled with promise. However, Calhoun couldn't be entirely sure just who was going to be seducing whom, or what precisely was going to be promised.

This "Vara Syndra" was unlike any woman he'd ever encountered. She was pure sex. Calhoun found it difficult to concentrate on the matter at hand, or even remember what the matter at hand was. But that wasn't what he needed to do at all. He had to stay focused, remember what his—

Grozit, look at those hips. The sway of them, and the arch of her back . . . the way she swivels when she walks . . .

He nearly had to slap himself across the face to try and bring himself back in line with what he was doing.

Vara Syndra was talking as she walked, and he came to the abrupt realization that he hadn't heard a word she said. At one point, though, she smiled at him in a way that seemed to indicate that she not only knew the effect she was having, but that she was accustomed to it. He wondered why she was suddenly so much further ahead of him, and suddenly noticed that he'd stopped walking. He was just standing there and admiring her.

Stop it. This isn't funny, he snarled at himself, and forced

147

his feet to go back into motion. It was incredible to him that this female appeared to be an associate of General Thul. One wondered how in the world the man got any work done. Then again, she was certainly eminently capable of making slacking off appear to be the single greatest pastime known to man.

They had been strolling about, apparently aimlessly, for more than an hour. But now they had arrived in a section of San Francisco that had been restored to much of the late twentieth century architecture. It was an architecture which had made that city so unique before the massive earthquake and fire had practically levelled the place in the first half of the twenty-first century. Vara Syndra was guiding him to one of those townhouses. It had an old-world elegance and charm to it, but at the same time it also had an air of dark foreboding. Calhoun allowed the possibility that he might just be projecting his own concerns upon it. There was the further possibility that, when compared to the vision that was Vara Syndra, *everything* had an air of dark foreboding.

"In here," she said, stopping at the door and gesturing that Calhoun should precede her.

Calhoun had a fairly reliable sixth sense for danger. So if there was an ambush of some sort waiting inside, for whatever reason, he would likely have been alerted to it. Then again, considering how distracted he was by Vara Syndra, it was possible that an entire regiment of Danteri nationals, thirsting to avenge themselves against the fabled liberator of Xenex, were concealed within and Calhoun still wouldn't know the difference. Still, there was enough of the cautious and experienced warrior about him that he was prompted to say, as suavely as he could manage, "After you, Vara."

"How very gallant," she said, and entered without hesitation. Calhoun followed a moment later.

There wasn't a single Danteri, or other such soldier, in sight.

There was, however, a full-size portrait of Vara Syndra decorating the portico, and she was gloriously nude in it. She was also discretely positioned, but still . . .

"Oh," said Vara Syndra in a teasing voice as she saw where his gaze was drawn. "That old thing. Do you really think it captures me?"

"I don't think a hundred big game hunters could adequately capture you," said Calhoun.

"Aren't you sweet." She ran a finger teasingly under his chin, and then sashayed up a long, winding flight of stairs. Calhoun took them two at a time.

At the top of the stairs she went through a door that Calhoun followed her through, which in turn led to a large suite of rooms. And seated rather comfortably in the elaborately furnished suite was General Thul. He was holding a drink, swirling the contents around casually, and he gestured to a cart nearby which had an assortment of beverages arrayed on it in assorted decanters. "Greetings, Captain Calhoun . . . or is it accurate to call you 'captain' anymore?"

"Simply 'Calhoun' will do for the time being."

"Really. Your friends, so I understand, address you as 'Mac.' I was hoping that we might become friends."

"Interesting that you should be aware of that. Been checking up on me, have you?"

"It wasn't all that difficult, Calhoun. After your rather unceremonious eviction from the gathering, you and your past 'antics' were very much the talk of the party for some time afterward."

"Indeed. I'm flattered."

"You needn't be. Much of it wasn't particularly complimentary. Still," and he stroked his yellowed beard thoughtfully, "even those who were less than flattering clearly had a measure of grudging respect for your . . . curious talents."

Calhoun said nothing.

"M'k'n'zy of Calhoun," continued General Thul. "A young Xenexian who watched his father beaten to death in the town square by Danteri oppressors, and was inspired by that incident to free his home world from Danteri rule. By the age of twenty, he had accomplished this rather remarkable feat, achieving the rank of warlord and becoming possibly the most admired man on his world. All of Xenex was at his feet, but he instead walked a different path at the behest of one Jean-Luc Picard. He joined Starfleet, developed a reputation as an independent thinker whose sheer bravery and resourcefulness got the job done, and then resigned after an incident that resulted in the death of his commanding officer aboard the *Grissom*.

Spent a number of years doing whatever jobs he could for whomever he could before rejoining Starfleet and being assigned command of the *Excalibur,* presently on extended assignment to my dear Thallonian space. And now . . . ?" He waited, but Calhoun still said nothing. "Now . . . what, Calhoun?"

"I don't know," Calhoun admitted. "I wasn't expecting this to happen. Then again, in retrospect, I suppose it was inevitable. Starfleet and I have never exactly been a smooth fit."

"I've thought as much myself." General Thul rose from his chair and slowly walked in a circle around Calhoun. Calhoun, for his part, simply stood where he was, his hands draped behind his back. "I may be able to make use of a man like you."

"Give him my regards."

"Who?" Thul seemed momentarily puzzled.

"The man like me."

The confusion remained for a second longer, and then Thul allowed a smile. "Very witty. That was very witty, Calhoun."

"Not really. But my head's a bit foggy. Give me about three hours, I'll have reduced you to helpless giggles."

"What do you think of this one, Vara?" Thul said.

Vara had draped herself over a nearby chair. Calhoun suddenly found that it was all he could do not to jump out of his skin. "I think a good deal of him, General."

"So do I. Then again," and he returned to his seat, "caution is always to be preferred. These are, after all, dangerous times."

"Not for you, I'd think," said Calhoun. "General Thul, doer of good works. Darling of the Starfleet upper rank. What danger have you to fear?"

"Oh, I'd rather not speak of such things. After all, we wouldn't want to upset Vara. Would we, Vara?"

Vara Syndra fanned her face with her hand as if she were a southern belle fighting off an attack of the vapors. "I should certainly hope not," she said.

Every movement, every gesture she made, even the rising and falling of her chest as she breathed, was alluring to Calhoun. *I must be losing my mind. She must be doing something. But I have no idea what. Moreover, I don't care all that much, which is even more disturbing.* "What things," he forced himself back on track, "should we speak of, then."

Thul didn't answer immediately. Instead he strolled with slow, measured steps toward a skylight that provided a splendid view of the starlit sky. He stood under it and gazed heavenward. "I have a small matter that I need attended to. You may very well be just the man for the job, and it would fulfill an old debt."

"I see," Calhoun said neutrally.

"You see, I've recently managed to track down a certain individual who is a 'guest' of the Andorian government." The contempt was evident in his tone. "They're holding him on trumped-up charges of espionage."

"But certainly a well-connected individual such as yourself would be able to have him freed through the use of your considerable contacts."

"I have my friends, Calhoun, but make no mistake: My influence is not quite as wide and all-encompassing as you obviously think it is. Andorians, you see, are members of the United Federation of Planets, and the UFP will not involve itself in how member worlds conduct themselves. However," and now he turned back to face Calhoun, "I was hoping you might be able to aid this individual's . . . recovery."

"You want me to break him out of wherever it is the Andorians are holding him?"

"Nothing goes past you, I see, Calhoun. That's very comforting to know. You should be aware, though, that participation in this matter will likely be the end of your association with Starfleet, particularly if they learn of your involvement."

"That association doesn't appear too promising at the moment anyway," said Calhoun.

Thul openly scoffed. "You mean that business with Jellico? Calhoun, I have enough contacts to know that Jellico has not earned himself quite as many friends as he would like to think he has. There are some who would probably applaud that you struck him. Although serious black marks on your record might appear as a result of the incident, that wouldn't necessarily spell complete doom for your career. My mission, however, likely would. So the question is, do you worm your way back into Starfleet? Perhaps apologize to Jellico in the hopes of smoothing matters over? Or do you acknowledge where your talents would best be suited?"

"And when I accomplish this mission of yours . . . ?"

" 'When.' Not 'if.' 'When.' Very confident, aren't you."

"When it seems warranted. If I didn't go into risky situations confidently, I'd never come out of them."

"Very well . . . when you accomplish the mission . . . then you and I shall speak again. We shall speak of things of . . . great importance. So . . . what say you, Calhoun?"

Calhoun found himself staring at Vara Syndra once more. She wasn't even looking at him at that point. Instead, in rather leisurely fashion, she was trailing her fingers along the curve of her leg.

"What does the job pay?" asked Calhoun.

"A man after my own heart," Thul said with a smile. "What would you consider to be adequate compensation for your time?"

Calhoun looked at Vara. Vara looked at him. Thul looked at both of them, and his smile widened.

"Everything," he said, "is open to negotiation."

XII.

BURGOYNE BURST ONTO THE BRIDGE, which was an unusual enough event in and of itself since s/he didn't tend to hang about the bridge all that much. Even more unusual, s/he went straight to Shelby and stood in front of her, hands on hir hips. "May I speak with you, Commander?" s/he asked.

Shelby was a bit surprised at the urgency to Burgoyne's manner. Granted, s/he was one of the more flamboyant individuals aboard the ship, but s/he never displayed the sort of outright consternation that s/he was now showing. Also, Shelby couldn't help but notice that McHenry was making a determined effort not to look in Burgoyne's direction. The normally near-comatose helmsman suddenly seemed extremely interested in checking over his instrumentation.

Riker, who'd been standing next to Zak Kebron and going over tactical relays in preparation for possible battle, looked up in confusion. "Is there a problem, Burgoyne?" he asked.

"Nothing that Commander Shelby can't handle, sir."

Riker took a step down from the upper ring of the bridge. "Indulge me. What's the problem?"

"All right," Burgoyne said after a moment's consideration. "I want to know why I just got a reassignment."

"What?" Riker said, glancing at Shelby. Shelby shrugged,

not knowing what Burgoyne was referring to. "Are you no longer chief engineer?"

"Oh, I'm still that, yes. But I've been rotated to a desk job. Instructed to remain in my office or work at the engineering station here on the bridge."

"But why . . . ?"

"I don't *know* why," said a clearly exasperated Burgoyne. "I got the message over my computer, and the computer simply said it was orders. I thought they were yours." Some of the ire was being replaced by simple confusion. "Because of . . . you know . . ."

"Payback, perhaps," suggested Riker. "For our little misunderstanding in the holodeck?"

"The thought did cross my mind."

"I don't operate that way, Lieutenant Commander. I had nothing to do with this reassignment."

"Lefler," Shelby called to Robin at ops, "run this one down, would you? See what's going on?"

It took Lefler only a few brief moments to track down the origin of the orders. "Captain Calhoun," she said, punching up the transfer records at her station.. "It came from Captain Calhoun."

"What?" said a stunned Burgoyne.

"Hold on. There's a notation here . . . oh," Lefler said after another moment's checking. "According to his log, he was concerned about keeping you in engineering, in proximity to potentially high levels of radiation. Because of, well . . ." She cleared her throat. " . . . you know."

"No, I don't know."

"Because of you being pregnant."

"I'm *not pregnant*," Burgoyne waved hir arms about in clear exasperation.

"Well, yes, but the captain didn't know that when he put in for the reassignment. Apparently he did it right before he left, and there hasn't been the opportunity to clear it up yet."

"Perfect," sighed Burgoyne. "Just perfect. Mark, tell them I'm not pregnant." When McHenry didn't answer immediately, Burgoyne repeated, "Mark?"

Shelby couldn't help but notice how strange McHenry's voice sounded when she spoke. Usually the most carefree-sounding of individuals, this time he came across as a bit stressed. "So you've told me, Lieutenant Commander. Then again, you also told me you were pregnant in the first place. I guess even in this high-speed age, it's hard to keep up."

Quickly Shelby stepped in. "I'll expunge the orders immediately, Burgoyne. Sorry for the confusion."

"That . . . would be appreciated, Commander," said Burgoyne, but s/he was looking with open curiosity at McHenry. "I hope I didn't come across as too belligerent."

"No, not at all."

"Mark," Burgoyne continued slowly, "is there something you wish to discuss?"

The entire bridge crew was watching, but McHenry didn't give any indication that he was aware of the scrutiny. If he was aware, he didn't seem to care. "No, Burgy. Nothing at all, thanks. If you'll excuse me . . . I'm kind of busy . . ."

Without missing a beat, Burgoyne turned to Shelby and said, "Commander, I have a few navigational issues that need to be attended to. May I borrow Mr. McHenry for a few minutes?"

"That sounds like it might not be a bad idea," Shelby said readily.

McHenry turned in his chair, looking slightly betrayed. "Commander . . ."

But Shelby simply said, "Go," and her tone of voice made quite clear that no dispute was going to be welcomed in the matter. With a heavy sigh, McHenry rose from his station and headed into the turbolift.

"Commander, a moment of your time, please," Riker suddenly said. Shelby frowned, because it was clear to her from his tone of voice that something was bothering him. She nodded and followed him into the ready room. Once they were inside, he didn't sit, but turned to face her and said, "I don't know if you've noticed, but there's a tendency among the crew to speak directly to you on all matters."

"No, I hadn't noticed," said Shelby.

"I doubt that, Commander, although perhaps you're just being too tactful to say so."

"I try not to let tact stand in the way of doing my job, sir."

"In that, you succeed admirably," Riker said drily. "The point remains that I've been noticing it repeatedly, on all matters great and small. And it's something that you've been encouraging."

"Encouraging? You mean I've been answering questions and dealing with problems? Is that your definition of encouragement?"

"You could, on occasion, make a point of consulting me, instead of acting as if I'm not even on the bridge."

"Permission to speak freely, sir," Shelby said stiffly.

"If I said 'no,' would that stop you?"

"Probably not."

"Permission granted, then."

"This isn't about the crew, Captain. This is about your ego. You're the cock of the walk on the *Enterprise* and you feel that now, as captain here, you're entitled to get the same sort of treatment."

"What I am entitled to get, Commander," he said hotly, "is the respect that is due the rank."

"A rank you've made no effort to obtain. You've practically had to have it shoved down your throat," retorted Shelby. "Will Riker, the reluctant captain. How is anyone here supposed to take you seriously."

"You listen to me, Shelby," Riker shot back. "I've been through enough battles, through more life-and-death situations than you can even begin to count."

"Not with us. I've been here. You haven't. Besides, how do you expect this crew to warm to you? You make it clear that you think they're all vastly inferior to the *Enterprise* crew."

"I've done no such thing."

"Oh, please!" she rolled her eyes. "With gestures, with looks, with tone of voice. You make it clear just how second-rate you think this crew is. Well, I'll tell you something, 'Captain,' this is one of the best crews I've ever dealt with. And they deserve better than to be condescended to."

"Don't tell me you've never felt separate from this crew yourself, Commander," Riker said. "That you weren't accepted, that you didn't fit in, weren't respected . . ."

"I don't know what you're talking about."

"Your log clearly stated—"

"My log?" That stopped the conversation dead. "My log?" she said again. "I never said anything like that in my public log. Only my . . . personal log . . . when did you read my personal log?"

"It . . ." Riker suddenly looked a bit uncomfortable. Falling back on regs, he said, "Captains and chief medical officers reserve the right to review all records of their command staff."

"That doesn't give you the right to read my personal log." She felt her cheeks starting to flush.

"Actually, it does. I was trying to familiarize myself with this crew and with all the pertinent attitudes. If I'm going to be leading you into potentially hazardous situations, I want to know where everyone's mind is. So a few hours ago, I reviewed entries relevant to—"

"You bastard," said Shelby.

"Watch it, Commander," Riker said. "Speaking freely or no, you're pushing it. The bottom line is that you've had a serious attitude problem with me for years, and I can't be in a position of having to tolerate . . ."

"Position? What do you know of positions?" she demanded. "The only position you know is standing in the cooling shade of Jean-Luc Picard's shadow. What is it with you, anyway? Getting in behind him and staying put. What are you, just lazy?"

"Not that it's any of your damned business, *Commander,* but have you considered that, after the *Enterprise,* command of another ship might be something of a come-down?"

"Nice little theory . . . except the *Enterprise* you were aboard for over half a decade blew up. So what's the new excuse? Oh, I know, maybe it's the name. Or maybe it's just that Picard fills some sort of need in your life that you didn't get elsewhere. What is he, some sort of father figure that you've just attached yourself to and can't let go, no matter what, because you'll feel like you're abandoning him or something . . . ?"

Her voice trailed off as she saw Riker's face become more darkly furious than she'd ever seen. For a moment, just the briefest of moments, she actually thought he might haul off and belt her.

"At least I've been offered command of my own vessel," Riker said with barely contained rage. "Perhaps before you start analyzing *my* problems, you might want to turn that piercing vision of yours inward and see just why it is that you *haven't* been given the same opportunity."

Then, slowly, through sheer force of will, he composed himself. He drew himself up to his full height and, as if speaking from high on a mountain, he told her in a flat, even voice, "Until further notice, all decisions and matters that are put forward in my presence are to be addressed to me. I will not be treated as if I'm not there. Is that clear, Commander?"

"Crystal," said Shelby.

"Turbolift, all stop."

The turbolift that had been carrying McHenry and Burgoyne came to a halt in immediate compliance with Burgoyne's directive. McHenry looked around, mildly puzzled. "This is going to make it take much longer to get to engineering."

"Okay, Mark, what's going on?" Burgoyne faced him, arms folded across hir breast. "You've been avoiding me."

"No, I haven't."

"Yes, you have."

"No, I haven't."

"Yes, you . . ." S/he shook hir head. "This isn't getting us anywhere."

"Yes, it is."

"No, it isn't."

"Yes, it is."

"No, it . . . *nyarrrh!*" snarled Burgoyne. "Stop it! Just . . . stop it! You're trying to make me crazy!"

"How am I doing?"

In the question, in the attitude with which it was asked, there was a flicker of the puckishness that had always characterized McHenry in the past. Burgoyne was extremely relieved to see it, if only for an instant. "You're doing quite well," s/he admitted. "Mark . . . is this about Selar and me? Because you said you could take it in stride. Nothing fazed you, is what you said. You said you were happy for us."

"Yeah . . . I know."

"What, was that true?"

"It was when I said it."

"But now . . . ?"

He leaned back against the railing of the turbolift. "I don't know."

"What don't you know?" S/he put a gentle hand on his

shoulder. "Mark, above everything else, we've always been able to communicate. I don't want to lose that."

"I'm just . . ." He sighed heavily. "Look . . . Burgy . . . the truth is that I'm not in touch with my feelings, okay? If you know anything about me, you should know that. There's just so many other things to think about, and wonder about . . . and if I have to start putting everything through the filter of how I 'feel' about it, I'll go kinda crazy. So I sort of like to live for the moment."

"All right. But it would be nice if, every once in a while, it was somebody else's moment as well. You do tend to go off into your own world, Mark . . . and it's hard for anyone to know what's going on in there."

"I know. It's . . ." He seemed to steady himself, and then the words all came out in a rush. "It's just that . . . I was very angry with you. There. I said it. Don't hate me."

"Hate you?" s/he said, bemused. "Why would I hate you? What were you angry about? Because I made a joke to see if I really could throw you off kilter, and it worked more than I could have hoped?"

"No, that's not it. It's that . . . well . . . after I came to, I had plenty of time to think about the whole idea before you wound up telling me it wasn't true. And during that time, I just . . . well . . . I got to like the idea. It seemed fun . . . and . . . I dunno . . . grounding, somehow. And that didn't seem to be such a bad thing . . . particularly the notion of having one with you, because you're so . . ."

"Maternal? Special? Intelligent?"

"I was going to say 'weird,' but those others apply too, I guess." He shook his head. "And you know me, I start thinking . . . and I just go off in my own world, and think of things, and I was building up this whole life together. I even had this whole weird family unit built up in my head, with you and Selar and that baby, and me and you and that baby, and maybe even the three of us working together . . ."

"Now *that* would be weird."

"I know. That's what I kind of liked about it. But that's not going to happen anymore. I mean, when it was just you and Selar and you guys having a baby, I had no trouble with that. I could handle that, accept it, even step aside. But for a while there, I just saw something different, and kind of liked it, and now it's gone, and I'm back to being an outsider again."

"Oh, Mark . . . you'll never be an outsider with me. You—"

"But I'll never be her," McHenry said with a sad smile. "I'll never be Selar. I was always a second-place choice to her, I understood that. And I thought that was okay. And it should be. But for a while I . . . Ohhhhh . . . never mind."

"Mark, you keep saying 'never mind' and shutting things off . . ."

"Yeah, I know. That's the way I am. I kind of like me that way."

"Do you?"

They looked at each other levelly for a moment that seemed to stretch out for quite some time. Finally he said firmly, "Yeah. I do. Turbolift, resume."

The turbolift promptly started up once again, and the two of them rode the rest of the way down to the engineering deck in silence. Burgoyne turned to McHenry. He didn't move. "I assume you didn't really need me down in engineering."

"No. Not really. But I do need you to be a friend—"

"Always. Well, I guess this is your stop then," he said a bit too quickly to sound sincere.

"I guess it is."

S/he disembarked, then started to say something to him, but he put up a finger to shush hir. "It's okay. Relationships are like turbolifts. Sometimes you just have to know when to get off."

"Yellow alert," Riker ordered. "All handles, battle stations."

As the *Excalibur* approached Narobi II, Riker stroked his chin as he contemplated the scene before him and came to two conclusions: First, Si Cwan's "tip" might have been groundless. And second, he really, really missed his beard.

"No Romulan vessels detected, sir," announced Zak Kebron from the tactical station. "But if they're cloaked, they're harder to pick up."

From the science post, science officer Soleta said, "Sensor scan to pick up emissions will take time."

"Understood," Riker said. "Proceed with scan. Hailing frequencies, Mr. Kebron?"

"Open, but we're not getting a response from Narobi."

"That could be a definite indicator of a problem," said Riker thoughtfully.

Abruptly Soleta looked up from her science station. "Two vessels with cloaking devices detected uncloaking, at 352 and 367 Mark 2."

She was absolutely correct. On the far side of the Narobi homeworld, two Romulan warbirds wavered into view.

"That," Shelby observed, "could be an even more definite indicator of a problem."

"Red alert. Shields up," Riker ordered crisply. "Weapons systems?"

"We are at weapons hot," Kebron said. "Good to go."

"Try to hail them. Warn them off." He leaned forward in the command chair, fingers interlaced, trying to determine what it was the Romulans were up to.

"Attempting to do so now, sir. No response. It is my belief that the warbirds are jamming transmissions from the planet."

"I suspected as much. Mr. McHenry, target both warbirds. Report on warbird readiness?"

"They are running weapons hot . . . but they are not targeting us, sir," said Kebron.

Riker turned to Soleta. "Can we confirm that?"

"Confirmed," Soleta said without hesitation. "They're ready to shoot if need be, but they're not doing so."

"Some sort of Romulan game," Riker said thoughtfully. "Trying to make us guess what they're up to."

"I don't like this," said Shelby.

"What's to like?" muttered Kebron.

"Bring us in slowly, Mr. McHenry," said Riker. "Let's get them to move off. I want them clear of that planet."

"Sir," Shelby said, turning to face Riker, "something's wrong here."

"Specify."

"They're just sitting there, as if they're daring us to get closer. Why would they do that?"

"Romulans are like cats, Commander. They like to arch their backs and hope that larger and more formidable enemies will be thrown by it," Riker told her confidently. "They have their weapons on line, but they won't target us because they know that'll provoke us into firing. They want to see if we'll hesitate to engage them. If we don't hesitate, if we don't show fear, they'll move off. If we do . . . they're that much more likely to attack. Except that most likely the ones they will attack will be the planet in an attempt to strong-arm us into surrendering. No hesitation, Commander, and no fear. It's all based on an old earth game called 'chicken.' "

"Captain, as much as I appreciate the assorted barnyard analogies, I maintain that something doesn't seem right. I suggest we hold our position. Make them come to us."

"I've had a lot more dealings with Romulans than you, commander, with all due respect," Riker said firmly. "I know how they operate."

"What if they've changed their method of operation?"

The eyes of the bridge crew were going back and forth, from Shelby to Riker and back, as if they were watching a tennis match. McHenry, meantime, operating on his last instructions, kept the starship moving forward.

"Sir, I'm telling you, they're up to something. I can feel it," Shelby said.

"And how would you suggest we find out just what it is they're 'up to,' Commander?" Riker tried to keep his voice even, but it was difficult to refrain from sarcasm.

"For what it's worth," offered McHenry, "we may be able to ask them face-to-face. At this course and speed, if they don't back down, we're going to collide with one of them in two minutes, ten seconds."

"It won't come to that," Riker said. "Even if they open fire, it won't be with anything our shields can't handle. We'll do far worse damage with return fire. They can't afford a pitched battle. They won't want to, either. It's not the Romulan way."

"Captain . . ." Shelby said, with clear exasperation in her voice.

But the more annoyed Shelby got, the calmer Riker felt. "Commander . . . we're not going to run from two Romulan vessels who don't even have us targeted. That would send a message that none of us wants to send. Understood?" he said in a tone that indicated no further discussion would be appreciated.

Shelby straightened up in her chair, moved her gaze solidly to the screen, and without looking at Riker, said, "Aye, sir."

The *Excalibur* drew closer, closer still. And still the Romulans weren't moving.

"Contact, one minute," McHenry said.

"Fire a warning shot across the lead ship's bow."

Kebron promptly did so, a phaser lancing out and narrowly missing the lead Romulan warbird's bow section. Still, the vessels didn't move.

"Attention Romulan vessels," Riker said firmly over the open hailing channels. "We are not turning off course, repeat, we are not turning off course. You are instructed to vacate the area immediately. If you do not, we will fire, repeat, we will fire. Reply."

"Sir!" Soleta informed him. "The ships are moving off. They are powering down their weapons."

McHenry, who was not particularly looking forward to the prospect of slamming the *Excalibur* into a Romulan warbird, let out an audible sigh of relief.

Riker turned to Shelby and said, "I would have to say that constitutes a reply, wouldn't you, Commander?" But Shelby said nothing in response. Riker could only chalk it up to being a poor sport. All-business, Riker turned to McHenry and said, "All right, Lieutenant . . . let's remember that the purpose of this is to track them to whatever base they may be operating from. They'll likely go into warp, and that's when we'll have to—"

And that was when McHenry's board shut down completely.

McHenry gaped at the sudden loss of his instrumentation. It wasn't as if he needed it, but nonetheless the fact that it had abruptly gone south was disconcerting. "Uhm, sir . . . we may have a problem . . ."

"Tactical systems down," Kebron announced.

"All sensors, all scanners down," Soleta said.

"Lefler, what the hell is going on with shipboard?" Riker demanded.

Lefler desperately tried to make sense of it, but the answer she was coming back with was virtually incomprehensible. Her fingers flew over the control padds, but nothing was coming back at her. "Sir . . ." she said with a tone of pure incredulity, "our computer's crashed."

"What?"

The entire bridge was promptly plunged into total blackness. The front viewing screen went blank. Moments later, the emergency lights came on, giving the ship's command center an eerie Halloween-esque glow. Riker was on his feet, leaning over Lefler's ops station. He couldn't believe it. "Our power is done . . . ?"

"Not a power loss, sir. Power's all still there. But the computer routes everything, unless we tell it otherwise," Lefler said. "The only thing that's functioning at the moment is the emergency life support system. That's a bottom line fail safe. But otherwise we're dead in space. No guidance systems, no weaponry, no shields . . . nothing!"

"Find a way to get us out of here," Riker ordered.

"Quick, let's crack out the oars," suggested McHenry.

"Stow it, lieutenant!" Shelby said, also out of her chair. "We have got zero time before the Romulans move in on us. Lefler, try to reroute via manual . . ."

Suddenly the air in the bridge began to shimmer, and an all-too-recognizable hum sounded within the confined area. And Riker knew, even before they materialized, what he was going to see.

A Romulan raiding party, fully armed and ready to annihilate anyone who opposed them, appeared dead center of the bridge. And standing foursquare in the front, with her finger on a trigger and a smirk on her face, was Sela.

"Hello, Will," she purred. "Miss me? Because this time, I won't miss you." And she aimed her phaser straight at his face.

XIII.

LODEC LOOKED AT HIS REFLECTION in the polished wall and barely recognized himself.

Naturally he still possessed the bronze skin that marked him as one of the Danteri race. But his hair was dirty and matted, his beard thick and scraggly. Oddly enough, it may have been that, even more than his imprisonment itself, that was the most depressing thing with which he had to contend. For Lodec had once been a soldier, and his training, his very essence, cried out for a neat and trim presentation to the world. Servitude, lack of freedom . . . these he could handle. But being reduced to looking like a slob? It was more than he should have had to bear.

Somehow, though, he suspected that those who were running the Andorian prison ship that he was being held upon weren't going to be sympathetic to his plight.

Lodec coughed again, but none of the other prisoners who were in the cramped barracks with him paid any attention. He felt a deep rattling about in his throat and would have been most grateful for some sort of medication to ease the congestion before it grew into something far worse. But nothing was forthcoming from the Andorians.

Gods, did he hate the Andorians.

The blue skin was almost hurtful to his eyes, it was so glaring. When they spoke, the Andorians did so in a sort of whisper that almost made them seem the most polite of races. But the ones who were running the vessel were among the most sadistic bastards that Lodec had ever had the opportunity of dealing with. They would deprive the prisoners of food for days on end, and when they did give them sustenance, it was so wretched that it became almost impossible to hold it down. In many instances it was, in fact, impossible, and the stench of the heaved food would hang in the air of the cells for ages until the hideously slow filtration system finally expunged them.

The worst thing of all was that there was really no need for the transportation of the prisoners to take so damned long. The transport was equipped with warp drive, and could easily have gotten to its destination within a few days. Instead, it was taking its own sweet time, proceeding mostly on impulse drive, utilizing warp only every so often when proceeding through areas of space where prolonged travel might result in jeopardy to the crew (since the crew didn't give a damn about the cargo). There were a couple of theories among the prisoners as to why it was taking so damned long. One was that the prison for which they were bound was overcrowded, and they were waiting either for prisoners aboard the transport or prisoners at the receiving end to die in order to free up space. Another theory was that it was simply part of the softening-up process. Prison officials didn't want to have to deal with prisoners who might have some fight left in them. So their spirits were battered and broken along the way, making them nice and malleable when they arrived.

And so one day stretched out into another for Lodec and the others who had been luckless enough to transgress against the Andorians.

He lay on his bunk in the cramped quarters that he shared with a number of other prisoners and murmured to himself, "This is not how my life was supposed to turn out."

Suddenly the door to the quarters slid open, the glare of light from the hallway outside nearly blinding as his eyes tried to adjust. Standing in the doorway was Macaskill, the transport commander who was exceptionally softspoken—even for an Andorian—and exceptionally ruthless—even for an Androian.

He was an older Andorian, his skin a more pale blue than the others, but that made him no less deadly.

"I'm looking for volunteers," he whispered, so much so that Lodec had to strain to hear him. As the prisoners blinked to get the sleep from their eyes, Lodec glanced around and then pointed at several in rapid succession: "You," he said, "and you . . . and you. And you." And one of the ones he chose was Lodec.

Slowly, Lodec sat up. He rubbed at his wrists which, as always, had the electronic manacles secured to them. He let out a long, unsteady sigh, but knew better than to ask what was so important that they had to be rousted from bed at that time of night. He wasn't likely to get any sort of answer in any event, and far more likely that he'd simply get a major shock pounded through him. That was certainly not aggravation that he needed. Besides, when one got right down to it, what did it matter if he knew what was going on or not? He was still going to have to do what he was told anyway. His life was not his own, and had not been for some time.

Then, to his surprise, one of the other prisoners asked the very question that he hadn't seen fit to risk punishment over: "What's this all about?" It was a Pazinian, a very small and harmless-looking species, with a perpetually wistful look on its vaguely avian face. His voice was high-pitched and reedy.

To his even greater astonishment, Macaskill answered without hesitation. "We've come upon a small freighter in distress, and will be requiring your volunteered aid to unload its cargo," he said. "We are not in the salvage business, of course. But it turns out that the pilot's carrying a shipment of gold-pressed latinum. Naturally, in good conscience, we could not turn away from a sentient being in need."

"Or from the latinum?" asked the Pazinian.

"Naturally," Macaskill said. "That goes without saying." Macaskill then tapped a small control device on his wrist . . . and energy lanced through the Pazinian, his arms flying out to either side as if he'd been crucified. He let out a shriek and collapsed to the ground, quivering and spasming as Macaskill continued calmly, "On that basis, you probably should not have said it.

He then turned to another prisoner, pointed and indicated

that he should take the Pazinian's place. "The freighter is presently in our main bay. We're drafting you to help unload it. May I safely assume there will be no further questions?"

It was an eminently safe assumption. And as they filed out, Lodec couldn't help but wonder if the Pazinian had simply been that anxious to get out of helping with the shipment. It seemed a rather extreme thing to do just to get out of some work. On the other hand, as the Pazinian lay there insensate, Lodec mused upon the fact that at least the Pazinian had gotten to go back to sleep.

They trudged down to the main bay in silence, several Andorian guards falling into step alongside them. In point of fact, they weren't really needed. The manacles were more than enough to keep the prisoners from fighting back or even, absurdity of absurdities, escaping. But their presence helped to pile on the feeling of hopelessness. Talking was actively discouraged, under all circumstances. The Andorians had means of eavesdropping even when the prisoners were by themselves. The captors didn't want to take any chances that the captives might put together some sort of breakout strategy. Lodec tried at one point to stifle a loud yawn, but was unable to do so. This got him a fairly fierce scowl from one of the guards, but no further recriminations, and he considered himself extremely lucky.

They arrived in the main bay, and sure enough, there it was: A reasonably small freighter. There was nothing particularly impressive-looking about it. In fact, it seemed rather old and worn out, the hull distressed and pockmarked with years of service in the harsh vacuum of space. The obvious captain of the ship was standing just outside the main door of the freighter, engaged in what appeared to be a fairly animated discussion with one of the Andorian guards.

The freighter captain turned and looked at Lodec with what appeared to be bottomless purple eyes. In a heartbeat, Lodec knew the man was a Xenexian. Then he saw the scar that ran down the side of the man's face . . .

. . . and he knew exactly which Xenexian it was.

He had absolutely no idea how to react. He had heard many conflicting reports about the life of the rebel outlaw who had broken Xenex from the control of Danter. Lodec had never had the opportunity to come face to face in battle with M'k'n'zy of Calhoun, but he had certainly heard enough about him. Moreover, he had lost a number of friends to Calhoun's fabled sword, strength and resourcefulness.

Ostensibly, he had heard that Calhoun had then left Xenex once freedom was established and joined Starfleet. But his awareness of Calhoun had eroded over the years. There had been rumors that he had left Starfleet, that he had taken up an aimless, freelance life. It seemed a rather pathetic existence for one who had once been the warlord of Xenex and one of his people's greatest heroes. Lodec had always thought, though, that people such as M'k'n'zy were simply destructive types at their core. When they turned their destructive tendencies outward, they could accomplish amazing feats that left enemies stunned. But when they had no opponents before them, that selfsame destruction often wound up turning inward, and they would slowly diminish themselves until their greatness faded to nothing.

And now here was evidence that all that he had heard was true. The great M'k'n'zy of Calhoun, reduced to being a common freighter pilot. Probably an underhanded one at that, transporting gold-pressed latinum. For all Lodec knew, Calhoun was even in the process of stealing it.

Macaskill had stridden up to M'k'n'zy, and in his customarily soft voice, he said, "So . . . I understand your name is Calhoun."

Calhoun nodded. Obviously he wasn't going by an assumed name. How very foolish.

"I am Macaskill . . . your savior."

"I appreciate the help," Calhoun told him. But there was an expression in his face that indicated he knew that the help would not come without a price. Sure enough, he said, "So . . . I assume that you'll be seeking some sort of finder's fee."

"We did find you," agreed Macaskill. "We have taken the time to expend our resources in aiding you. Your ship is not functioning; you will require us to repair it, I trust."

"How much are we talking about?" asked Calhoun, clearly resigned to the inevitable.

"Does ten percent seem fair to you?"

Calhoun looked surprised. "It . . . does indeed. I have to admit, I thought you'd be looking for much more than that. But a ten percent commission seems more than fair."

"No . . . you don't understand," Macaskill said. His smile displayed a perfect row of white teeth. "Ten percent of your cargo . . . is what you will be left with."

"What!" Calhoun clearly couldn't believe it. He stomped back and forth a few feet, shaking his head and gesticulating wildly. *"What!"* he said again. "Look, you don't understand! This isn't my latinum! I'm just transporting it! A ten percent loss, at least I can cover that by giving up a portion of my fee . . . *grozit,* probably all of my fee. But if you walk off with ninety percent of the cargo, the people I'm supposed to be delivering it to aren't going to be happy! To be specific, they're going to be rather angry, and they'll be taking out that anger on me! If you gut me that much, I'm dead!"

"No. If we toss you into space, you're dead," the Andorian politely corrected him. "If we fix your ship and leave you ten percent of your cargo, we are giving you a fighting chance. But if you do not wish to have that chance . . ."

And he extended a hand in the general direction of the airlock.

"I will give you precisely two standard minutes to make up your mind," said the Andorian, "although I strongly suspect what your answer will be."

Calhoun, looking stunned, walked in the general direction of the prisoners. He was shaking his head in disbelief, clearly unable to deal with what had happened. The pity that Lodec felt for him grew and grew. Poor devil, indeed, to have fallen this low.

And then, as Calhoun drew within a few feet of the prisoners, his gaze shifted—ever so slightly—in Lodec's direction. And something seemed to come alive in his face, an almost fearful determination that Lodec had no idea how to interpret.

Then Lodec saw Calhoun's mouth move silently, addressing the mute question to him: *Lodec?*

Lodec nodded imperceptibly. He had no clue as to what to expect.

Calhoun mouthed two more words: *Hold on.*

At which point, Lodec forgot himself. Out loud, he said, "Hold on? To what?"

The confused comment drew a puzzled look from Macaskill. "Prisoner . . . who told you you could speak? Calhoun . . . it's time for you to admit the hopelessness of your situation. If you will cooperate, perhaps we can be generous and provide you with an additional five percent of—"

Calhoun turned to face Macaskill, and his attitude had completely changed. He was standing straighter, more determined, and utterly confident. And he called out, "Freighter! Execute offensive preprogram one!"

"What are you—?" Macaskill demanded.

He didn't get the entire question out as the freighter—which had previously been thought dead in space—roared to life.

From the sides of the vessel, white mist blasted out in all directions. Lodec stared, still not grasping what in the world was happening, and suddenly Calhoun was at his side. He was slapping some sort of unit on Lodec's face, a breathing device with goggles attached. Calhoun already had an identical device affixed to his own face. "Come on. We're leaving," Calhoun told him curtly.

"But—" Lodec had no idea what to say, no clue as to what was going on. Something screamed a warning though in his mind, and the warning said, *The deadliest Xenexian who ever lived is trying to make off with you.* To Lodec, there could only be one reasonable conclusion. For whatever reason, M'k'n'zy of Calhoun had decided to hunt down, kidnap and murder Lodec of Danter.

It wasn't as if a prison world such as the one that Lodec was being transported to was any great place to be, but at least he would be alive there, and where there was life, there was hope. But if Calhoun got away with him, he'd have no hope at all.

Blind panic seized Lodec, and as Calhoun tried to drag him forward, Lodec abruptly began to struggle. "What are you doing?" demanded Calhoun. "Will you come on!"

All around them, people were dropping. Macaskill, who had been closed to the ship, went down first. Others were tumbling just as fast. As they lay on the ground, Lodec saw that they were virtually frozen in position. They weren't frozen in the sense of people covered with ice. Rather, they were paralyzed, every muscle in their bodies apparently completely taut.

Lodec struggled all the more, trying to claw the mask off

Calhoun's face. "You idiot!" snapped Calhoun, and he punched Lodec just once on the side of the head. Lodec sagged, not lapsing into unconsciousness, but the fight momentarily knocked out of him. From that point on, he had no choice at all. Calhoun half carried, half dragged him to the freighter. The engines of the freighter were roaring to life; obviously the entire business about the ship being helpless had been a ruse.

"Let me . . . go . . . you'll kill me . . ." Lodec managed to get out, although his voice was muffled by the mask.

"Fool! If I wanted to kill you, I'd just do it here and now! Snap your neck and rip your head off as proof!" Calhoun said angrily as he approached the freighter. The main door automatically swung open and Calhoun shoved Lodec into the main cabin. Calhoun continued, "I wouldn't be going to all this trouble if your murder was my only concern!"

"Oh . . ." The panic was beginning to slip away from Lodec, even though he still didn't comprehend just what was going on. "That . . . hadn't occurred to me."

"I bet it hadn't. Hard to believe your kind ruled my world for years."

The door slammed shut as Calhoun swiftly operated the computer interface on the control panel. "What are you doing?" asked Lodec.

"Ordering the transport's computer to open up the bay doors. . . . there!"

The massive main bay doors of the transport ship began to open wide. The stars beckoned as the freighter lifted off.

Then Lodec heard shouting from outside, and several shots ricocheted off the freighter's hull. "Damn," muttered Calhoun.

The doors began to slide shut again.

"Hold on," Calhoun said, and gunned the ship forward.

Lodec gasped. The doors were closing far too fast, and there was absolutely no way that the freighter was going to make it. He looked to Calhoun . . . and saw what he could only describe as a demented grin on Calhoun's face. Either the man was utterly suicidal . . . or else he simply really loved a challenge.

With astounding dexterity, Calhoun manipulated the controls and the freighter leaped forward even faster, half-turning sideways and sliding out just before the bay doors slammed shut.

"You did it!" shouted Lodec. "That . . . that white stuff! That mist! What was that?"

"Cyro-mist. Put them into temporary suspended animation . . . uh oh."

"Uh oh? What is . . . uh oh?" Lodec asked, scrambling to the front of the freighter.

Then he saw it. There, tracking on the screen, were two plasma torpedos, coming in fast. They'd been launched by the prisoner transport, and they were going to overtake the freighter in no time.

Calhoun didn't appear to be the least bit concerned. Instead he flipped open a panel and tapped a blue square inside.

The freighter shuddered slightly and an alarmed Lodec said, "Are we hit?!"

"If we'd been hit," snorted Calhoun, "you wouldn't be here to ask that question. Those were torpedo counter-measures. Watch," and he tapped another panel.

The viewscreen showed a rear view of the vessel, and the transport was clearly in evidence. And then, to his astonishment, he saw the plasma torpedos that had been pursuing them . . . streaking straight back toward the transport. "There's something small . . . leading them . . ." Lodec said after a moment.

"You've got good eyes," Calhoun admitted. "That's the counter-measure. It's a false beacon. Draws the torpedos away from the intended target and toward one that I far prefer. Such as . . ."

The torpedos slammed into the rear of the transport. The ship shuddered under the horrific impact. The transport had shields which it had barely managed to get up in time, but it was not designed to be a combat vessel and the shields were minimal at best. The first of the torpedos didn't get through, but it did damage the shields sufficiently that the second one blasted into the hull. Plasma tore through the bulkhead, and the ship sparked furiously. All along the transport vessel, the lights went out and within seconds the entire ship was dark.

"That should take them some time to repair," Calhoun said calmly. "If it's repairable at all, that is. In the meantime, they'll be the ones who are floating in space. Let's hope that anyone who comes upon them will be a bit more generous than they were going to be with me."

"There was never any latinum on this ship," Lodec said.

"That's right."

"And you were never actually crippled. This ship, I mean. It was a lure to get aboard the vessel."

"Also right. You pick up things quickly."

"So all of this . . . was to get me out of there." He paused and then asked, with a sense of dread, "Why?"

"Because someone wants you out. That's all you need to know at the moment. That, and the fact that we rendezvous at Wrigley's Pleasure Planet."

"A desirable rendezvous point if ever I've heard one."

The freighter, under Calhoun's guidance, surged forward and leaped into warp space, leaving the crippled prison transport far behind.

Out of range of the transport, the manacles were no threat to Lodec. He looked around the interior of the freighter with interest. "Is this your ship?"

"It is now," said Calhoun. "I've used it from time to time, but it's been out of commission for a while. It's good to be back, though." He patted the console in what almost appeared to be the type of gesture that a person would use with a pet.

"Listen . . . I suppose I should—"

"Don't." As if reading his mind, Calhoun briskly cut him off. "Don't thank me. Don't give me gratitude. I don't want it, I don't need it. I know who you are. What you are. Just as you know who and what I am."

"M'k'n'zy the Destroyer," Lodec said softly. "M'k'n'zy the monster."

"Those and many other names," Calhoun agreed readily. "I'd like to think I earned them all. And I do not suggest you press me about old times, because I assure you the years have not made me think more kindly about your race. There's little forgiveness in my heart."

"In your heart?" scoffed Lodec. Part of him screamed a warning, that engaging in discourse with this man could result in a very quick and painful death if Calhoun were so inclined. But Calhoun was clearly operating on someone else's behalf, and it was obviously in Calhoun's interest to bring Lodec back in one piece. That gave Lodec a certain amount of boldness. "In *your* heart? You were personally responsible for the deaths of friends of mine. Good friends, good men, who deserved better than to die on some damnable foreign planet at the hands of barbarian heathens. Do you think that we . . ."

"What?" Calhoun cut him off, and there was danger in his eyes. "Do I think what?"

Lodec laughed softly to himself and shook his head. "Do you think . . . that we wanted to be there? Most of us didn't give a damn about Xenex. We did what we were told. We followed orders."

"The oldest excuse in the universe."

"It works for Starfleet officers."

"Yes. It does. Notice that I'm not one," Calhoun pointed out.

Lodec's back was against one of the bulkheads. Suddenly feeling all the strength ebbing from his legs, he allowed himself to slide to the floor. Drained, he said, "It was all . . . a very long time ago. And I suppose none of it matters anymore."

"No," said Calhoun. "I suppose it doesn't."

And then, after a long pause, Lodec said, "Thank you anyway. For getting me out of there." And after a hesitation, he added, "You don't have to say 'you're welcome.' "

Calhoun didn't.

XIV.

THE SITUATION IN THE ENGINEERING ROOM of the *Excalibur* had not come close to panic . . . but it wasn't all that far away from it, either.

Burgoyne 172 and Ensign Beth were sorting through the isolinear chips with a finely controlled franticness. Throughout the engine room, the rest of Burgoyne's people were checking every circuit, every possible route that might explain what in hell had just happened to cause the ship's computers to come tumbling around their ears.

S/he held a stack of the thin, hard chips in hir hand. "These things are useless . . . *useless,*" Burgoyne said, the "s" in "useless" extending to a snake-like hiss. "The only way we're going to get things back on line is to bypass the computer altogether. Everything's got to be done manually." S/he glanced in the direction of the warp core. The power emanating from it was still comfortingly humming away. "At least power still exists in the ship. Thank the Great Bird for that. If the engines were out and we had to do a cold start . . ."

"If there's power, then why isn't it getting to the rest of the systems?" Beth said, her frustration mounting. Even as she complained, though, she was rerouting systems to get around the stalled computer. "Henderson! Camboni! Punch this pulse through subsystems A1 through A7!"

"It's like a body that's had a stroke," Burgoyne said as s/he started reracking the isolinear chips in hope that s/he could find some sort of short cut s/he hadn't spotted before. "The brain is functioning fine. The rest of the body may be in perfect shape. But the connectors have been cut. If we can—"

Suddenly they heard the sound of transporters. And there, materializing not ten feet away from Burgoyne, were four Romulans, heavily armed and clearly ready to take possession of the engine room.

Burgoyne had no weapons on hir. S/he hadn't been expecting trouble. The Romulans, for their part, looked prepared to start shooting the moment they finished their materialization. Immediately what came to the forefront for the Hermat was concern about the safety of hir ship and the safety of hir people. Hir crew, hir engineers who looked to hir for guidance and leadership. And these no-good Romulans were going to show up and wreak havoc in hir engine room?

Not bloody likely.

At first glance, Burgoyne did not look particularly daunting. One would not readily appreciate hir strength and speed until one found oneself in a dire situation . . . which was more or less what the engineering crew of the *Excalibur* had on its hands. Burgoyne, however, did not hesitate.

S/he snatched an assortment of isolinear chips from their receptacles. And the moment that the Romulans materialized, s/he let fly, one after the other, in rapid succession.

Several years ago, Burgoyne had seen a magician, a card master who billed himself simply as Jay, entertaining at a local pub during one of hir pubcrawling expeditions. His mastery of simple pasteboard cards had been nothing short of astounding. Claiming to be descended from a long line of master cardsmen stretching back centuries, the most impressive stunt that he had pulled was hurling playing cards with such velocity that they had actually lodged in solid objects, such as fruit. Burgoyne had been incredibly fascinated by the stunt, and with hir long fingers and quick-snap wrists, had long felt that s/he would be eminently capable of imitating the act. And so s/he had taken up card flipping as a hobby, developing superb accuracy so that s/he had been able to hit a target from a reasonable distance away.

S/he had never, however, been able to get sufficient velocity for the cards actually to pierce anything . . . even a fruit. However, s/he had never had quite the incentive that s/he had at that moment. Furthermore, isolinear chips were harder and nastier than playing cards.

Consequently, as s/he tossed the chips with a vicious sidearm snap of hir wrist, the things shot across the distance like bullets, and had about the same devastating effect. The chips were relatively harmless when they were stationary. When they were hurtling at high speed, however, they were astoundingly nasty.

One Romulan took one square in the base of the throat. He choked on his own blood while the second turned and got one right in the eye socket, and went down, shrieking. The third took a step in Burgoyne's direction while bringing up his gun, which proved to be a mistake . . . not the motion of the gun, but the movement toward Burgoyne, because the increased proximity resulted in the thrown chip literally cleaving straight into the Romulan's skull. He went down without a whimper. It had all happened to fast, all within split seconds, that the fourth Romulan's jaw dropped open in amazement. This proved to be a spectacular blunder as the chip sailed through his open mouth and lodged in the back of his throat. He went down gagging.

Four appeared, four dropped, in less time than it took for the engineering staff to fully comprehend that they were under attack. Beth turned pale as she saw the Romulans piled up, one atop the other on the floor. The only one who was still alive was the one with the chip in his eye, and then he stopped moving a moment later, apparently dead from shock.

Burgoyne regarded them with remarkable calm and then glanced at the chips remaining in hir hand. "Hunh. I was wrong. These things were useful after all." Then, without hesitation, s/he shouted, "Shields and warp drive, first and second priorities! We want to stop these bastards from beaming on, and we want to get the hell out of here! Move!"

The largest raiding party, composed of about twenty Romulans, had materialized in deck 10. There had followed a furious pitched battle with an *Excalibur* security team which had resulted in casualties on both sides. The security crew, which had been far outnumbered, had managed to whittle the Romulans down to twelve, but the *Excalibur* team was hurt far more badly, and with only three of them still alive, had gone into full retreat. The Romulans, sensing victory, had gone in pursuit, and the trio of badly wounded, barely alive security guards had been certain that their time was up.

They had rounded a corner, hearing the pounding of the Romulans right behind them . . . and then they had come upon Si Cwan. The Thallonian noble was simply standing there. His palms were pressed together, his eyes closed, and he looked as if he were delving deeply into some sort of inner strength.

"Go," he said softly. "I will hold them."

The security team was in no shape to argue. One of them tried to thrust his phaser into Si Cwan's hands, but Si Cwan waved it off. "I don't like weapons," he said. "One tends to rely on them too much. Go. I will be fine."

Moments later, the attacking Romulans came around the corner, and Si Cwan was still standing there, just as calm as he'd been moments ago. The fact that a dozen Romulans had weapons angled squarely at him did not seem to bother him particularly.

He put his hands over his head in complete surrender. "I'm not one of them," he said, walking slowly toward the Romulans. "I'm just a passenger. In fact, I'm . . ." he started to stammer. "I'm a rich passenger. Rich and influential. See? I've . . . I've no weapons. No way of hurting you. Please . . . don't kill me . . . please . . . take me prisoner . . ."

"Romulans," said the foremost one in the group, "don't take prisoners." And he aimed his weapon at Si Cwan.

Si Cwan, hands over his head, was still several feet away. It did not, however, matter. He leaped straight up, swinging his legs upward as he did so. In one smooth movement, both of his feet caught the closest Romulans squarely in the pits of their stomachs. They doubled over. He had barely landed before he jumped again, this time nailing them squarely in the face. Both of their weapons flipped into the air, and Si Cwan caught them on the way down. He criss-crossed his arms and opened fire.

It was true. Si Cwan generally preferred not to use weapons. However, he prided himself on his adaptability.

Within seconds, six more Romulans were lying strewn about the floor. The remaining half dozen opened fire on Si Cwan, but he grabbed up the fallen body of the nearest Romulan and used it as a shield. A disruptor shot disintegrated the top half of the Romulan, and then Si Cwan hurled the remainder of his carcass, knocking down two more of the Romulans.

And then Si Cwan laid into the remaining Romulans. They fired at him, point blank . . . and missed. He scrabbled across the floor, moving like a gigantic spider, and then forward-rolled and came up with his feet planted in their faces. Just that quickly he was back on his feet, and he snapped the neck of another without slowing down, grabbed yet another and smashed him against the wall with such force that his face was little more than a red smear.

Blood jetted from his opponents as Si Cwan waded into them. His hands like spears, his movements economical and with machine-like precision, he bobbed and weaved through the increasingly frantic—to say nothing of diminishing—crowd of Romulans.

When Sela aimed the phaser at William Riker, she did not for one moment think that there was any question of missing.

She was also under the impression that the four Romulans she had with her would be able to handle matters. They were, after all, heavily armed. The average bridge complement was usually less than a dozen, and only one of them—the on-bridge security guard—was ever armed. Plus, she was all too familiar with the ways of the Federation. They liked to talk, to discuss, to debate. When they appeared on the bridge, "What do you want!" would be the first defiant words to leap from the throat of the ship's commander—in this case, as delightful luck would have it, Will Riker himself. After that would follow a dialogue, a back and forth, vituperation, sneering and cutting remarks, and so on.

A substantial threat, though? That truly didn't cross Sela's mind. That was why she knew that she could execute Will Riker with impunity. The boldness, the viciousness of her act would be enough to completely paralyze the battle-unready crew. As his lifeless body tumbled, so would their resistance. She was absolutely positive of that.

Which was why it was all the more confusing to her when she heard the sound of tearing metal. She had no idea what the cause was. She didn't have long to wait to find out.

As hard as it was to believe, she had not noticed the Brikar when she had arrived on the bridge. He had been crouched behind his tactical board. For a large individual, Zak Kebron had a surprising way of coming across as less substantial than he truly was. Now, however, he made no such effort. He emerged from behind his station, gripped the hand railing that ran across the upper section of the bridge . . . and pulled.

The railing tore out of its moorings. It took the Brikar no more than an instant to be clutching the massive piece of metal, and the instant the Romulans were turning to see what in the name of the Praetor had caused that ear-splitting racket, Kebron was already swinging the railing like a baseball bat.

Sela saw it coming and ducked. The Romulan standing directly behind her was far less fortunate. The railing struck him squarely in the head. The humanoid neck is actually one of the weakest links in the body, the flexibility of the neck coming at a high price. Romulans shared the same weakness as humans. Consequently the Romulan's head was sent flying from his shoulders. Sela jumped back, emitting a most un-Romulan shriek, and even as the horrified Romulans tried to react, Kebron took a step forward and shoved the jagged-ended metal railing squarely forward into the chest of another Romulan. A third Romulan let out yelp that was actually higher-pitched than Sela's as the impaled Romulan crashed into him.

It had all happened within seconds, and Sela had been so distracted that she had actually forgotten about Riker. But she had a forceful reminder as Riker lunged forward, grabbed her gun hand and shoved the phaser straight up.

He was strong, but she was no slouch either. Giving as good as she got, the two of them struggled hand-to-hand, and then with a grunt, Riker shoved Sela back. She tripped over one of the fallen bodies, sprawled . . . and that was when Riker spotted what appeared to be a small comm device on Sela's wrist. He noticed that all of them were wearing similar equipment. "Get that thing off her!" shouted Riker.

At that moment, the fourth Romulan managed to open fire with his disruptor. He nailed Zak Kebron squarely in the chest. Kebron rocked back on his heels and then announced, "Ouch," before getting the Romulan to drop the gun through the simple expedient of crushing his hand so that he couldn't hold it ever again.

Shelby, meantime, moving with remarkable speed, literally hurled herself atop the fallen Sela. With a snarl, she got a grip on Sela's arm and received a punch in the head for her trouble.

"Ha!" shouted Sela right in her face.

In response, Shelby slammed her fist down against Sela's head. She heard a satisfying crunch of bone; it would have been far less satisfying had it actually been her own bone.

"Ha!" Shelby shouted right back, and tore the comm device from Sela's wrist. "Zak!" she shouted as she tossed it in Kebron's direction. It landed on the floor at his feet, and Zak simply stepped on it. The Romulan communications device . . . and her locator for beaming . . . crunched rather pleasingly beneath the massive foot of the Brikar.

The other Romulan who remained alive had already hit his comm device, and he was shouting, "Get me out!" As Kebron tried to grab at his comm link as well, the other two Romulans, along with the corpses, vanished in a haze of molecules. Sela, without her communicator link which would have enabled them to home in on her, didn't go anywhere.

But she was hardly finished. From the folds of her tunic, she pulled a long-bladed knife and lunged straight at Riker. At that moment, a slim hand clamped down upon her shoulder. Sela's head snapped around, her eyes rolled up into the top of her head, and she sank to the floor without a sound. Standing directly behind her, Soleta simply shook her head. "If you had simply allowed me to get close enough to apply the nerve pinch," she said to Shelby and Riker with mild reproof, "we could have terminated this violence far more quickly."

"Captain!" Lefler suddenly called from her station. To her credit, she had never budged from it even as chaos had unleashed itself on the bridge. "We've got shields back on line . . . and engines, too!"

Riker, who was envisioning the warbirds moving in on the still blind and weaponless starship, allowed a quick sigh of relief. "Bless you, Burgy!" he called to the engineer who obviously couldn't hear him. "McHenry, take us out of here!"

"We can't set coordinates," McHenry replied. "That's run through the computer. Of course, I could probably . . ."

The ship suddenly shuddered under a blast to her starboard, and then another to port. Obviously the warbirds were moving in, and it was impossible to fire back. Although shields were back on line, that was hardly going to save them for an extended period of time.

"McHenry, I know we'll be flying blind, but at this point if we wind up in the middle of a supernova, we won't really be much worse off than we are!" Riker told him.

"True enough," admitted McHenry. "Hold on."

He closed his eyes. Riker found that disconcerting for a moment, and then realized that it didn't make all that much difference. Not only did they have no instrumentation, they didn't even have the viewscreen.

The warp engines flared to life, and seconds later the wounded, but still active, *Excalibur* leaped into warp and was gone.

"We were set up! That's got to be what happened!" Shelby said furiously.

Shelby, Riker, Soleta, Sela, Lefler and Kebron were in the conference room. Kebron was there mostly to keep Sela in line, and he did so through the simple expedient of keeping one hand firmly on her shoulder with his hand on her. The handbinders were simply a formality. This was more effective than one might have thought, because every time Sela tried to stand or shrug Zak's hand away, she failed utterly. She had, by that point, given up, and was just sitting in place with a rather irritated expression.

"Set up," Shelby continued, and she looked angrily at Lefler. "Si Cwan should have known."

"We don't know that we were 'set up,' Commander, and even if we were, there was no way that he could have known. He's only as good as his information," Lefler said defensively.

"Then his information should have been better," Riker said, no happier about the situation than Shelby. "Mr. Kebron, where is Si Cwan?"

"Intraship communications are still down," rumbled Kebron. "I've sent a security team to find him and bring him to this meeting, since you said you wanted to see—"

The door slid open. Lefler's gasp could be heard immediately. The others contained themselves, but just barely.

Si Cwan was covered with blood, and since it was for the most part green, it obviously wasn't his. Blood on his tunic, on his face, and on his hands. He had clearly been in a massive pitched battle with the Romulans. Seeing all the Romulan blood on him, Sela visibly paled.

Riker half rose from his chair. "Lord Cwan . . . are you all right?"

Si Cwan seemed puzzled that Riker would even have to ask. "Of course. Why?"

"Uhm . . ." Riker hesitated a moment, looked at the others in the room who nodded silent assent with what was clearly going through his mind. "Why don't you head back to your quarters . . . get cleaned up, relax . . . you've . . . clearly had a rough time . . ."

"You said you wished to see me. You sent a security guard to escort me here for that purpose."

"We'd heard that you'd been in a fight, that's all," Shelby said quickly.

"That is true. Is that all you wished to know?"

"Yes," said Riker.

"Very well." With that, he turned and left the conference lounge.

Somewhat more sedate in her tone, but still with no less conviction, Shelby continued, "These Narobi natives . . . Si Cwan said they were machine beings. And our computers went down. That certainly suggests . . ."

"That it was not a coincidence," Soleta agreed. "I have been doing further research since Si Cwan brought them to my attention. Their cybernetic make-up would appear to give them some sort of affinity for computers. That would put the odds of their involvement, and a possible alliance with the Romulans, at 83 percent."

"I had heard that 92 percent of all statistics are made up," Kebron observed.

This small attempt at levity actually drew smiles from several people in the conference room which, considering the circumstances, was quite the achievement. But then, turning serious once more, Riker turned to Sela and said, "It's more than that, isn't it, Sela. A lot more."

"Scamper back to the *Enterprise,* Riker," Sela said contemptuously. "Without Picard to show you how it's done, you're no threat . . . and certainly of no interest to me."

Riker didn't rise to the bait, keeping his cool. "You're going to tell us, Sela. You're going to tell us everything that's going on. About the Romulan involvement, about the raid on Daystrom . . . everything."

"Over my dead body, Riker."

And there was something in Riker's voice that caught Sela's attention as he said very deliberately, and very menacingly, "If necessary, Sela. Only if absolutely necessary."

XV.

THERE WERE FEW WORLDS in the galaxy that were more of an assault on the senses than Wrigley's Pleasure Planet. Actually, Calhoun really couldn't think of any, now that he put his mind to it.

They walked through streets that were in perpetual celebration. Lights garishly flickered on and off all day and all night, loud music blared from buildings all around them. Calhoun couldn't help but wonder when the natives slept, and came to the conclusion that the likely answer was "never."

Wrigley's Pleasure Planet was entirely a manufactured world, bought and paid for by one Horatio Wrigley several centuries ago and run by his family after his death . . . a passing, it was rumored, that resulted from an extended stay upon his own world. Supposedly he went with a smile on his face. There were certainly, Calhoun reasoned, worse ways to go.

Ostensibly, Wrigley had taken the hedonistic lifestyle that he had found on such worlds as Argelius and Risa and decided to heighten it, jack the level up to an unprecedented degree. Wrigley's was the only world where you could see spotlights shining while in orbit.

Calhoun and Lodec were not exactly allowing themselves to be swept up in the perpetual celebratory mood. Calhoun observed the gaiety around him as if he were watching from outside himself. It didn't seem to have anything to do with him or with his life. What underscored that the most for him was that he was walking down the street with a living reminder of the oppression his people had suffered under. A Danteri, right there, right next to him, and he himself had freed him. He would just as soon let him rot, and yet he had risked himself to set the man free.

It was all ... a very long time ago. And I suppose none of it matters anymore.

Those had been Lodec's words, and the thing was, Calhoun couldn't help but wonder if Lodec was correct. Two decades. Could it have been that long? Two decades since he had spearheaded the liberation of Xenex. He hadn't really dwelt on what that passage of time meant, not really. Twenty years. There were Xenexians who were adults now who had absolutely no recollection of a time when Xenex had been anything other than free. For whom the name M'k'n'zy of Calhoun was simply a name in a history book (plus a name attached to several statues which dotted the Xenexian landscape, none of which he thought looked a damned thing like him). Indeed, there were Xenexians to whom the Danteri meant nothing in any threatening sense.

The fact was that the leadership which had come in after Calhoun had itself made many inroads and wound up working quite closely with the Danteri—a leadership that had been spearheaded by Calhoun's own brother. That alliance, that willingness to work with their former oppressor, had driven a wedge between Mac and his brother that continued in force more or less to the present day.

Do you think ... that we wanted to be there? Most of us didn't give a damn about Xenex. We did what we were told. We followed orders.

... And I suppose none of it matters anymore ...

That wasn't how he wanted to think of the Danteri. It didn't fit into his view of the universe at all. The Danteri were uniformly oppressive monsters who wanted nothing but to reestablish their chokehold on Xenex and hated all things connected with that world. They were heartless bastards who would just as soon kill Calhoun and his kind as look at them.

They weren't allowed to come across as simply . . . mortal. Fallible mortals, tired of fighting, or perhaps grateful to a Xenexian, or even friendly . . . it simply wasn't allowed.

None of it matters . . .

Should it? Should it matter? Was there a statute of limitations on hatred? Was Calhoun being unreasonable, intransigent? Truthfully, Lodec seemed a decent enough sort. Once he'd gotten rested, cleaned up, he actually came across as a man of quick wit and ready tongue, a man who took a slightly skewed view of the universe.

And his crime against the Andorians? If he was to be believed . . . and he had, at that point, no reason to lie . . . it had nothing to do with crimes of violence, or spying, or anything that one would normally have expected in such a situation. No, Lodec had made the hideous mistake of having an affair with the wife of an Andorian high government official. He had not taken kindly to being cuckolded, and when he'd learned of the involvement, had Lodec brought up on charges of high crimes against the state. Lodec would have been more than happy to tell his side of the story, had he not had an electronic gag slapped across his mouth during the trial. And so a casual tryst by Lodec, who had just been passing through the homeworld of the Andorians, had turned out to be the beginning of a fifteen-year prison sentence. Granted, absconding with the affections of someone's wife was hardly an act that warranted having a medal pinned on you, but losing one's freedom for fifteen years because of it seemed a bit excessive. Even Calhoun had to admit that. But part of him wanted to feel that anything bad which happened to any Danteri was deserved and not to be mourned. That any ill fortune which befell any Danteri was something he had coming to him . . .

Except . . . that didn't hold up, either. After all, if there were Xenexian adults who had never been the slaves of Danteri, then it was also an inevitable conclusion that there were Danteri who not only had never been party to the oppression of Xenex, but had no inherent interest in Calhoun's world in the first place. Hell, if one could believe Lodec, he never "gave a damn" about Xenex to begin with. Of course, he didn't know for sure just how much he *could* believe Lodec, for the Danteri had been deliberately vague about what he himself had done during the war. He had basically admitted to being involved on a military level, but he had not gone into specifics. As near as Calhoun was able to determine, militarily Lodec was not much above a grunt.

None of which explained why in the world he was of such interest to General Thul.

Then Calhoun suddenly became aware of the fact that several Thallonians were following them.

Mentally he chided himself. That had been unforgivably sloppy. He had no idea how long they had been behind him. Had they just shown up? Were they there for several blocks? No way to tell. And he had been too wrapped up in his own musings to pay attention.

His first instinct was to confront the Thallonians following him. If nothing else, the notion pleased his ego. The thought of anything believing that they could tail Mackenzie Calhoun without his knowledge was galling to him.

But then he reconsidered. The fact was that they weren't making any aggressive moves against him. Furthermore, Thul had given Calhoun an address to which he was supposed to bring Lodec. It was possible that the Thallonians were there simply to observe, and report any questionable behavior back to Thul.

If one were to follow that reasoning, one would also assume that anything construed as being on Thul's side would likewise be reported.

With that notion in mind, Calhoun abruptly draped an arm around Lodec's shoulders. Lodec was clearly startled, and looked at Calhoun in surprise. "Is something wrong?" he asked.

"You're right. It was a long time ago," Calhoun said. "There's no need to hold grudges."

Lodec let out an obvious sigh of relief. "You can't believe how glad I am to hear you say that," he told Calhoun. "You've seemed to be wrapped up in your own thoughts since we got here . . . I have to admit, I was getting worried. I felt as if you were trying to figure out the best way to kill me or some such."

"No, no," and Calhoun laughed heartily. If one had looked closely, one would have seen that there was no touch of humor reflected in his eyes, but Lodec didn't look closely at all. "No, that's just my way. I've just been considering the situation, and concluded that there's nothing to be gained by obsessing about the past. We should only be concerned about the future, correct? That is, after all, where we all intend to live."

"I know I do," said Lodec, and he laughed. The noise was almost painful to Calhoun's ears, but he maintained his outward appearance of good humor, anyway. He took pains not to glance back at the Thallonians who were pacing them, since he didn't want to take any chance of giving away to them that he knew they were there.

They arrived at the prescribed address, and were promptly escorted upstairs to a private suite. There, in somewhat the same environment as he'd seen him on earth, was Thul. He was dressed far more festively than he had been on earth, much more in keeping with the general atmosphere of Wrigley's.

Vara Syndra was also there. Draped alluringly across a chair, winking at Calhoun, she was wearing an incredibly skintight yellow . . .

No. She wasn't. Calhoun's eyes widened. She was wearing body paint. That was it.

He promptly zoned out of the first minute and a half of the conversation, and only managed to re-enter it through sheer force of will as Thul was pouring drinks for all of them. Calhoun, cautious as always, mimed sipping from it but actually left the contents intact. Thul and Lodec were seated opposite each other, and appeared to be catching up on old times. At that moment, Thul was busy speaking directly to Calhoun. It was fortunate that he'd managed to get his head back on track, as it would have been rather embarrassing if Thul had asked him a question and Calhoun had been too busy staring at the thimbleful of paint which constituted the entirety of Vara Syndra's present wardrobe to answer.

"Lodec here was a close friend of my son, Mendan Abbis," Thul was saying. "As such, I had promised Mendan that Lodec would remain under my protection. Up until recently, that promise was merely words, as Lodec here," and he patted the Danteri's knee, "had always been more than capable of taking care of himself."

"Oh, yes," Lodec said with amused sarcasm. "I certainly

was doing a wonderful job of caring for myself, wasn't I. If it hadn't been for you and Calhoun, Thul, I'd still be en route to the Andorian prison world right now."

"Everyone needs assistance from time to time in their lives, my dear Lodec," Thul said.

"The thing is, Thul . . . poor Mendan is gone," Lodec said, and there seemed to be genuine sorrow in his voice. "If you had not assisted me . . . if you had left me to my fate . . . then Mendan would never have known."

"Granted," admitted Thul. "But I, General Gerrid Thul, made a promise to my son nonetheless, and our family name has always stood for integrity. Whether Mendan Abbis is alive or not, if my word is not to be trusted, then truly, what kind of Thul am I?"

"True. Very true." Lodec held up his glass after a moment and said with quiet conviction, "To Mendan Abbis."

"To Mendan Abbis," echoed Thul, and so did Calhoun.

"So," Lodec continued, "what now? You have obtained my freedom for me. Your debt is fulfilled . . ."

"Hardly," laughed Thul, although there was an odd undercurrent to that laugh. "If my promise of protection is to be seen through, then I am personally going to have to attend to your safety in the times ahead."

"The times ahead? What is that supposed to mean?"

"It means, good Lodec, exactly what it means. I am going to assure that you survive all that is to come." He rose. "Attend, then . . . we will pass the night here, enjoying the hospitality this world has to offer. Tomorrow we will depart, rendezvous at my headquarters . . . and all will be made clear. Calhoun . . ." and he extended his hand. Calhoun shook it firmly as Thul continued, "You have done well. Extremely well. No one could have done better. Vara," and he inclined his head toward her, "will see you to your room. I can count on you to depart with me tomorrow?"

"Absolutely," Calhoun said. And as he shook Thul's hand, his ring implanted a transponder directly into Thul's palm. Calhoun was taking no chances; the last thing he needed was for Thul to depart during the night, leaving Calhoun high and dry.

The next thing Calhoun knew, Vara Syndra was hanging on

his arm. "Come along, Mackenzie," she whispered softly in his ear. "Let me take you to your . . . room . . ."

At which point every hormone in his body completely stopped paying any attention whatsoever to whatever it was that Thul wanted to do or had in mind. Without hesitation he followed Vara out the door.

The moment they were in the hallway, out of sight of Thul, she began to kiss Calhoun. He did nothing to stop her. It was doubtful he could have done anything to stop her. He returned the kisses with equal passion, and hungrily locking lips with one another, they sidled down the hallway to the room that had been reserved for Calhoun. They eased in through the door, which obediently slid shut behind him.

It was a perfectly serviceable room, although nowhere near as opulent as Thul's. Somehow, though, opulence was not at the top of Calhoun's concerns at that particular moment. All he was concerned about was whether or not the place had a bed. Actually, it didn't matter all that much. The odds were sensational that the room had, at the very least, a floor, and the way he was feeling, that was all that he was going to need. But as luck would have it, there was indeed a bed there, large enough for an entire security team to wrestle with Vara, were such needed.

He ran his hands along the length of her body as they tumbled onto the bed, kissed her hungrily. Then he stopped long enough to look her in the eyes and say, "Why? Why me?"

She smiled at him. "Why not you? Don't you deserve it? Aren't you brave and heroic? Aren't you," and she ran her hands across his chest, "aren't you remarkably handsome?"

"And it doesn't have to mean more than that?"

"Of course not. Do you think it has to?" She actually seemed amused by the notion.

"No. No, it doesn't." He kissed her again, and his entire body was screaming at him to just get *on* with it already, she was wearing *body paint* and she was ready, willing and eager, how long should this possibly *take*. She pulled his shirt over his head. Naked from the waist up, he pressed against her. He groaned as she ran her tongue under the line of his chin, and he whispered her name . . .

"What's an 'Eppy'?" she asked.

He stopped, stared at her. "What?"

" 'Eppy.' Just now." There was laughter twinkling in her eyes. "You said, 'Eppy.' "

"I . . . said I was . . . happy. I whispered the word 'happy.' "

"Oh. Okay." She shook her head and chuckled once more. "Thul said you would be an interesting one. He had no idea, though, did he?"

"Thul. You're . . . here because Thul told you to be here," Calhoun said slowly.

"I'm here because I want to be here," Vara Syndra said firmly. "I'm here for my own reasons. Thul is part of it, yes. But you," and she fondled the lobe of his ear, "you are the main part of it. You rescued Lodec. You rescued . . . so many people, I'm sure."

"Yes. Yes, I did. I have."

She ran her fingers down his back, and he trembled from her touch. "Thul kept talking about how important it was to save Lodec. Kept talking about how he'd met Mendan Abbis, back in the days when Lodec worked for some man . . . Faulkner, I think, or Falcon, something like that . . . they'd stayed so close, and when Lodec was captured, Thul just knew that you'd be the man to get him out. Just like I—" She gasped. "You're hurting me!"

And he was. Because he'd had his hand on her wrist, but suddenly he was gripping it tightly.

"I'm . . . sorry." He let go of it immediately. She sat up, looking far more irritated than seductive. "Falkar?"

"What?"

"The man he worked for . . . was his name Falkar?"

She frowned a moment, concentrating, and then her eyes widened. "Yes!" she said, eager and cheerful, the momentary pain on her hand apparently forgotten. "Yes, that's right. Falkar. He worked for a man called Falkar. Lodec was apparently his main lieutenant, did all the tough jobs for him. That sort of thing."

His mind reeled as he sagged back onto the bed.

"Mackenzie? Are you all right?" She looked down at him with genuine concern. "Do you know this 'Falkar' person? What's happened? What's wrong, you seem so upset . . ."

Slowly, absently, Calhoun ran a finger down the scar on his

cheek. The scar that a Danteri general named Falkar had left there, as if it were a gift to wish him luck as an adult. And in his mind's eye, he called up images long buried, recollections of his father, strapped to a post in the public square, being beaten by a Danteri officer at Falkar's direction.

Twenty years unravelled in an instant, and he put a beard on the then-beardless youth with the whip, and he aged him in his mind's eye . . .

"Mackenzie!" she called loudly.

Before, it had taken him tremendous effort to focus on anything besides Vara Syndra. Now it was a formidable task to concentrate on her. "What?" he said in confusion.

"What's going on? Can you tell me what's going on?"

"I . . ." He couldn't find the words.

No. No, he knew the words. *That man I rescued . . . that man I almost started to like . . . that man who was a friend of Thul's son . . . that man who executed my father. He beat him to death in the town square, and the man who ordered the beating is long dead by my hand, but the man who actually did the job is right down the hallway, tossing back drinks with your boss and if you'll excuse me now, I've got to go kill him . . .*

He started to rise from the bed.

"Mackenzie," and for the first time, there was a sound of warning in her voice. "I don't appreciate the notion of men walking out on me. It's never happened before. It had better not happen now."

He turned his attention back to her and realized that the last thing he needed was Vara Syndra complaining to General Thul that the merest mention of Lodec or his former employer was enough to send Calhoun over the edge. He was trying to get himself on Thul's good side, after all. Besides, what was he going to do? Kill Lodec? Run in there screaming his father's name, announce that Lodec would pay for his deeds, rip out his beating heart and show it to him? The idea had some merit, granted, but ultimately it was counter-productive. Calhoun still had no true idea what it was that Thul was up to, and no certainty of where he was hiding, what it was he was hiding, or who it was he was hiding it from.

The only thing he knew for sure was that if he didn't give

Vara Syndra what she wanted, it was going to look bad for him. Very, very bad.

So he looked at her for a moment as if appraising her, and then he forcibly rolled her onto her back and brought his mouth ruthlessly down upon hers . . . and then proceeded to give her what she wanted.

But he didn't enjoy it.

Not especially, at any rate.

XVI.

XVI.

"I WILL NOT DO IT."

There was nothing in Doctor Selar's attitude that suggested she was going to change her mind anytime soon. Nonetheless, Riker did not appear remotely prepared to back down. Standing with him in Selar's office were Shelby and Soleta. Soleta kept her face, as always, impassive, while Shelby looked concerned and uncomfortable. She was no more happy with what Riker was proposing than Riker himself was, she had made that quite clear. But, to her credit, she was there as a sign of support for the commanding officer.

"Doctor," Riker began again, "it's not as if we have a great deal of choice here."

"You, Captain, may not have a choice. I, however, do." She shifted her gaze to Soleta, and there was a hint of disapproval in her eyes. "And you have agreed to this . . . proposal?"

"It is necessary," replied Soleta, sounding rather formal. "The Romulan woman, Sela, knows information that is potentially of great importance. The Romulans are not in the habit of acting in a capricious or haphazard manner. The raid on the Daystrom Institute, their presence in Thallonian space, their possible alliance with Narobi . . . they are pieces of a puzzle that Sela apparently knows."

"And that gives you the right," Selar said to her, "to forcibly thrust your mind into hers?"

"No," Soleta admitted. "It does not give me that right. It does, however, make it an obligation."

"If you must do this thing, and are committed to this deplorable course, then that is your own consideration," Doctor Selar said. "But to seek to involve me in the matter is adding insult to injury . . ."

"I have performed initial probes into her mind. Very mild. However, I can already sense that she has had training in psychic combat."

"So you believe that you alone cannot accomplish the job?"

"That is correct."

"And you would have me disgrace myself because you are incapable of doing so yourself."

"Doctor," Shelby said impatiently, "it is not a 'disgrace' to do something on behalf of a greater good. Furthermore, when you're in a service, such as Starfleet, it's your duty."

"Duty. Duty." Selar shook her head. "Commander . . . throughout history there have been those who were presented with situations where they were asked to make a choice that was morally repugnant to them . . . usually during a war when they were 'serving' the interests of their country in some way. More often than not, they went ahead with those repugnant efforts, even though they knew them to be wrong. Even though the cost may have been the purity of their very *katra* . . . their soul. And the excuse they invariably fell back upon was that it was their duty. The duty I attend to, Commander . . . Captain . . . Soleta . . . is the duty to do no harm. As a doctor, that is not only my first priority, it is my only priority. I will not force myself into the female's mind. You will have to find another way, or Soleta will simply have to do it alone. But that is my final word on the subject. Now, will there be anything else?"

"Doctor," Soleta said slowly, "a moment of your time . . . alone? If you please?"

"Lieutenant . . ."

"It will be all right, Commander," she said to Shelby.

Shelby seemed no more thrilled than did Riker by the situation, but finally she nodded and she and Riker walked out of the room, leaving Selar and Soleta alone.

"Do you desire to have me talk you out of this course?" Selar asked calmly.

"Doctor . . . there was a time some months ago when you needed me. I am telling you now that I need you."

"Soleta . . ."

Soleta leaned forward on the edge of Selar's desk, and the careful reserve that she maintained, with effort, slipped somewhat. " 'I believe I am ill. Mentally ill. And I require your services to ascertain that.' That is what you said to me, Selar, when you needed my help. When you were so convinced that you could not possibly be undergoing Pon Farr that you asked me to help you. No . . . no, you begged me. You asked me to grant you succor, you were so wretched . . ."

"I know that," Selar said. "I was there. I know what I did. I know what I went through. And you helped me, and for that I shall be forever grateful. But this is a different situation . . ."

"It would be, to you. I'm the one asking for help this time. Selar," she said in a lowered voice as if someone were eavesdropping, "I am not full Vulcan. You know this. I am impure, my mother Vulcan but my father a Romulan. They are expecting me to meld with a half Romulan woman, against her will, who is quite likely capable of resisting me. And she has had training . . . what if she turns it back against me? What if she uncovers my background? The risk to myself, the—"

"You are scared." Selar almost sounded sympathetic.

"Yes. I admit that freely. I am afraid of what I am being asked to do."

"Then do not do it. I am refusing."

"The difference is," Soleta said, "that you are refusing based upon moral principles. If I refused, however, it would be predicated purely on fear."

"Not necessarily. When you granted me succor, realized that it entailed a mind meld that you did not wish to perform, and further realized that I was just desperate enough to force you to do it anyway, you were morally and ethically repulsed by the notion. You felt that forcing one to perform a mind meld was repellant."

"Yes. I did. I still do."

"Then that is the basis upon which you can refuse. For is it not a small step from being forced to perform a mind meld, to having one forced upon you. The woman, Sela, does not want to have her mind probed. On the basis that such matters are best left to personal choice, you can and should refuse."

And then, to Sela's complete astonishment, Soleta let out a low roar of fury and, with a sweeping gesture, knocked everything off Selar's desk and sent it scattering to the floor. The clatter grabbed the attention of everyone in sickbay, and whatever anyone was doing came to a complete halt as all eyes turned to Selar's office.

Selar's eyes were wide with astonishment; not even her Vulcan training could repress that. As for Soleta, she was gripping the edge of the desk and trying to restore her breathing to normal. "Have you lost your mind?" Selar asked her, recapturing her customary calm.

"I need you," she said in a low voice. "And I need Starfleet. I am an impure bastard offspring of a violent rape. I have nowhere else to go in this universe where I can be at home except Starfleet."

"You are not limited or defined as a person by the circumstances of your birth, Soleta . . ."

"Yes. I am. And I have been asked by Starfleet, by my commanding officers, to do this thing. They believe that there may be something very terrible at stake, and Sela holds the key. I care about Starfleet. I care about people possibly being hurt or killed by the machinations of this woman. I have asked for your help. When you asked for mine, I provided it; as much as it cost me, I provided it. The short-term result was your coming to terms with, and understanding, what was happening to you, and the long-term result is the baby you carry in your belly. You owe me," she said in a low and angry voice. "You owe me, Selar, and if you won't help me, then to hell with you."

Selar did not even hesitate. "I cannot help you. It is a question of principle. For what it is worth, however . . . I am sorry."

Soleta drew herself up, her facade of reserve firmly back in place. "No. You're not sorry at all. What you are . . . is Vulcan."

She turned and walked out of Selar's office.

Shelby and Riker were standing in the corridor just outside sickbay, and Shelby was saying, "I don't know about this. I'm . . . uncomfortable about it."

"Truth to tell, I'm not happy with it either."

"Really?" Shelby seemed surprised. "I wouldn't have known it. If you ask me, you seem perfectly sanguine about it."

"I know I do. If there's one thing I've learned, it's that whether you make a good decision or a bad decision, what's just as important—if not even more so—is making a decision and sticking to it. You can't be a commanding officer and not be committed to your commands."

"Yes, well . . . that would explain why some of the CO's I've worked with should be committed."

They both laughed at that, and then Riker turned to Shelby with mock astonishment and said, "Why, Commander. Did we just have a moment there?"

"I don't think it was a whole moment, sir. Maybe half a moment."

"Half."

"Three quarters at most."

"I see." He paused. "You were right about the Romulans."

"I know. But then again, in retrospect, so were you."

He raised an eyebrow. "What do you mean?"

"I mean ninety-nine times out of a hundred—hell, maybe nine hundred ninety-nine times out of a thousand—the way you played it was absolutely right. Who knew that they had some bizarre scheme or ability to break into our entire computer system and cause the kind of havoc that they did?"

"You knew."

She shook her head. "No. I guessed. I had a gut feeling . . . which, I have to tell you, is damned peculiar for me. I've always been by-the-book, follow-the-rules."

"Perhaps you've been hanging around with Captain Calhoun too long. You're starting to pick up some of his seat-of-the-pants method."

"Perhaps. Or perhaps it was just, with you here, my inclination was to second-guess what you were doing. Maybe . . . that's my basic nature. I've never thought about it before, but maybe it's the way I operate. When Mac is here and being all gut-feeling, I'm all rules and regs. When you're here, doing things by the numbers, I'm suddenly advocating acting on impulse. Maybe . . ." and she sighed deeply. "Maybe that's why I've never gotten command. Maybe I don't have my own command style, but instead I simply react to other people. But a captain needs to be a leader, to set the tone. Maybe I just don't have that in me."

"Nonsense," Riker said. "You're selling yourself short, Shelby. Way short."

"Oh really. And why do you say that?"

He grinned readily. "Call it instinct. Hey . . . even I have to go by it sometimes."

She returned the smile, but before she could reply, Soleta walked out into the corridor. She had never seen the Vulcan science officer look quite that deliberately stone-faced before. "Soleta . . . ? Are you all right?"

"I am perfectly fine, Commander . . . Captain," she took in both of them with a glance.

"Is Selar going to help you? Give you back-up?" asked Riker.

"No. And I will endeavor to respect her decision. So . . . let's get this over with." And she headed toward Sela's cell.

Soleta didn't like the look of things from the moment she got to the cell.

Sela was sitting there looking infinitely smug and infinitely composed. There wasn't the slightest flicker of fear in her eyes. "Well, well, little lieutenant . . . going to take a shot at visiting the dark side, are you?"

Riker and Shelby were standing on the other side of the security field, as was Zak Kebron. But for all that their presence mattered, they could have been on Mars. The struggle, on all levels, was purely between Soleta and Sela.

"I will give you one last chance to cooperate," said Soleta.

"That's very gracious of you," Sela replied in a throaty voice. "Ever so gracious. But I don't need your chances."

"You may not have as much luck with resisting a mind probe as you think you will," Soleta warned her. "You are, I understand, half human. That will hamper you."

"And you are a fool, so that will hamper you."

Soleta did not rise to the obvious bait. Instead, she nodded her head in Kebron's direction as she extended her hands in preparation. "I feel it necessary to warn you that if you resist my making physical contact, Lieutenant Kebron will enter this room and hold you down. That will be most uncomfortable for y—"

"Resist? Why? What possible reason would I have? Do you think I'm afraid of you?"

"I am simply . . ."

Sela was on her feet, and in two quick strides she was directly in front of Soleta. She grabbed Soleta's wrists and, with that confident grin of hers, said, "Take your best shot." And she slammed Soleta's hands onto either side of her own head.

For the briefest of moments, Soleta hesitated, but she knew that way lay utter defeat. So she cast away her doubts and plunged headlong into Sela's mind.

Sela had not overspoken when she talked of walking on the dark side. Soleta felt completely overwhelmed by darkness. Darkness all around her, impenetrable and chilling. Somewhere deep in the distance, she was sure she heard Sela laughing at her. The contempt irritated Soleta, fired her forward, and she plunged further, further on.

Run while you can, little Vulcan, came the warning, but still Soleta moved forward. All round her reality shifted and twisted, because there was no reality, there was only the subjective aspects of what she was perceiving within Sela . . . and within herself. For a meld was not simply a one-way connection. She was risking making herself as vulnerable to Sela as Sela was to her . . .

. . . except Sela didn't seem vulnerable at all.

Soleta crashed into something.

It was huge and black and unmoving, and now the laughter was coming in from all around. She pulled back, withdrew her perspective, and she saw it in her mindscape. It was a gigantic image of Sela, a mile high it seemed, her face reflected in some sort of gargantuan mirror. The world twisted and turned back on itself around her, and still the image of Sela loomed over all. The blackness with which she had collided was the gaping maw of Sela's mouth, wide-open and laughing at her.

There was no delicacy, no finesse to Soleta's probe. She simply hurled herself with brute force against the image of her opponent. She slammed into it and she felt a painful shudder throughout her body, except of course she had no true body there, the pain was all in her mind and somehow that made it worse. But she could not go back, nor could she go around, she had to go through.

Having problems, Lieutenant? The image of Sela sneered at her, and then added, *Here come a few more problems.*

Black tendrils seemed to expand from all around, wrapping themselves around Soleta, and she did everything she could to shake them off. For a moment she was free and then once more she crashed into Sela's massive face, and once more there was the pain of collision, and once more she got nowhere, and this time she was a bit more tired, a bit more frustrated, and even a bit more

Frightened? Are we having problems, Lieutenant? What's frightening you? The prospect of failure? Or the prospect of something more? Her voice was everywhere, not just all around her but inside her, inside her head, there was nowhere to go, nowhere to escape.

Escape? Is that your concern? Why would you want to run away? Is there something you are concerned I'll learn? Come, come, Soleta, you wanted to find out my secrets. You should be willing to trade some of yours in turn. This is just girl talk, after all . . .

And the tendrils were back, and this time there was no shaking them off. Sela's training had been too thorough, and it was more than just training, she burned, she burned with a dark and fearsome intensity that was painful in and of itself. And Soleta tried to pull away, tried, but Sela was everywhere now, penetrating and violating her, and she was thinking of what her mother must have suffered except she didn't want to think of that because that way lay madness, and there was Sela's face as huge as a star, filling up everything . . .

. . . and suddenly Sela's face changed. It went from smug triumph to alarm. Soleta didn't understand at first, but as the tendrils slipped away from her, she saw the first cracks appearing in the mirror image of Sela.

And a voice said, *Calmly, Soleta. Calmly. That is what is needed here. Calm and focus.*

She did not see the image of Selar next to her, did not perceive her in that way. But she sensed her, sensed the steadying presence.

Sela discerned the cracks that were appearing in her image,

and a snarl of animal fury that carried psychic repercussions blasted out from her. *Get out! Both of you! Get out while you can!*

Are you with me, Selar? Soleta asked.

I am here. My hands are upon your brow. Our minds have merged. Do as you need.

GET OUT! Sela howled, and that howl translated into winds so massive, so deafening, that they threatened to blast Soleta right out of the mindscape.

But she drew strength from Selar's presence, drew focus. And more, she began to draw upon herself. For she knew that Sela's heritage was hers too. The fires of fury that burned within Sela raged within her as well. It was that pure, raw, fierce emotion that she drew upon now. *Not calm, Selar,* she thought, *not just calm. You bring the calm . . . but it's the calm before the storm.*

And she summoned that rage, then, the rage and pure emotion that was part of the Romulan make-up, the rage that she felt over the circumstances of her own birth, the rage from the confusion and frustration and sense of desolation and separation that she had carried with her for year after year. All that she pulled to her, clutching to herself, and then she hurled herself forward straight toward the mirrored image of Sela.

Sela screamed in protest, but it was too late, far too late as Soleta smashed through. The image, the psychic shield that Sela had created, cracked and splintered and fell completely apart. And it poured out, it all poured out, images, awareness, facts, tumbling one over the other, and Sela was desperately trying to prevent the strip-mining of her thoughts; however, not only could she not slow it down, but Soleta was enjoying it with a primal fury that was terrifying to perceive.

Tell me what I want to know! Show me! You have no choice! GET OUT!

Tell me, you Romulan bitch!

And it was there, everywhere, the Thallonian and the plan and the location and she just needed a few more details to help it all fit together and then she saw a horrible, horrible landscape, bodies, bodies piled up in mountains stretching so high that they blotted out the sun hanging in the sky, except it wasn't the sun, it was something glistening and metal . . .

And then the world crashed in around Soleta.

Her body collapsed, and the only thing that stopped her from hitting the ground was Selar. It wasn't that Selar caught her; Selar also collapsed, but as it turned out, Soleta fell on top of her so that her fall was slightly cushioned.

There was nothing to prevent Sela from hitting the ground, though, which she did with all the elegance of a sack of rocks.

Shelby and Riker were through the door in a heartbeat, Riker helping up Selar while Shelby attended to Soleta. "Soleta . . . are you all right?" she called to her.

Soleta stared at her, trying to focus her eyes. "You don't have to shout, Commander. I'm right here."

"Oh, thank God. I . . . I heard this shriek . . . and . . ." Shelby turned to Riker. "Did you hear it, too . . . ?"

He nodded. "In my head. Nothing spoken."

"Psychic backlash," Selar now spoke up. Riker was helping her to her feet. "Even those who have no telepathic leanings can sense such an event."

"What happened to her?" Although Shelby was propping up Soleta, she was now looking at Sela. The Romulan was lying flat on her back, staring up at nothing. Her eyes were glazed over. "Doctor . . . ?"

The doctor was already tapping her comm badge. "Selar to sickbay."

"Sickbay," came Maxwell's quick response.

"We need a team up to the brig, immediately." She was checking Sela over briskly even as she was speaking to Maxwell. "Blood pressure, vital signs all appear minimal but within safety limits . . ."

"What's happened to her?" demanded Riker.

"Brain fried," Soleta said tonelessly. They all looked at her, and she noticed that Selar was nodding. She continued, "To put it in human terms . . . we strip-mined her. Forced our way in, took what we needed. She fought . . . valiantly . . . but realized that she was losing the fight. So she . . . burned herself out."

"You mean deliberately?" said Shelby, appalled.

"In a manner of speaking, yes. It wasn't that difficult, really. Everything that she was turning outward for the purpose of resisting us . . . she turned inward instead. Like burning the crops so that the attacking forces can't use the food."

"Will she recover?"

"I . . . don't know," Soleta said. "I've never actually seen this technique used. I've heard whispers about it, stories of people who had done it to themselves as a sort of mental suicide out of extreme depression . . . but I've never witnessed it myself. I have absolutely no idea of what to expect in terms of her recovery."

"And as long as she's like this . . . we can't find out anything from her?" asked Riker.

Selar shook her head. "It would be like trying to read a book with blank pages. She has done to herself what her people did to us: She has crashed her computer."

"Which leaves us right back where we started."

"No, Commander Shelby," Soleta said. "Not quite. I . . . learned some things. Some terrible things. Saw visions of what's to come . . . saw those involved, or at least some of them . . ."

"Do you know where they are? Where to find them?" asked Riker.

She nodded, but then added, "What I don't know . . . is whether we can do a thing about it."

XVII.

CALHOUN STARED OUT at empty space and tried to figure out what in the world it was that he was supposed to see.

In his freighter, he had arrived at the designated coordinates at the same time as General Thul, who was piloting his own vessel, a sleek mini-cruiser that looked as if it was more than capable of handling itself in most combat situations. Truth to tell, Calhoun had been concerned if, once he was out in space, he might be subject to some sort of sneak attack or ambush arranged by Thul or his minions. That was why he was somewhat relieved that Vara Syndra was with him.

She was wearing something a bit more substantial than body paint this time, but the clothes were still extremely tight and rather revealing. She positioned herself in the co-pilot chair in such a way that he wondered if he would ever be able to look at anyone else sitting there in quite the same way.

"Why are we sitting here?" Calhoun said after a brief time. "There's nothing out here. What's the point?"

"Oh, you'll see. The General likes to be mysterious," and she said the word 'mysterious' in a deliberately dramatic manner. "That's just his way. You know," and she leaned forward, displaying her ample cleavage, "instead of simply complaining, I can think of ways in which we could pass the time."

He looked at her, regarded her thoughtfully. He'd had a lot of time to think about her. When he had woken up in the middle of the night, she had been lying on his shoulder, snoring softly. He had studied her for some time, giving matters a good deal of consideration. He knew himself. He knew what others were capable of. And he had come to some rather interesting conclusions.

"Pheromones," he said.

He got precisely the reaction he was hoping he would get: Startled. He'd said something that she had not remotely anticipated. "Wh-what?"

"Pheromones. You generate them in such a way that I, and any other male, couldn't help but be affected by them. You can regulate it however you wish, 'turn on the charm,' as it were. You can crank it up to high heat, which is what you did with me, depending upon what it is that Thul wants you to do. Problem is, you did too good a job on me. You made it so that I couldn't think straight. Except I can always think straight."

"I . . . don't know what you're talking—"

"Yes, you do." When he interrupted her, he did so with no rancor. Indeed, he sounded a bit sad. "I don't know whether you come by it naturally, or if it's somehow been implanted into you. Don't know, don't care, really. The most depressing aspect of all is, I have absolutely no idea whether I would have been attracted to you just because of you yourself, or whether you need something like being able to artificially stimulate male hormones in order to function. If I had to guess, that's probably a bit depressing for you, too. Not to know, I mean. Considering the way you look, it's somewhat sad to think that you would have to depend on something chemical. Or . . . do you really look that way . . . ?"

She turned away from him, then. "Here's my back," she said with far more anger than he would have thought she was possible of generating. "Just stick a knife into it and be done with it."

"Vara," he said softly, "listen—"

"No," she snapped, looking back at him. "God, you're all the same. The surface is all that matters to you. And you know what? I thought you were different. I thought you'd know me. That you, of all people, would know me. But you don't know anything. You know what I wanted to do after you fell asleep last night? Leave. That's what I usually do. But not with you, no. With you, I stayed. I totally, totally let down my guard with you . . ."

"Why?" he asked.

"Because I thought I could. Because I thought we had connected on a deeper level than simply the physical. Because . . ." A tear trickled down her cheek and she wiped it away angrily. "It doesn't matter," she said finally. "None of it does, I guess."

"Why are you hooked up with General Thul?" he asked. "Look what he's doing to you. He uses you."

She stared at him with eyes that were glistening. "And I use him. Everyone uses everybody else, Mackenzie. And anyone who says otherwise is probably one of the biggest users of all."

"Vara . . ."

Suddenly Calhoun's ship-to-ship comm channel flared to life. "Calhoun. Are you still with us?" Thul sounded particularly jovial.

"I'm here, yes. Although I'm wondering why, exactly. Is there some deep, hidden meaning to the fact that we're sitting here?"

"Just being cautious. I generally like to do a detailed scan of the area before going home, just to make sure that there's no one about who shouldn't be here. But I'm pleased to report that the area is clear."

"It's certainly clear of anything that could possibly be called 'home,' " Calhoun observed.

"You should not always believe what your eyes tell you, Calhoun. First appearances do not necessarily mean anything."

"Yes, I think I've heard that occasionally," he said with a sidelong glance at Vara. She was looking resolutely away from him.

"Welcome to my home, Calhoun."

Calhoun still had absolutely no clue what Thul could possibly be talking about.

And then, in the near distance, space began to ripple. At first Calhoun thought it was something dropping out of warp space, but then he realized it was a ship dissolving its cloaking field. His immediate instinct was to prepare for battle, for when Romulan vessels dropped their cloak, it meant that they were about to open fire.

Then he realized that the dissolution field was too wide. It wasn't just one ship, it was a fleet of ships. A huge fleet . . . but . . . there was no space between the ships . . . it was one, big, solid, wavering mass . . .

"Grozit," whispered Calhoun.

It was a gigantic sphere, massive beyond belief. The thing could have contained the entirety of Starfleet within itself and had room left over for the Klingon fleet and a few others as well. It blotted out everything. Calhoun had his viewscreen on maximum reverse magnification, and he still couldn't make out the whole thing. He prodded the freighter into reverse.

"Don't run away, Calhoun, it won't bite," came Thul's voice.

"I'm not running away," said Calhoun, "I'm just trying to get a better view of the thing."

Within moments he'd backed up far enough away so that he could see it in its entirety. "It's a Dyson Sphere," he said.

"I believe that is what terran technology refers to such a structure as, yes. Call it what you will. As I mentioned, I call it home."

"But it's impossible! Cloaked? How can you possibly cloak something that big?"

"I've been working with the Romulan empire for some time now, Calhoun. You would truly be amazed what a few people with determination, resources, and sufficient hatred for the Federation can accomplish. Follow me, if you please."

Thul's ship moved toward the sphere, and Calhoun fell in behind him. The closer he got, the bigger it got. His instrumentation gave him readings as to the size, but knowing it intellectually and seeing it up close were two entirely different things. "How did he build it?" he asked Vara. "How long did it take? How—?"

"You can ask him," Vara Syndra replied. "I'm just here for my looks."

Calhoun rather wisely decided not to press the point.

They moved through the massive entrance bay, passing through to the interior of the sphere itself. It was, to all intents and purposes, hollow. This hardly meant that it was empty, however. For starters, there were dozens, perhaps hundreds of ships, parked within. Furthermore, the walls of the sphere itself were lined with walkways, residences, work areas. Toward the top and bottom of the spheres, Calhoun spotted hydroponics growing fields where fresh food was being cultivated. And straight down the middle of the sphere was a huge, pulsing device that Calhoun immediately recognized as an infinitely larger version of a Romulan cloaking device. He saw that it was feeding off a core that was a modified version of a warp core. The Dyson sphere had no means of propulsion, however. It simply utilized the combination of matter and anti-matter explosions to feed its energy needs. He also saw workers casually walking vertically along the outside of the core, getting from one point to the other, and he realized that the sphere was creating an artificial gravity by the simple expedient of rotating on an axis.

"Incredible," he breathed.

"Follow me, please," came Thul's voice over the comm. "You'll see a docking beacon flashing. That will guide you in."

Calhoun did as he was told. It wasn't particularly difficult maneuvering, really. If it had been remotely difficult, they probably would have had a computer come on line and handle it for him. As it was, he followed Thul's lead across the vast interior and locked into position at a docking bay on the far side.

Moments later Vara and Calhoun had exited the freighter and were in what appeared to be a large reception area. People were walking briskly about on their business, but every single one of them paused in their stride to nod and acknowledge Thul's presence. It was an impressive variety of races represented there . . . and Calhoun noticed that the vast majority of them were not members of the Federation. Of those individuals who were, Calhoun recognized a number of them from records that had been circulated to all Starfleet captains, warning about individuals who posed a hazard to life and liberty.

"This way," said Thul. Lodec was next to him, and as Vara and Calhoun joined them, they made their way to what appeared to be some sort of turbolift.

As they walked, Calhoun found it more and more difficult to so much as look in Lodec's direction. Every time he did so, he risked betraying the depth of fury that the merest proximity to the Danteri provoked within him. One of the few things that

Calhoun had never been able to accomplish was to learn from the Danteri government the name of the individual who had wielded the whip that killed his father. Intellectually, he had always known that it was Falkar who had ordered the deed. That gave him the responsibility, and that scale had been balanced. But part of Calhoun had always wanted to crush the throat of the man who had actually done the deed. He longed to feel that pulse beneath his fingers, struggling and beating its last before falling forever silent.

And now, after all these years, he had the motherless scum at arm's length. But he couldn't touch him. The object was to stay in Thul's good graces, and slaying the best friend of Thul's late son was hardly going to accomplish that goal. Calhoun was anxious to learn what it was that Thul was up to, and determined to stop it. But now he had an additional incentive, something that—perhaps not surprisingly—gave him something more personal at stake than simply the entirety of the Federation's survival.

At one point, Lodec seemed to sense that Calhoun was eyeing him. He glanced in Calhoun's direction, but by that point Calhoun was looking off somewhere else. Lodec shook his head slightly, as if endeavoring to sort out his imagination from reality, and Calhoun simply watched him through half-lidded eyelids, like a great cat waiting in the high grass.

They stepped into the turbolift car. The doors hissed shut as Thul said, "General Thul, command level." The turbolift immediately started moving, sliding noiselessly toward the instructed destination. The lift was situated on the inside wall of the Dyson Sphere, which meant that they had a dazzling view of the entirety of the place as they moved downward.

"What do you think of my little endeavor, Calhoun?" he asked. "I noticed you studying some of the other residents of my home quite carefully."

"Well . . . if you're really asking me . . ."

"Oh, I am. I am," Thul said sincerely.

"As near as I can tell, a goodly number of the individuals here are . . . how should I put this delicately . . ."

"Scum?"

"Yes. Thank you. That's the word I was looking for. And the

problem with filling a place with the scum of the galaxy, with some of the least trustworthy individuals around, is that you're going to have a hell of a time watching your back."

"I could not agree more, Calhoun," Thul said readily. Calhoun could feel the lift slowing to a stop. "On that basis, I've taken great care to have the best people watching my back. Here's one of them now."

The doors slid open and Calhoun stepped out, looking around.

Zolon Darg was standing there.

Clearly he had been waiting for Thul to show up. Perhaps Thul, in a rather perverse bit of amusement, had requested that he show up and meet them there. Whatever the occasion might have been, the fact was that Darg was there and it took him all of two seconds to recognize Calhoun.

For his part, Calhoun couldn't believe how massive Darg looked. Bigger, wider than when Calhoun had last seen him, with arms, legs and chest so thick that one could only conclude that he had rippling muscles beneath his clothes, the likes of which no one had ever seen.

"Darg, this is—" began Thul.

That was as far as he got. With a roar of inarticulate fury, Darg charged forward and grabbed Calhoun by the front of the shirt. He slammed the Starfleet officer against the far wall with such fury that Calhoun felt every bone in his body rattle. His eyes felt as if they were ricocheting off his brain.

"Miss me?" he managed to get out.

Darg howled again and threw Calhoun to the floor. When Calhoun crashed into it, he barely managed to absorb the impact with his arms. If he hadn't pulled it off, the impact would likely have broken his neck.

Calhoun couldn't believe his strength; it surpassed understanding. Darg would have given Zak Kebron a run for his money, and perhaps even beaten him. Then there was no time to think as Darg drove a boot straight down toward Calhoun's face. Calhoun barely managed to roll out of the way as Darg's foot crashed down where Calhoun's head had been moments before.

"I'll kill him!" Darg shouted, which was the first coherent thing he had managed to get out since he'd first seen Calhoun.

All things considered, it was a somewhat wasted pronouncement. His actions had already spoken far more loudly.

"Stop it, Darg. Right now," said Thul, and there was an iron sense of command in his voice that snagged even Darg's attention.

Darg rounded on Thul, and he looked like a barely contained nuclear detonation. "He's mine, Thul! Mine to kill! Mine!"

"That's enough, Darg. The idea! Throwing a guest of mine around," and he helped the shaken Calhoun to his feet. "Are you all right, Calhoun?"

Calhoun was woozy, his knees starting to buckle. "Well . . . fortunately, I'm still alive. Except . . . that might be a bit unfortunate, too, because I don't really feel like being alive at the moment."

"I'll remedy that!" snapped Darg, and he started to advance on Calhoun once more. " 'Calhoun,' eh? So that's the name you're going by. I've never known it . . . but by God, your face has been seared into my memory long enough! And I'm—"

"I said enough!" and if there was any doubt until that moment as to who precisely was in charge, that strident bellow more or less demolished it. Darg froze where he was, in midstep, as he had been advancing on Calhoun.

"I warn you, Darg. Do not cross me on this matter. Calhoun has done me a great service. Because of that, he is not to be harmed."

"He nearly killed me," Darg said slowly, as if addressing a child. "He . . . tried to kill . . . me . . ."

"Yes, he did. And the only reason that you're still alive is because of me," Thul reminded him. This appeared to be getting through, and he continued, "Because of Calhoun, Lodec stands with me now."

"I could have gotten Lodec for you," Darg said with contempt, as if the feat of freeing Lodec was a simple conjuring trick that could be performed by the average eight-year-old with a home starter magic bag.

"You were busy elsewhere. You cannot be everywhere, Darg, and I need others I can count upon."

"You would put . . . that . . ." and his finger quavered as he pointed in Calhoun's direction, " . . . that . . . thing . . . on the same level with me? You would depend on both Calhoun and myself equally? That is madness!"

"Grow up, Darg," Thul said, and he certainly sounded as if he meant it. "What is past is past. Reliving grudges and offensive acts taken toward one another is a fool's errand. And I am no fool. Now . . . Mackenzie Calhoun . . . Zolon Darg . . . you will work in tandem with each other, in a spirit of cooperation. I do not want to hear rumors of either of you trying to kill the other one. That would be unacceptable. And a mysterious midnight poisoning . . . ? That would be unacceptable as well." Calhoun wasn't sure, but he thought perhaps that Darg had looked a bit crestfallen upon learning of the further edict. "You will work together. You will trust each other as much as can possibly be expected. If there are any disputes, they will be mediated through me. And gentlemen . . . think of it this way . . ."

"What way?" Calhoun asked, still rubbing the parts of his body that had been badly bruised while being tossed around.

"It will be in both your best interests to lead a long, healthy and productive life here in the Thul Sphere. Because if either of you dies, I will automatically assume that the other had something to do with it, and act accordingly."

"Wait a minute," Calhoun said, "you can't hold us responsible in such an open-ended manner. What if one or the other of us dies of natural causes?"

"That might be almost impossible to determine," Thul said reasonably. "There are too many drugs and poisons that can simulate demise from a certain cause . . . and the poisons themselves are undetectable within minutes after doing the job. Therefore, we would likely err on the side of caution, decide that the means of death was actually murder, and act accordingly."

"You can't do that!" protested Darg.

"Darg . . . Calhoun," Thul said slowly, with tremendous warning in his voice, "this is my place. I cannot suggest strongly enough that you do not tell me what I can and cannot do. Understood?"

Calhoun and Darg looked at each other. Calhoun did not think for a moment that Darg was going to let it drop quite that easily, and was fully aware that he was going to have to watch himself every waking minute—and, even more importantly, those minutes when he was not awake. Still, he simply nodded and said, "Understood."

"Understood," muttered Darg.

"Good. That's settled then."

"Mackenzie Calhoun," Darg said slowly. "I know that name. You are with Starfleet. I've heard your name bandied about in Thallonian space. There are some who worship you as a god."

Calhoun shrugged indifferently. "Some. I don't encourage it."

"You're not wearing a Starfleet uniform. What is a Starfleet man doing here, anyway?"

"He is late of the fleet, Darg," Thul assured him. "This is a place where new lives are started. All I care about is what a man brings with him, not what he leaves behind. Now then, Darg . . . the recruitment drive on Argelius. How did that go? We are running short on time, and are rapidly drawing to the 'now-or-never' moment."

"It went quite well, actually," said Darg, casting one more sidelong glance at Calhoun before continuing his comments to Thul. "Of the twelve representatives I met with, nine showed up in force several hours ago, bringing the required payment along with the people they represent. The population of the Thul Sphere has increased exponentially."

"Perfectly acceptable," smiled Thul. "That is perfectly acceptable. The resources of the sphere have been carefully built up. You see, Calhoun," he continued, turning back to the officer, "this has hardly been an overnight project. I have labored many years to bring this to fruition."

"You must be very proud."

"Very, yes. And who is this?"

Calhoun didn't understand the question, and then realized it wasn't being addressed to him. Someone else was walking toward them from behind him, joining the group. It was Darg to whom Thul had been speaking.

"This fellow," Darg said, "was of tremendous use to me on Argelius. I have taken the liberty of inviting him to join our operation. General Thul . . . this is Kwint. Kwint, this is our glorious leader, the great General Thul. And this is Thul's glorious associate, Vara Syndra, and Lodec of Danter, and . . ." he growled the name reluctantly, as if hating to acknowledge that it needed to be spoken, "Mackenzie Calhoun, late of Starfleet. Gentlemen, lady . . . this is Kwint."

Calhoun turned and saw a man with silver hair and beard, but a face that otherwise he recognized instantly. His voice caught in his throat as he found himself staring straight into the eyes of Jean-Luc Picard.

XVIII.

"WE WERE SET UP, SI CWAN. I'm sorry, but that's one of the
things I drew from her mind," said Soleta. She looked around a
conference lounge that was occupied at that point by Shelby,
Riker, Selar, and Burgoyne, and Si Cwan. Cwan's face, in particular, was deathly serious. "This ostensibly 'peaceful' race
you spoke of had actually allied itself with the Romulans. Because of their machine make-up, they were apparently the perfect tools to help put into place the final elements that were
needed for Thul's plan. And they decided to test those elements on our computers. They were simply able to take our
computer system over with no problem, punching through all
the safeguards and security codes as if they weren't even
there."

"So their plan is to try and take over computers of star-
ships?" asked Burgoyne. "But why? It sounds somewhat ab-
stract to me."

"You mentioned Thul. That would be Gerrid Thul," Si Cwan
said slowly.

"You know him, then," asked Riker.

"More by reputation, although I seem to have a vague recollection of meeting him when I was quite young. A rather
power-mad individual. At the time he was a second-level

218

Thallonian nobleman. Very eloquent, but that eloquence helped to cover a ferocity of ambition that was rather chilling. My father once said that Thul is a man who uses lies the way a surgeon uses a scalpel, and assigned him to be in charge of one of the farthest-flung of our outposts. But Thul craved power, and decided that the best way to go about it was to court the emperor's sister, my aunt. My father thwarted that, feeling that Thul wasn't good enough for her. This infuriated Thul. Then there was a rebellion . . . Thul's son was killed, I believe . . . and then one thing led to another, and Thul wound up in prison."

"Well, he's out, and apparently he has no love for the Federation. What I managed to draw from Sela's mind before she collapsed is, unfortunately, spotty at best," admitted Soleta. "Thul has been experimenting with some sort of virus . . . a virus that apparently is one of the most devastating that the Federation has ever dealt with."

"Dealt with? You mean it's surfaced before?" asked Riker.

"Apparently it has, yes," said Soleta. "The *Enterprise* first encountered it several years ago on Archaria III. It then resurfaced on Terok Nor a few years later. A variation was used to attack the Romulan royal family, and finally, just before his defection, Tom Riker reported dealing with the virus on a planet in what was then the demilitarised zone between the Federation and Cardassia."

"But what's been the point of it all? These repeated attempts at a virus . . . ?" But then Shelby realized it. "He's planning to unleash it on the Federation, isn't he."

"Apparently so," said Selar. "From what I have garnered, this virus crosses races with the ease that we cross warp space. If Thul does manage to unleash it somehow, it could annihilate every living organism it comes in contact with."

"But a virus can't travel through space. How can he possibly do it?" asked Si Cwan.

There was dead silence for a moment as they looked at one another.

Then Riker's eyes widened. "I get it. Good lord . . . I get it."

"Get what?" asked Shelby. "I don't understand . . ."

Riker leaned forward, his fingers interlaced. "Federation races share technology. That's one of the fundamentals of the alliance. That technology includes such standard items as holotech . . . computers . . . and *replicators*."

"So?" asked Shelby . . . and then she understood. "Oh, my God."

Riker nodded. "Replicators work via computers. They tap into a data base and use that information to replicate food, clothing, whatever's needed. It's one of the underpinnings of our way of life, because as long as replicators exist, no one wants for anything. With the aid of the artificial intelligence equipment and research that Thul has stolen, via such catspaws as Zolon Darg, and the help of the Narobi, Thul has found a way to access any and all computers throughout the Federation. Because computers are the connecting tissue of the entire Federation."

"Thul has come up with the ultimate computer virus," Soleta said, comprehending.

"That's right," said Riker. "He's going to take over the data base of every computer in the Federation, just as easily as he took over ours. Every homeworld, every colony, every starship, everything in the shared computer environment. Once he's 'in,' he's going to program the replicators to produce this virus of his."

"But replicators can't create living things," said Shelby. "Aren't viruses partly alive?"

"Partly, yes. But there are ways around it," Soleta said. "I can think of several."

"So can I," said Riker, "And either it'll put the virus right into the food, or the clothing, or he might just pump it right into the air. We should consider ourselves damn lucky that he didn't decide to try and replicate the virus aboard the ship or we'd all be goners."

"We can probably thank the Romulans for that, ironically enough," Soleta said. "I know them, I know how they think. We did them some serious damage. They probably wanted to beam aboard first and obtain some personal vengeance for the ships of theirs that we destroyed. Once done with that, they likely would have started pumping their virus throughout the ship after they left . . ." Her voice trailed off.

All eyes turned toward Burgoyne. But s/he shook hir head quickly. "No. No, nothing like that's been done. We got out of the area fast enough to avoid any such stunts."

"But we might be carrying something within the computer base . . ."

"No, that's the problem. We're not carrying anything in the computer base. When they got into our mainframe, they wound up erasing all the data. Everything. This ship is a damnable blank slate. All of the fundamental material and information needed for its running is gone."

"Gone? Completely?"

"Information is never gone completely from a computer, Captain. It's there somewhere. But when it's wiped clean, what basically happens is that we can't get at it. I'll find a way . . . but it'll take time."

"How much time?"

"I don't know," s/he admitted. "I have all my people working on it, but I simply do not know. And that's not all."

"What, it gets better?"

"That's an understatement. Our preliminary probes reveal imprints of mental engrams left behind, like fingerprints. This wasn't simply a virus or a machine wipe. A mind . . . an actual mind . . . entered the computer and nearly wiped it, and us, from existence."

"The Narobi. It has to be," said Si Cwan.

"Perfect. So what have we got?" asked Riker. "In terms of capabilities, I mean."

"Minimal, being routed through manual control. We've got life support systems on line. Warp drive is up, as you know, which is how we managed to throw ourselves to . . . wherever the hell it is that we are."

"Have we got coordinates as to our present location?" asked Riker.

Shelby nodded. "McHenry says he knows where we are. I have no reason to doubt him."

"We jumped blind through warp space and he knows where we came out?"

She nodded again. "He's rather talented that way."

"So I hear. All right: Life support, warp drive . . . what about communications?"

"Not yet," said Burgoyne. "Besides, even if we did have communications up and running and could get through to the Federation . . . what would we say? '*Excalibur* to UFP: Shut

221

down everything throughout the entire Federation. We're celebrating the bicentennial by reverting to the Stone Age. Cease and desist in your entire way of life until you hear from us again. And by the way, we have no proof.' Oh, that's going to go over very well, I can assure you. They'd probably shunt the message over into a committee which would debate about it for three weeks before resolving to tell us that we're idiots."

"You've made your point, Burgoyne," Riker said. "Is anything else functioning around here."

"Manual guidance control just came back on, and we've got the viewscreens up and running. Basically, we can move, at warp speed if we need to. But navigation is still off-line. It would be like trying to steer in the dark while blindfolded. It's impossible. Besides, we have no idea where we would go anyway."

"Yes. We do," Soleta said. "That was the one other piece of information I . . . we," she amended with a glance toward Selar, " . . . managed to get out of Sela. The coordinates of where Gerrid Thul is."

"But as Burgoyne said, trying to plot, to navigate without the computers . . . unless these coordinates are practically next door, it's just not possible," Riker said.

"I wouldn't be so quick to say that," Shelby told him. "I suggest we run it past McHenry."

"Are you sure?" he asked.

She smiled thinly. "Trust me."

"All right," he nodded slowly. "I don't see that we have much of a choice. Let's do it, people."

As they cleared out of the conference lounge, Soleta found herself momentarily alone with Selar. She moved toward her and said, "Doctor . . ."

But Selar shook her head. "Lieutenant . . . do not."

"I was just . . ."

"Going to thank me?"

"Yes."

"Do not," she said again. "I do not wish to be thanked. You have done me service in the past. I found that I could not turn away from you when you were in need. But I compromised myself . . . my sense of ethics . . . my very morality. I did harm, Lieutenant."

"For the greater good, Doctor. That should make it easier."

"It should. I agree. But . . . it does not. If you will excuse me," and she walked out of the conference room.

Mark McHenry stared out at the stars. So many. So many of them. Riker stood behind him on the bridge, as did Shelby. "They are gorgeous, you know," McHenry said softly. "I see them in my head last thing before I go to sleep . . . and first thing when I wake up. I know them. Know them all."

"And you know where we are in relation to them right now?"

"Yes, sir."

"And these coordinates that Soleta has given you . . . you know where those are, as well?"

"Yes, sir."

Riker found it hard to believe. He had been treading the spaceways for over half his life, but like virtually everyone else he knew, he required starcharts, computer-generated readouts, and whatever else could be provided for the purpose of making his way around the vastness of space. To just . . . *know* . . . to be able to look out into the galaxy and have that clear an idea in one's head of exactly where one was . . . it was astounding.

"And you can get us there?" Riker said.

McHenry closed his eyes a moment. It seemed as if he'd gone to sleep. Riker started to say something, but Shelby touched him gently on the arm and shook her head. Then McHenry opened his eyes once more and said, "Yes, sir. Not a problem."

"All right, then. Lay in a course—" His voice trailed off, and he corrected himself, because it was impossible to plot a course. All the steering would have to be done manually. "Take us out, Mr. McHenry. Warp factor . . ." He hesitated and then shrugged. "Whatever you feel comfortable moving at. And let's hope to hell that Burgoyne has the weapons on line by the time we get there."

"Aye, sir. May I ask a question, sir?" he inquired as he urged the ship forward.

"Absolutely."

"What's going on? I mean, I can get us there, but it's not without risks. Without navigation on line, it's going to be a bit trickier avoiding, oh . . . black holes, asteroid fields and the like. I can do it, mind you . . . but it's trickier. The smart thing to do would be to remain where we were until everything is back up and running. So what's the rush? What are we trying to do?"

"Fair enough." He glanced around the bridge and said, with sufficient graveness of tone to put across the gravity of the situation, "A deadly virus is threatening to wipe out the lives of everyone we hold dear . . . and only the good ship *Excalibur* has a hope of stopping it. Does that answer it?"

"Yes, sir."

"You're frowning, Lieutenant. I hope you're not feeling daunted."

"No, sir," said McHenry. "Just the strangest feeling of déjà vu, that's all. Don't worry. It'll be gone soon enough."

XIX.

CALHOUN HAD BEEN in his quarters for all of two minutes when Kwint showed up at the door. He entered without a word and they faced each other as the door slid closed.

"Are you out of your mind!" Calhoun fairly exploded the moment they were in private. "What the hell are you doing here? You almost gave me a heart attack!"

"Calm down, Mac," Picard said stiffly. "Having apoplexy is not going to help the situation."

"That's putting it mildly! It was everything I could do not to react when I saw you! Why are you here? With the hair? And the beard? And Darg?"

"I was sent in by Jellico . . ."

"Jellico? But he was working with Nechayev! He helped stage an entire confrontation at the big diplomatic reception to make it seem as if I was storming out of Starfleet! It's how we got Thul's attention!"

"So it would seem. I was unaware of that. Jellico called me in, summarized the situation for me, and sent me on a mission to get in good with Zolon Darg. He chose me because Jack Crusher and I had dealings in the past with Thul. Jellico had heard the rumors that Thul was involved and wanted to make certain, one way or the other."

"But if he knew about—" Then Calhoun actually half-smiled to himself. "He didn't trust me. He didn't trust me not to screw things up. So he sent you in as back-up, without telling Nechayev or me."

"Charming," said Picard.

"And this disguise," and he tugged slightly at the beard, "was supposed to fool him? It didn't fool me."

"First, you've seen me far more recently than Thul. He hasn't laid eyes on me for a good many years, and Darg has never met me. Second, you're Xenexian. You have a heightened sensitivity to such things. Besides, I didn't know for sure that I would wind up face to face with Thul. In any event, he hasn't recognized me, nor has Darg. So we're safe enough . . . for the moment. We have to stay steady, though . . ."

"That was easy until this got personal," said Calhoun, tightly.

Picard looked at him in confusion. "What do you mean?"

"Lodec . . . the Danteri that you saw . . . ?"

"Yes? What about him?"

"He killed my father."

Picard's eyes widened in concern. "Are you certain?"

"Absolutely. Absolutely positive." He paced the room like a caged tiger. "The longer this goes on, the more I think of my father crying out . . . think of what he did . . . Picard . . . there's so many people here now. It could be covered."

"What could be covered?"

"I could kill him, make it seem as if it was a random act of violence. There's enough disreputable individuals that the suspicion wouldn't fall on me, and—"

"Mac," and Picard grasped him by the shoulders, "you can't lose focus. Letting feelings get in the way is not a luxury we can afford."

"Laying my father's soul to rest is not a luxury, Picard. It's a mandate. It has to be done."

"Not here! Not now!" Picard said harshly. "If you do anything to jeopardize the mission we're on now, Mac, just out of a personal sense of vengeance, I will . . ."

"You will what? Have me busted in rank? Slap my wrist? Give me ten lashes? Do you think I seriously give a damn what happens to me?"

"Probably not. But I would hope you give a damn what happens to everyone else. Mac . . . I appreciate your anger and your frustration. But you simply cannot indulge in those feelings at the moment. It could be ruinous for everyone and everything. We have to determine what Thul is up to and stop him. The Mackenzie Calhoun I know wouldn't elevate his need for vengeance over the needs of those who are depending upon him."

"Maybe you don't know Mackenzie Calhoun, then."

"Maybe I don't. But the brutal, simple truth, Mac, is that killing Lodec won't bring your father back. . . . and it could result in the death of many more. Are you prepared to take that chance? Or are you going to do what's right?"

"And who knows what's right, Picard. You?"

"Not always. But in this instance . . . yes."

Slowly, Calhoun sat. He rubbed the lower half of his face in thought, and finally said, "All right. For now . . . for now I do nothing against Lodec. But I'll tell you something, Picard . . . I never thought that doing nothing would be a hundred times more difficult than doing something. Do you have any idea what it's like, Picard? That there's someone you hate so much . . . that with every fibre of your being, all you want to do is hold their head in one hand, their neck in another, and with one quick movement, break it?"

For a moment, Picard saw the skinless, gleaming skull and spine of the Borg queen in his hands, and the cathartic cleansing that came with that glorious snap.

"Believe it or not . . . I do," said Picard.

The summons had come.

Everyone had been informed that they were to come to the grand hall, and come they did. The lifts were operating at peak capacity throughout the sphere as the entire populace converged on the main meeting area.

There had been those who had doubted. Even though they had shown up with the one hundred thousand bars of latinum as promised, still there had been doubts and discord. But the revelation of the sphere's existence, in and of itself, was enough to quell their initial concerns. They knew, beyond question, that they were now part of something special, something incredibly significant in the entire history of the galaxy. There were still questions, still worries, but there was also enough faith that Gerrid Thul actually had a plan. That he knew what he was doing.

And now they were going to find out. All their questions were to be finally, ultimately, answered.

Calhoun and Picard had resolved that going together would not be the brightest move. There was no intrinsic reason for them to be especially friendly with one another, and so it was advisable that they keep their distance, at least until such time as it was unavoidable. So Calhoun headed toward the turbolift on his own upon receiving word of the summons. He stepped into the lift, and froze.

Lodec was standing there. It was just the two of them.

Calhoun couldn't believe it. What was this, some sort of perverse joke that the cosmos was playing on him? He forced a smile as he stepped onto the lift and the doors shut behind him.

"Impressive set-up, isn't it," Lodec said after a moment.

Calhoun managed a nod. He pictured himself with his sword in his hand, plunging it into Lodec's heart. It gave him a minuscule amount of satisfaction, but not much.

And then Lodec said, "I'm sorry."

"Sorry." Calhoun repeated the word tonelessly. "Sorry . . . for what?"

"You were right. My saying that I was simply following orders . . . that was just an excuse. A nice, tidy way of shirking my responsibility. The things that we did . . ." He shook his head. "Inside . . . I was screaming. Screaming. But Falkar—that's who I was connected to—Falkar was the liege-lord of our family. Our patron, as he was to a number of us. So when he selected me to serve him, I had no choice. At least, that's what I told myself. My family sent me off to war, and I'll never forget my father looking at me so sternly, giving me the admonition, 'Don't dishonor us, son. Don't dishonor us.' And me, young and foolish . . . I would have done anything to make my father proud. Do you know what that's like?"

"No," Calhoun said hollowly.

"Oh. Well . . . that's all I cared about. Pleasing him, pleasing my family. But I hated every moment of it. It got so bad . . . there was a time there where we were posted to Xenex, and I thought of leaving the camp and walking into the nearest Xenexian town and picking a fight, and then allowing myself to be killed. That way . . . that way it would have been over. I didn't have the nerve, though. I didn't want to throw my life away because part of me kept saying, 'Stay steady. Things will get better. You won't have to live this way forever.' Except the problem is . . . even when you're not living it . . . it stays with you for as long as you live. The things we did," he said again, shaking his head, looking lost. "The helpless people we killed . . . the beatings . . . lord . . . they put me in charge of whippings, can you believe that?"

"Indeed. Why you?" Calhoun's voice was strangled. But he saw that Lodec was so far in his recollections that he wasn't noticing.

"I'd practiced with whips ever since I was a kid. To me, it wasn't a weapon. It was a tool of skill. I could knock over a particular rock from thirty paces without disturbing anything around it. Falkar saw me showing off one day, and on the spot, stated that I was his new whip master. He had me beat people . . . the screams . . . the blood . . ."

"Beat them to death, did you?"

"Sometimes," he whispered. "Sometimes, yes. I'd be there, torturing the poor devils, and in my head I was taking myself away, somewhere far away . . ."

"What are you telling me this for?" demanded Calhoun abruptly. "What do you want from me? Absolution? You want me to tell you that it's okay, you're forgiven?"

"Perhaps. You were their warlord. If you said you understood . . . if you . . ." Then he saw the look in Calhoun's hard purple eyes. "No. No, I suppose not. My apologies. It was foolish of me even to try."

The door slid open and he walked out, leaving Calhoun drained in the turbolift, his hands shaking.

The viewscreen was massive, and on it, everyone could see the celebration of the bicentennial well under way. It was in the great plaza of the United Federation Headquarters, and it was a wonder to behold. a veritable sea of races and faces, smiling or doing whatever their respective physicality allowed them to do when it came to expressing pleasure. Calhoun even fancied that he could make out Jellico's face somewhere in all that hubbub.

Gerrid Thul was standing upon a raised platform, looking down at the assemblage that he had gathered. He looked stronger, more vital than he had before. "Thank you, my friends," he said. "Thank you for coming. Thank you for . . . believing. For many months now, you have heard the whispers . . . you have had revealed to you, in small amounts, the truth of the time to come. And you see there, now, on this screen, on the planet earth, the United Federation of Planets celebrating its own birth. As it so happens, we shall be celebrating as well. We shall be celebrating . . . its demise.

"It is ironic somehow that we are witnessing a celebration on earth. Earth has many interesting and intriguing end-of-the-world myths from its many cultures. The details differ, but the outcome remains the same: The old is washed away, while the new rises to take its rightful place.

"The time has come for a new cleansing. The Federation has become too huge, too insensitive, interested only in maintaining its own existence and status quo rather than attending to the true needs of various sentient beings. There is too much need for commonality, and there is a loss of individual identity. You see on that screen a dazzling array of species . . . but as year upon year has gone by, they have slowly lost that which made them unique, special. The Federation must pay for that loss. And the Federation must, and shall, pay for the disservice that it has done to you. You, the outcasts, who for whatever reason, do not fit in with the Federation's grand scheme of the way things should be. Rejoice, my friends, for the days of your living in a galaxy that attends to the Federation's beck and call are soon over."

Thul gestured to his right, indicating that someone should join him on the podium. In the meantime, Calhoun looked around, trying to catch a glimpse of either Picard or Vara Syndra or, most particularly, Zolon Darg. Darg was the only one he managed to spot, but that wasn't too surprising. With his bulk, he towered above everyone around him. Picard might have been standing right next to him, but thanks to the crowd, Calhoun couldn't possibly see him.

A rather unassuming human was now standing next to Thul

on the podium. "This . . . is Doctor David Kendrow, one of the premier computer scientists in the quadrant. Wave to the good people, Kendrow." Kendrow obediently waved. He seemed none too thrilled to be there. "Doctor Kendrow," continued Thul, "has been instrumental in aiding us. He has helped us to coordinate an astounding amount of information about artificial intelligence. His greatest aid has come in helping us to understand a remarkably advanced computer called the Omega 9 . . . a computer which sets new advances in the art of interfacing with existing mainframes. Working in tandem with the Omega 9, assorted other research, and dissident residents of a world called Narobi II, we are going to accomplish what no one else in the history of the Federation has managed to do: We are going to connect, at one time, with every computer mainframe through the entire UFP.

"The very commonality which has made the UFP into such a tightly-knit organization is going to be used against it. But we are not simply going to use the Omega 9 to destroy the computers, oh no. Far from it. You see, the computers are tied in with, and control, food replicators which are common technology on all the member planets. The Omega 9 is going to cause all the computers to replicate a virus which I call the Double Helix, which I have spent years perfecting. Now . . . replicators are limited. They cannot create something that is alive. They can, however, create a string of chemicals which will replicate the disease, and as the disease is introduced into the food or textiles that the replicators generate, that—I assure you—will be more than sufficient.

"But that is too slow. Oh yes . . . too slow, my friends, and too inefficient. So what will, in fact, happen, is that at the precise same moment, all replicators everywhere will go active, and a gas will be issued by them. That gas will contain the Double Helix virus, and will spread as an airborne menace in no time at all, over every single planet.

"The Federation representatives are scheduled to re-enact the signing of the charter. That will be the moment when the virus will be released on all the Federation worlds simultaneously via the replicators. It will be galaxy-wide, and the entire Federation will be obliterated in one stroke. Those worlds which are not part of the Federation will naturally survive . . . as will anyone who is safe within the Thul sphere." He smiled out at the crowd, spreading his arms wide. "And that will be that. In one grand, glorious stroke, the entire United Federation of Planets will become a thing of the past!"

A huge buzz of conversation had been building and building as Thul had continued, and when he stopped and waited for a reaction, he very much got one. There was a gigantic cheer, a roar of approval so loud that Calhoun thought he was going to go deaf. The applause and huzzahs seemed to go on forever, and when it finally did subside, it was only at Gerrid Thul's urging as he clearly had more to say.

Calhoun, in the meantime, was endeavoring to drift toward the back of the room. He had no problem making sure that no one was watching him; every eye in the place was rivetted on Thul. He tapped the inside of his left heel, and the long-range communicator slid smoothly out of the heel and into his palm.

Thul started to speak again. His voice was amplified, and it was so loud that Calhoun knew he was going to have trouble getting anyone to hear him.

"Yes, my friends. The Federation has become weak," said Thul. "The Federation has become stupid. And the most insulting of all . . . the Federation thinks that we, ourselves, are so stupid, that we will easily be fooled by whatever pathetic plan they might come up with. See for yourself the pathetic spy that they have sent into our midst."

Calhoun's head snapped around . . . and he saw himself. To be precise, he saw his face on the gigantic screen behind Thul, having replaced the image of the UFP celebration. There he was, right in the midst of the crowd, palming the device that he was about to speak into.

Those who were standing around him naturally recognized him immediately and lunged toward him. Calhoun tried to fight his way out, but it was hopeless before he even began. Innumerable hands surrounded him, shoving him toward the floor, and the communicator flew out of his hand. It skidded to a halt several feet away and he could see it, just out of his reach.

And then it was trampled, simply crushed beneath the stampede that was converging on the spy who had been named by Gerrid Thul.

Calhoun was hauled to his feet, still struggling. Even as he did, though, he knew that it was futile. It was almost more out of misplaced pride than anything else, because in point of fact, he didn't stand a chance.

"Up here, my friends! Bring him up here!"

They shoved Calhoun forward, laughing and shouting, and within moments he had been thrown at the feet of Gerrid Thul. He started to get to his feet, and then an immense foot came down on his back. He knew who it was immediately, even as his spine creaked under the weight.

"Zolon Darg," Thul said conversationally to Calhoun, "has been asking for this opportunity."

"I'm not a spy—" Calhoun began. Then he couldn't get another word out as Darg increased the pressure, chortling as he did so.

"It is possible," Thul allowed. "On the other hand, that is merely a possibility . . . whereas I consider your being a spy to fall far more into the realm of likelihood. Darg . . . do as you like."

"As I like?" Darg said, and made as if to slam his foot completely through Calhoun's torso. Then he paused and said, "No. Why should I keep the fun to myself? You know . . . there are many things I can do with you, Calhoun, after you're dead. So why not give others the opportunity to actually escort you to the other side." He pulled his blaster from his holster and called out, "Kwint!"

Kwint appeared at his side, his face one big sneer. "Yes, sir?"

"Here," and he handed the blaster to Kwint. "Execute him."

Calhoun, very carefully and very deliberately, did not look up at the disguised Picard. To do so would have come across as pleading, and that was not something he could risk. Calhoun was done for, he knew that. But if Picard foolishly attempted to save him, they would both be finished. One of them had to complete the task. And if Calhoun was going to be the one to fall, then so be it.

He just prayed Picard wouldn't be so foolhardy as to try some insane rescue ploy. Surely Picard had to know that it was hopeless, that Calhoun had to be sacrificed. That was simply the way it had played out. No offense, no foul, see you next lifetime.

In a way, it was almost a relief. At that point, Calhoun had absolutely no idea what to do about Lodec. At least dying first would resolve that quandary.

He had always understood that, when one is about to die, one's life flashes before one's eyes. He waited for that to happen.

There was no flash. There was no life.

This made him edgy, as it seemed to indicate that he wasn't about to die. If that were the case, then it was most unfortunate because that meant—

"*Nobody move!*" shouted Picard.

"Oh, hell," muttered Calhoun.

Picard considered, for a moment that was in fact brief but, to him, seemed endless, the option of shooting Calhoun. There didn't seem to be any other options being presented to him.

His finger even started to squeeze the trigger . . . and that was when Picard knew that he simply couldn't do it. If one was dealing with sheer numbers—the death of one man, Calhoun, versus the potential death of trillions of beings—obviously there was no choice. But Picard refused to accept that it was that simple. There had to be other choices.

Moving with surprising speed, Picard vaulted the distance between himself and Thul and put the blaster straight at Gerrid Thul's head. Darg didn't budge. Neither did Thul. The crowd started to converge, to surge forward, and Picard called out, "Tell them to back off! We're going!"

"Are you?" Darg asked calmly. "And if you're prevented from doing so . . . ?"

"Then Gerrid Thul dies," Picard said firmly. "I'll kill him . . ."

"As you killed my son?" Gerrid Thul asked.

The words froze Picard. Did Thul actually know him? What was that possible? But if he did, then that meant—

"Go ahead," Darg was saying. "Shoot. See if I care."

That more or less clinched it for Picard. He looked down at the energy indicator on the blaster he was holding, but was reasonably certain about what he was going to find.

It read "empty." The blaster was completely out of power.

Picard looked up and saw that he was ringed by half a dozen blasters, all aimed squarely at him.

"Now these," Darg said conversationally, "all work."

Slowly Picard put up his hands, knowing there was no choice. He was grabbed from all sides, and he saw Calhoun being hauled to his feet as well.

"I never trusted you for a moment, 'Kwint,' " Darg told him. "So I had a DNA check run on you from scrapings taken off a glass at Kara's. By the time we arrived here, Gerrid Thul was already quite aware that the man who killed his son was going to be making a return visit."

"I was not responsible for the death of your son, and you know it," Picard said to Thul.

"You can believe that, if it pleases you to do so," Thul said. "I, however, know otherwise. Darg . . . take them away. Put them in lock-up."

"What? Why? I'll just kill them . . ."

"You'll do no such thing," Thul admonished him. 'I want them in lock-up, with a screen that broadcasts the Federation ceremonies. I want them to witness their Federation's fall. I think . . ." and he smiled broadly, "I think my son would have liked it that way."

XX.

"WHAT DID YOU EXPECT me to do?" demanded Picard.

From within their cell, Calhoun glowered at him. "I expected you to pull the damned trigger, that's what I expected you to do."

"And kill you in cold blood."

"If it meant preserving the mission, yes."

Just outside the cell, two guards were visible through the force field that was blocking the door. They appeared to be smirking as the two captains disagreed rather vocally about the direction that Picard should have followed in the given situation.

Calhoun was sitting disconsolately on one of the hard benches that constituted the entirety of the furniture in the cramped cell, while Picard was standing and facing him. "So you expected me to shoot you down?"

"Absolutely," said Calhoun. "I knew there were hazards to this mission . . ."

"For God's sake, Mac, there are hazards to any mission. But this was . . ." He paused and then said, "If the situation were reversed, would you have shot me."

"With the safety of the entire Federation on the line?"

"Yes."

Without hesitation, Calhoun said, "In a heartbeat."

They stared at each other for a long moment, and then Picard said softly, "And if it were Shelby?"

Calhoun looked away. "This is a stupid discussion. It's all moot anyway. The game was up before they even handed you the blaster."

"True."

"So . . ." Calhoun slapped his thighs and stood. Then he walked over to the forcefield that barred the way and he stroked his chin thoughtfully. The guards outside watched him through narrowed eyes. "Here's what we have to do. We have to get out of here, destroy their computer system, take down Gerrid Thul and Zolon Darg, and do it all before they have the signing ceremony back on earth that's going to signal the beginning of the end."

The guards clearly thought this to be a hilarious proposition. They laughed out loud as Calhoun stared at them. "Is something funny?" he asked quietly.

"No, nothing at all," said one of the guards. "We'd be most interested in seeing you get out of here. Wouldn't we, Benz?" he said to the other.

"Absolutely, Zeen," said Benz.

"I just need to warn you," Calhoun said calmly, "that if I do get out of here, the first thing I'm going to have to do is kill the both of you. Nothing else to be done for it, I'm afraid. I can't take the chance of either of you recovering and sounding an alarm prematurely."

"Oh, we understand that perfectly. We won't hold it against you. How are you going to kill us, by the way? Weapons scan revealed no weapons on you."

"I'll just have to do it with my bare hands."

"Very well. You go right ahead," grinned Zeen.

"You're sure you won't be upset?"

"Not at all. We understand you have a difficult job to do. Far be it from us to resent you for it."

"That's very kind of you. Activate transporter, right."

The grin remained on their faces for another moment or two . . . and then, to their shock, Calhoun vanished in a burst of molecular rearrangement.

"What the hell!" the one called Benz roared.

They were both facing the cell when Calhoun rematerialized directly behind them. They spun, faced him.

Benz was closer. Calhoun's right hand speared out, nailed Benz in the throat, crushing his windpipe. It was effectively over for him at that moment as he collapsed to the floor, unable to breathe.

Opening his mouth to shout out a warning, Zeen brought up his weapon at the same time. Calhoun didn't even slow down. Moving with incredible calm, he grabbed Zeen's gun, angled it backward and fired. The blast struck the forcefield, ricocheted, and hit Zeen in the back. Zeen's eyes went wide as his spine sizzled, but he didn't feel the pain for long as Calhoun grabbed either side of his head and twisted with brisk efficiency to the right. Zeen's neck broke with remarkable ease and he sagged to the floor.

As he fell, Calhoun pulled the gun from his lifeless fingers and glanced down at Benz, gasping on the floor, unable to draw in air. Calhoun fired off a quick shot into his head and Benz stopped thrashing about.

From the moment he'd reappeared outside the cell to the moment that the guards were dead, the entire incident had taken no more than four seconds.

Calhoun shoved the blaster into his belt, picked up Benz's, which he'd never even had the chance to pull out, and then tapped the controls deactivating the cell forcefield. Picard stepped out and looked down in astonished horror at the unmoving guards . . . and then up at the cold purple eyes of Calhoun.

"Let me guess," he said coolly to Picard. "You wouldn't have done it."

"I would have found another way, yes."

"I guess you're not a savage, then."

There was an element of pity in Picard's eyes that Calhoun found most annoying, "I guess not."

He handed one of the blasters to Picard. "That's too bad. It's a savage galaxy. Let's go."

Suddenly they heard a footfall behind them, someone else coming down the corridor. Calhoun spun, levelling his weapon and fully prepared to annihilate almost anyone who appeared around the corner.

Vara Syndra, however, fell into the "almost anyone" category, and so it was that when she came into view, she did not immediately die. Instead she looked at the fallen bodies, and up at Calhoun, with a remarkable lack of surprise.

"I should have known," she said, and for some reason her voice sounded different. Less airy, less seductive, more hardened. "I show up to free you, and you're already out."

"Free us? Why?" demanded Picard.

"Because I owe him," she said, indicating Calhoun, "and I always pay my debts."

"You don't owe me anything," Calhoun said. "I mean, granted, it was good, I thought, but—"

"This isn't about sex, you idiot!" she said in exasperation. "Don't you know anything? Don't you—?"

And then, from behind Vara, came three guards. Like the fallen ones, they were Thallonians. Unlike the fallen ones, they had their weapons up and they were ready to start firing. Picard and Calhoun had their blasters up, but Vara was squarely in the way.

"Hold on a moment," she sighed, and then she spun and she was holding a knife in either hand. Before the guards were even aware they were under attack from her, they were already dead. A thick pool of blood began to spread from their fallen bodies as they lay on the floor, one piled atop another, dark liquid pouring from the vital arteries that Vara had effortlessly cut.

Vara grinned. There was nothing seductive about her. The woman who had been radiating sex not so long ago had changed into something completely different. Feral, wild, brutal and—

And Calhoun laughed.

"What," Picard asked him stiffly, "is so damned funny?"

"She knows what's so funny," said Calhoun. "Don't you, Vandelia."

"It took you long enough, you Xenexian jerk," said Vandelia of Orion.

In the main computer lab, Kendrow studied the final link-ups very carefully. The last thing he wanted at this point was for something to go wrong, because he knew all too well that any sort of failure at this point would be the end of him.

He kept glancing, equally nervous, at the Narobi who was standing nearby. His name, loosely translated, was simply Silver, which was his color. He had another designation which was used to distinguish him from other Narobi, but since there were none others around at that point, he had seen no need for its use. When it had been made clear to him that human interaction almost required that he be called *something,* he had chosen simply "Silver" and recommended that that be the end of it.

Silver was the leader of the dissidents of Narobi. Normally a peaceful people, it had been Silver who had felt most strongly that they were capable of so much more than simple peace, and he had been more than accommodating when he had been approaching by Gerrid Thul. Silver, like all his people, was tall and glistening and almost entirely machine. There were some small elements of the mortal left within him. Those were doubtlessly the ones that made him dissatisfied with the Narobi philosophy of peace.

When he spoke, his lips did not move, for the simple reason that he had none. No mouth, for standard food was not a requirement; he was solar powered. No nose, for of what interest was scent. He did, however, have eyes, not so much for sight as it was that the Narobi had discovered other races like to have eyes they could look into when they were talking.

Standing nearby, observing the final preparations, were Gerrid Thul and Zolon Darg. "Everything will be ready, will it not, Kendrow?" asked Thul in that silky voice he had that was half pleasantry, half warning.

"Yes, sir."

"Good, Quite good. We wouldn't want anything to go wrong, would we?"

"Definitely not, sir."

There was an observation window in the computer center that opened up onto the grand square. The screen was up and running, once again focused upon the events at the Federation gathering. Many of Thul's followers who had gathered there were still there, watching the drama unfold that was going to spell the end of the Federation. Thul smiled down at them. His people. His followers. He very much liked the sound of that. And Mendan Abbis would have liked the sound of it, too. The thoughts of his son momentarily saddened him, and he pushed them away. Now was not the time for distractions.

"Darg . . ." he glanced around. "Have you seen Vara? She seems to have disappeared."

"No, sir. I have not."

"See if you can find—"

And suddenly there was a *breep* that came over Darg's comm unit. "Yes. Go ahead," he said brusquely into it.

"Sir! The prisoners are out! We found the cell deactivated! Five guards down!"

Darg looked at Thul in a most accusing, "told you so" manner. "Alert the security force. But do it quietly. We don't need alarm bells howling, getting everyone upset and also letting the prisoners know that we know they're out. I'll be right there." Then he stabbed an angry finger at Thul. "I told you this would happen! I told you I should have killed them immediately!"

"I simply have endless confidence in you, Darg, that you'll be able to handle them. In fact, you should thank me. You see . . . you made a muddle of attending to Calhoun last time you faced him. If I hadn't found you and . . . attended to you . . . you'd be long dead by now. So I'm generously giving you an opportunity to get it right this time. Do not disappoint me, or yourself."

With an irritated growl, Darg headed out. Thul, meantime, turned back to Kendrow and said calmly, "Don't slow in your preparations, Kendrow. Timing, after all, is everything."

At the site of the great Federation assemblage, Admiral Nechayev, in full formal dress, felt a tap on her shoulder. She turned and saw Admiral Jellico behind her, with his customary polite-but-pained expression. "Greetings, Admiral," he said. "I don't usually see you at such functions, particularly at such crowded ones."

"I know that, Admiral. But even an office-bound old thing like me likes to get out every now and then. Mingle. That sort of thing."

"So," and he folded his arms, "your boy Calhoun staged quite an exit, didn't he, Alynna?"

"You cooperated admirably, Eddie."

"Cooperated? He hit me! In the head!"

"He was simply improvising."

"In the *head*," repeated Jellico.

"Oh, well, Eddie, it's not as if you were using it for anything."

"You're a riot, Alynna. We were supposed to stage an argument. Not get physical."

A slightly tipsy Tellarite bumped into her. He grunted an apology and moved on. She shook her head in annoyance, although she was more irritated with Jellico than the Tellarite. "And how convincing do you think it would have been if you threatened to throw him out of Starfleet after a simple argument. I don't blame Mac for slugging you. It all serves a higher purpose, Eddie, just remember that."

"So you say." He looked around. "Except I don't see him here. In fact, I don't see any danger of anything at the moment."

"That's why he's involved, Eddie. To attend to whatever it is we don't see."

"And maybe he's not needed. Maybe there are others who are attending to it just fine."

She looked at him askance. "What is that supposed to mean?"

"Nothing." He smiled enigmatically. "Not a thing."

Rolling her eyes, she said, "Fine, Eddie. Whatever you say. It means nothing. Oh," and she pointed toward the front of the room. "They're starting."

"Starting what?"

"The re-enactment of the Resolution of Non-interference. Come along, Eddie. We're about to see history."

XXI.

ALL THOSE YEARS AGO, even after Calhoun had freed her, Vandelia had lived in fear of Darg. For she had heard rumors that Darg had somehow survived the destruction of his headquarters. That he was back in the business, building up his strength, making his connections once more. That he was more powerful and nastier than ever. And that he had never, ever, given up the notion of tracking down Vandelia and the mysterious man who had freed her, and making them both pay. On at least two occasions, Vandelia had narrowly missed him, arriving at a performing spot mere days after Darg had been there.

Vandelia was a brave and fierce woman, as was typical of Orions. But even she had her breaking point. Night after night she would lie awake, listening, wondering whether this would be the night that Darg tracked her down. She had no interest in facing him and teaching him one final lesson, nor did she desire to track him down first so she could put an end to him. For Vandelia had had the most uncanny feeling that she had gotten off quite luckily the first time, and to encounter Darg again would be to tempt fate in a manner that would ultimately rebound to her detriment.

She saw only one way out . . . and she took it.

Vandelia disappeared . . . and Vara Syndra was born.

It had not been all that difficult, really. The changes were mostly cosmetic. She hadn't really been transformed into a Thallonian. Shaving her head, changing the pigmentation of her skin from green to red, all had been fairly simple. Her physicality, however, and the ability to give off waves of sex appeal in the same way that stars gave off light was another matter, however.

For that, she had turned to a supplier of all things exotic, questionable and, for the most part, illegal. His name had been Brace Carmel Mudd, and the first time that she had encountered him, she had felt unclean. Purported to be a "family business," it had been his name which she had heard bandied about most often when she'd made inquiries as to obtaining Venus drugs. She had managed to track him down and, for a healthy price (not to mention a substantial loss of her self-respect), had obtained the drugs.

The drugs had been around for nearly two centuries, and the core suppliers—whose real names were unknown to all but a handful, Mudd included—had spent much of that time perfecting them. In the old days, their effects had been fairly temporary, and the alterations they made relatively modest. They had simply enhanced those features that the users felt were their strongest. But it had been as much in the mind as in the body.

Not anymore. The Venus drugs of the modern era were far more sophisticated. They had put inches on Vandelia in all the right places, reconfigured her into an absolute sexual magnet. They had even altered the shape of her face, to the point where she was unrecognizable. Mudd had given her a ten-year supply and gone on his way, and Vandelia had used it extremely well. She had gone into Thallonian space, which on the surface of it seemed insane. It was, after all, the native territory of the one man she never wanted to encounter again. But she had decided to play the concept of hiding in plain sight to the hilt. If Darg was busy checking the far reaches of the galaxy for Vandelia, it would never occur to him to look in his own backyard. And even if he did, he wouldn't think at all about a sultry Thallonian woman who went by the name of Vara Syndra.

Everything had been going fine . . . until the drugs had run out prematurely. For Mudd, as it turned out, had not exactly dealt fairly with her. The ten-year supply was, in reality, half that, the rest of it simple colored gelatin. It meant that she had overpaid significantly. It also meant she was in tremendous danger.

It was around then that she had fallen in with Gerrid Thul. Thul had taken an immediate liking to her. He did not know her true name, or even that she was originally an Orion. What he did know, however, was where to obtain the Venus drugs which she now desperately needed as her supply of the real drugs was dwindling to nothing. It became an eminently workable arrangement. She became his full-time aide, generating her considerable sex appeal whenever he needed it, and he kept her in supply of the Venus drugs. It worked out rather nicely.

Nonetheless, she nearly panicked when Zolon Darg came on the scene.

At first she couldn't believe it was he when Thul "introduced" them, he had become so huge. Then she waited for some glimmer of recognition from him. She had steeled herself for this possibility for many years, but once it arrived, it was everything she could do not to run screaming from the room.

Darg grunted.

That was it. End of encounter. He grunted. Whenever he would see her in the future, it would always be the same terse acknowledgment of her. She couldn't believe how fortunate she had been; he had no idea who she was. In fact, at one point, he even asked her if she knew of an Orion dancer named Vandelia. It was all she could do not to scream the truth in his face to display her contempt for him. That, however, would not have been a wise move, since he would then have killed her in short order, so she managed to restrain herself.

"Vandelia? Never heard of her," she had said, wide-eyed, and he never inquired again.

He also never displayed any physical interest in her. For the first weeks after encountering him, she had dreaded the day that Gerrid Thul might tell her that she was required to "entertain" the formidable Zolon Darg. But it had never happened. He wasn't remotely drawn to her. She couldn't quite figure out whether she should be relieved or insulted. Ultimately she opted for the former.

Thus had her life gone, hiding in plain sight. Living the life of Vara Syndra, adored by more males than she had ever known. It was artificial, it was a shadow, but at least she was alive and enjoying herself.

But every so often she would think about her dancing . . . and also about the scarred man who had rescued her back when she was another person entirely . . . the scarred man who had, amazingly, not immediately succumbed to her charms as an Orion dancing girl, even though the pheromones that she generated (as did all of her kind) should have made her irresistible. She was sure, though, that the Venus drugs enhancing her pheromones would prove irresistible even to Calhoun.

She'd proven right.

She was, for some reason, a little disappointed . . .

Calhoun, Picard and Vandelia headed down the corridor as quickly as she could. "Down this way," she said. "We've got to get you out of here."

"We can't," Picard said. "We have to stop Thul's plan."

She was about to try and talk them out of it, and then she mentally shrugged. "Yes. You would have to, wouldn't you?" Calhoun was staring at her. "Well? Any questions, Mac?"

"No," he said after a moment's thought. "Shaved the head, retoned the skin, Venus drugs, hid in plain sight. Correct?"

She blinked back her astonishment and then said in the most bored tone she could muster, "Wrong. Completely wrong. Now come on."

"Where's the central computer room. He must be programming it from somewhere," said Picard.

"Up," she said. "It's up at the top level. Here," and she suddenly walked over to a computer station that was built into the wall. She tapped in an identification code and, moments later, a schematic of the sphere appeared on it. "Here it is," and she pointed out the location.

"Are there laboratory facilities?" asked Picard.

"Yes. Here. Two levels below the top. Why?"

"Because if we don't manage to stop the initial launch of the virus, and it does get loose, we need to know if there's some sort of cure for it," Picard said. "And if he was doing research on it—"

A blaster bolt struck the computer station and smashed it apart.

The three of them whirled, just in time to see a squadron of Thul's men charging toward them.

Picard and Calhoun immediately fell back, firing as they went, desperately trying to keep their pursuers off balance. Vandelia, who had lifted a blaster from one of the Thallonians who had tried to take them down earlier, was also firing. They picked off several of their pursuers, and the others ducked for cover. "Come on! This way!" shouted Picard, and they bolted down the corridor.

Blasts ricocheted off the walls around them as they ran. One of them struck an overhead pipe, and coolant blasted out, filling up the entire walkway with thick, white smoke. Vandelia took a deep breath of air before it became impossible to do so, and then she couldn't see anything. There were forms, shadows ahead of her, and she ran after them. She went around another corner, and then another.

And suddenly she was alone.

She looked around, tried to figure out where she had become separated from Calhoun and Picard. There were no sounds of pursuit; perhaps they had decided to go around another way, she must try to catch up with them. Even so, retracing her steps would not be the best idea. So she decided to keep going forward.

As she did, she mulled over the fact that she could easily have ducked out of the situation. She could have pretended that Calhoun and Picard had just now taken her hostage. The guards that she'd killed were dead, so they weren't going to talk. The Federation men would certainly have played along so that she wasn't at risk. She could have kept her life going . . .

Except it wasn't her life, not really. It was Vara Syndra's life, and she realized that she had grown rather tired of her. She missed the woman she was. She wanted Vandelia back. And this was the only way to recapture her.

She saw a figure ahead of her in the mist, turning and looking at her. "Mac!" she called. "Mac! Over here!"

The figure suddenly seemed to stand up, looming large in front of her. Zolon Darg emerged from the mist and looked at her as if seeing her for the very first time.

"Hello, Vandelia," he said.

Then he killed her.

XXII.

PICARD HAD ABSOLUTELY NO IDEA how he had become separated from Calhoun, but there was no time to worry about it at that point. What was of far greater concern were the men who were pursuing him.

He turned quickly, spotted an open lift, and charged toward it. He ducked, weaved, ran as fast as he could. A blast bolt singed his shoulder and he staggered, but he tumbled into the lift, losing his grip on his blaster as he did so. "Level 3A!" he called, which was how he had seen it demarcated on the schematic.

The doors slid closed . . . but just before they did, a Thallonian leaped the distance and fell into the lift car atop Picard. The car started up.

The Thallonian snarled into Picard's face, tried to bring his blaster up. Picard gripped his wrist and they struggled furiously as Picard tried to aim it away from himself. The blaster discharged, blasting through the clear backing of the lift that overlooked the dizzying interior of the sphere.

Picard and the Thallonian struggled to their feet, pushing and shoving against one another. The blaster went off again, ricocheting and striking a glancing blow against the Thallonian's heavily armored back. It wasn't sufficient to hurt him. It was, however, enough to knock both the Thallonian and Picard back and out the gaping hole in the back of the turbolift.

For a moment, there was nothing between Picard and a drop except air, and he was floating in the zero-g environment. Then he snagged the shattered exterior of the lift. It sliced up his hand fiercely, but it held firm.

The Thallonian was less fortunate. He tumbled away from the lift, but he did so in extreme slow motion. He tried to make it back to the lift, looking for all the world as if he were swimming in the air. But he simply drifted backward, faster and faster, heading toward the core of the sphere where the massive cloaking device was.

Picard knew immediately what was going to happen. When he hit the gravimetric center of the sphere, he was going to make a fairly significant splat. And if Picard didn't manage to haul himself back into safety, he was going to go the same way.

The slicing of his hand was excruciating—it was like massaging broken glass—but Picard had no choice. Setting his jaw determinedly, he dragged himself into the lift, fighting against the zero G which seemed so buoyant but was, in fact, so deadly. In a moment he was tumbled to the floor, and then looked up as the door opened on the level that he had requested.

He picked up the blaster that he had dropped on the floor of the turbolift and staggered out. His blood-covered palms made it difficult to grip the gun securely, but he had to do the best he could. He looked around desperately and saw signs pointing to the lab. How exceptionally convenient.

He followed them quickly, got to the lab, and just as he arrived, ran into another squadron of guards. They had their weapons out, he was ten feet short of the door to the lab, and they absolutely had him cold.

At that point, Mackenzie Calhoun ran by.

And another. And another still.

"Get him!" the lead attacker shouted, but they had no idea which "him" to get. "And him!" he added, and pointed at Picard.

Several of them indeed fired right at Picard, and he would have been dead if Calhoun had not thrown himself into the blaster's path. The shot took him down from the back, and Calhoun collapsed into Picard's arms.

"Mac!" Picard cried out.

At which point, Calhoun abruptly got to his feet and started running back the other way.

By then, everyone was so confused, that they totally missed it when Picard charged into the laboratory.

There were workers and people whom Picard presumed to be scientists within the lab. They were milling about in confusion, clearly concerned over the shots that they were hearing just outside. One of them, not realizing that Picard was the target of those shots, demanded, "What's going on out there? Are you people insane! We can't have blasts flying around here! We can't—"

Picard aimed his blaster squarely at the scientist's face. "You can't . . . what?"

He froze. They all did. When he spoke again, it was with a stammer. "We . . . there are dangerous chemicals . . . things here that can't . . . that mustn't . . ."

"Things such as the Double Helix virus?" Picard said, his blaster never wavering. His hands were throbbing. It was everything he could do to hold his weapon steady.

There were apprehensive nods from everyone in the room.

"And that means it would be very, very bad if something were to be broken . . . wouldn't it . . . because it might release something that you don't want released. . . ."

At which point, he swung his blaster around in a sweep of the room. He didn't fire . . . he just aimed. But when he was pointing to one corner in particular, that caused an alarmed jump by nearly everyone in the room.

A-ha, he thought as he crossed quickly. Several of the scientists made a move toward him, but he held them back with a glance that spoke volumes.

There were vials, samples lining the wall where he was standing. "Which one?" he demanded. "Which one is the Double Helix? And which one is the cure?"

"There is no cure!" one of the scientists said, and the others bobbed their heads in agreement.

It was too spontaneous a reply to be a falsehood. Picard's heart sank when he heard it, but then he reasoned that if the Federation got their hands on a pure sample of the virus, perhaps their researchers could find it. "A sample. a sample of the virus. I need it, now."

"But . . ."

"Now!"

They pointed to one of the tubes, and he snatched it up.

"No, that's the wrong one! It's not the standard virus . . . that one's highly concentrated!" one of them said. "Ten times more virulent! You—!"

Suddenly the pursuing guards burst in through the door, their weapons ready to blast holes into anything and everything.

Considering the inflammatory nature of the moment, Picard was remarkably calm. He simply held the vial up and said, coolly, "You would not like me to drop this?"

In spite of themselves, the guards cast a glance at the scientists. There were rapid and very anxious shakings of heads from all of them, verifying the notion that shooting at Picard at that moment in time would be an extremely bad idea.

Slowly Picard moved toward the door, holding the vial in front of him. "That's it. That's fine. Everyone stay right where they are," he said. "My hands are slippery enough with blood, you see. Wouldn't want me to be even more clumsy, would you? Now, clear the way." They didn't move. His voice dropped even lower, so low that one would have been inclined to check and see if he still had a pulse. "Clear . . . the . . . way," he said very slowly, very methodically, and very dangerously.

They cleared the way.

Calhoun had run to the upper levels and no one stopped him. He had done so through a rather crafty subterfuge that he was, in fact, rather proud of. He had circled around to where Vandelia had dispatched the group of guards, torn off a piece of cloth from one of them, soaked it in the widening pool of blood, and then held it up to the right side of his face. He then proceeded to run as fast as he could, using stairwells and ladders rather than the lifts which he felt would be watched more carefully. He kept the cloth pressed against his face.

The first time he encountered a squadron of guards, he said nothing, but simply pointed and gesticulated while groaning. What the guards saw was a man who had clearly been badly injured by the escaped prisoners who were somewhere behind him. They promptly ran right past Calhoun and, grinning to himself, he kept on going. It happened three more times as he made his way up the sphere, and each time played out in exactly the same manner.

The fourth time, while on the third level, it didn't work.

It worked at first as they started off down the hall. But then around the corner came Lodec, and he and Calhoun froze, face to face. Lodec wasn't fooled for a second, but for a moment—just a moment—doubt seemed to play across his face.

Calhoun brought his blaster up, operating completely on instinct, ready to shoot Lodec down. And he, likewise, hesitated for a moment.

And then Lodec shouted, "Calhoun! He's here!"

The guards, as one, turned and charged back.

Calhoun shoved his tongue against the replicator inside his mouth, and suddenly multiple versions of himself sprang into existence and started running in all directions. The guards were frozen in confusion, and when they did start opening fire, it was too late. As for the real Calhoun, he paused only long enough to swing a roundhouse punch that flattened Lodec. He hoped he had broken his jaw, and would have liked to do more, but it was all he had time for.

Just ahead of him, on the uppermost floor, was the computer room. He braced himself, holding his blaster firmly, and then he thrust himself in, coming in low, getting ready to fire . . .

There was no one there.

That wasn't entirely true, actually. Vandelia was there, her body tilted back on the chair, blood trickling from her mouth. Calhoun could see from across the room that she was dead. God knew he had seen it enough.

Even so, he didn't want to believe it was true. He approached her slowly, hoping against hope that somehow she would just get up, come back to life. That it was all some sort of a sick joke. Then he heard her voice, and she was whispering, "I wanted to dance . . . for just you . . . Mac . . . one more time . . ." And then her voice rattled in her throat.

And then she repeated it . . . and died again . . . and again . . .

He turned and saw Darg's image on the screen. He was smiling. It was not a pleasant expression.

"Those were her last words, Calhoun. I recorded them for

you. I knew you'd want to hear them. If you're hearing this . . . which I assume you are . . . I can further assume that you're in the main computer room. That's where you would naturally come to try and head off Thul's plan. That is naturally where we would be . . . if we didn't mind being easy targets for you. We're secured in another part of the station, I assure you, preparing for the great moment. I'm afraid there's nothing you can do to stop it. It would be most appreciated, however, if you would kindly . . . die."

At that moment, Calhoun had no idea where to go.

At that moment, Calhoun didn't care.

The door to the computer room slid open, as he knew it would. Darg was standing there, as he knew he would be. He was empty-handed, and he waggled his fingers toward Calhoun. Pressing in around him, from all sides, were armed guards. They had their weapons trained on Calhoun. The slightest move and they could easily blast him to free-floating atoms.

"If you drop the weapon . . . you have an opportunity at me . . . man to man. If you don't drop the weapon . . . my men drop you." He paused and then said softly, "Come on, Calhoun. You know you want it."

Calhoun allowed the blaster to drop from his fingers. At that moment, they could easily have killed him where he stood.

They didn't. Instead, they simply watched and grinned. Clearly they were all of the opinion that Darg was in absolutely no danger at all. But at that moment, Calhoun didn't give a damn what they thought. Instead he charged toward the far bigger man, building up speed with every moment, and he slammed into Darg with everything he had.

And bounced off.

His head spun around him as he hit the floor. He had no idea what had just happened. It had been like crashing into a bulkhead at full tilt. His eyes crossed and then uncrossed and he looked up at Darg who was coming right toward him, his fist cocked and ready to slam home. He barely managed to roll out of the way in time as Darg smashed the floor where he'd just been and made a hole in it the size of a watermelon.

Calhoun stumbled out the door. Darg's men made no effort to stop him. They seemed to be having too good a time. Darg lumbered after him, coming toward him like a tidal wave, just as easy to reason with, just as unstoppable.

"A little different this time," he rumbled. "Come back here, Calhoun. We have old scores to settle."

He closed on Calhoun, swung an uppercut that could have taken off Calhoun's head had it connected. Calhoun barely dodged it, moved out of the way of a second thrust, dodged a third. "Stay still!" snarled Darg, but Calhoun did not feel inclined to oblige.

Once more Darg swung, and once more Calhoun got around him, and this time Darg was slightly off balance. Calhoun moved quickly and drove a punch to Darg's jaw. Darg let out an angry yelp and staggered, and Calhoun hit him in the head a second time, staggering him. But then he pressed his luck and this time Darg caught his hand, yanked him off his feet, and slammed him against the wall as if he were a beanbag.

Calhoun felt his face starting to swell from the impact of hitting the wall face-first. He saw Darg advancing on him. Trying to stall for time, he pushed his tongue against the false tooth to activate it. Nothing. Instead he felt the broken shards of the device crumble in his mouth. The impact had shattered it. He spit it out and made a mental note to write a memo to Nechayev about the durability of SI devices.

Darg extended his hands . . . and razor-sharp blades snapped out of the ends of his fingers. He swiped at Calhoun, slashing across his tunic, and Calhoun barely managed to avoid more serious injury. He stared at the blades uncomprehendingly.

"You still don't understand, do you," Darg said. "All right. I'll make it clear for you." He turned the blades toward himself and slashed open his shirt. It fluttered to the ground in several pieces, to reveal Darg's glistening metal silver torso.

"Thul found me, damned near dead. He was impressed I'd survived that long on sheer hatred. He kept me alive and took me to Narobi. They built me this body. My head, my brain's all that's left. I'm not a man anymore. I'm a walking weapon, a machine that pretends it's vaguely alive. A freak. And it's your fault, Calhoun. *Your fault!*" Upon the last words, he succumbed to total rage and charged at Calhoun.

Calhoun twisted loose the heel of his boot. It came clear and he aimed and fired. The phaser blasted out, smashing Darg squarely in the chest. It knocked him back and he fell with a startled grunt.

Calhoun did the only thing that seemed reasonable under the circumstances. He turned and ran.

One of Darg's men tried to fire after him, but Darg slapped the weapon from his hand. "No! He's mine! After all this time, he's mine!" He charged after Calhoun, the floor trembling under his footfall.

In the back-up computer room to which they had been relocated, Kendrow was making the final adjustments under the watchful eyes of Silver and Gerrid Thul. "We're running out of time, Mr. Kendrow," Thul said. He didn't sound nearly as jovial as he usually did.

"I'm very aware of that, sir," said Kendrow nervously. "But I'm getting some odd readings off the Omega 9. Having a bit of trouble locking down some of the neural nets . . ."

"I have far too much riding on this, Kendrow." He pointed below him at the masses who were watching the ceremony about to start. "When one makes the sort of announcements that I have made, it is incumbent upon me . . . for the purpose of my sustained credibility . . . to see them through. I do not need last-minute glitches ruining my plans."

"Neither do I!" Kendrow shot back, sounding rather nervous. "Do you think I don't know what you'll do to me if I—"

"Steady, Kendrow, steady," said Thul gently. "Just do your job. Silver . . . are you prepared?"

Silver was seated in front of the interface panel. He had his palm flat, prepared for the process to begin. "I am ready," he said in that flat and rather unappealing voice of his.

"Excellent." Thul's eyes glittered with anticipation.

Calhoun found an access port directly in front of him, and then he heard the thundering footfall of Darg coming in fast behind him. He ripped open the access port and dropped through.

He landed lightly on a narrow maintenance bridge and made the hideous mistake of looking down.

"Down," in this instance, went on forever. Because he was at the uppermost point of the sphere, standing on a very small bridge which ran across the top of the gigantic column that fed energy into the cloaking device. It was anchored to the top of the sphere by support struts overhead.

Far, far below him, in the center of the great sphere, the cloaking device hummed powerfully.

Clutching onto the railings, Calhoun started running the length of the maintenance bridge. He had almost made it to the far end when he heard a tearing of metal, and then Zolon Darg dropped onto the bridge in front of him. Darg looked utterly confident. There was no reason for him not to be.

"Shoot me again," Darg challenged him. "Go ahead."

Calhoun aimed for Darg's head and fired. But Darg easily blocked the shots by raising his huge metal arms in front of his face and deflecting the blasts. Quickly, Calhoun squeezed the sides of the heel-shaped phaser instead, increasing the intensity of the blast. This actually caused Darg to stagger under the barrage, but it also seemed to anger him more. Despite the sustained assault, Darg advanced step after steady step. His arms outstretched, he was within five feet of Calhoun, then four and then three, and the phaser blast was starting to falter. Calhoun realized that he was reaching the limit of the small phaser's energy capacity.

Calhoun backed up, further and further, and cast a desperate glance behind and up. He saw Darg's men clustered at the access port above and behind him. They didn't seem about to let him climb out. Instead they grinned and pointed and clearly were waiting for the inevitable moment when Darg would get his mechanical hands on him.

He glanced up at the support struts . . . levelled his phaser, and fired.

Darg's smug grin of triumph flickered and then vanished as he saw what Calhoun was doing. "Wait! Hold it, you idiot! Stop!"

But it was too late. The phaser blast tore through the support struts, weakened it sufficiently, and the entire thing tore loose. The maintenance bridge, with a groan of metal, angled wildly downward, affixed to the ceiling only by the struts behind Calhoun. Calhoun clambered toward the section that was still secured, holding on to the railing for dear life as the bridge slanted wildly beneath him, threatening to send them both tumbling off.

Darg leaped forward and upward toward Calhoun, trying to forestall sliding down and off. Calhoun tried to swing his legs up and clear away from Darg's desperate grasp, and almost managed it. But Darg, at the last second, snagged Calhoun's leg. Calhoun let out a yell as he felt his leg practically being torn right out of its socket. Then he lost his grip on the railing and both of them slid off the maintenance bridge and fell.

Gerrid Thul grinned in triumph as the Narobi named Silver pressed his hand flat against the interface board. "Contact processing," announced Silver.

Suddenly a clipped voice called from behind him, "Disconnect him."

He whirled, and couldn't quite believe what he was seeing.

It was Picard. He was standing there with a blaster and an extremely irritated expression. The insensate bodies of a couple of guards could be glimpsed out in the corridor. "You," he said, "have been a very difficult individual to locate."

"Indeed," said Thul slowly. "How did you do it?"

"I asked around. I believe you will find that several of your guards are no longer functioning at full capacity. Have him back away from the computer. Shut it down."

"That's not going to happen, Picard," said Thul.

"I think it will." Picard aimed the blaster and fired almost point blank at Silver.

The blast coruscated around Silver. He paid it no heed.

Picard couldn't quite believe it. Thul, however, didn't seem the least bit thrown. "Very dense material that the Narobi are made from," he said mildly. "Resistant to blasters, phasers, disruptors . . . just about anything. And you'll find that the exterior of the computer bank is coated with the same material. Just one of the several contributions that the Narobi provided. You see, Picard . . . I tend to think ahead. I was not *expecting* that some foolhardy Federation idiot would come charging in here at the last moment and try to disrupt it . . . but I *anticipated* it. I try to anticipate everything."

Picard swung the blaster around and aimed it at Thul. "You," he said sharply, "are not blaster proof. Shut this down, now, or I'll—"

"You'll what? Kill me?" There was no longer any trace of

amusement in his voice. "You already killed me, Picard. You killed me years ago, when my son died because of you." Slowly he started to walk toward Picard. "You know . . . when I considered the possibility of the Federation sending someone . . . when I contemplated, imagined that I might find myself facing a desperate emissary trying to stop me . . . I always fantasized it would be you. Isn't that interesting? No one else. Always. In my mind's eye, I saw it just this way, with the two of us face-to-face, and you standing there feeling the same sort of helplessness as Double Helix was unleashed that I felt when I lost my son. Lost him because of you. Because of your damnable Federation."

"And everyone, every man, woman and child is to suffer because of your loss?"

"That's right. That is exactly right."

"You won't live to see your triumph."

"Don't you understand? *I don't care!* Do your worst, Picard! I assure you it will pale next to what I have already done to myself! But in the meantime, nothing you will do will matter one iota, because in the final analysis, I will still win! And there's absolutely nothing you can do to—"

That was when the lights when out and the sphere was rocked by a massive explosion.

In other sections of the Dyson Sphere (or the Thul Sphere, as it were) the gravity was zero, as Picard had learned. But in the center the gravity was near normal. Calhoun tumbled, end over end, trying to find something that he could grab onto, but there was nothing. Far, terribly far away to his left, was the docking port where his ship was comfortably anchored. It operated on voice recognition, but it had to hear him to respond, and he was simply too far away.

Then Calhoun slammed into something. He landed badly, wrenching his shoulder, and he lay there a moment, stunned. He realized that he had struck the outer edge of the cloaking device. He could feel the power of the mighty machine humming beneath him.

He slid a few feet but then managed to halt his skid. Slowly he tried to push his way back up toward the center of the cloaking device, in the meantime looking around and trying to catch a glimpse of where Darg had gone to. His main hope was that Darg had not landed quite as fortunately as he had. That he had instead clipped an edge and bounced off, or perhaps missed it entirely, and was sent tumbling the rest of the way to the bottom of the sphere.

Suddenly he felt the surface of the cloaking device tremble beneath him in a manner that was in excess of the power rumbling beneath it. He craned his neck around and saw Darg charging him.

The top of the cloaking device was slightly angled downward, and Calhoun did the only thing he could: He stopped fighting the pull of gravity and allowed himself to skid toward the edge. Darg was right after him. Calhoun got to the edge of the device and saw a yawning drop beneath him. He also saw that the side of the device was not smooth: There were handholds, or at least protruding surfaces that could be utilized as handholds. The only hope he had was that Darg's metal fingers were so thick that he wouldn't be able to utilize them.

Calhoun swung his body over the edge. His toes sought and found something to break his fall. He started clambering down the side like a monkey scaling a mountain. He just couldn't help but wish that he had some clear idea as to just where the hell he thought he was going.

And in the meantime, his mission was still unfulfilled. He knew that he had almost no time before the Double Helix was unleashed. He had to stop it, somehow.

There was absolutely no choice.

He reached up to his face, grabbed the fake scar that was adhering to his own, and pulled. It came loose with a soft tearing sound, and he slapped the adhesive against the side of the cloaking device. He twisted the edges around each other, and he realized that he had no idea as to whether it was actually activated or not. Well, within fifteen minutes, he'd know for sure . . . and if the thing really were as powerful as claimed, it would wind up being the last thing he knew.

He then continued his descent, and he'd made it fifteen feet, moving quickly in the slightly lighter-than-normal gravity when he saw Darg reach the edge and look down at him with cold, implacable fury. But it would still take Darg time to find a way to come down after him.

Darg jumped.

Son of a bitch, thought Calhoun.

Darg's hand lashed out and he snagged a crossbar, halting his fall. The bar held. Damned sturdy devices these Romulans designed. He was clinging, bat-like to the surface of the cloaking device, only a few feet to Calhoun's right. He advanced on Calhoun, and Calhoun looked around frantically, up and down, trying to determine if there was a direction he could go fast enough that would carry him out of Darg's reach. Nothing presented itself.

Darg was closer, closer, and the blades were fully extended on his hand. Within less than a second, he would be close enough to slash out at Calhoun and cut him to ribbons. Beneath Calhoun's fingers, he could feel the power of the cloaking device surging beneath him. If there were some way to disrupt it, maybe . . .

Too late. Darg's fingers lashed out, trying to slice through Calhoun's grip. Calhoun desperately shifted handholds, swinging his body out of the way, buying himself perhaps another second or two. But Darg had him cold, they both knew it.

And then Darg spotted the explosive that Calhoun had affixed to the surface of the cloaking device. He didn't recognize it for what it was, clearly, but he didn't like what he saw. With one glance at Calhoun's expression, he could tell that Calhoun wasn't happy about his noticing it either. That was more than enough reason for him to reach for it and start to peel it off. As he did so, he said almost conversationally, "Any last words?"

"Actually . . . yes. Three, to be exact," said Calhoun. He yanked the pip off his shirt where he had secreted it and slapped it on Darg's arm. "Activate, transporter right."

Darg looked at him in confusion, and suddenly he dematerialized. He let out a roar and lunged at Calhoun, but his now-phantom hands went right through him, and then Darg vanished. Seconds later, he materialized in the heart of the cloaking device.

Calhoun had no real idea what would happen when that occurred. The energies required to power a cloaking device that big were like nothing that Calhoun had ever encountered before. He didn't know what powered it, nor did he know what powered Darg's robotic body. All he knew was that he was combining two elements, and hoping for the best.

What he got was far more than he had bargained for. For he felt a violent rumbling beneath him, and he heard, or thought he heard, a truncated scream from Darg before the energies within the cloaking device ripped him apart, even his powerful mechanical body not impervious to the power and energy that was buffeting him.

And then Calhoun heard an explosion, muffled but huge, and he suddenly realized that the explosive adhesive had been stuck to Darg when he rematerialized, and he had the further flash of understanding that the explosive had been detonated prematurely thanks to the forces roiling within the cloaking device.

He did the only thing he could. He hurled himself off the cloaking device into mid-air, hurtling down and away from the immediate blast area.

A split second later, the cloaking device erupted.

XXIII.

THERE WAS ALARM throughout the sphere as the cloaking device erupted in flame. The entire manufactured world trembled from the detonation.

Thul saw it from a distance and couldn't believe it. From his vantage point he could see the crowd that had been milling about in the great square, waiting to witness the signing of the document that would be the cue for the annihilation of the Federation. Except the picture on the huge screen had disappeared as systems shorted out and went down all over the sphere. Not only that, but they could see and hear, as he just had, the terrible explosion that had originated at the very core of the sphere.

Silver stood up, gingerly pulling his hand from the surface of the computer.

"What are you doing!" said an alarmed Thul in the now-darkened room. "I need you to interface with the Omega 9! The job's too big for a normal human mind! You have to—"

"I have to do nothing," Silver said calmly. "I have analyzed the present situation, including the obvious sabotage to this sphere. It is my belief that, within three minutes, at the present rate of destruction, this sphere will be destroyed. I have no desire to accompany it. So . . . I am leaving."

And suddenly there was a fearful looking weapon in Thul's

hand, pulled from the folds of his cloak. "Get back there, Silver!" he snarled.

"I am leaving," said Silver.

Thul fired.

Picard watched the entire scene unfold with a sort of distant disbelief.

Thul fired upon the being whom he called Silver. But the blast from Thul's own weapon was no more effective upon Silver than anything that Picard might have wielded. The blast ricocheted harmlessly off Silver . . .

. . . and struck Kendrow.

With a howl of agony, clutching at his blackened chest, Kendrow went down. He flopped about on the floor like a just-landed marlin, making incoherent babbling noises.

Thul paid him no mind. Instead he fired once more at Silver, and had no more luck than he'd had the previous time. Silver walked past him, completely ignoring him.

Everything forgotten except his boiling rage and desperation to carry out the final demise of the Federation, Thul charged at Silver. All pretensions of dignity, all of his superiority, were gone, vanished, boiled away by pure fury. It made him a very easy target. Picard reversed his gun, bringing the butt-end around, and as Thul passed him, Picard slammed him across the side of the head. Thul collapsed at his feet.

Silver paused a moment to cast a glance at Picard. "I would leave here if I were you," he said simply, and then the silver-metal being turned and walked away.

Picard turned quickly and headed over to Kendrow. He knelt down next to him, saw the severity of the wound, saw the despair in the man's eyes. Kendrow clearly knew he was dying . . . and yet he was looking up at Picard with heartbreaking despair, silently pleading for him to help hm. Picard hesitated, unsure of what he could possibly do . . .

And that was when Gerrid Thul leaped upon his back.

A huge piece of metal, buffeted by the shock wave, slammed into Calhoun as he hurtled through mid-air. His head rang from the impact, but then he quickly realized that it was the single luckiest thing that could have happened to him.

The shock wave from the explosion hit, radiating outward, propelling Calhoun toward the far edges of the sphere. He tumbled end over end, but because he was clutching with all his strength at the large shard of metal, his body pressed flat against it, he managed to avoid losing consciousness altogether. He was like a crazed surfer riding out a massive wave.

Before he knew it, he slammed into the interior surface of the sphere. He lost his grip on the metal shard and it spiralled away from him. Once again in a zero-G area, Calhoun hung there for a moment, dazed, banged up, barely able to string a coherent thought together.

Then he started to float back toward the center, toward the massive conflagration which was building upon itself exponentially.

It was at that moment that he saw his freighter, docked and waiting. It was some distance away and he prayed his voice would carry as he shouted at the top of his lungs, "Freighter! Voice response activate! Pick up!"

For a moment he was certain that it hadn't heard him, and then the running lights suddenly flared to life. Wasting no time, the freighter pulled away from its moorings and angled obediently down toward its pilot.

Another explosion roared from within the heart of the sphere as the lower half of the cloaking device went up in flames.

Calhoun was now plummeting toward it, and then the freighter was there, main door open. Calhoun tumbled into the cabin, kept rolling and slammed into the far wall. He lay there for a moment, stunned, muttering, "I'm not getting paid enough."

Then he stumbled to his feet and seized the controls of the freighter . . .

. . . and was abruptly faced with a very difficult choice.

Picard tried to stagger to his feet and barely managed to do so. Thul was on his back, howling in fury, and Picard barely managed to shove him off. They faced each other, both their weapons fallen. Thul had a look of dementia in his eyes.

"It's over, Thul. We have to get out of here—!"

"No." Thul was shaking his head like a man deep in denial.

"No . . . they have to die . . . you have to die . . . the Double Helix . . ."

"I said it's over! Snap out of it, man! Nothing is going to be accomplished by staying here and being incinerated!"

Thul didn't listen. He was beyond listening, beyond caring. Instead he came right at Picard, his attack so sudden that Picard barely had time to defend himself against it.

And Picard abruptly found himself in the hands of one of the most devastating hand-to-hand combatants he had ever encountered.

One wouldn't have known it to look at Thul. The Thallonian was clearly an older man, older than Picard. He wasn't all that tall, not especially wide. But in close-quarters combat, he was a terror, an absolute terror. Picard wasn't exactly helpless in such situations, a fair hand-to-hand combatant himself, with some good moves and a rather nasty right hook, if he said so himself. But he couldn't even begin to mount a defense against Gerrid Thul.

Thul's hands were lightning. Picard would try and block a punch, and even before he had time to realize it was a feint, Thul had landed two blows, a third and a fourth. He struck Picard at will, doubling him over, straightening him up with an uppercut. Picard never even laid a hand on him.

Thul picked him up and threw him out into the main corridor, advancing on him mercilessly. All around them, panicked residents of the sphere were running like mad, trying to get to whatever ships were nearest so that they could get the hell out of there. Thul didn't seem to notice any of them. He was focused, with laser-like efficiency, on Picard.

Picard felt the world swimming around him, tried to get to his feet, and then Thul was there and he kicked Picard in the gut, causing him to curl up like a fetus, and he kicked him over and over, howling, "You, Picard! It's all your fault! You're the living symbol of everyone and everything that destroyed my life! But you're not going to be living much longer!"

David Kendrow's desperate, questing hand stretched out toward the hand padd for the Omega 9. His body trembled from the exertion, and he was certain that he wasn't going to make it. But then, at the last moment, like a gift from God, he had a small surge of energy that was small, ever so small, but it was enough. He lunged forward and his hand came into contact with the padd.

He trembled as the nannites, careless of the environment that was crumbling around them, did their job. They joined with him, penetrated his mind, his body, and seconds later his consciousness was pulled from his body and sent hurtling into the depths of the Omega 9.

What he had, at that point, was a plan that could most charitably be called a long-shot. What he was hoping was that his consciousness would survive the passing of his body if it was buried deep within the Omega 9. The problem was that, all too soon, the Omega 9 would be dust, gone with the rest of the sphere.

But the intention had been for the Omega 9 to interface with computers on other worlds. Granted, it had been too massive a job for Kendrow to do himself. Silver was supposed to bridge that gap with his machine mind. But Kendrow was still capable of at least projecting himself to some other computer data base . . . earth, perhaps, or another world. And perhaps . . . just perhaps . . . he could use the replicators wherever he wound up to fashion himself some sort of body. There were other possibilities as well, but before he could explore any of them, he had to survive.

He plunged into the heart of the Omega 9, the glistening circuitry singing gently to him. It was the first time that he himself had done it, and it was glorious, it was like nothing else. He floated there, feeling as if he had somehow managed to return to his mother's womb. There was peace, there was security, there was . . .

Darkness. Something was moving in around him, something that seemed alien to the Omega 9. Kendrow's consciousness looked around, tried to perceive, tried to understand . . .

And a voice echoed all around him, a voice that said, *I'd been trying to get your attention, David. Causing glitches here and there, doing what I could in my own small way . . . how kind of you to finally brave the interior of the Omega 9 . . . it took you quite some time, didn't it . . . but you always were a bit of a coward at heart, you know that, don't you, David . . . ?*

Kendrow looked around frantically. It was everywhere, the dark and cold, and he called out, *Who is it? Who's there?!?*

I brushed against the Omega 9, David . . . with Darg and the others standing there, and you, and all you bright people, and you didn't spot it. Didn't spot the final connection. What did you think, Dave . . . that you were the first person to hit upon the idea of putting his consciousness into the Omega 9? You always were more of a follower than a leader . . .

And then he understood. *Fro . . . Frobisher . . . but . . . but you're dead . . .*

Yes, Dave. I was dead. But you know, Dave . . . I'm feeling a lot better now . . .

The laughter was everywhere and Kendrow screamed as the darkness enveloped him.

Picard rolled over onto his back and then Gerrid Thul was upon him. He was straddling Picard, his hands at Picard's throat, and he slammed the captain's head against the floor. Stars exploded behind Picard's eyes, and Thul wasn't letting up, not for a second.

"I made a son . . . and you destroyed him. I created the perfect virus . . . and you destroyed my plan to implement it," and as he spoke the pressure of his hands upon Picard's throat was steady and unyielding. "You call me the destroyer? It's you, Picard! You are the bringer of pain! You are the slayer of dreams! You!"

The test tube rolled out from Picard's pocket.

It made a gentle, tinkling sound as it rolled. Thul cast a confused glance in the direction of the tube . . .

And the distraction was all Picard needed. He broke Thul's grip and shoved as hard as he could, sending Thul off-balance as he gasped and drew in air. Thul tumbled to the side, hit the floor hard.

Picard heard something break.

He clambered to his feet and saw Thul, on his back, starting to tremble. Instantly Picard understood. Thul had landed atop the test tube and crushed it . . . and the Double Helix virus was rampaging through his body. But it was doing so in highly concentrated form.

Gerrid Thul, creator of the Double Helix, writhed in the grasp of his own creation. His back arched, his tongue lolled out, and his eyes went wide with horror as he realized what had happened. For all his speeches about not caring about life, about being dead already, he certainly seemed to have the expression of someone who was suddenly terrified about being hurled into oblivion. Or perhaps it was simply the way that it was occurring.

Thul's eyes shrivelled, collapsed into their sockets, his tongue began to blacken even as he voicelessly screamed his terror, the skin started to pucker and blister, pus oozing out from sores that had appeared spontaneously all over.

Picard was transfixed, and then it suddenly occurred to him that if the damned thing became airborne, this was going to be the perfect time to get the hell out of there. He tore his gaze away from Thul and ran like mad.

His legs and arms pumping, Picard dashed down the corridor. He hoped that he remembered where the docking area was, and also prayed that he would be able to find a means of escape once he got there. The sphere rumbled around him and he knew there wasn't much time left as the systems ate themselves, one explosion feeding upon another. Bleakly, he wondered what had happened to Calhoun and Vara Syndra, or Vandelia, or whatever her name was. He could only pray that they were all right and that somehow they were going to manage to get themselves clear.

He saw a sign marked for one of the docking areas, turned right, and saw huge double doors that were just sitting open, which led to the docking ports. He dashed out into the vast docking area which opened out to the interior of the sphere. From that viewpoint, he could see flame erupting from spots throughout the sphere. The far side of the sphere was already a massive wall of flame, and it was spreading wildly. He was witnessing the death of a technological marvel. From a purely scientific and even aesthetic view, it was a tremendous waste and tragedy.

All this he saw from where he was standing. What he did not see were any ships. He spotted the last of the small transports moving away, and there was nothing left in his immediate area. There were other docking ports, but they were too far away for him to get to in time.

He saw the firewall racing toward him from either side. There was nowhere to go.

He took a deep breath, faced his death, and thought about a book his mother had read to him several times in his youth: *Peter Pan*. He thought of the time that Peter was crouched on the rock, having just been stabbed by Hook, unable to fly, unable to save himself, and he had looked at the rising tide and mused philosophically about his impending doom.

"To die," Picard whispered, "would be a great adventure."

At which point he promptly disappeared in a haze of sparkles.

Seconds later, he materialized in what appeared to be a small freighter. He looked around in confusion . . . and then a smile broke across his face. "I should have known."

"Yes, you should have," Calhoun said reprovingly from the control panel. He hadn't even bothered to turn around. "I was on my last sweep of the place looking for you. You certainly took your sweet time getting somewhere that I could see you. Thanks to you, I've had to cut this a lot thinner than I would have liked."

"It's getting thinner still. Where's the woman?"

"Dead," Calhoun said tonelessly. "Darg killed her. But considering there's not two molecules of him left to rub together, I doubt he'll be hurting anyone else. Where's Thul?"

"The same, but more grisly. Get us out of here."

"That's why you've been captain longer than me. You know how to make the tough decisions."

Even as he spoke, he was sending the freighter hurtling toward one of the few areas that was not completely aflame. The sphere was collapsing on itself, gigantic flaming shards smashing into one another. Calhoun coolly maneuvered the shuttle between the debris, dodging left and right as he called out, "Hold on. This is going to be a little tricky."

He saw an escape route and went for it, and the freighter darted forward just before a huge piece of debris could smash into it. Then they were clear of the sphere, moving away from it faster and faster as the last of the explosions utterly consumed it.

Other ships were all around, scattered, confused, unsure of where to go or what to do. Then, after a few moments, they slowly started to move away from the area of the destruction. Picard watched them go, shaking his head, and—like an old-time policeman—he said, "Show's over. Nothing more to see here."

"Yes," Calhoun said slowly, "yes . . . there is."

He was angling his freighter toward one particular ship. "What is it, Mac?"

"That's Thul's ship. But you said he's dead."

"He is."

"Then I'm going to take a shot in the dark," Calhoun said.

He touched several controls and Picard heard the distinctive whine of phasers powering up. "What are you doing?"

But Calhoun had opened up a ship-to-ship channel. "Lodec. I have you targeted. I'm coming in at 273 Mark 2. This is it, Lodec."

There was dead silence as Picard looked in puzzlement at Calhoun . . . and then Lodec's voice came back over the channel. "Hello, Calhoun."

"Do you want an opportunity to fight back . . . or should I just blow you out of space?"

"Calhoun, back off," Picard said sharply, "this is absurd—"

Calhoun looked at him with blazing eyes and said, "No. This is personal. Well, Lodec?"

Again a moment of silence, and then Lodec said, "I was going to let you go, you know. In the corridor. I saw you there, and I was all set to keep my silence. And you had to draw on me, so that I thought you were going to shoot me. You left me no choice. But it's all about choices, isn't it, Calhoun? So fine. I leave you the choice you didn't leave me. Shoot or don't. It's of no consequence to me. Death will just silence the voices that have been crying out in my head for so many years. Do as you like."

With that, he cut the connection.

Picard said nothing. He simply watched Calhoun, who stared out at the ship that was hanging there, a huge target. It offered no defense. It would have been so easy.

And then, unmolested . . . the ship moved off. a moment later, it kicked into warp space and was gone.

Picard let out a slow, relieved breath, and he patted Calhoun on the back. "Mac . . . believe it or not . . . I know how difficult it is to let go of the need for revenge. But—and I don't mean to sound patronizing here—I think you've taken a tremendous step forward in your personal growth and—"

"The phaser banks are empty," Calhoun said.

"What?" Picard leaned forward and looked. It was true. The phasers had powered up, but had been unable to sustain it.

"They're empty. And it's not just them. Thul must have drained the ship's systems. Engines, life support, all going. He had quite a knack for thinking ahead. Here was a man who thought, Well, just in case Calhoun and/or Picard escape, I'll leave them just enough power to get away. To make them think they're safe. And then all the systems will . . ."

The lights in the freighter suddenly went out.

". . . cut out," he concluded.

On earth, the closing ceremonies for the bicentennial went without a hitch. As they did, Jellico turned to Nechayev and said, "Well, well . . . it would appear that we got all concerned for nothing."

"Apparently so. Unless, of course, someone just saved the galaxy as we know it from total disaster and we're simply unaware of it."

"I doubt it," Jellico replied. "I mean, I think I'd know if something like that had happened."

"Yes," said Nechayev. "It'd be fairly difficult to slip something like that past you, Eddie."

Picard and Calhoun spent the next several minutes seeing what they could possibly do to reverse the situation, but nothing seemed to present itself. Furthermore, all the other ships had moved out by that point. Not that their being present would have offered any great options. Calhoun and Picard had already been named as traitors and enemies by Thul. Finally, options expended, they simply sat there, looking at each other.

"Had you already decided not to kill Lodec before you saw the phasers were out? Or did you notice that the phasers were out and realize that the decision was out of your hands?"

Calhoun said nothing.

"You're not going to answer, are you."

"Picard," Calhoun said slowly, "you are probably one of the brightest men I've ever met. You've known me for twenty years. You know my background. You know what I stand for.

272

And you know that, ultimately—even if there are some bumps along the way—I'm going to end up doing the right thing. So I think you really know the answer to that question, don't you."

"Nice try, Mac."

"All right . . . I suppose I knew I wouldn't get away with it that easily. The truth, Picard . . . is that I was in the same situation once before. The indecision led to my resigning from Starfleet because the universe was very black and white to me. This time around . . . I have to admit that, once again, I don't know what I would have done. I still might have given in to the impulse for vengeance. Or I might not. I'm just not sure. But at least this time, I'm not going to let the lack of knowledge get to me. It took me a long time and a lot of learning to realize that it's all right not to know everything . . . including every aspect of oneself. That it's acceptable to live within the shades of gray on occasion. Good enough?"

"Not really. But I suppose it will have to do."

They sat there for a time more, and then Calhoun said, "What are you thinking about?"

"All the people I've known. All the opportunities I've had in my life, and whether I would do it all the same. About Thul's son, and whether his death could have been prevented . . . whether I could have done anything differently, for if I had, all this could have been avoided. Lives wouldn't have been wasted and lost, and incredible forays of ingenuity wouldn't have been dedicated to such a useless endeavor as a hollow need to destroy in the quest for useless revenge. I'm thinking about the universe in general, of free will, and of man's place within that universe and whether we really have a place at all, or how much we matter in the grand scheme of things. I'm wondering . . . what the ultimate answers to all reality are, and whether we'll ever get to know them." He paused, feeling the chill of space beginning to work its way into his bones. "And you? What are you thinking about?"

"I'm thinking about how nice it would be if the *Excalibur* showed up and rescued us."

Picard laughed softly to himself, starting to feel a bit lightheaded as the carbon dioxide began to build up. And at that moment, space in front of them rippled, a hole in the space-time continuum opened up, and the starship *Excalibur* dropped into normal space a mere five hundred kilometers away.

Picard gaped at the sight and then turned to Calhoun, who maintained an absolute deadpan as he said, "I don't know about the ultimate ones, but I guess some answers come more quickly than others."

XXIV.

CALHOUN AND SHELBY were escorting Picard and Riker to the transporter room. "Sela's already been beamed aboard the *Enterprise,* as per your request, Captain," said Calhoun. "I'm afraid there's been no change in her condition."

"I'm hoping that Starfleet will be able to give her the help she needs," Picard said. "Perhaps even leave her better than when she started. No matter what it is that she's become . . . she remains the daughter of an old, dear friend. If there's any way to salvage the influence of the good person that Tasha Yar was, then we have to take it."

"Looking for the best in people. It's comforting to know that some things about you don't change, Captain," Calhoun said.

"It is equally comforting, Captain, to know that some things about you do change," Picard replied with a carefully neutral expression, which drew a wary grin from Calhoun. Picard continued, "Number One . . . how went your temporary assignment to the *Excalibur?*"

"Good question," seconded Calhoun. "Commander Shelby, did you two get on with each other? Or were there any problems I should know about?"

Shelby and Riker cast a glance at each other, and then Shelby said, "Actually . . . it went about as expected."

"It was a learning experience . . . for all concerned," Riker added.

"It would appear, Captain Calhoun," Picard said, "that the crew here is beginning to imitate your rather enigmatic way of expressing yourself. Perhaps you—"

He stopped in his tracks.

A dark haired woman was approaching him. And she looked like . . . but . . . it couldn't possibly be . . .

"Leaving, Commander? I hope you enjoyed your stay. Well, have to rush. Good day to you," said Morgan Lefler as she breezed past.

Picard gaped after her, then looked back to Riker. "What was . . . was that . . . how?"

"Captain," Riker said in a firm but understanding voice, "I've learned that around this ship . . . it's best not to ask too many questions."

"Is it finished yet?"

Burgoyne lay on the examination bed in sickbay while Doctor Selar studied the readouts. "Almost, Burgoyne. But let me see if I understand this. Medical scans and similar procedures are privileged information . . . but you want me to post this scan publicly? To everyone on the ship?"

"Yes. That's correct," Burgoyne confirmed. "I'm tired of everyone congratulating me on my pregnancy. It's gotten very old, very quickly. And some of them even think I'm being coy when I deny it. So if I just publicize it in one shot, with the scan confirming that I'm not pregnant, that should put an end to it."

"That sounds like a commendable plan. I wish I could oblige."

"But Selar, I told you, I'm waiving the confidentiality—"

"It is not a matter of that. But if you wish to circulate this scan as proof of what you are claiming, that is not going to be possible."

"What?" Burgoyne was completely confused. "What are you talking about?"

"You are pregnant."

"What?" The blood drained from Burgoyne's face. "But . . . but I can't be . . ."

"You are. Look for yourself."

Burgoyne took one look at the readout and fainted dead away.

Selar stood there and regarded hir with very mild amusement. And then McHenry emerged from hiding nearby and grinned down at the unconscious Hermat. "Well, well, Burgy. You told me you were pregnant, except you really weren't . . . and I passed out . . . and you teased me about it. So now, with the good doctor's help here, you get told you're pregnant, except you're really not . . . but you handled the unexpected fake news as well as I did. For some reason, I find that very comforting. Don't you think that's comforting?"

"I think you are all insane, and I think I am just as insane for cooperating," sniffed Selar. And she turned away to hide the slight smile that she couldn't quite repress.

Pocket Books
Proudly Presents

Double Helix #6

THE FIRST VIRTUE

Michael Jan Friedman
& Christie Golden

Available Now from Pocket Books

Turn the page for a preview of
The First Virtue. . . .

As Governor Gerrid Thul walked through the doors and entered the throne room of his emperor, Tae Cwan, he reflected on how different the place now looked.

After all, the three prior occasions on which Thul had visited were all elaborate state gatherings of nobles and high-ranking officials in the empire. He was only a small part of them, though his standing had grown surely and steadily over the years.

But this, the governor told himself, looking around at the cavernous, high-ceilinged hall and the splendid furnishings . . . this was different. He frowned. He was all alone now, without a crowd to hide him.

And at the end of the rich, blue carpet that bisected the chamber's white stone floor, the illustrious Tae

Cwan himself waited for Thul. The blue-robed emperor sat between two armed guards on a chair of carved nightwood that had given his forbears comfort for more than a thousand years.

It was daunting. Or it would have been, if the governor were one who allowed himself to be daunted. But he hadn't risen to a rank of esteem and power by being timid.

Lifting his chin, Thul set foot on the carpet and approached Tae Cwan's presence. The chamber magnified every sound—the flutter of his cape, the padding of his feet on the blue path, even the drawing of his breath—as if the room weren't filled with simple air at all, but something infinitely more sensitive and unstable.

Finally, the governor reached the end of the carpet and stopped. His emperor gazed down at him from the height of his chair, his features long and perfect, his expression a tranquil one.

Thul inclined his head out of respect—or at least that was the nature of the gesture. Then he smiled his best smile. "I believe you know why I have come," he told Tae Cwan, his voice echoing in the chamber like stormwaves on a rocky beach.

"I believe I do," the emperor replied without inflection, though his voice echoed just as loudly.

Abruptly, he gestured—and a door opened behind him. A couple of attractive handmaidens came through, followed by someone else in the deep blue color that could be worn only by imperial blood. It was Tae Cwan's younger sister, Mella.

The resemblance was difficult to ignore. However, as often happens in a family, the clarity of feature that made the brother a handsome man made the sister look plain and austere.

Nonetheless, the governor turned his smile of smiles on Mella Cwan, and the woman's eyes lit up in response. Dark and vulnerable, her eyes were by far her best attribute.

"Proceed," said the emperor.

Thul inclined his head again. "As you wish, Honored One." He paused, as if gathering himself. "I have come to profess my love and admiration for your sister, the Lady Mella."

A demure smile pulled at the corners of the woman's mouth. Unfortunately, it didn't make her any more pleasant to look at.

"I ask you for permission to make her my wife," Thul continued.

Tae Cwan considered the governor for a moment. He had to know that nothing would make his sister happier than the prospect of marriage to Thul. And yet, the governor noted, the emperor hesitated.

It was not a good sign, Thul knew. Not a good sign at all.

"I withhold the permission you seek," said Tae Cwan, his expression stark and empty of emotion.

To the governor, it was more than a disappointment. It was like a blow across his face, with all the pain and shame such a blow would have awakened in him.

The Lady Mella, too, seemed shocked by her brother's reply. She stared at him open-mouthed, her face several shades paler than before.

Still stinging from Tae Cwan's words, Thul asked, "Is it possible you will change your mind in this matter, Emperor? Or perhaps reconsider my request at a later date?"

Tae Cwan shook his head from side to side, slowly and decisively. "It is not possible," he responded flatly.

Thul felt a hot spurt of anger, but managed to stifle it. After all, it was forbidden to show excessive emotion in the presence of a Cwan.

"I see," he said as calmly as he could. "And am I permitted to inquire as to the emperor's thinking in this matter?"

"You need not inquire," Tae Cwan informed him. "I will give you the insight you want."

The emperor leaned forward on his throne, his features severe and impassive. But his eyes, as dark as his sister's, flickered with what seemed like indignation.

"I do not wish you to be part of the royal family," he told Thul. "Certainly, you have been a dedicated and efficient servant who has made considerable contributions to the Empire. However, there is also something dangerous about you—something I do not entirely trust."

The governor's teeth ground together, but he said nothing. After all, it was he who had requested Tae Cwan's response.

"Beyond that," said the emperor, "you are well inferior to my sister in station. No doubt, she would be willing to overlook this difference now. But in time, she would come to see it as a problem, as I do."

Mella averted her eyes, her brow creased with disappointment. But like Thul, she was forced to keep her emotions in check.

"These are my reasons for disallowing your request," Tae Cwan finished. "I assume I have made my decision clear."

"Eminently," said the governor, though he felt something twist inside him as he said it. "And though I have not been granted my request, I remain grateful for the audience, as befits a loyal servant of the empire. May you continue to reign in splendor, Emperor."

Tae Cwan inclined his head, his eyes sharp and alert, though the rest of his features were in repose. "Go in peace, Gerrid Thul."

The governor cast a last, wistful glance at the Lady Mella. But with her brother's pronouncement still hanging in the air, she didn't dare return it.

Thul cursed inwardly. As his wife, the woman would have brought him immeasurable power and prestige—more than enough for him to overlook his lack of attraction to her. But with a few words, the emperor had taken away that dream of power and prestige.

Enduring his loss—one that was no less painful for his never having had the thing to begin with—the governor inclined his head a third time. Then he turned and followed the length of blue carpet to the doors and made his exit.

But as soon as the doors closed behind him and he was left alone in the hallway outside, Gerrid Thul turned and glowered in the direction of Tae Cwan. Emperor though he might be, the governor reflected bitterly, he had gone too far this time.

He had humiliated one of his most determined servants—one who had risked much and accomplished much on behalf of the Empire. He had told Thul in no uncertain terms that he would never be more than what he was—the administrator of a farflung outpost.

The governor swore again. Maybe he couldn't ascend to power by marrying the Lady Mella, but he was still no beast of burden to wallow in self-pity. He was intelligent. He was resourceful. And he was every bit as Thallonian as the feared Tae Cwan.

For some time now, Thul had toyed with an alternative to marrying the Lady Mella—one that would allow him to enjoy the prominence he craved without the need to seek the emperor's blessing. With his first option closed to him, the second came to the fore in his mind.

And the more he thought about it—the more he considered how badly he had been treated by Tae Cwan—the more inclined he was to pursue it.

Look for
The First Virtue
Available Now
Wherever Books Are Sold

OUR FIRST SERIAL NOVEL!

Presenting one chapter per month . . .

The very beginning of the Starfleet Adventure . . .

STAR TREK
STARFLEET: YEAR ONE

A Novel in Twelve Parts

by
Michael Jan Friedman

Chapter One

Commander Bryce Shumar felt the labored rise of his narrow, dimly lit turbolift compartment, and sighed.

The damned thing hadn't been running as smoothly as he would have liked for several months already. The cranky, all-too-familiar whine of the component that drove the compartment only underlined what the commander already knew—that the system was on its last legs.

Under normal circumstances, new turbolift parts would have appeared at the base in a matter of weeks—maybe less. But lift parts weren't exactly a tactical priority, so Shumar and his people were forced to make do with what they had.

After a few moments, the component cycled down and the commander's ascent was complete. Then the doors parted with a loud hiss and revealed a noisy, bustling operations center—

Ops for short. It was packed with one sleek, black console after another—all of them manned, and all of them enclosed in a transparent dome that featured a breathtaking view of the stars.

The first day Shumar had set foot there, the place had impressed the hell out of him—almost enough to make him forget the value of what he had lost. But that was four long years ago. Now, he had learned to take it all for granted.

The big, convex viewer located in the center of the facility echoed the curve of the sprawling security console below it. Fixing his gaze on the screen, Shumar saw two ships making their way through the void on proximate parallel courses.

One was a splendid, splay-winged Rigelian transport vessel, its full-bellied hull the deep blue color of a mountain lake. The other was a black, needle-sharp Cochrane, capable of speeds as high as warp one point six, according to some reports.

It was hardly an unusual pairing, given the Cochrane's tactical advantages and the dangerous times in which they lived. Vessels carrying important cargo were almost always given escorts. Still, thought Shumar, it wouldn't hurt to make sure the ships were what they appeared to be.

"Run a scan," he told his redhaired security officer.

Morgan Kelly shot a glance at him over her shoulder. "Might I remind the commander," she said, "no Romulan has used subterfuge to approach an Earth base since the war began? Not even once?"

"Consider me reminded," Shumar told her, "and run the scan anyway."

"Way ahead of you," said Kelly, only half-suppressing a smile. She pointed to a monitor on her left, where the vessels' energy signatures were displayed. "According to our equipment, everything checks out. Those two are exactly what they're cracked up to be—a transport and its keeper."

Shumar frowned. "Tell them I'll meet them downstairs."

"Aye, sir," said the security officer. "And I'll be sure to tell them also what a lovely mood you're in."

The commander looked at her. "What kind of mood would *you* be in if you'd just learned your vessel had been destroyed?"

Kelly grunted. "Begging the commander's pardon, but it was nearly a month ago that you got that news."

Shumar's frown deepened. Had it really been that long since he learned what happened to the *John Burke?* "Time flies," he remarked drily, "when you're having fun."

Then he made his way back to the turbolift.

Though not a human himself, Alonis Cobaryn had seen his share of Earth bases floating in the void.

The one he saw on his primary monitor now was typical of the breed. It possessed a dark, boxlike body, four ribbed cargo globes that vaguely resembled the legs of a very slow quadruped on his homeworld, and a transparent bubble that served as the facility's brain.

There was also nothing unusual about the procedure he had been instructed to follow in his approach. And now that he was within a few kilometers of the base, Cobaryn was expected to begin that procedure.

But first, he pulled a toggle to switch one of his secondary monitors over to a communications function. After all, he always liked to see in whose hands he was placing his molecular integrity.

The monitor screen fizzed over with static for a moment, then showed him the Earth base's security officer—a woman with high cheekbones, green eyes and red hair pulled back into a somewhat unruly knot. What's more, she filled out her gold and black jumpsuit rather well.

All in all, Cobaryn mused, a rather attractive-looking individual. *For a human, that is.*

It took her about a second to take note of the visual link and look back at him. "If you were planning on cutting your engines," the woman told him, "this would be as good a time as any."

Cobaryn's mouth pulled up at the corners—as close as he could come to a human smile. "I could not agree more," he said. Tapping the requisite sequence into the touch pad of his helm-control console, he looked up again. "I have cut my engines."

"Acknowledged," said the security officer, checking her monitors with admirable efficiency to make sure all was as it should be.

Next, Cobaryn applied his braking thrusters until he had reduced his vessel's momentum to zero and assumed a position within half a kilometer of the base. The facility loomed larger than ever on his primary monitor, a dark blot on the stars.

"That'll be fine," the redhaired woman told him.

"I am pleased that you think so," he responded.

The officer's green eyes narrowed a bit, but she wasn't adverse to the banter. At least, that was how it seemed to Cobaryn.

"I suppose you'd like to beam over now," she said.

"If it is not too much trouble."

"And if it is?" the woman asked playfully.

Cobaryn shrugged. "Then I would be deprived of the opportunity to thank you for your assistance in person."

She chuckled. "You Rigelians don't lack confidence, do you?"

"I cannot speak for others," he remarked thoughtfully, "but as for myself . . . I do indeed believe that confidence is a virtue."

The officer considered him a moment longer. "Too bad your pal in the Cochrane doesn't have the same attitude."

Cobaryn tilted his head. "And why is that?" he inquired, at a loss as to the human's meaning.

A coy smile blossomed on the officer's face. "No offense, Captain, but the Cochrane jockey's a lot better-looking." Then she went on, almost in the same breath, "Get ready to beam over."

Cobaryn sat back in his chair, deflated by the woman's remark—if only for a moment. Then he recalled that humans often said the opposite of what they meant. Perhaps that was the case here.

"Ready," he replied.

"Good," said the security officer, embracing a lever in each hand. "Then here goes."

Commander Shumar stood in one of his base's smallest, darkest rooms and watched a faint shimmer of light appear like a will-o'-the-wisp over a raised transporter disc.

Gradually, the shimmer grew along its vertical axis. Then a ghostly image appeared in the same space—a vague impression of a muscular humanoid dressed in loose-fitting black togs.

The transport captain, Shumar remarked inwardly. Obviously, he had been nicer to Kelly than the pilot of the Cochrane, or the security officer would have beamed the other man over first.

The base commander watched the shaft of illumination dim as the figure flickered, solidified, flickered again and solidified a bit more. Finally, after about forty-five seconds, the process was complete and the vertical blaze of light died altogether.

A moment later, a host of blue emergency globes activated themselves in a continuous line along the bulkheads. By their glare, Shumar could make out his guest's silvery features and ruby-red eyes, which gleamed beneath a flared brow ridge reminiscent of a triceratops' bony collar.

He was a Rigelian, the commander noted. More specifically, a denizen of Rigel IV, not to be confused with any of the other four inhabited planets in the Rigel star system. And he was smiling awkwardly.

Of course, smiling was a peculiarly Terran activity. It wasn't uncommon for aliens to look a little clumsy at it—which is why so few of them even made the attempt.

"Welcome to Earth Base Fourteen," said the human.

"Thank you," the Rigelian replied with what seemed like studied politeness. He stepped down from the disc and extended a three-fingered hand. "Alonis Cobaryn at your service, Commander."

Shumar gripped the transport captain's offering. It felt much like a human appendage except for some variations in metacarpal structure and a complete lack of hair.

"You shake hands," the base commander observed.

"I do," Cobaryn confirmed.

Shumar studied him. "Most nonhumans don't, you know."

The Rigelian's ungainly smile widened, stretching an elaborate maze of tiny ridges that ran from his temples down to his jaw. "I have dealt with your people for a number of years now," he explained. "Sometimes I imagine I know as much about them as any human."

Shumar grunted. "I wish I could say the same about Rigelians. You're the first one I've seen in person in four years on this base."

"I am not surprised," said Cobaryn, his tone vaguely apologetic. "My people typically prefer the company of other Rigelians. In that I relish the opportunity to explore the intricacies of other cultures, I am considered something of a black sheep on my homeworld."

Suddenly, realization dawned. "Wait a minute," said the human. "Cobaryn . . .? Aren't you the fellow who charted Sector Two-seven-five?"

The alien lowered his hairless silver head ever so slightly. "I see that my reputation has preceded me."

Shumar found himself smiling. "I used your charts to navigate the Galendus Cluster on my way to—"

Before he could finish his sentence, the emergency illumination around them dimmed and another glimmer of light appeared over the transporter disc. Like the one before it, it lengthened little by little and gave rise to something clearly man-shaped.

This one was human, the base commander noted—the pilot of the Cochrane, no doubt. Shumar watched the shape flicker and take on substance by turns. In time, the new arrival became solid, the shaft of light fizzled out and the emergency globes activated themselves again.

This time, they played on a tall, athletic-looking specimen with a lean face, close-cropped blond hair and slate-blue eyes. His garb was civilian, like that of most escort pilots these days—a brown leather jacket over a rumpled, gray jumpsuit.

"Welcome to the base," said the commander. "My name's Shumar."

The other man looked at him for a second, but he didn't say a thing in return. Then he got down from the platform, walked past his fellow human and left the transporter room by its only set of sliding doors.

As the titanium panels slid closed again, shutting out the marginally brighter light of the corridor outside, Shumar turned to Corbaryn. "What's the matter with your friend?" he asked, as puzzled as he was annoyed.

The Rigelian smiled without much enthusiasm. "Captain Dane is not very communicative. The one time we spoke, he described himself as a loner." He regarded the doors with his ruby red orbs. "Frankly, given his attitude, I am surprised he takes part in the war effort at all."

"The *one* time?" Shumar echoed. He didn't get it. "But he was your escort, wasn't he?"

"He was," Cobaryn confirmed in a neutral tone. "Still, as I noted, he was not a very loquacious one. He appeared to be troubled by something, though I cannot imagine what it might have been."

Shumar frowned. "It wouldn't hurt him to say a few words when he sets foot on someone else's base. I mean, I'm not exactly thrilled about my lot in life either right now, but I keep it to myself."

The Rigelian's eyes narrowed. "You would rather be somewhere else?"

"On a research vessel," Shumar told him unhesitatingly, "conducting planetary surveys. That's what I did before the war. Unfortunately, I'll have to get hold of a new ship if I want to pick up where I left off."

"The old one was commandeered, then?" asked Cobaryn.

Shumar nodded. "Four years ago, when I was given command of this place. Then, a little more than a month ago, it was blown to bits by the Romulans out near Gamma Llongo."

The Rigelian sighed. "You and I have much in common, then."

The commander looked at him askance. "Don't tell me they pressed *you* into service. You're not even human."

"Perhaps not," said Cobaryn. "But it is difficult to pursue a career as an explorer and stellar cartographer when the entire quadrant has become a war zone." His eyes crinkled at the corners. "Besides, it is foolish to pretend the Romulans are a threat to Earth alone."

"A number of species have done just that," Shumar noted, airing one of his pet peeves.

The Rigelian nodded wistfully. "Including my own, I hesitate to admit. However, I cannot change my people's minds. All I can do is lend my own humble efforts to the cause and hope for the best."

The commander found the sentiment hard to argue with. "Come on," he said. "I'll arrange for some dinner. I'll bet you're dying for some fresh muttle pods after all those rations."

Cobaryn chuckled softly. "Indeed I am. And then, after dinner . . ."

Shumar glanced at him. "Yes?"

The Rigelian shrugged. "Perhaps you could introduce me to your security officer? The one with the splendid red hair?"

The request took the commander by surprise. "You mean Kelly?"

"Kelly," Cobaryn repeated, rolling the name a little awkwardly over his tongue. "A pleasing name. I would be most grateful."

The commander considered it. As far as he knew, his security officer wasn't attracted to nonhumans. But then, the Rigelian had asked for an introduction, not a weekend in Tahoe.

"If you like," Shumar suggested, "I can ask the lieutenant if she'd like to dine with us."

"Even better," said Cobaryn.

The Rigelian looked like a kid in a candy shop, thought the commander. He wasn't the least bit self-conscious about expressing his yen for Kelly—even to a man he had only just met.

Shumar found it hard not to like someone like that.

As Connor Dane entered the rec lounge at Earth Base Fourteen, he didn't even consider parking himself at one of the small black tables the base's crew seemed so fond of. Instead, he made his way straight to the bar.

The bartender was tall, thin, and dourfaced, but he seemed to perk up a little at the sight of the newcomer. Of course, he probably didn't see too many new faces in his line of work.

"Get you something?" he asked.

Dane nodded. "Tequila, neat. And a beer to chase it with."

"We've got a *dozen* beers," said the bartender.

The Cochrane jockey slid himself onto a stool. "Your choice."

The bartender smiled as if his customer had made a joke. "You sure you wouldn't want to hear our list?" he asked.

"Life's too short," said Dane. "Just close your eyes and reach into the freezer. I promise I won't send it back, whatever it is."

The bartender's brow knit. "You're not kidding, are you?"

"I'm not kidding," the captain assured him.

The bartender shrugged. "Whatever you say."

A moment later, he produced a shot glass full of pale gold liquor. And a moment after that, he plunked a bottle of amber beer down beside it, a wisp of frosty vapor trailing from its open mouth.

"There you go," he said. He leaned back against the shelf behind him and folded his arms across his chest. "I guess you'd be the Cochrane jock who checked in a couple of minutes ago."

Dane didn't answer, hoping the man would get the message. As luck would have it, he didn't.

"You know," said the bartender, "my brother flew one of those needlenoses back before the war." He looked at the ceiling as if he were trying to remember something. "Must have been ten, eleven—"

"Listen, pal," Dane snapped, his voice taut and preemptive.

It got the bartender's attention. "What?"

"I know a lot of people come to places like this for some conversation," the captain told him. "Maybe your commander does that, or that foxy redheaded number behind the security console. But I'm not looking for anything like that. All I want is to kick back a little and pretend I'm somewhere besides a hunk of titanium in the middle of—"

Suddenly, a high-pitched ringing sound filled the place. Scowling at the interruption, Dane turned to the emergency monitor above the bar—one of hundreds located all around the base.

A moment later, the screen came alive, showing him the swarthy, darkbrowed visage of the man in charge of the place. What was the commander's name again? he asked himself. Shumac? No . . . Shu*mar*. He didn't often pay attention to things like that, but this time the name seemed to have stuck.

"Attention," said the base commander, the muscles working in his temples. "All hands to battle stations. Our long-range scanners have detected a Romulan attack force at a distance of twenty-six million kilometers."

The Cochrane jockey bit his lip. At full impulse, the Romulans would arrive in something under eleven minutes. That didn't leave him much time.

As the lounge's contingent of uniformed officers bolted for the door, Dane raised his glass of tequila and downed it at a gulp. Then he took a long swig of his beer and wiped his mouth with the back of his hand.

The bartender looked at him as if he'd grown another head. "Didn't you hear what the commander said?" he asked.

The captain nodded. "I heard." Ignoring the man's concern, he held his beer up to the light, admiring its consistency. Then he raised the bottle's mouth to his lips and took another long pull at its contents.

"But . . ." the bartender sputtered, "if you heard, what the devil are you still *doing* here?"

Dane smiled grimly at him. "The Romulans may rip this base in half, pal. They may even kill me. But I'll be damned if they're going to keep me from enjoying a refreshing beverage."

Finally, he finished off his beer and placed the bottle on the bar. Then he got up from his stool, pulled down on the front of his jacket and headed back to the base's only transporter room.

His message to his staff delivered, Commander Shumar turned from the two-way viewscreen set into the Ops center's comm console and eyed the officer seated beside him.

"Have you got the *Nimitz* yet?" he asked.

Ibanez, who had been Shumar's communications officer for the last two and a half years, looked more perturbed than the commander had ever seen him. "Not yet," the man replied, making adjustments to his control settings.

"What's wrong?" Shumar asked.

"They're just not responding," Ibanez told him.

The commander cursed under his breath. "How can that be? They're supposed to be listening twenty-four hours a day."

The comm officer shook his head from side to side. "I don't know what the trouble is, sir."

Shumar glared at the console's main screen, where he could see Ibanez's hail running over and over again on all Earth Command frequencies. Then he gazed at the stars that blazed above him. Why in blazes didn't the *Nimitz* answer? he wondered.

According to the last intelligence Shumar had received from Command, the Christopher-class vessel was within ninety million kilometers of Base Fourteen. At that distance, one might expect a communications delay of several seconds, but no more. And yet, Ibanez had been trying to raise the *Nimitz* for nearly a minute without success.

Without the warship's clout, the commander reflected, they wouldn't be able to withstand a Romulan attack for very long. No Earth base could. Clearly, they had a problem on their hands.

Of course, there was still a chance the *Nimitz* would respond. Shumar fervently hoped that that would be the case.

"Keep trying them," he told Ibanez.

"Aye, sir," came the reply.

Crossing the room, the commander passed by the engineering and life support consoles on his way to the security station. When he reached Kelly, he saw her look up at him. She seemed to sense his concern.

"What's the matter?" the redhead asked.

Shumar suppressed a curse. "We're having trouble raising the *Nimitz*."

Kelly's eyes widened. "Tell me you're kidding."

"I'm not the kidding type," he reminded her.

She swallowed. "That's right. You're not."

The commander leaned a little closer to her. "This could be a mess, Kelly. I'm going to need your help."

She took a breath, then let it out. It seemed to steady her. "I'm with you," the security officer assured him.

That settled, Shumar took a look at the monitors on Kelly's console. The Romulan warships, represented by four red blips on the long-range scanner screen, were bearing down on them. They had less than ten minutes to go before visual contact.

The commander turned his attention to the transporter monitor, where he could see that someone was being beamed off the station. "That Cochrane pilot had better be good," he said.

Kelly tapped a fingernail on the transporter screen. "That's not the Cochrane pilot. That's Cobaryn."

Shumar looked at her. "What . . .?"

The woman shrugged. "The Rigelian showed up in the transporter room and the Cochrane jock didn't. Who was I to argue?"

The commander's teeth ground together. True, Cobaryn had a valuable cargo to protect—medicines and foodstuffs that might be of help to some other Earth base—and technically, this wasn't his fight.

But the Rigelian had seemed so engaging—so *human* in many respects. And by human standards, it seemed like a slimy thing to abandon a base at the first sign of trouble.

"Transport complete," said Kelly, reading the results off the pertinent screen. "Cobaryn is out of here."

Shumar forced himself to wish the Rigelian luck. "What about the Cochrane pilot? He's got to be around the base—"

His officer held her hand up. "Hang on a second, Commander. I think our friend has finally arrived." Her fingers flying over her controls, she opened a channel to the transporter room. "This is security. Nothing like taking your sweet time, Captain."

"Better late than never," came the casual response.

Obviously, Shumar observed, Dane wasn't easily flustered. But then, that might be a good thing. After all, the Cochrane might be all the help they would get.

"Get on the platform," said Kelly.

"I'm on it," Dane answered.

The security officer took that as a signal to manipulate her controls. Pulling back slowly on a series of levers, she tracked the dematerialization and emission processes on her transporter screen. Then she glanced meaningfully at the commander.

"He's on his way," said Kelly.

Shumar nodded soberly. "I sincerely hope the man's a better pilot than he is a human being."

The first thing Connor Dane noticed as he materialized in his cockpit was the flashing proximity alarm on his control panel.

He swore volubly, thinking that the base's scanners had been off a few light years and that the Romulans had arrived earlier than expected. But as he checked his external scan monitor, the captain realized it wasn't the Romulans who had set off the alarm.

It was the Rigelian transport.

Craning his neck to look out of his cockpit's transparent hood, Dane confirmed the scan reading. For some reason, that idiot Cobaryn hadn't taken off yet. He was still floating in space beside the Cochrane.

Shaking his head, Dane punched a stud in his panel and activated his vessel's communications function. "Cobaryn," he said, "this is Dane. You've got to move your blasted ship!"

He expected to hear a response taut with urgency. However, the Rigelian didn't sound the least bit distressed.

"I assure you," said Cobaryn, "I *intend* to move it."

The human didn't yet understand. "For Earthsakes, when?"

"When the enemy arrives," the transport captain replied calmly.

"But it'll be too late by then," Dane argued, fighting the feeling that he was swimming upstream against a serious flood of reality.

"Too late to escape," Cobaryn allowed. "But not too late to take part in the battle."

The human didn't get it. Maybe the tequila had affected him more than he'd imagined. "You've got no weapons," he reminded the Rigelian. "How are you planning to slug it out in a space battle?"

"I would be perfectly happy to discuss tactics with you," Cobaryn told him reasonably, "but I think the time for discussion is past. It appears the Romulans have arrived."

Spurred by the remark, Dane checked his scan monitor. Sure enough, there were four Romulan warships nearing visual range.

Bringing his engines online, he raised his shields and powered up his weapons batteries. Then he put the question of the transport captain aside and braced himself for combat.

Shumar eyed the Romulan vessels, each one a sleek, silver cylinder with a cigar-shaped plasma nacelle on either side of it and a blue-green winged predator painted on its underbelly.

No question about it, the base commander mused grimly. The enemy had a flair for the dramatic.

"Shields up," he said. "Stand by, all weapons stations."

Kelly leaned forward and pulled down on a series of toggles.

"Shields up," she confirmed. She checked a couple of readouts. "Weapons stations standing by, awaiting your orders."

Shumar's stomach had never felt so tight. But then, in the past, Romulan assault forces had been deflected from the base by the *Nimitz* or some other Terran vessel. In four years as commander, he had never had to mount a lone defense against an enemy attack.

Until *now*.

"Fifty kilometers," said Kelly. "Forty. Thirty. Twenty . . ." Suddenly, she looked up at the transparent dome and pointed at a swarm of tiny silver dots. "There they are!"

Continued
Next Month . . .

Continued
Next Month . . .

Look for STAR TREK Fiction from Pocket Books

Star Trek®: The Original Series

Star Trek: The Next Generation®

Encounter at Farpoint • David Gerrold
Unification • Jeri Taylor
Relics • Michael Jan Friedman
Descent • Diane Carey
All Good Things • Michael Jan Friedman
Star Trek: Klingon • Dean W. Smith & Kristine K. Rusch
Star Trek VII: Generations • J. M. Dillard
Metamorphosis • Jean Lorrah
Vendetta • Peter David
Reunion • Michael Jan Friedman
Imzadi • Peter David
The Devil's Heart • Carmen Carter
Dark Mirror • Diane Duane
Q-Squared • Peter David
Crossover • Michael Jan Friedman
Kahless • Michael Jan Friedman
Star Trek VIII: First Contact • J. M. Dillard
Star Trek IX: Insurrection • Diane Carey
The Best and the Brightest • Susan Wright
Planet X • Michael Jan Friedman
Ship of the Line • Diane Carey

#1   *Ghost Ship* • Diane Carey
#2   *The Peacekeepers* • Gene DeWeese
#3   *The Children of Hamlin* • Carmen Carter
#4   *Survivors* • Jean Lorrah
#5   *Strike Zone* • Peter David
#6   *Power Hungry* • Howard Weinstein
#7   *Masks* • John Vornholt
#8   *The Captains' Honor* • David and Daniel Dvorkin
#9   *A Call to Darkness* • Michael Jan Friedman
#10 *A Rock and a Hard Place* • Peter David
#11 *Gulliver's Fugitives* • Keith Sharee
#12 *Doomsday World* • David, Carter, Friedman & Greenberg
#13 *The Eyes of the Beholders* • A. C. Crispin
#14 *Exiles* • Howard Weinstein
#15 *Fortune's Light* • Michael Jan Friedman
#16 *Contamination* • John Vornholt
#17 *Boogeymen* • Mel Gilden

Star Trek: Deep Space Nine®

The Search • Diane Carey
Warped • K. W. Jeter
The Way of the Warrior • Diane Carey
Star Trek: Klingon • Dean W. Smith & Kristine K. Rusch
Trials and Tribble-ations • Diane Carey
Far Beyond the Stars • Steve Barnes
The 34th Rule • Armin Shimerman & David George
What We Leave Behind • Diane Carey

Star Trek®: Voyager™

Flashback • Diane Carey
Pathways • Jeri Taylor
Mosaic • Jeri Taylor

Star Trek®: New Frontier

Star Trek®: Day of Honor

Book One: *Ancient Blood* • Diane Carey
Book Two: *Armageddon Sky* • L. A. Graf
Book Three: *Her Klingon Soul* • Michael Jan Friedman
Book Four: *Treaty's Law* • Dean W. Smith & Kristine K. Rusch
The Television Episode • Michael Jan Friedman

Star Trek®: The Captain's Table

Book One: *War Dragons* • L. A. Graf
Book Two: *Dujonian's Hoard* • Michael Jan Friedman
Book Three: *The Mist* • Dean W. Smith & Kristine K. Rusch
Book Four: *Fire Ship* • Diane Carey
Book Five: *Once Burned* • Peter David
Book Six: *Where Sea Meets Sky* • Jerry Oltion

Star Trek®: The Dominion War

Book 1: *Behind Enemy Lines* • John Vornholt
Book 2: *Call to Arms . . .* • Diane Carey
Book 3: *Tunnel Through the Stars* • John Vornholt
Book 4: *. . . Sacrifice of Angels* • Diane Carey

Star Trek®: My Brother's Keeper

Book One: *Republic* • Michael Jan Friedman
Book Two: *Constitution* • Michael Jan Friedman
Book Three: *Enterprise* • Michael Jan Friedman

1252.01